FIVE HIGHLY ACCLAIMED AUTHORS
BRING YOU
THE JOY AND ROMANCE OF CHRISTMAS

MARY BALOGH won the *Romantic Times* Award for Best New Regency Writer and the Reviewer's Choice Award for Best Regency Author in 1985, and the *Romantic Times* Award for Best Regency Author in 1989. She lives in Kipling, Saskatchewan, Canada. She is also a three-time winner of the Waldenbook Award for Bestselling Regency.

CARLA KELLY was the winner of the 1989 *Romantic Times* Award for Best New Regency Author. She lives in Springfield, Missouri.

ANITA MILLS won the *Romantic Times* Award for Best New Regency author in 1987. She lives in Kansas City, Missouri.

MARY JO PUTNEY has won four writing prizes, and was the winner of the 1988 *Romantic Times* Award for Best New Regency Author. She lives in Baltimore, Maryland.

SHEILA WALSH's first Regency novel, *The Golden Songbird,* won her the award for best novel presented by the Romantic Novelists Association in 1974. She lives in Southport, Lancashire, England.

D0059362

A Regency Christmas II

— Five Stories by —

Mary Balogh · Carla Kelly
Anita Mills · Mary Jo Putney
Sheila Walsh

A SIGNET BOOK

SIGNET
Published by the Penguin Group
Penguin Books USA Inc., 375 Hudson Street,
New York, New York 10014, U.S.A.
Penguin Books Ltd, 27 Wrights Lane,
London W8 5TZ, England
Penguin Books Australia Ltd, Ringwood,
Victoria, Australia
Penguin Books Canada Ltd, 10 Alcorn Avenue,
Toronto, Ontario, Canada M4V 3B2
Penguin Books (N.Z.) Ltd, 182–190 Wairau Road,
Auckland 10, New Zealand

Penguin Books Ltd, Registered Offices:
Harmondsworth, Middlesex, England

First published by Signet, an imprint of New American Library,
a division of Penguin Books USA Inc.

First Printing, November, 1990
11 10 9 8 7 6 5 4 3

 REGISTERED TRADEMARK—MARCA REGISTRADA

Printed in the United States of America

Contents

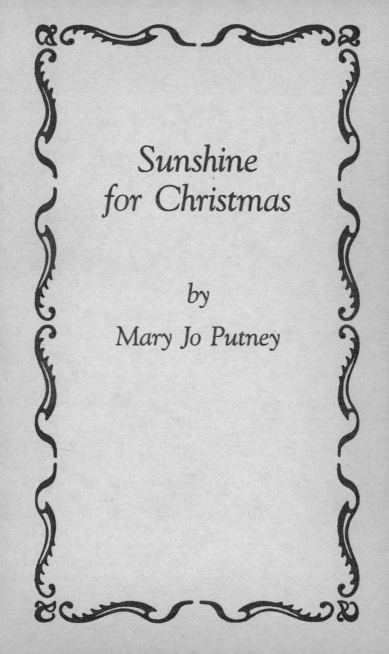

Sunshine
for Christmas

by

Mary Jo Putney

It was raining again. It had rained yesterday and the day before that. His hands clasped behind his back, Lord Randolph Lennox gazed out the window of his bedroom at the slick gray streets of Mayfair. "Burns, do you know how many days it has been raining?"

"No, my lord," his valet replied, glancing up from the wardrobe, where he was stacking precisely folded neckcloths.

"Thirty-four days. Rather biblical, don't you think? Perhaps it is time to order an ark."

"While the autumn has been a wet one," Burns said austerely, "it has not rained continuously day and night. Therefore, if I recall the scriptural precedent correctly, an ark should not be required."

Between amusement and depression, Lord Randolph considered the question of arks. Somewhere on Bond Street, among the tailors and bootmakers and jewelers, was there a shop that would supply an ark suitable for a gentleman? But that would never do, for arks were meant for pairs, and Randolph was alone. Had been alone for thirty-four years, save for one brief spell, and undoubtedly he would be alone for the rest of his life.

With disgust, Randolph realized that he was in danger of drowning in self-pity. Damn the rain. He was a healthy, wealthy man in the prime of his life, with

friends and family and a variety of interests, and he
had no right to complain of his lot. He knew that he
should be grateful for the rain that kept "this scepter'd
isle, this demi-paradise" green, but the thought did
nothing to mitigate the bleakness outdoors, or in his
soul.

He would have enjoyed snow, which was clean and
pure and forgiving, but snow seldom fell in southern
England. Farther north, in Scotland or Northumbria,
soft white flakes might be floating silent from the sky,
but in London the weather was merely miserable.

In a few weeks it would be Christmas, doubtless a
drab, wet one, and Randolph was not sure which
thought was more depressing: the rain or the holiday.
As a boy growing up on the great estate of Dunbar,
he had loved Christmas, had ached with excitement
from the celebrations and the sense of magic in the
air.

Randolph and his older brother, Edward, more formally known as Lord Westkirk, would burrow into the
Dunbar kitchens with the glee of all small boys. There
they stole currants and burned their fingers on hot
pastries until chased out by the cook, who had a fondness for children except when a holiday feast was
threatened.

Dunbar had been a happy house then; indeed, it still
was. Randolph's parents, the Marquess and Marchioness of Kinross, enjoyed robust good health and liked
nothing better than having their family about them.
Edward and his wife and three children would be at
Dunbar for Christmas, as would numerous other Lennoxes. The great house would be drenched with love
and laughter and happiness, and it was expected that
Randolph would be there as cherished son and brother,
uncle and cousin.

He couldn't bear the thought.

It was only midafternoon, but the light was already
failing because of the rain. Randolph detachedly stud-

ied his reflection in the darkening window glass. Above average height, dark-gold hair, slate-blue eyes, regular features. During their courtship, his wife had said that he looked like a Greek god. It had been a sad disappointment to her when he had proved merely human, and not an especially dashing speciman at that.

He did not have to spend Christmas at Dunbar. There were other houses, other friends, more distant relations, who would welcome him for the holidays, but he no more wished to go to any of them than to his father's house. He did not want to be an outsider at the feast of other people's happiness. Neither did he want the good-hearted matchmakers of his acquaintance trying to find him another wife.

What did he want? Sunshine and anonymity. Bright skies, warm air, a place where no one knew or cared who he was.

An absurd idea. He could not just pack up and run off on impulse.

Why not? Why not indeed? First with surprise, then excitement, Randolph realized that there was nothing to stop him from leaving England. Winter was a quiet time at his estate and his presence was not required. And now that the long wars were done, the Continent awaited, beckoning staid Englishmen to sample its decadent charms. If he answered that siren call, his family would regret his absence, but he would not be missed—not really. His presence was essential to no one's happiness.

Quickly, before the impulse could dissipate, he turned from the window. "Burns, commence packing. Tomorrow we shall take ship to the Mediterranean."

The usually imperturbable valet so far forgot himself as to gape at his master. "Surely you jest, my lord?"

"Not in the least," Randolph answered, a sparkle in his eyes. "I shall go into the City to book passage directly."

"But . . . but it isn't possible to arrange such a journey in twenty-four hours," Burns said feebly.

Randolph considered all that must be done, then nodded. "You're right. We shall leave the day after tomorrow instead." He grinned, feeling lighter than he had in months. "We're going to find some sunshine for Christmas."

With a lamentable lack of regard for his expensive coat, Lord Randolph crossed his arms and leaned forward on the brick wall, drinking in the grandeur of the scene before him. Even under damp gray skies, Naples was beautiful.

Having made the decision to leave London, he had booked passage on the next available Mediterranean-bound passenger ship. Its destination had seemed a good omen, for Naples was said to be one of the most sophisticated and enchanting of cities. As further proof that his journey was blessed, Randolph had found lodgings at the best hotel in the city, with glorious prospects visible from every window. Naples seemed a magical place, and he had gone to bed the first night full of hope, sure that even a staid Englishman could find magic here.

The next morning he awoke to rain, and the local variety was every bit as dismal as the London kind. The hotel manager, heartbroken at being the bearer of bad news, had admitted that December was the height of the rainy season, then hastened to add that the weather might well improve momentarily, if not even sooner.

Perhaps the sun would come out, perhaps not, but that morning the weather exactly resembled a bad English November, which was what Randolph had tried to escape. His brief spark of hope had flickered and died, leaving resignation. It had been foolish to think that he could run away from either rain or loneliness.

But, by God, he was here on the holiday of a lifetime, and he was going to enjoy himself if it killed him.

He hired a guide, and for three days he had dutifully viewed churches and monuments. He had bought antiquities and *objets d'art*, and an exquisite doll in native dress for his niece. He had also admired the handsome Neapolitan women, had even been tempted by one or two of the sloe-eyed streetwalkers. But he did not succumb to temptation, for the price might be too high: it was said that the prostitutes of Naples often gave men souvenirs that could be neither forgotten nor forgiven.

Yesterday his guide had taken him to view a religious procession. For reasons incomprehensible to a northern Protestant, a statue of the Blessed Virgin was removed from its church and paraded through the streets. Men carrying fifteen-foot-tall torches had led the way, followed by musicians playing small tambourines, castanets, and enormous Italian bagpipes. Black-clad sweepers wielded brooms to clean the street for the Madonna, a most useful activity, and another confraternity strewed the cobbles with herbs and flowers.

The street and balconies were thronged with watchers, and at first Randolph had enjoyed the parade and the contagious enthusiasm of the crowd. Then, after more musicians and phalanxes of solemn dignitaries, came a body of grim, barefoot penitents, with knotted cords around their necks and crowns of thorns seemingly spiked into their skulls. Behind them marched ominous beings dressed all in white, their heads covered by slant-eyed hoods. Most disturbing of all, six of the cowled figures were shirtless, and they scourged themselves as they walked, rivulets of blood trickling down their shredded backs and arms to stain their white garments.

The whole concept of flagellation was repellent to a rational Englishman, and Randolph shuddered, his pleasure in the spectacle destroyed. Even through the general clamor, he heard the sickly thud of iron-tipped whips against raw flesh.

To his guide's mystification, Randolph turned and began elbowing his way through the crowd. He had been a fool to think that he would be less lonely in an alien land; quite the contrary, he had never felt more of an outsider. He was deeply different from the Neapolitans, and just as he would never understand that orgy of self-abusive piety, he would never be able to match their passion for living.

Seeking comfort among his own kind, that evening Randolph had attended a small gathering at the British ambassador's residence. The English community was a sizable one, and clearly eager to welcome a lord into their midst. There were numerous invitations for him to come to dinner on Christmas Day and have some proper plum pudding, not heathen food like the locals ate. But it was not authentic plum pudding that Randolph wanted. With the gracious vagueness of which he was a master, he had declined all invitations and returned to his hotel thoroughly depressed.

This morning had dawned overcast but no longer raining, and the sky hinted at possible clearing later in the day. Heartened by the prospect, Randolph had dismissed the guide and set off on foot to explore the city himself. He had marveled at the juxtaposition of magnificence and cramped poverty, at the fierce pulse of a city whose inhabitants insisted on living their joys and sorrows in public for all the world to see. His obvious foreignness had attracted attention, and he had had to fend off small street boys whose innocence was dubious, no matter how young they were, but he had had no serious problems.

In late morning his wandering brought him to a quiet residential square on one of the higher hills. Modest but respectable houses surrounded the piazza on three sides, while the fourth was bounded by a brick wall.

The hill fell sharply away below the wall and there was a splendid view of the whole bay. Pleased, Randolph crossed his arms on top of the wall and studied the city that sprawled so wantonly below.

He inhaled deeply, thinking that the air smelled different from England, the breeze redolent with the rich, intriguing scents of unfamiliar vegetation and kitchens. The clouds were beginning to break up, and as he watched, the first shafts of sunlight touched the famous bay, changing the sullen gray waters to teal and turquoise.

On the far side of the bay loomed the indigo bulk of Vesuvius. This was the first day clear enough for Randolph to see the volcano, and he was intrigued by the small, ominous plume of smoke wafting from the top. What would it be like living by a volcano? Perhaps that constant, smoldering reminder of mortality was one reason that Neapolitans lived life with such intensity.

The only other person visible was a bespectacled woman perched on a bench at the opposite end of the square. Oblivious to Randolph, she sketched in a pad balanced on her knees. Fair-skinned and soberly dressed, she must be another tourist. Randolph thought that it was rather adventurous of her to be walking out alone, then dismissed her from his mind.

One of the skinny Italian cats jumped up on the wall by Randolph, examined him with feral yellow eyes, then crept along the wall, stalking a bird that flew away at the last minute. Several chickens wandered across the piazza, pecking hopefully at the ground, and somewhere nearby a dove was cooing. It was the most peaceful spot he had found in Naples, and he closed his eyes for a few minutes, content to absorb the welcome warmth and brightness of the increasing sunshine.

Then a scraping sound caught his attention, and Randolph glanced over to see a young girl emerge from a house in the corner of the piazza, a bucket in one hand and a low ladder in the other. Paying no attention to the two tourists, she propped the ladder against the wall and scampered up, bucket in hand, and began washing one of the windows.

The girl was very pretty, with olive skin, raven hair tied back with a scarlet ribbon, and a pair of trim ankles visible below her full skirts. Randolph watched her idly, enjoying the sight as he would any of Naples' other natural wonders.

After vigorously washing the nearest panes, the girl leaned over and began working on the far side of the window, the ladder swaying beneath her. Randolph frowned, thinking that she would be wiser to move the ladder, then shrugged. Doubtless she had been washing windows that way for years. And even if she fell, the distance was not dangerously great.

Ready to resume his explorations, he started across the square, but before he had taken three steps, he heard a noisy clatter of falling objects, followed by a cry of pain. Cursing himself for not having attempted to caution the girl, Randolph hastened to where she lay in a dazed heap and knelt beside her.

"Signorina?" he said, gently touching her shoulder.

Long black lashes fluttered open to reveal melting dark eyes. The girl murmured something, probably an oath, then pushed herself to a sitting position and gave Randolph a shaky smile. She was very young, perhaps fifteen, and had the breathtaking Madonna face that seemed to be a Neapolitan specialty.

"I'm glad to see that you have survived your fall," he said, though he was sure that she would not understand. He started to rise so that he could help her up, but suddenly she swooned forward and he found himself with an armful of nubile young womanhood. From the feel of the lush curves pressed against Randolph's chest, it was true that the females of the Mediterranean matured earlier than their northern sisters.

The girl tilted her head back dizzily, and this close, it was obvious that her mouth was the kind usually described as kissable. For a moment Randolph's arms tightened around her. It had been far too long since he had held a woman, and he was only human. But he was also a gentleman, and gentlemen did not take advantage of stunned children, be they ever so nubile.

He decided that the best plan was to lay her down on the street, then summon help from her house. But before he could do so, he heard hoarse masculine shouting behind him, followed by the sound of heavy pounding feet.

He looked up and saw two men racing across the piazza, a strikingly handsome youth and an older man. From their noisy concern, they must be family or neighbors of the injured girl. Hoping one might know some English or French, Randolph opened his mouth to speak as they skidded to a stop next to him.

Before he could say anything, the older man snatched the girl from his arms with an anguished howl, and the youth hurled a vicious punch at Randolph's jaw.

"What the devil!" The reflexes honed in Jackson's Salon took over and Randolph ducked his head and twisted away from the blow, his hat falling to the ground. As he scrambled to his feet, another fist connected solidly with his midriff.

As he doubled over, gasping for breath, Randolph realized that these two maniacs must think he had assaulted the girl. The wooden ladder had fallen nearby, and he grabbed it by two rungs and used it to hold his furious assailant at bay.

The situation was so ludicrous that Randolph almost laughed. Then he saw the wicked glitter of a knife in the young man's hand, and his amusement congealed. This was no longer a joke—it was entirely possible that he might be killed over a stupid misunderstanding. If that happened, doubtless the Kingdom of the

Two Sicilies would express profound regret to the British authorities, but that would do Randolph no good.

Yelling, the youth swung the knife wildly. Randolph blocked the blow with the ladder, then retreated to the wall of the house so that his back was protected. Amazing how noisy two Neapolitans could be. No, three, the girl had recovered her senses and was shrieking as she clung to the older man's arm, preventing him from joining the attack.

Then a smartly swung umbrella cracked across the young man's wrist, knocking the knife to the ground. The female tourist had entered the fray. Moving between Randolph and his assailants, she began speaking in fluent, staccato Italian. After a startled moment, the Neapolitans began addressing her, all three jabbering simultaneously.

Randolph had already noticed that Italians talked with their bodies as much as their voices, and he watched the pantomime with deep appreciation. The older man's impassioned gestures made it crystal clear that he had been struck to the heart by the sight of his treasured daughter lying lifeless in the arms of a foreigner. As Randolph recollected, the *signorina* had felt far from lifeless, but no matter. Less clear was the young man's role, but he was equally distressed. Meanwhile, the girl, an angel of innocence, was apparently declaiming that it was all a misunderstanding.

Since it appeared that farce was prevailing over force, Randolph lowered the ladder and studied his defender curiously. She was somewhere around the age of thirty, slim and quite tall. And, to his fascination, she combined the no-nonsense air associated with governesses with the lively body language of the Neapolitans. Perhaps she was also Italian? But she had the pale translucent complexion usually associated with England.

By sheer volume, the young man managed to shout down the other speakers. Arms waving, he made an impassioned diatribe, which he concluded by spitting at Randolph's feet.

The tall woman hesitated, took a quick glance at Randolph, then responded, a soulful quiver in her rich alto voice. She ended her address by gesturing toward him, then clasping her hands to her bosom as her eyes demurely fluttered shut behind her gold-rimmed spectacles.

Whether it was her action or her words, the two men looked at each other, then gave mutual shrugs of acceptance. With a soft sentimental sigh, the older man took the woman's hand and kissed it lingeringly, murmuring a baritone *"Bellissima."*

The handsome youth, anger vanished as if it had never been, bobbed his head to Randolph, then offered a sunny smile.

The woman turned to Randolph. "Act as if you know me," she murmured in native-born English. "Smile graciously, bow to the young lady, and we can leave."

Randolph retrieved his hat and obeyed. Obviously recovered from her fall, the girl gave him a bewitching smile while her father beamed benevolently. Accompanied by a chorus of good wishes, the two Britons crossed the piazza. On the way, the woman collected the canvas bag that held her sketching materials, thrusting her umbrella into loops on the side. Taking Randolph's arm, she steered him into a street leading down the hill.

When they were out of sight of the square, he said mildly, "Would you care to explain what that was all about?"

The woman smiled cheerfully and released his arm. As they continued down the street, she said, "The two gentlemen are the father and betrothed of young Filomena, both of them stonemasons. They were returning home for lunch when they found Filomena in your arms. Being protective and volatile, they feared the worst.''

She wrinkled her nose. ''In truth, the situation was more complicated than that. If it were just the father, he would probably have chastised Filomena for immodest behavior. But since her intended, Luigi, was present, her father could not admit that his daughter was a designing baggage. Hence, any fall from grace must have been your fault.'' She gave a gurgle of laughter. ''It would not have been as serious if you were not so handsome, but I'm afraid that Luigi was expressing his regret for the fact that he will never look like Apollo.''

Randolph found himself blushing. ''Why should Luigi have regrets? He looks like Michaelangelo's *David*.''

''Very true,'' the woman said with an unladylike amount of approval. ''But that kind of male beauty is not uncommon here, while you have the charm of novelty.'' Taking pity on his blushes, she continued, ''Incidentally, I am Miss Elizabeth Walker.''

''I'm Randolph Lennox, and very much in your debt.'' He gave her a rueful smile. ''I was imagining the London headlines: 'English Tourist Accidentally Murdered in Naples.' ''

''That's better than 'English Tourist Assaults Innocent Italian Miss and Is Executed on the Spot.' ''

''Definitely.'' He looked at her curiously. ''Just what did you say that convinced them of my harmlessness?''

A hint of color showed on Miss Walker's cheek. ''Since they were unwilling to accept that you were motivated only by a spirit of helpfulness, I finally said that you were my husband, that we were on our honeymoon, and how could they possibly believe that a gentlemen like you would dishonor me by making improper advances to a young girl right in front of my face?'' She held up her bare left hand. ''Fortunate that

Luigi and company were not close observers, or they might have doubted my story. I'm sorry, but strong measures were called for; rational arguments weren't working.''

''No harm done,'' Randolph said, amused. Remembering her earlier comment, he went on, ''You said that the girl was a designing baggage?''

''Oh, she is. I'm a governess, you see, and I'm up to all a young girl's tricks. Filomena watched you from an upstairs window for a while until she struck on a way to further her acquaintance. You should have seen her expression—like a cat watching a bird.''

''Surely a girl so young would not behave in so forward a fashion!''

''You would not say that if you knew many young females,'' Miss Walker said feelingly. ''But I doubt that she was interested in serious immorality—merely a bit of flirtation. My most recent charge was a girl much like Filomena, and let me tell you, getting Maria safely to the altar was a challenge to make Hannibal's crossing the Alps look like a stroll in Hyde Park.''

Randolph remembered how Filomena had conveniently fainted into his arms, and how rapidly she had recovered when her menfolk appeared on the scene. ''I thought that Italian girls were very modest and strictly brought up.''

''They *are* strictly brought up, but human nature being what it is, some are modest while others are the most amazing flirts.'' She glanced at him for a moment. ''Now I am shocking you. I have lived too long in Italy and quite forgotten proper English restraint.'' With a grin, she continued, ''I could give you a lengthy dissertation on Italian behavior, but it is a rather warm lecture and, as I said, quite lengthy.''

Randolph laughed out loud. It occurred to him that he had not laughed like this since . . . since September. Preferring to think of this refreshing female rather than the past, he said, ''I should like to hear your

dissertation some time. I know we have not been properly introduced, but if you are willing to overlook that,
perhaps you will let me take you to lunch as a sign of
appreciation for your most timely rescue? And you can
also explain Italian behavior to me.''

A wise woman would not casually accept a stranger's invitation, so she hesitated, studying his face as
if looking for traces of dangerous derangement under
his respectable appearance.

''I'm a very harmless fellow,'' he said reassuring.
''Besides, knowledge of local customs might save my
life. Look at what almost happened.''

Smiling, she replied, ''How can I refuse such a re-
quest? A luncheon would be very pleasant. Did you
have a particular place in mind? If not, there is a *trattoria* near here that has good food.'' Her gaze flickered over Randolph's very expensive coat. ''That is, if
you are willing to eat as Neapolitans do.''

It was easy to guess her thoughts. During his first
days in Naples, Randolph's guide had insisted on taking him to boring establishments that specialized in
English-style cooking. ''Do I appear to be such a paltry fellow that I cannot survive on native fare?'' he
asked, reaching over to take her canvas bag. ''I would
be delighted to broaden my culinary horizons.''

The *trattoria* was about ten minutes' walk away, on
a market square. Unlike the residential square on top
of the hill, this piazza bustled with activity. The *trattoria*'s proprietor greeted Miss Walker with enthusiastic recognition and hand-kissing, then seated them
at an outdoor table.

After the proprietor had bustled off, Miss Walker
said, ''I trust you don't mind alfresco dining? Raf-
faello wants everyone to see that his establishment is
frequented by discriminating foreigners. Also, while
the day is rather cool by local standards, he assumes
that it will seem warm to Englishfolk.''

"A correct assumption," Randolph agreed. "It feels like a fine summer day in Scotland."

Miss Walker chuckled. Then the proprietor returned with two goblets and a carafe of red table wine. After pouring wine for both of them, he rattled off a spate of suggestions. Miss Walker responded in kind, with vivid hand gestures, before turning to her companion. "How adventurous are you feeling, Mr. Lennox?"

Randolph hesitated. He had never been the least adventurous, particularly where his stomach was concerned, but when in Naples . . . "I throw myself on your mercy. I will attempt anything that will not try to eat me first."

Eyes twinkling, she gave an order to the proprietor, who bowed and left. "Nothing so fearsome. What I ordered is a simple Neapolitan dish. Peasant food, really, but tasty."

For a few minutes they sipped their wine in silence. As he swallowed a mouthful, Randolph gazed over the piazza, enjoying the shifting throngs of people. Housewives, cassock-clad priests, costermongers and workmen, all moved to a background of joyously conflicting street musicians. This was what he had come to Naples for: sunshine, exotic sights, enjoyable company.

His gaze drifted to Miss Walker, who was looking pensively across the square. Her appearance was unremarkable but pleasant, with nut-brown hair, a faint gold dusting of freckles, and spectacles that did not manage to conceal fine hazel eyes. She looked like the sort of woman who should be raising children and running a vicarage. She would counsel the villagers, help her husband with his sermons, and all would agree that the vicar was fortunate to have such a capable helpmeet. What had brought her so far from the English countryside? "I gather that you have lived in Italy for some time, Miss Walker."

She glanced over at him. Very fine hazel eyes. "Over

six years now. At first I lived in this area, but for the last two years I was entirely in Rome, teaching—or rather, standing guard over—the young lady whom I mentioned earlier.''

"How did you come to Italy in the first place?'' he asked. "That is, if you don't mind my asking.''

"Not in the least,'' she replied. "After my parents died, there was no reason to stay in England, so I jumped at the chance to become governess to a British diplomatic family that was coming to Italy. When they returned home, I decided to stay on. I am quite valuable here, you see. Aristocratic Italian families like having English governesses, both as a mark of consequence and in the hopes that cold English temperaments will act favorably on hot-blooded daughters.''

"Do you never miss England?''

Her gaze slid away from his. "A little,'' she admitted softly, taking off her spectacles and polishing them, a convenient excuse for looking down. "A sad consequence of travel is that the more one sees of the world, the more impossible it is to be satisfied with any one location. Sometimes—especially in the spring and summer—I long for England. Yet, if I were there, I should pine for Italy. Here at least I command a better salary than at home, and there is more sunshine.'' Then, almost inaudibly, she added, "And fewer memories.''

It was a motive Randolph could understand. To change the subject, he said, "I envy your command of the language. I wish I had studied Italian, for I find it very strange to be unable to communicate. When someone addresses me, I find myself starting to reply in French, because that I do know.''

Miss Walker replaced her spectacles and looked up, collected again. "The Italian taught in England would have been of limited value in Naples. Standard Italian is really the Tuscan dialect, for that was used by Dante and many of the other great writers. I knew Tuscan when I came here, but learning to communicate in Naples was almost like learning a new tongue.''

"Not just tongue—also arms, torso, and facial expressions,'' he pointed out.

"Very true. One cannot stand still and speak properly. Italians are so expressive, so emotional.'' Absently she tucked an unruly brown curl behind her ear. "I suppose that is one reason why Italy fascinates the English.''

"Fascinates, yet repels,'' Randolph said slowly, thinking of the flagellants in the religious procession. "I've seen more visible emotion in Naples than I have in a lifetime in England. Part of me envies such freedom of expression, but I would probably die on the rack before emulating it.''

She regarded him gravely. "Is it that you could not, or would not, act in such a way?''

"Could not.'' Wryly Randolph thought that it was typical of his English reserve to find himself embarrassed at what he was revealing. Fortunately a waiter appeared and set plates in front of each of them. He studied the dish, which was some kind of salad consisting of vegetables, olives, and less definable substances. "This is the local specialty you warned me of?''

"No, this is *antipasto,* a first course consisting of bits of whatever is available. *Antipasti* are served throughout Italy.''

The salad was lightly dressed with olive oil, herbs, and vinegar; after finishing, Randolph gave a happy sigh and said, "This is the best thing I've eaten since I arrived.''

"Either you have been most unfortunate, or you are new to Naples.'' She neatly speared the last bite of her own salad. "The Italians, like the French, take food very seriously indeed. The main course will not appear for some time, for our hosts do not believe in rushing anything as important as a meal.''

"I've only been here for four days," he explained. "I came on impulse, looking for some sunshine for Christmas, and felt sadly betrayed to arrive in Italy and find rain." As the plates were cleared away, his eye fell on her portfolio, which was peeping from the canvas bag. "Are your drawings for public view, or do you prefer to keep them for yourself?"

She eyed him doubtfully. "They are not private, but neither are they very interesting."

"If they are of Naples, I'm sure that I will enjoy them."

"Very well." She pulled the portfolio out and handed it to him. "But remember, you have been warned."

Randolph smiled and opened the portfolio. The not-quite-finished drawing on top was the one she had been working on when the altercation broke out. Most of the sketch was devoted to a hazy, atmospheric rendering of the bay and the volcano beyond—how did she achieve such an effect with only pencil?—but what made it really unusual was the skinny cat in the right foreground. The beast sat on the wall, sinuous tail curling down the weathered stone, its feral gaze fixed on the city below.

Randolph began leafing through the portfolio. Her drawing was technically excellent, and it was amazing how much she could convey with a few deft lines, but what was remarkable was the imaginative way she viewed the world. Over a Roman ruin arched the gnarled, ancient trunk of an olive tree, fishing boats were seen through a veil of nets, and the massive medieval bulk of Castel Nuovo was framed by its Renaissance triumphal arch.

Most striking of all, Vesuvius was drawn from the point of view of a bird looking down on drifting smoke and stark craters, one powerful wing angling across the lower part of the picture. "You have great talent," he said. "It is extraordinary how the viewpoints you choose enhance and intensify the scenes."

Her cheeks colored becomingly. "Drawing is a common accomplishment, like embroidery or music."

"That does not mean it is always well done." He turned back to the first drawing, admiring how the thin, restless cat symbolized the passionate, demanding life of the city's slums. "But you have more than skill. You have a unique artist's eye."

Miss Walker opened her mouth to speak, then closed it. After a moment she said, "I was going to make a modest self-deprecating remark, but what I really want to say is 'Thank you.' That is a fine compliment you have given me, and I shall cherish it."

"Do you do watercolors or oils?" he asked as he closed and returned the portfolio.

"Watercolors sometimes. I would like to try oils, but I have little time." She made a face. "It would be more honest to say that I'm afraid that if I started serious painting, I would lose track of the world, and lose my situation along with it."

A pity that she lacked the leisure to develop her gift. With his independent income, Randolph would have been able to find the time to cultivate talent, but unfortunately he had none. Perhaps he should follow a fine old Italian custom and become her patron so that he could bask in reflected glory. But, alas, with a male patron and a female artist, the modern world would put a different construction on the arrangement, even though Miss Walker was an improbable choice for a mistress.

The waiter returned, this time placing a sizzling platter in the middle of the table. On it was a crispy circle of dough spread with herbs, sliced sausage, dried tomatoes, and hot bubbling cheese. Randolph regarded the dish doubtfully. "You are sure that this fulfills my minimum condition of not attempting to eat me first?''

Miss Walker laughed. ''I've never heard of anyone being assaulted by a *pizza*. I think you will be agreeably surprised.''

And he was. The *pizza* was gooey, undignified, and delicious. Between the two of them, they managed to eat almost the entire platter, and he was eyeing the last slice speculatively when someone called, ''Lord Randolph, what a pleasant surprise.''

He looked up and saw a female detach herself from a group crossing the piazza. It was a woman whom he had met at the ambassador's dinner, and as he stood, he ransacked his memory to identify her. Mrs. Bertram, that was her name. A lush blond widow with a roving eye, she lived with her wealthy merchant brother. Both were prominent in the local British community.

Ignoring Miss Walker, Mrs. Bertram cooed, ''So lovely to see you again, Lord Randolph. Are you enjoying your visit?''

''Yes, particularly today. Mrs. Bertram, may I make you known to Miss Walker, or are you already acquainted?''

The widow gave Elizabeth Walker a sharp assessing glance, then dismissed her as possible competition. Randolph saw and understood that glance, and felt a small spurt of anger. So had his wife, Chloe, reacted whenever she met another woman. ''Miss Walker and I are old friends,'' he said pleasantly, ''and she has been kind enough to show me some of the sights of the city.''

Mrs. Bertram's eyes narrowed in irritation. ''I should have been delighted to perform that service. I have lived here long enough to know what—and who— is worthwhile.'' She looked at the last congealing section of *pizza* and gave a delicate shudder. ''One cannot be too careful. There is a distressing lack of refinement in much of Neapolitan life.''

Randolph's expression must have warned her that her cattiness was not being well-received, for she went on, ''I do hope you will be able to join us for Christmas dinner.'' There was a smudge on his sleeve from the earlier altercation, and she reached out and brushed at it, her fingers lingering. ''One should not be alone at Christmas. You are very far from home. Let us stand as your family.''

''You are most kind,'' he murmured, ''but you need not be concerned for my welfare. I have other plans. Pray give my regards to your brother.''

It was unquestionably a dismissal, and Mrs. Bertram was unable to ignore it. After a venomous glance at Randolph's companion, she rejoined her group, which was entering a jeweler's shop.

Relieved to be free of her, Randolph sat down again. Miss Walker regarded him thoughtfully. ''Lord Randolph?''

He nodded. ''My father is Marquess of Kinross.'' He wondered if she was going to be either awed or intimidated: those were the two most common reactions.

Instead, she planted one elbow on the table and rested her chin on her palm, her hazel eyes twinkling. ''I presume that you did not use your title when you introduced yourself because you weary of being toadeaten. It must be very tedious.''

''It is,'' he said fervently. ''And I have only a meaningless courtesy title; my father and brother must tolerate far worse.''

''In fairness to Mrs. Bertram, I imagine that it is not only your title that interests her,'' Miss Walker said charitably. ''By the way, am I an old friend on the basis of my advanced years, or the fact that we have known each other easily two hours?''

He pulled his watch from his pocket. "By my reckoning, it is closer to four."

"Good heavens, is it really so late?" She glanced over at the ornate clock suspended over the jewelry shop. "I must be on my way." She began to collect her belongings. "Lord Randolph, it has been an exceptional pleasure making your acquaintance. I hope you enjoy your stay in Naples."

He stared at her, disconcerted. She couldn't just disappear like this. She was the most congenial soul he had met since coming to Naples. No, far longer than that. He stood. "I should hate to think that I have endangered your livelihood. Let me escort you back. If necessary, I can explain that you are late because you saved me from grievous bodily injury."

She laughed. "Lord Randolph, can you think of anything more likely to be injurious to a governess's reputation than having a handsome man say it is all his fault?" When he looked sheepish, she continued, "You needn't worry. My livelihood is not threatened. I am between situations, gloriously free until I take up a new position after Epiphany." She wrinkled her nose. "Twins! The prettiest little vixens you can imagine. I don't know how I shall manage."

"Very well, I'm sure." The proprietor appeared, and Randolph settled the bill with a gratuity that put an ecstatic expression on the man's face. When the proprietor had left, Randolph continued, "Since it will not cost you your situation, will you accept my escort?"

She hesitated, and he felt a constriction somewhere in his middle. Probably the *pizza* fighting the *antipasto*. Then she smiled. "That would be very nice. I am going back to my *pensione,* and it is not in the most elegant part of the city."

As they made their way through the piazza, Randolph carrying her canvas bag, she explained, "I am giving drawing lessons to my landlady, Sofia, who has been a good friend to me over the years. She is free for only an hour or so at the end of the afternoon, and if I am late, she will be deprived of her lesson.''

Would Mrs. Bertram have abandoned the company of a man in order to fulfill a promise to a landlady? Randolph knew the question was so foolish as not to merit an answer.

As they threaded their way through increasingly narrow, crowded streets, Miss Walker gave an irreverent and amusing commentary on the sights. While she did not neglect splendors like the recently rebuilt San Carlo opera house, her real talent lay in identifying Neapolitan sights like the ribbons of wheat paste drying on backyard racks, and the ancient statue of a pagan goddess, now rechristened and worshiped as a Christian saint in spite of a distinctly impious expression.

All too soon they arrived at the *pensione,* a shabby town house on a noisy street. Miss Walker turned to take her farewell. ''Thank you for the luncheon and the escort, Lord Randolph. While you are in Italy, stay away from designing young baggages, no matter how dire their straits seem to be.''

Impulsively Randolph said, ''The discerning eye that makes you an artist also makes you a fine tour guide. Since you are at liberty now, would you consider acting as my cicerone? You could protect me from the designing baggages directly.'' When she frowned, he said coaxingly, ''I would be happy to pay you for your time, at double the rate of the boring fellow who insisted that I eat only English food.''

''It is not a matter of money,'' she said, uncertain in the face of his unusual offer. ''Why do you want me for a guide?''

''Because I enjoy your company,'' he said simply.

For a moment her serene good humor was shadowed by vulnerability. Then she gave a smile different from her earlier expressions of amusement. This smile came from somewhere deeper, and it transformed her plain face to fleeting loveliness. "Then I will be very glad to be your guide."

Elizabeth woke with a glow of anticipation, and at first she could not recollect why. Then she remembered. It was not yet time to rise, so she opened her eyes and gazed at the ancient fresco on the ceiling. In truth it was badly drawn, but without her spectacles, it looked splendid, a magical landscape inhabited by flawless lads and lasses. One golden lad looked rather like Lord Randolph Lennox must have at eighteen.

She tucked her arms under her head and reveled in the strange and wondrous chance that had brought them together. Perhaps heaven was giving her a special Christmas present as a reward for managing to keep Maria pure until her marriage? Elizabeth chuckled at the thought; the longer she lived in Italy, the more superstitious she became.

Eager to begin the day, she swung her legs over the edge of the bed and slid her feet into the waiting slippers. Then she began the slow process of brushing out her hair, which was thick and very curly. In the morning it tumbled over her shoulders in a wild mass and at least once a week she considered cutting it, but never did. A governess had little-enough femininity.

Patiently she unsnarled a knot. He had said that he was harmless, but that was only partially true. Certainly he would not threaten her virtue, for he was a gentleman and she wasn't the kind of woman to rouse a man to unbridled lust. Heavens, not even bridled lust!

But that didn't mean Lord Randolph was harmless, because of course she would fall in love with him. Any lonely spinster worth her salt would do the same if thrown into the company of a man who was charming, kind, intelligent, and handsome as sin. And he would never even notice, which was as it should be.

After a day or two he would tire of sight-seeing, or

go north to Rome, or become involved in the glittering circle of court life for which he was so well qualified. And she would begin the task of taming the terrible twins, and tuck the image of Lord Randolph away in her heart, next to that of William.

She might cry a little when he was gone for good, if she wasn't too busy with the twins. But she wouldn't be sorry to have known him. Though magic must sometimes be paid for with pain, that was better than never knowing magic at all. When she was old and gray and dry, she would take his image out and dream a little. If anyone noticed, they would wonder why the old lady had such a cat-in-the-creampot smile on her withered lips.

Elizabeth glanced into the cracked mirror. With her glasses off and her hair curling madly around her face, she looked more like a blowsy baroque nymph than a governess.

For just a moment she let herself dream. Lord Randolph would fall in love with her beautiful soul and marry her out of hand. England would be home, but they would make long visits to Italy. They would have three children; she might be starting late, but she was healthy. She would paint, powerful unusual canvases that some people would love and others would loathe. His aristocratic family would be delighted that Lord Randolph had found a wife of such fine character and talent.

Her mouth thinned and she put her spectacles on and began tugging her hair back. As the nymph vanished into the governess, she knew that he would not fall in love with her, and that even if he did, she could not marry him. Even in her wildest flights of fancy, she could not escape the knowledge that her actions had put respectable marriage forever out of reach.

But that did not mean that Elizabeth could not enjoy this rare, magical interlude. And she did.

In Rome, she had been told of an Englishman who

had decided that the main point of seeing sights was to say that one had seen them, so he had hired a carriage and crammed the Eternal City into two fevered days so he could devote the rest of his time to dissipation. Fortunately Lord Randolph proved to be a visitor of quite a different stamp, interested in everything and willing to take the time to absorb as well as see.

She began by taking him to all of Naples' famous sights, and when it became clear that he shared her taste for the unusual, she expanded the itinerary to include more eccentric amusements. Over the next week they explored Naples' narrow, teeming streets, ate fresh fruit, pasta, and ices purchased in the markets, and stopped to enjoy arias of heart-stopping purity that soared from the open windows of tenements.

When it rained they searched dark churches for neglected paintings by great masters, and smiled together at signs that offered, "Indulgences Plenary, daily and perpetual, for living and the dead, as often as wanted." As Lord Randolph remarked, it was precisely the way a London draper would advertise.

Tactfully, Lord Randolph did not again suggest hiring her services; instead, he paid for all admissions, meals, and other expenses. On fair days he hired a carriage and driver and they went into the countryside. They visited Baia, which had been a fashionable Roman bathing resort, and speculated about the palaces that now lay beneath the sea. At Herculaneum they marveled at the city that had emerged after almost two thousand years beneath volcanic mud, and Elizabeth did sketches that populated the ruins with puzzled, ghostly Romans.

It was Lord Randolph who had suggested that Elizabeth bring her sketchbook. While she drew, he would sit quietly by, smoking his pipe, a man with a gift for stillness. It was not uncommon for rich tourists to hire artists to record what they saw, and Elizabeth quietly resolved to give Lord Randolph this set of drawings when they parted. When he looked at them to remember Naples, perhaps he would also think of her.

In the meantime, she utilized the governess's skill of watching unobtrusively, memorizing the angle of his eyebrows when he was amused, the way the winter sun shimmered across his dark-gold hair, and a hundred other subtle details.

Alone in her *pensione* in the evenings, she tried to draw Lord Randolph from memory, with frustrating results. He would have been an easier subject if he were less handsome, because his regular features looked more like an idealized Greek statue than a real man. She did her best to capture the quiet humor in his eyes, the surprising hint of underlying wistfulness, but she was never satisfied with the results.

As an escort Lord Randolph was thoughtful and impeccably polite, and Elizabeth knew he enjoyed her company, but she also knew he was scarcely aware that she was a woman. Had he come to Italy because he was disappointed in love? Hard to imagine any woman turning him down. But she would never know the truth. Though their conversation flowed with ease and wit, they spoke only of impersonal things; her companion kept his inner life to himself, as did Elizabeth.

For the first few days they spent together, she was able to maintain a certain wry detachment about her growing infatuation with Lord Randolph. But the day that they visited the Fields of Fire, detachment dissolved as she fell blindly, helplessly, irrevocably in love with him.

The Campi Flegrei—Fields of Fire—lay north of Naples. The poetic name described an area of volcanic activity, a sight not to be missed by tourists. After spending the morning in the nearby town of Pozzuoli, they had driven to Solfatara, an oval crater where the earth was sometimes too hot to touch and noxious fumes oozed from the holes called fumaroles.

A local guide led half a dozen visitors into the crater, and as part of his tour he held a lighted brand over a boiling mud pot. Immediately the steam issuing from the mud pot flared furiously, as if about to explode. Even though Elizabeth had seen this before, she still flinched back.

Lord Randolph touched her elbow reassuringly. "That is just an illusion, isn't it?"

She nodded. "Yes, the fumarole doesn't really burn hotter, but whenever I see that, I can't help feeling that the sleeping volcano is lashing back at impudent humans who disturb its rest."

After tossing the brand into the fumarole, the guide stamped on the ground, sending a deep, ominous echo rolling through the hollow mountain under their feet. Then he led the group away.

Having had enough demonstrations, Elizabeth and her companion wandered off in another direction.

"It's an interesting place," Lord Randolph remarked as they picked their way through a field of steaming fumaroles. The pungent odor of sulfur hung heavy over the sterile white soil. "Rather like one of the outer circles of hell."

"Exactly. Solfatara is a place every visitor to Naples should see, but I dislike it intensely." Elizabeth gestured around the barren crater. "When I come here, I always think it is the loneliest, most desolate spot on earth."

"No," her companion said softly, his voice as bleak as the dead earth crumbling beneath their feet. "The loneliest place on earth is in a bad marriage."

That was when the fragile remnants of Elizabeth's detachment shattered, for in that instant she came to really understand Randolph. It was not a shock to learn that he was married; she had never understood why a man so attractive and amiable did not have a wife. Nor did she feel betrayed that he had not mentioned his wife before, because she had always known there could be nothing between him and her but fleeting friendship.

What Elizabeth did feel was a disabling flood of love and tenderness. It was tragic that a man so kind and decent should be so unhappy, that loneliness had driven him so far from home.

Even more than tenderness, she felt a sense of kinship. Impulsively she said, "You mustn't surrender to it."

"Surrender to what?" he asked, turning to face her, his slate eyes shadowed.

"To loneliness," she stammered, embarrassed at her own impertinence. "To give into it is to dance with the devil and lose your very soul."

Under his grave gaze, she felt hot blood rise in her face. She looked away, bitterly sorry that she trespassed beyond the limits of friendship by alluding to intimate, solitary sorrows.

Quietly he said, "If you have danced with the devils of loneliness, you have escaped with your soul and learned wisdom into the bargain."

Elizabeth took a deep, steadying breath, grateful that he had forgiven her lapse. "I think I hear our guide calling. Come, it is time we went back, before he decides that we have fallen into a mud pot."

The Via Toledo had been called the gayest and most populous street in the world, but Randolph paid little attention to the blithe people swirling around him as he strolled through the lamplit night. He had been walking for hours, his thoughts occupied by an alarming but deeply appealing idea.

He had enjoyed Elizabeth Walker's company from the moment they met, but he had thought her self-sufficient, completely comfortable with her life as it was. That belief had changed in an instant that afternoon at Solfatara. In a moment of weakness he had lowered his guard, and rather than ignoring or despising him for his lapse, Elizabeth had done the same. By the act of reaching out to him she had revealed a loneliness as great as his own, and her blend of warmth, generosity, and vulnerability was so potent that he had very nearly said that if they joined their lives, they might banish the worst of their mutual loneliness.

Naturally he had restrained the words; he was too skeptical, too wary, to propose marriage on impulse. Yet the idea had taken hold, and now he found himself wondering what kind of wife Elizabeth would make. And the more he thought, the more his conclusions agreed with his first impression of her. She would make an excellent wife.

He smiled wryly, thinking of Samuel Johnson's remark that a second marriage was the triumph of hope over experience. Randolph had thought that life had cured him first of love, then of marriage, and he had resigned himself to spending the rest of his life alone. Yet here he was, thinking that seeing Elizabeth Walker across a breakfast table would be a very pleasant sight indeed. Chloe had seldom risen in time for breakfast, and when she did, she was invariably irritable and self-absorbed.

Elizabeth was not a beauty, but one beauty was enough for a lifetime. Hard experience had taught Randolph that humor, honesty, and a tolerant mind were far more important in a marriage. And she was far from an antidote. While her face was unremarkable, it was engagingly expressive. He found frank pleasure in the supple grace of her slim body, and a mischievous whirl of wind had revealed that her long legs were truly outstanding.

Realizing that he was hungry, he stopped at a small café. The proprietor spoke enough French to take an order but not enough to carry on a conversation, leaving Randolph free to continue his thoughts over wine and *pollo alla cacciatora*. He was not in love with Elizabeth Walker, nor was he coxcomb enough to think that she loved him, but that didn't matter, for he was not convinced that love was an asset to a marriage.

What mattered was friendship, and in a short time they had become good friends. He knew that most people would think he was a fool to be considering marriage to a woman he had known only a week, but they had spent a great deal of time together, long enough that he felt he knew her better than either of the other women who had been important to him.

He thought the chances of her accepting him were excellent. She seemed to enjoy his company, he was presentable, and his wealth would allow her the time and money to paint. Yes, a marriage between them would work out very well. They were both old enough to know their own minds; if she were willing to marry him, there would be no reason for a long engagement.

Now all he had to do was find the courage to ask her.

The morning air was cold but the sky was glass clear; December 24 promised to be the warmest day since Randolph had arrived in Naples. His driver and carriage showed up scarcely a quarter-hour late, which was stunning punctuality by Neapolitan standards. Vanni was a cheerful fellow with a splendid baritone and villainous shaggy mustaches. His English was no better than Randolph's Neapolitan, but over the last several days he had learned to drive directly to Elizabeth Walker's *pensione*.

Elizabeth was ready when the carriage arrived, but punctuality was no surprise in her case. It was one of the things Randolph liked about her.

"Good morning," she said cheerfully. "Are you game for a drive in the country? My friend Sofia has a mission for us. It is the end of the olive harvest, and she has asked that we collect her year's supply of fresh oil. A respectable cook insists on knowing where her olive oil comes from, and Sofia swears that her cousin presses the best oil in Campania.''

''Which means that it is the best in the world?'' he asked with a smile.

''Exactly. You are beginning to understand the Neapolitan temperament, Lord Randolph.'' Elizabeth lifted a lavishly packed basket. ''As reward for our efforts, Sofia has packed a most sumptuous picnic for us.''

He helped her into the carriage, then he and Vanni stowed the basket of food and a large number of empty stone jugs behind the passenger seat. After a staccato exchange with Elizabeth, Vanni turned the vehicle and began threading his way through the crowded streets. Leaving the city, they headed south to the fertile farmlands near Vesuvius. To Randolph it seemed odd that lifeless volcanic ash eventually became rich soil, but the luxuriant fields confirmed the fact.

The ride through the hills was spectacularly lovely, and having someone to share the sights made them lovelier yet. After two hours of driving they reached their destination, an ancient rambling farmhouse surrounded by silvery olive trees. The two Britons were welcomed joyfully and given a tour, from the vineyards to the hand-operated olive press. As a farmer himself, Randolph enjoyed it thoroughly, and through Elizabeth he and Sofia's cousin exchanged farmer comments.

After Sofia's jars were filled, Randolph and Elizabeth were offered oven-hot bread spread with fresh-squeezed olive oil. Randolph accepted his in the spirit of being a good guest, but his first bite showed him that he had been honored with a matchless delicacy, a local equivalent of the first strawberries of spring. When he finished the first piece, he accepted a second, then a third, to the unconcealed satisfaction of his hosts.

As Elizabeth took a proper leave, a lengthy business, Randolph wondered how many members of the local English colony had experienced such simple pleasures. Probably very few. It was impossible to imagine the likes of Mrs. Bertram enjoying "unrefined" rural life. And had it not been for Elizabeth, he would have seen only the usual sights, met only socially prominent Neapolitans, and never known what he was missing.

Bread and oil takes the edge from an appetite, and after they left the farm, they decided to delay their midday meal and visit Balzano, a nearby hilltop town with a famous church. The inside of the church was dim after the bright sunshine, and Randolph paused in the door while his eyes adjusted. Vaguely aware that several people stood in front of the altar, he inhaled the scents of wax and incense.

"Look," Elizabeth murmured, "they've erected the *presepio*."

He followed her down the aisle and discovered that the figures he had assumed to be local worshipers were wooden statues, life-size, lovingly painted, and very old. The grouping formed a Nativity scene featuring Mary, Joseph, two shepherds, the Three Kings, and a family of sheep.

Softly his companion explained, "You see how the manger is empty? That is because the Child has not yet been born. During the service tonight, a real infant will be placed in the manger. They say it was St. Francis of Assisi who invented the *presepio*. He enacted it with a real mother and father and their babe, to remind people that Christmas was a season for holy celebration rather than profane pleasures."

"A most effective demonstration of the fact that the origin of the word 'holiday' is 'holy day,' " Randolph agreed. "Tonight, by candlelight, it will seem very real."

After viewing the rest of the church, they decided to stroll through the narrow medieval streets before leaving the town. As they neared the bustling market square, they were intercepted by an enterprising peddler who pulled a handful of small figurines from his basket and pressed them on Elizabeth, along with a torrent of enthusiastic words.

"These are *pastori,* figures for a Nativity scene," Elizabeth explained. She handed one to Randolph. "You might find them interesting. They are made of lapis solaris."

He accepted it from her, seeing only a rather crudely formed Madonna. "Stone of the sun?"

"Yes, the material holds light and will glow in the dark for hours. It was invented by an alchemist who was searching for the philosopher's stone. He never found that, but lapis solaris became very popular for rosaries and crucifixes and the like."

Randolph regarded the small figure thoughtfully. "I'm not sure if the basic idea is sublime or ridiculous."

"Both." Elizabeth's lovely hazel eyes danced. "Because he can see that we are *inglesi* of rare discernment, he will offer us a complete *presepio* of lapis solaris for a price so low that it will shame him before all of Balzano if we tell anyone."

Suddenly the ground moved beneath their feet, a subtle, disquieting shift that made the peddler's figurines chatter together in their basket. Randolph tensed, though this was not the first tremor he had experienced since his arrival. He doubted that he would ever get used to them, though Elizabeth and the peddler seemed unconcerned by the earth's betrayal.

As the tremor faded, the peddler spoke to Elizabeth with a smile and a triumphant lift of his hand. She burst out laughing. "He says that his price for the complete *presepio* is so low that God Himself was shocked, and that is why the earth moved."

Randolph joined her laughter. He had already observed that the local peddlers had an audacity that would make a gypsy horse coper blush. He decided that this peddler deserved to make a sale, but for the honor of the English, Randolph bargained over the price for the next quarter-hour.

When they were done, the peddler wrapped the set in an old rag and presented it to Randolph with a flourish. As they walked away, Elizabeth said, "Well done. You brought him down to half the original asking price."

"Which I estimate is at least double what the things are worth," Randolph said with amusement. He removed the top figurine from the bundle. It was the Bambino. "Why do I have the feeling that this was made in Birmingham?"

"Cynic." Elizabeth chuckled. They had reached the market square, which was crowded with people buying the last ingredients for their holiday feasting. "I'm sure that it was made somewhere in Italy. Glowing religious artifacts are just not very English, are they?"

She stopped by a stall that featured marzipan shaped into exquisite imitation fruits and flowers. Knowing that the confections would be popular with the younger Lennoxes, Randolph bought a large number. While the marzipan was being wrapped in silver paper, Elizabeth suddenly jumped, at the same time giving a smothered squeak.

Alarmed, Randolph asked, "Is something wrong?"

"Just someone pinching me," she explained. "A little harder than usual, or I would scarcely have noticed."

"Someone pinched you? Outrageous!" Indignant, Randolph turned toward the square with the vague idea of calling such impertinence to book, but Elizabeth caught his arm.

"Don't be upset, it was not meant as an insult. Quite the contrary." She smiled at him. "It's one of the things I love about Italy. Even though I am much too thin and not at all in the local style, at least once a

day someone will perjure himself by saying or imply-
ing that I am beautiful. I doubt there is another place
in the world where a plain old spinster is made to feel
so desirable.''

Adding the marzipan fruit to his bundles, Randolph
took her arm and began steering her through the
crowd. "You do yourself an injustice, Miss Walker.
You are not old, and what is thin to a Neapolitan is
elegantly slim to an Englishman."

She gave him a startled glance. "Is that a compliment?"

He smiled down at her. "Yes, it is." She looked
quite adorable in her astonishment. If they had not
been surrounded by people, he would have proposed
to her on the spot. What they needed was a place with
a little privacy, which shouldn't be hard to arrange.
"Shall we ask Vanni to find us a suitably scenic site
for a late luncheon? I suspect that Sofia would be outraged if we returned her basket intact."

They had reached the carriage, and as Randolph put
his purchases away, Elizabeth and Vanni conferred.
Eventually she asked, "What say you to a ruined Roman temple, high on a hill, gloriously private, and
possessing a matchless view of Vesuvius?"

"Perfect." Randolph helped her into the carriage,
then swung up beside her. He was beginning to feel a
little nervous. One would think that a man who had
twice before proposed marriage would be a little
calmer about the prospect, but that didn't seem to be
the case. Still, his qualms did not run too deep. At
heart he did not believe that Elizabeth would turn him
down.

The trail had been growing narrower and narrower,
and finally Vanni pulled the horses to a halt and turned
to speak to Elizabeth. She explained to her companion, "This is as close as a carriage can go. Vanni says

the temple is a ten- or fifteen-minute walk along this path.''

Lord Randolph nodded agreeably and took the picnic basket in hand and they started upward. The condition of the path explained why the site was seldom visited. It was narrow and irregular, not much more than a goat track, and had been washed out and repaired more than once. The mountain face rose sheer on the right, then dropped lethally away to the left. Elizabeth went first, keeping close to the rock face and being very careful about where she put her feet.

She rounded the last bend in the trail, then stopped, enchanted. The path widened into a large ledge, with a steep wall on the right and a sheer drop on the left. Perhaps a hundred yards long and fifty wide, the site had soil rich enough to support velvety grass and delicate trees. As Vanni had promised, the view of Vesuvius was spectacular. But all that was simply a setting for the temple, which looked as if it had floated down on temporary loan from fairyland.

Behind her, Lord Randolph said admiringly, ''Anyone who ever built a false ruin would give his left arm to have this instead. It's the ultimate folly.''

The small round shrine was built of white marble that held a hint of rose in its translucent depths. A curving wall formed the back half of the building, with dainty Ionic columns completing the front part of the circle. The roof was long gone and vines climbed the columns for an effect that was beautiful, wistful, and altogether romantic.

Elizabeth said, ''Do you think we should invite Byron to visit? This deserves to be immortalized in poetry.''

''Never,'' Lord Randolph said firmly as he set the picnic basket down. ''If Byron wrote of it, the path would become so jammed with people coming to admire and languish that someone would surely fall down the mountain to his death, and it would be our fault. Much better to let it stay Vanni's secret."

The ruins of an old fire proved that the site was not precisely a secret, but certainly it was seldom visited, for the floor of the shrine was entirely covered with drifted leaves. Elizabeth knelt and carefully brushed them away, finding a charming mosaic of birds, flowers, and butterflies. "I wonder what god or goddess was worshiped here."

"A gentle one, I think."

Glancing up, she saw an odd, assessing look on Lord Randolph's face. Inexplicably she shivered, wondering if there were really tension in the air, or just another example of her overactive imagination.

Seeing her shiver, he offered his hand to help her up. "In spite of the sunshine, in the shade it is still December."

His hand was warm and strong as he lifted her effortlessly. Elizabeth released his clasp as soon as she was on her feet. Her awareness of Lord Randolph's strength and masculinity was acute and uncomfortable. She decided that it was because, in spite of a week of constant company, they had never been quite so alone.

She moved away from him quickly, knowing that her dignity depended on her ability to remain collected. She would rather throw herself from the cliff than let her companion know of her foolish, hopeless passion. Removing the folded lap rug that protected the contents of the basket, she asked, "Shall we see what Sofia has given us? I think we are going to benefit from her Christmas baking."

"There's enough food for an army, or at least a platoon." Randolph reached in the basket and removed the shallow oval bowl. After investigating the contents, he said, "Eel pie?"

"Very likely. The day before Christmas is meatless, and eels are a tradition," Elizabeth explained as she unpacked the basket. "We also have fresh fruit, two cheeses, braided bread, three kinds of Christmas cakes, *pizza rustica*—you'll like that, it's sort of a cheese pie with slivered ham, among other things— and enough red wine to wash it all down."

Randolph blinked. "If the laborers are worthy of their hire, I suppose this is an indication of how much she values her olive oil."

"That, plus the fact that she is continually trying to fatten me up. She thinks you are too thin also." Remembering what else Sofia had said about the English milord—all of it complimentary and some of it decidedly improper—Elizabeth concentrated on laying food out on the cloth. What was wrong with her? A simple picnic with a gentleman and she was behaving like one of her own hot-blooded, romantic charges, every thought revolving around the man at her side. The incredibly handsome, amiable, interested, courteous man at her side. Stop that! she scolded herself. She was glad to see that her hand did not tremble as she poured wine in the two stone cups provided.

The meal was a leisurely one. As they chatted amiably about the day, Elizabeth's nervousness subsided. She considered asking Lord Randolph how much longer he intended to stay in Naples, then decided she would rather not know. Later would be soon enough.

After they had eaten, Elizabeth pulled out her tablet and began sketching the temple, though she despaired of doing justice to it. Having seated himself downwind of her, Randolph smoked his pipe in apparent contentment.

Eventually the lengthening shadows caught her attention and she glanced up. "Heavens, it's getting late. You should have stopped me earlier. I lose track of time when I'm drawing." She closed her tablet and slid it and her pencils into the picnic basket. "The weather is so warm that it's hard to remember that this is one of the shortest days of the year, but it will be dark by the time we reach the city.''

''Miss Walker . . . Elizabeth . . . there is something I want to say before we start back.''

Startled, she sat back on her heels and looked at Lord Randolph. Though he was still seated on the ground, his earlier ease was gone and his lean body was taut with tension. He looked down, fidgeting with his pipe, and she realized that he was using it as an excuse to avoid her eyes.

Taking out his penknife, he started carefully loosening the charred tobacco. ''I have enjoyed this last week immensely.'' He gestured vaguely with his left hand, as if hunting for words, and instead spilled cinders on his fawn-colored breeches. Ruefully he brushed them away, then glanced up at her. ''I'm sorry, I'm not very good at this. I had a speech memorized, but I've entirely forgotten it. Elizabeth, I am very partial to your company, and . . . and I would like to have more of it. Permanently.''

If breathing was not automatic, Elizabeth would have expired on the spot. At first she just stared at him in disbelief. Then his eyes met hers, hope and uncertainty in the depths, and she realized that he meant what he said.

A stab of pain cut through her, anguish as intense as when she had heard of William's death. Amazingly, Lord Randolph wanted her to become his mistress. It was the best offer she would ever get—and she, Elizabeth acknowledged miserably, was too much a child of the vicarage to agree.

Tears started in her eyes and she blinked fiercely, refusing to let them overflow. Her voice a choked whisper, she said, ''I'm sorry, my lord, but I couldn't possibly accept.''

The hope in his eyes flickered and died, replaced first by hurt, then withdrawal. He had never worn the mask of the cool English gentleman with her before, but he donned it now. "No, of course you couldn't. My apologies, Miss Walker, it was just a foolish fancy."

He put his pipe and penknife in his pocket and stood, then lifted the basket. "Pray forgive me if I have embarrassed you. Come, it is time we left. The afternoon is almost over."

It wasn't just the afternoon that was over, but their friendship; Elizabeth knew from his expression that she would never see Lord Randolph after today. She scrambled to her feet unassisted, ignoring his proffered hand. Desiring him and racked with her own loneliness, she daren't touch him, for doing so would cause her to break down entirely.

Wordlessly she led the way back to the path, waging the battle of her life with her conscience. She was sure that his offer sprang not from casual immorality but from a lonely man's yearning for companionship. If he were free to marry, he would ask a younger, prettier woman, but she guessed that he was too honorable to destroy a marriageable girl's chance for respectability. There was no risk of that with someone like Elizabeth, who had been on the shelf for years. Yet he must care a little for her as well, for he could have his choice of a thousand more likely mistresses.

She had known that she loved him, yet had not realized how much until now, when she found herself seriously considering abandoning the training of a lifetime so that she could give him the comfort he sought. But as Elizabeth picked her way along the narrow path, Lord Randolph silent behind her, she knew that her motives were only partly altruistic.

Yes, she wanted to ease his loneliness, but she also wanted to ease her own. She wanted his kindness and wry humor and beautiful body. And almost as much, she wanted to resurrect the Elizabeth Walker she had been before "the slings and arrows of outrageous fortune" had worn her hope away.

Intent on her despairing thoughts, she did not feel the first warning tremor, did not take the action that might have saved her. Her first awareness that something was wrong came when she staggered, almost losing her balance. For an instant she wondered if she had drunk too much wine, or whether her thoughts were making her light-headed.

Then everything seemed to take place at once as disaster unfolded with excruciating slowness. The ground heaved and a low, terrifying rumble filled the air, the vibrations so intense that her skin tingled.

The path began to crumble beneath her feet. Elizabeth tried to scramble to safety, but it was too late, there was nothing left to cling to. She screamed as she pitched sideways from the cliff, falling helplessly. How far was it to the rocks below? And would she feel the shattering of her bones?

Randolph's deep voice shouted, "Elizabeth!" Between one heartbeat and the next, powerful arms seized her and dragged her back to solid ground. She slammed into the rocky path with rib-bruising force.

As she gasped for breath, Randolph pulled her farther from the edge, then threw himself over her, his body shielding her from a torrent of falling earth and gravel. In the midst of chaos and confusion, her sharpest awareness was of Randolph's closeness, the warmth and strength that enfolded her. If they were both going to die, she thought dizzily, she was glad that it would be in his arms.

The earth tremor was an eternity of fear that must have lasted less than half a minute. When the ground had steadied and the last of the rumbling died away, Randolph lifted himself away, gravel showering from him. His voice ragged, he asked urgently, "Elizabeth, are you all right?"

Shakily she pushed herself to a sitting position and straightened her glasses, which by some miracle had not fallen off. "I think so. Thanks to you." She inhaled some dust and doubled over coughing. When she could speak again, she continued, " 'Thank you' doesn't seem strong enough. I thought my hour had come. How are you?''

"A fairly sizable stone hit my shoulder, but nothing seems to be broken." He winced as he stood and brushed himself off, then examined a ripped sleeve ruefully. "However, my hat is gone forever and my coat seems unlikely to recover. My valet will be heartbroken—this coat is one of his favorites."

This time Elizabeth was grateful to accept his assistance in rising. "Is it one of your favorites as well?"

"I am not permitted to have opinions about matters that fall within Burns' purview, and that definitely includes coats." He looked beyond Elizabeth, then gave a soft whistle. "Fortunate that Sofia gave us so much food, for I fear that we may be here longer than we expected."

Still a little unsteady, Elizabeth turned cautiously, grateful when Lord Randolph put a firm hand on her arm. She bit her lip in dismay at the sight behind. About ten feet of the path had disappeared completely, and it made her dizzy to look down, knowing how near an escape she had had. Beyond the gap, the path seemed intact but was covered with rubble until it curved out of sight around the hill. "I hope Vanni is all right," she said, "for both his sake and ours."

"I'm sure he is," Lord Randolph said. "He and the carriage were on solid, level ground."

Confirmation came almost immediately when the driver's voice shouted from around the corner, *"Signorina, signore!"*

Elizabeth called back, reassuring him that they were well, then explaining that part of the path had collapsed so they could not clear the rubble away themselves. After the driver replied, she translated for her companion. "Vanni say the path is clear and solid just around the corner, so it shouldn't be too hard to remove the fallen earth from that direction. He will go back to Balzano to get men to dig and planks to bridge the gap.''

"What if the town has been badly hit by the earthquake?" Randolph asked grimly. "They may have more serious concerns than two stranded foreigners."

Elizabeth relayed his comment, then the driver's response. "Vanni says that this was only a little tremor. If the earth had not been soft from rain, there would be no problem here."

"Let us hope he is right. Tell him that I will pay the men he brings an exorbitant amount of money for their help, and double that if they can get us out this evening."

Another round of shouting and answer. Elizabeth shook her head at the reply. "Vanni says that it would be impossible to get anyone to come tonight since it's Christmas Eve, but he swears that tomorrow we will be free sometime between Mass and the midday meal."

Randolph sighed. "I suppose that will have to do." He turned and picked up the basket from where he had dropped it when the tremor hit. It had survived intact, if somewhat the worse for wear.

Elizabeth followed him back to the temple site. Still a little shaky from her escape, she was content to sit and watch while he explored the whole area, foot by foot. Eventually he returned to her. "If, God forbid, Vanni doesn't return, I think I could manage to climb over and around the landslide area, so we won't be trapped here indefinitely."

She looked at the steep rock face and shuddered. "Let us hope that it doesn't come to that."

"I don't think it will, but I am happier for knowing that there are alternatives." He looked at the sky and frowned. "The sun will be down in another hour, and it is going to be very cold here without any shelter. Fortunately I brought my flint and steel, so we can

light a fire, but there is precious little fuel. I imagine
that previous visitors used most of what was available.
Still, we should find enough wood to keep from freezing tonight.''

For the next half-hour, the two of them gathered
wood and stacked it by a shallow depression in the
rocky cliff. It wasn't even remotely a cave, but it offered the best available protection from the weather.
Elizabeth wrinkled her nose at the results. "It isn't a
very impressive wood pile.''

"No, but it should be enough.'' He retrieved the lap
rug from the basket and handed it to her. "You had
better wrap yourself in this.''

She accepted the lap rug gratefully and wrapped it
around her shoulders, wishing that it was twice as large
and thrice as heavy. "Women's clothing is not designed for winter, just as men's clothing is usually too
heavy for hot weather,'' she said philosophically, "but
with this I will do well enough.''

For lack of anything more productive to do, Elizabeth sat down with her back to the cliff, drawing her
knees up and linking her arms around them. To the
southwest, the massive black silhouette of Vesuvius
dominated the horizon. The only signs of man were
occasional distant farm buildings. The scene could as
easily have been Roman as in this civilized year of
1817.

Above the rugged hills, the sky was shot with gold
and vermilion, while a nest of violet clouds hugged
the horizon and welcomed the molten sun. Nodding
toward the sunset, she said, "We may have a long,
uncomfortable night ahead, but that is almost adequate
compensation. How often do we take the time to enjoy
a sunset?''

"Not often enough,'' Randolph agreed, settling
down on the temple steps so he could admire nature's
flamboyant artistry.

But in spite of the spectacular sky, Elizabeth found

that more of her attention was on her companion, who sat less than a dozen feet away. Hatless and disheveled, his hair touched to liquid gold by the waning sun, he was no longer the impeccable English gentleman. Now the power that underlay his gentle courtesy was visible, and she felt a faint sense of disquiet. Might Lord Randolph decide to take advantage of their enforced proximity to attempt seduction? If he did, she would be helpless before his superior strength. . . .

With an appalled shock, Elizabeth realized that she wanted him to try to seduce her. In fact, her devious lower nature was delighting in a situation that would allow her to submit with a clear conscience, absolved of sin. Unfortunately, her vicarage morals were not so easily fooled.

Hugging her knees closer, she chastised herself for being a shameless, disgusting creature. If Lord Randolph was the sort of man who would take advantage of their situation to force his attentions on her, he was not the man she had fallen in love with and she wouldn't want him. Besides, she doubted that he had any such interest in her; he had said himself that his offer was foolish fancy. By now, he was probably thanking his lucky stars that she had refused.

But if he wasn't, this temporary captivity must be even more awkward for him than for her. He was the one who had been rejected. He must be hating the sight of her.

Oblivious to her lurid thoughts, Randolph said with a trace of wry amusement, "I knew Christmas in Italy would be different from home, but I never dreamed just how different."

"Yes," Elizabeth agreed somberly, "but at least we're alive. If we had started down the path a few seconds sooner . . ."

"Very true," he said, his voice dry. "So I suppose there was some value to my misbegotten proposal, since it delayed us."

"I know that being trapped here with me must be difficult for you. I'm sorry," she said in a small voice.

He shrugged his broad shoulders. "Don't apologize—the fault is mine. I should have known that one seldom gets a second chance where love and marriage are concerned. For my sins of bad judgment, I must pay the price."

His words cut too close to the bone, and she drew a shuddering breath. "You are right. For whatever reason—bad judgment, bad luck—most of us only get one chance for happiness. We think it will last an eternity, and then it vanishes like smoke in our hands."

He turned to face her, a silhouette against the bright sky. "What happened to your chance, Elizabeth? Why are you spending your life raising other women's children rather than your own?"

She sighed. "It's not a very dramatic story. William and I were childhood sweethearts. He was the younger son of the squire, I was the daughter of the vicar. Our families were not enthralled by the match, for neither of us had any prospects, but we were young, optimistic, willing to work hard. We had our whole lives planned. William's father bought him a pair of colors and off he went to the Peninsula. I was teaching and saving my salary. When he became a captain, we would marry and I would follow the drum."

"But that didn't happen."

"No," she whispered. "Within a year he was dead. Not even nobly, fighting the French, but of a fever."

"I'm sorry," he said gently. "That was a dreadful waste of a brave young life, and a tragic loss for you."

In her fragile mood, his compassion almost broke her. She made an effort to collect herself. "I feel fortunate for what little we had, even if it was much less than we had expected." She tried a smile, without complete success. "Really, it was a great stroke of luck that even one man wanted to marry me. I'm not the sort to inspire a grand passion, and without a portion I wasn't very marriageable. If William and I hadn't grown up together, I doubt he would have looked twice at me, but as it was, we . . . well, we were part of each other.''

"I wish you would stop demeaning yourself," Randolph said sternly. "Beauty and fortune have their place, but they are not what make a good wife."

"As you learned to your cost?" she asked quietly.

"As I learned, to my cost." He stood abruptly. "I'd better start a fire while there is still a little light."

It was fortunate that Lord Randolph had flint and steel, and a penknife to whittle dry wood shavings from the inside of a branch. Soon a small fire was crackling away. He sat back on his heels, staying close enough to feed the blaze easily. "Having a fire brings civilization a little closer."

Elizabeth did not agree. Even with a fire, civilization seemed very distant, and she found herself speaking with a boldness that normally she would not have dared. "You said that you had committed the sin of bad judgment," she said tentatively. "If your sin was falling in love with a beautiful face, then finding that the lady's character was not so fine as her features, that is not such a reprehensible crime. Many young men do the same."

Lord Randolph must have felt the same lessening of civilized constraints, because he answered her comment rather than giving her the set-down she deserved. "True, but that is not what I did. My crime was much worse. Like you, I fell in love young. Unlike you, our families were delighted. Lady Alyson was a great heiress, and I was a good match for her—of similar rank, wealthy enough so as not to be a fortune-hunter. And as a younger son, I would have ample time to devote to managing her property when she inherited."

Throwing the last shred of her manners to the winds, Elizabeth asked, "Was the problem that she did not love you?"

The muscles of his face went taut in the flickering light. "No, she did love me. And I, in one moment of foolish cowardice, hurt her unforgivably and wrecked both our lives."

The silence that followed was so long that finally Elizabeth said, "I realize that this is absolutely none of my business, but I am perishing of curiosity. Is what happened so unspeakable?"

His face eased. "Having said that much, I suppose I should tell the rest. I made the mistake of calling on Alyson with one of my more boisterous friends along. While we were waiting for her in the drawing room, my friend asked why I was marrying her. If Alyson had been a little golden nymph, he could have understood, but she wasn't at all in the common way."

Randolph sighed. "I should have hit him. Instead, because my feelings for Alyson were too private to expose to someone who might make sport of them, I said breezily that I was marrying her for her money. I knew that was a reason he would understand."

Elizabeth had a horrible feeling that she knew what happened next. "Alyson overheard and cried off?"

"Worse than that." Carefully he laid two larger pieces of wood on the fire. "I didn't learn the whole story until quite recently. She did overhear and told her father she wouldn't marry me if I were the last man on earth, but wouldn't explain why she had changed her mind. Thinking she was just being missish, her father became very gothic and locked her in her room, swearing that he would keep her there until she agreed to go through with the marriage. Feeling betrayed by both her father and me, Alyson ran away. She stayed away for twelve long years. Just this last September she returned and reconciled with her father."

"Good heavens," Elizabeth said blankly. "How did she survive so long on her own?"

"First she taught. Later, by chance, she became a

land steward, quite a successful one. As I said, she
was not in the common way. You remind me of her.''
Randolph glanced up from the fire, which he had been
watching with unnecessary vigilance. ''After Alyson
vanished, I wondered if it was my fault, so when she
returned I asked her. She confirmed that she had overheard me, and that was why she had run away.'' He
gave a bitter laugh. ''This story would be better told
at Easter than Christmas. I felt like Peter must have
when he realized that he had denied his Master three
times before the cock crowed.''

Elizabeth's heart ached for both of them—two young
lovers shattered by a moment of foolishness. No wonder Randolph could not forgive himself. And the fact
that Lady Alyson had run away from her whole life
was vivid proof of the anguish she had felt at the apparent betrayal of the man she had loved and trusted.

Elizabeth tried to imagine what Randolph's meeting
with his former love had been like, but imagination
boggled. ''Calling on her must have taken a great deal
of courage.''

''I decided that it was easier to know for sure than
to continue to live with guilty uncertainty,'' he said
shortly. The corner of his mouth twisted up in wry
self-mockery. ''In fact, Alyson was amazingly easy on
me. I wouldn't have blamed her if she had greeted me
with a dueling pistol, but instead she said that the fault
lay as much with her and her father as with me, and
that her life had not been ruined in the least.''

''Your Alyson sounds like a remarkable woman.''

''She is, but she's not my Alyson anymore. A few
weeks after emerging from exile, she married one of
the most notorious rakes in England, and I have it on
the best authority that he is a reformed man: sober,
responsible, and as besotted with her as she is with
him. Alyson is happy now, and she deserves to be.
She is one of those rare people who forged herself a
second chance for happiness.'' Randolph linked his

fingers together and stared into the fire. "I've been telling myself since September that it all worked out for the best. Her strength of character would have been wasted on me. I have no interesting vices to reform, and doubtless would have bored her very quickly."

"Do you still love her?"

He sighed, his face empty. "The young man I was loved the young woman she was. Neither of those people exists anymore."

It wasn't quite an answer, but at least now Elizabeth understood why he had offered her a *carte blanche:* it was because she resembled the woman he had loved. Where did his wife fit into the picture? In the lonely years after Lady Alyson disappeared, he must have married without love, and lived to regret it. Elizabeth did not dare ask about his marriage; she had already been unpardonably inquisitive. Sadly she said, "Perhaps it is only the young who are foolish enough, or brave enough, to fall in love, and that is the reason why there are few second chances."

Having let her hair down metaphorically, Elizabeth decided that it was time to do so literally as well, or she would have a headache before morning. After removing her hairpins and tucking them in the basket so they wouldn't get lost, she combed her tangled curls with her fingers in a futile attempt to restore order. When Randolph glanced over, she explained, "In case any wolves or other beasts find their way up here, I am letting my hair down so that I can play Medusa and turn them to stone."

He chuckled, his earlier melancholy broken. "You should wear your hair down more often—it becomes you."

Elizabeth rolled her eyes in comic disbelief, and he wondered if she ever believed compliments. In truth, by firelight and with her brown hair crackling with red and gold highlights, she looked very winsome. Perhaps not beautiful, but thoroughly delectable.

He hastily looked back at the fire, knowing that that was a dangerous train of thought under these circumstances, when she had made it clear that he did not fit into her plans for the future. Apparently, having loved well and truly, she did not want to marry without love. Perhaps she was wiser than he, for he had tried that once, with disastrous consequences. Nonetheless, the more he saw of Elizabeth Walker, the more he thought that they would deal very well together, if she were willing to lower her standards and accept him.

Perhaps speaking so openly of their pasts should have made them more awkward with each other, but the reverse was true. The evening drifted by in companionable silence, broken by occasional desultory conversation. They sat a couple of feet apart with their backs against the cliff wall, which offered some protection from the bitter December wind. Vesuvius was close enough for a faint glow to be visible against the night sky. It was a dramatic but disquieting sight. Fortunately the little fire offered cheery comfort as well as some warmth.

Eventually they made further inroads on the picnic basket and still had enough food for another meal or two. After they had eaten and drunk some of the wine, Randolph asked, "How are you managing? It's cold now, and it will be considerably colder by tomorrow morning."

"I'm fine, thank you."

Elizabeth's voice sounded a little stiff, and when Randolph looked more closely and saw how she was huddled into the lap rug, he understood why. "You're freezing, aren't you? And too practical to say so when we haven't enough wood to burn it at a faster rate."

"You said it, not I."

Randolph peeled his coat off and handed it to her. "Put this on."

"Don't be silly," she said, refusing to accept it and keeping her hands tucked under the lap rug. "That would just mean that you'd freeze, too. I will do very well.'' There was a suggestion of chattering teeth under her brave words.

"You don't appear to be doing well. Come, take my coat,'' he coaxed. ''Cold has never bothered me much, while six years in Italy have probably thinned your blood to the point where you are more sensitive to cold than the average Englishwoman.''

Elizabeth looked mulish; she definitely had much in common with Alyson. Why did tall, stubborn, independent females who were not in the common way appeal to him so much? He smiled a little, realizing that his question contained its own answer. "Very well, if you won't accept my coat, we will have to resort to a time-honored method of keeping warm.''

He put his coat back on. Then, before she realized what he had in mind, he leaned over and scooped her into his arms. She squeaked in surprise, as she had when she was pinched in Balzano. It was a very endearing squeak.

"You really are freezing,'' he commented as she shivered against him. He arranged her across his lap and settled comfortably against the cliff wall as he began rubbing her back, shoulders, and arms, trying to get her blood moving again. She had a delicious scent of rosewater and oranges.

"This is most improper,'' she murmured into his lapel.

"Yes, but warmer for both of us. Think of your duty, Miss Walker,'' he admonished. "You may prefer to solidify into a block of ice yourself, but will you condemn me to the same fate?''

She pulled her head back and gave him a darkling look. ''You're teasing me.''

He grinned. "Making your blood boil should keep you warm.''

Elizabeth knew that she really should not permit

this, but she lacked the will to resist. It wasn't just his wonderful physical warmth, which was beginning to thaw her out; it was the intimacy of being in his arms. This was surely the most romantic thing that was ever going to happen to her, and she might as well enjoy it. She nestled closer, savoring the faint aroma of apple-scented tobacco that clung to his coat, but total comfort was prevented by a hard object pressing into her hip. She shifted her position. "If that is your pipe in your left pocket, I may be in danger of breaking it."

"Wrong pocket. I thought that one was empty, actually. Excuse me while I investigate." He removed his arm from around her and dug into the pocket, finally withdrawing an object in triumph. "Here it is."

His whole body stilled. Elizabeth twisted to see what had caught his attention, then sighed with delight. The lapis solaris figure of the Bambino had seemed crude by daylight, but now darkness transformed it. Cupped in Randolph's palm, the Holy Infant glowed with a soft, magical light, a miracle child come to bring hope to the hearts of men.

"I took it out of the *presepio* set earlier and must have slipped it into my pocket by accident," he murmured.

Elizabeth smiled and shook her head. "Not by accident. The Bambino came to remind us that tonight is a special night, the night of his birth. Remember that the Italian climate is similar to that of the Holy Land. It might have been just such a night as this in Bethlehem when the angels visited the shepherds." Quietly she began quoting from the book of Luke, beginning with the words, " 'And it came to pass in those days that there went out a decree from Caesar Augustus, that all the world should be taxed . . .' " Not for nothing had she been raised in a vicarage; word-perfect, she retold the immortal story.

" 'For behold, I bring you tidings of great joy,' "

Randolph repeated softly when she had finished. "Thank you, Elizabeth. You have just delivered the most moving Christmas service I've ever heard."

The only sounds were the crackle of the fire, the occasional distant bleat of a sheep, and the sighing of the wind. When the fire began to die down, Randolph asked, "Are you warm now?"

"Wonderfully so." She did not add that the heat that curled through her body was more than just temperature.

"Then it's time to make some adjustments. I don't suppose either of us will sleep much, but we might as well be as comfortable as possible."

To her regret, he removed her from his lap, so he could tend to the fire. When it was burning steadily again, he positioned the rest of the wood so that it could be easily added, a piece at a time. "If you lie down on your side between me and the fire, you should stay fairly warm, though I'll probably disturb you whenever I add wood to the fire."

She took off her spectacles and put them in the basket, then stretched out as he had suggested, the lap rug tucked around her. Randolph lay down behind her and wrapped his arm around her waist, pulling her close so that they were nestled together like two spoons. The ground was hard and cold and not very comfortable; Randolph was warm and firm and very comfortable indeed. Elizabeth gave a sigh of pleasure and relaxed in his embrace, thinking that this was even better than being on his lap. "Merry Christmas, Randolph," she whispered. She had never been happier in her life.

Randolph did not precisely sleep, but between bouts of tending the fire he dozed a little. Elizabeth was a delightful armful as she cuddled trustfully against him and unlike him, she had slept soundly. The fruits of a clear conscience, no doubt.

As the sky began lightening in anticipation of dawn, he carefully lifted himself away and added the next-to-last piece of wood. The air was bitter cold, but fortunately the night had been dry and within an hour or so the temperature should start to rise.

Before he could settle back, Elizabeth stretched and rolled over on her back, then opened her eyes and blinked sleepily at him, her hair curling deliciously around her face. There was something very intimate about seeing her without her spectacles—rather as if she had removed her gown and greeted him in her shift. Thinking improper thoughts, he murmured, "Good morning."

She gave him a smile of shimmering, wondering sweetness, as if this morning were the dawn of the world and she were Eve greeting Adam for the first time.

It seemed the most natural thing in the world to lean forward and give her a gentle kiss. Elizabeth's mouth was soft and welcoming—and sweet, so sweet. He lay down beside her and drew her into his arms, wanting to feel the full length of her slim, supple body against him.

As the kiss deepened, her arms slid around his neck, and her responsiveness triggered a wave of fierce, demanding desire that brought Randolph to his senses. Knowing that if he did not stop soon, it would be impossible to stop at all, he pulled abruptly away from her. His breathing unsteady, he said, "I'm sorry, Elizabeth. You have a most extraordinary effect on me."

She stared at him, her eyes wide and stark. Then she sat up and grabbed her glasses from the basket, donning them hastily as if they were a suit of armor. Under her breath, she said, "The effect seems to be mutual."

Spectacles and propriety once more in place, she said, "Since the fire won't last much longer, shall we toast some of the cheese and spread it on the last of the bread? Hot food would be very welcome.''

Randolph did not know whether to feel grateful or insulted that she was ignoring what had been a truly superior kiss. Dangerously superior, in fact; the idea of kissing her again was much more appealing than bread and cheese, and the results of that would warm them both through and through. With difficulty, he turned his attention to practical considerations. ''An excellent idea,'' he said, ''though I think I would trade everything in the basket for a large pot of scalding hot tea.''

''That is a cruel thing to say, Lord Randolph,'' she said severely. Longing showed in her face. ''Strong Italian coffee with hot milk would do equally well. And lots of sugar.''

He laughed. ''We shouldn't torture ourselves like this. Tomorrow morning we will be able to drink all the tea or coffee we want, and will appreciate it more for today's lack.''

The melted cheese and toasted bread turned out to be an inspired choice for fortifying themselves for the rigors of the day. By the time the fire had flickered down to embers and the sun had risen over the horizon, Randolph felt ready to face the difficult conversation that he had known was inevitable. Leaning back against the wall, he said, ''Elizabeth, there is something we must talk about.''

Daintily she licked the last crumbs from her fingers, then gave him a bright smile. ''Yes, my lord?''

''Since we have spent the night together, I'm afraid that you are now officially ruined,'' he said baldly. ''There is really only one recourse, though I know it is not agreeable to you.''

She shook her head. ''Nonsense,'' she retorted. ''I'm only ruined if people learn about last night, and probably not even then. I'm not an English girl making her come-out, you know. As a foreign woman of mature years, I exist outside the normal structure of Italian society and won't be judged by the same rules. Therefore I won't be ruined even if what happened becomes generally known.'' A glint of humor showed behind her spectacles. ''Indeed, most Italian women would envy me the experience of being 'ruined' by you.''

Ignoring her levity, he said, ''Do you think the family of the terrible twins, who want a cold-blooded Englishwoman to govern their hot-blooded daughters, will be so tolerant? Or other potential employers?''

Uncertainty flickered across her face as his words struck home. ''There could be problems if last night became generally known,'' she admitted, ''but I still think that is unlikely. I am not really part of the Neapolitan English community. Who would bother to gossip about me?''

''You think that everyone in this part of Campania hasn't already heard that there were two *inglesi* trapped up here on Christmas Eve? If the story hasn't already reached Naples, it will today.'' Randolph grimaced. ''Unfortunately, I was engaged to dine at the British Embassy last night, and my absence will have been noted. The local gossips know we have been spending time together. How long will it take someone to guess who the marooned *inglesi* are? Your reputation will be in shreds and you will be unemployable, at least as a governess.''

Her face was pale, but she said, ''Shouldn't we wait and see before assuming the worst?''

''Perhaps my anxiety is premature, but I don't think so.'' His mouth twisted. ''I know you don't want to marry me, Elizabeth, but if there is the least hint of scandal, I swear I will drag you off to the nearest Protestant clergyman. Even if you have no concern for your reputation, I'll be damned if I want to be known as a man who refused to do the right thing by you.''

Elizabeth was staring at him, her shock palpable.

Cursing inwardly for having upset her, Randolph said in a softer voice, "I swear that I won't force you to live with me, or to do anything else you don't want to do. I will settle an income on you and you can live wherever you choose and paint until you lose track of what year it is. But I will *not* let you be injured by an accident that would never have happened if you had not been acting as my friend and guide."

She swallowed hard. "But how can you marry me? What about your wife?"

"My wife?" he asked, startled. "Where did you get the idea that I was married?"

"When we were at Solfatara," she faltered, "you said that the loneliest place on earth was a bad marriage. You sounded so much as if you were speaking from experience that I was sure you must be married. It seemed to explain so much about you."

Randolph was silent as he thought back. "You're very perceptive, Elizabeth," he said finally. "I *was* speaking from personal experience, but my wife died three years ago, after not much more than a year of marriage." Then he remembered the day before and frowned. "Good God, did you refuse my offer yesterday because you thought I was setting up to be a bigamist, or lying in order to seduce you?"

She was so surprised that she let go of the lap rug and it slid from her shoulders. "You were asking me to *marry* you?"

"Of course. What did you think I was doing, offering you a *carte blanche?*" He said it as a joke, and was appalled to see her nod. "I would never have offered you such an insult, and I think I should be angry that you believed me capable of it."

Her face flamed and she looked down. In a choked whisper, she said, "I didn't feel insulted, I felt flattered. I was just too cowardly to accept."

Seeing the humor in the situation, Randolph began laughing. "I certainly bungled that proposal, didn't

I?'' he said ruefully. He stood and crossed the half-dozen feet to where she sat regarding him uncertainly. Going down on one knee, he caught her hands between his. "I will try again and see if I can get this right. Elizabeth, will you marry me? Not to save anyone's reputation, but a real marriage, because we want to be together?''

Her cold hands clenched convulsively on his. Behind her spectacles, her eyes were huge and transparent as silent tears began welling up. "Randolph, I can't,'' she whispered.

She tried to pull away, but he kept a firm grip on her hands. Yesterday he had accepted rejection too quickly, and that was not a mistake he would make again. "Why not? Is it that you can't abide the thought of having me for a husband?''

She shook her head miserably. "I can think of nothing I would like more.''

He smiled; they were making progress. Patiently he asked, "Do you have a husband somewhere so you aren't free to marry?''

She gave him an indignant look. "Of course not.''

"Then, why won't you say yes? I warn you, I will not let you go until you either accept me or offer a good reason for refusing.''

She turned her head away, her face scarlet with mortification. "Because . . . because I could not come to you as a bride should.''

He thought about that for a minute. "Do you think you could be more specific? I want to be sure I understand.''

"Before William went into the army," her breath was coming in ragged gulps, and she could not meet his eyes, "we . . . we gave ourselves to each other.''

"I see.'' At her words, profound tenderness welled up inside him, and another emotion too unfamiliar to name. Releasing Elizabeth's hands, he wrapped his arms around her and pulled her close so that her head was tucked under his chin. She was trembling. Gently he stroked her unruly curls, trying to soothe away the unhappiness he had caused. "Because you gave yourself in love to the man you were going to marry, you think that you are unfit to be a wife? Quite the contrary. I can think of no better qualification for marriage. Will you marry me, Elizabeth? Please?"

She pulled back and stared at him. Her glasses had steamed from her tears and she took them off so she could study his face better. "Do you really mean that, Randolph? Or would you have second thoughts later and feel cheated?"

"Yes, I mean it." He stood and drifted over to the steps of the shrine, searching for the best way to explain his feelings so that in the future she would never doubt him. Absently he laid one hand on a smooth marble column, tinted rose in the early-morning light. "As you guessed, my marriage was not a happy one," he said haltingly. "I wasn't really in love with Chloe, but I had given up hope that Alyson would ever return and I wanted to marry. Chloe was well-bred and very beautiful, and she made it clear that she would welcome an offer from me. Everyone said what a 'good match' it was. She was very proper and reserved, but I thought that was just shyness, which would quickly pass once we were married.

"I was wrong." He turned to face Elizabeth, who was standing a half-dozen feet away in grave silence. "I had thought her desire for matrimony meant that she cared for me, but soon I realized that though Chloe wanted the status of wife, she did not want a husband. Perhaps it was me in particular that she couldn't bear, but I don't think so."

He looked away, swallowing hard, thinking that it was simple justice that he must speak of something that was as painful for him as Elizabeth's confession had been for her. "She did not like to be touched, ever. Nor did she ever touch me, except in public sometimes she would take my arm, to show other women that I belonged to her.

"I don't mean just that she disliked marital relations, though she did. As soon as she had done her duty and conceived, she told me not to come near her again. Being denied her bed did not bother me half so much as her total lack of interest in giving or receiving any kind of affection. Perhaps the need for warmth and affection is deeper than physical desire." He shook his head vehemently, as if he could throw off the misery and yearning of the past. "Even when she was dying, she would not take my hand. There was nothing she ever wanted from me except my name and fortune."

He inhaled deeply to calm himself, then caught Elizabeth's gaze. "Do you understand now why I welcome the knowledge that you are a warm and caring woman? If you could give me even half as much warmth as you had for William, I would think myself the luckiest man alive."

"Unfortunate Chloe, to be unable to accept any love or affection," Elizabeth said with deep compassion. In a few swift steps she closed the distance between them and flowed into his arms. "And unfortunate Randolph, to have so much to give and no one to value the gift or the giver."

Her embrace was more than passionate, it was loving. And as he crushed her to him, Randolph identified the emotion that had been growing inside him. "I was wrong," he said softly. "There are second chances. I thought I wanted to marry you for companionship, but my heart must have known before my head did. I love you, Elizabeth. I came to Italy for sunshine, and I found it when I met you, for your smile lights up the world."

"Truly?" She tilted her head back. "You hardly know me."

"Wrong." He rubbed his cheek against Elizabeth's curly hair. She was a very convenient height. "We may have not known each other long, but I know you better than I knew Alyson, and infinitely better than I knew Chloe.'' He gave her a teasing smile. ''Is it safe to interpret your shameless behavior as a willingness to wed?''

''It is. You were quite right, Randolph, I *am* ruined, so hopelessly, madly, passionately in love with you that I shall be good for nothing unless you marry me.'' Elizabeth gave him the heart-deep smile that made her incomparably lovely. ''Just as Lady Alyson is your past, William is mine. I loved him and part of my heart died when he did, but the woman I am now, plain middle-aged spinster that I am, is yours, body, heart, and soul. Will that do?''

''No,'' he said severely. ''You are going to have to stop talking such nonsense about how plain and middle-aged you are. Just how old are you?''

''Thirty.''

''A wonderful age. Thirty-one will be better, and fifty better yet.''

Randolph kissed her with rich deliberation, working his way from her lips to a sensitive spot below her ear. She gasped, thinking that her knees had turned to butter.

He whispered, ''Do you think I would want you this much if I thought you were plain?''

Elizabeth was twined around him so closely that she had no doubts about just how much he did want her. ''I think that you need spectacles more than I do,'' she said breathlessly, ''but since beauty is in the eye of the beholder, your opinion is inarguable.''

''Good. I can think of much better things to do than argue.'' Randolph was about to start kissing her again when a shout sounded from the direction of the path. Elizabeth twisted her head so she could hear better, then called out an answer. After a lengthy exchange, she reported, ''Vanni says that they will have us out within two hours, so we can be in Naples for Christmas dinner.''

"Tell them not to rush," Randolph murmured. His slate-blue eyes warm with love and mischief, he removed her spectacles and tucked them in his pocket. "We don't want your glasses to steam up while we wait, do we?"

Her heart expanding with joy, Elizabeth lifted her face to his, and as the Christmas sun rose in the sky, they celebrated the season of hope. Together.

The Last Wish

by

Anita Mills

"Well, I ain't staying. Don't know why I came in the first place—don't know why you did either, Win," the thin, pale exquisite insisted. "As for Drew, he don't need the money."

"Lower your voice, George," his brother ordered. "He's not dead yet."

"No, and it don't look to me as he's about to pop off anytime soon, if you want my opinion of it," George Allyn complained peevishly. "Ten to one, 'twas all a hum to get us here for Christmas, don't you know? And I can tell you, I'd as lief be anywhere else on earth."

"Then go."

Both brothers turned suspicious eyes on the gentleman who lounged easily against the carved marble mantel. George's gaze traveled over their cousin, taking in Hoby's finest riding boots, the glove-smooth buff breeches, Weston's exquisitely cut coat, the snowy cravat executed in a fall of his own making, the finely chiseled, albeit slightly arrogant face, and the glossy black windswept hair, and his indignation grew.

"Don't know why you bothered to come, Drew," he muttered nastily. "Got more money than the old man, anyways, ain't you? A regular Corinthian, too— looks, address—don't tell me as you wouldn't rather

75

spend Christmas somewheres else, for I'll not swallow the tale.''

"Greed,'' Edwin Allyn uttered succinctly. "Plain greed.''

For a moment, the object of their resentment appeared to consider the charge, then a faint smile played at one corner of his mouth. "Actually,'' he drawled, "I am in retreat.''

"You?'' George sneered. "Coming it too strong, Drew! If you was to pay half the tradesmen in England, your purse'd still be nigh full.''

"Plain as a pikestaff—he's here to cut us out.''

The smile vanished entirely, and the hazel eyes turned to ice. "Not at all. Marchbanks thought to count my money a trifle too soon.''

The two brothers exchanged looks, then George blurted out, "You mean you ain't going to offer for the chit? But it was as good as done. I heard it from Revenham myself. Of all the—''

"For heaven's sake, George, keep your voice down. Uncle Jack—''

"Why? Old gent don't like me above half, anyways. Ought not to have come—bound to remind him of it. Can't think why Bagshot sent for me, if you want the truth of it, unless 'tis a jest. And now Drew says he ain't going to offer for Miss Marchbanks. 'Tis all of a piece, ain't it?''

"I advised you to wager the other way,'' Edwin reminded him. "I knew it was a hum from the outset.''

"And you bet against it. Well . . .'' George stopped, flushing guiltily, and cast a quick look at his cousin. "Well, dash it, Drew. Pockets were to let, and how else was I to come about? What the devil's the matter with Melissa Marchbanks, anyway? Deuced fine-looking female.''

"She's a pretty peagoose,'' Edwin answered. "Drew don't favor that kind.''

"And he don't marry the high-flyers,'' his brother

retorted. "But he's nigh thirty-five, ain't he? Time to settle down." Turning to Andrew Carstairs, he appealed with outstretched hands. "Ain't nothing wrong with Miss Marchbanks—got looks, breeding—do you credit, in fact."

"And he's got a thousand pounds on the match," Edwin added smugly. "Pay him no heed, coz."

"Don't listen to Win. He's got at least five hundred down against it," George pleaded.

"Actually, all I said was that Swynford don't marry ere a twelvemonth is out. I would not for the world distress an innocent female—even an empty-headed one—by using her name."

"Got to have an heir," George persisted desperately.

"I am three-and-thirty," Drew answered dryly. "And not the least likely to sacrifice myself at the matrimonial altar to satisfy anyone's debts, George. You, of all, ought to know that."

"Got no feeling—that's what it is. Don't care if I was to go to Newgate, do you?"

"Gentlemen . . ." Josiah Bagshot stepped into the room, then turned to shut the door behind him. "Most regrettable, I admit, but—"

"Regrettable," George exploded. "Could it not wait until after Christmas? He don't look like a man about to stick his spoon in the wall to me."

"George!"

"Cut line, Win. You wouldn't be here neither, if you wasn't thinking it had something to do with the will, and you know it."

"Perhaps Uncle Jack merely wishes to spend his last Christmas on earth with his loving family," Drew hazarded.

"Pack of nonsense! He don't like me, he don't like Win, and if he likes you, I ain't never heard of it. Uncle Jack," George pronounced definitely, "don't like nobody. And if the truth be told, we ain't overly fond of him neither. A man as would turn away from his own son . . . Well, if he's summoned me to toadeat him, he's—''

"Stifle it, George," Edwin snapped. "We'll both toadeat him, if we have to, and well you know it. Drew's the only one as can afford not to."

"Just so," their cousin agreed mildly. Turning to Bagshot, he directed, "Do continue."

The solicitor nodded stiffly. "As I was about to explain, my lord, Sir John Grey is in truth quite ill, and it is the opinion of Dr. Hatch and other consulting physicians that there is no recovery. Indeed, but his disease has already progressed to the point where laudanum is required to ease his suffering." He looked directly at George. "Two weeks ago, I was informed that he might not live past Christmas, and it was then that I decided to write, apprising you of his condition. Now it appears that he may linger longer."

"How much longer?" George asked suspiciously.

"That, sir, is in the hands of the Almighty alone. Dr. Hatch is of the opinion that 'tis fear that keeps him alive."

"Never heard such a farradiddle in all my life! There—you hear that, Win? Drew? If fear kept a man here, wouldn't nobody go. Well, I ain't stayin' to wait. Ten to one, he ain't dying at all." Pushing past Bagshot, he reached for the doorknob.

"If you leave, I'll do my damnedest to cut you out of the will, George," his brother promised him. "And I won't cover the thousand pounds you've got on the books at Brooks's."

"Damn it, Win, you got no right—"

"I'm serving you notice that I won't look after your interests for you. And you know Drew won't."

"Humph! The way I see it, he'll get it all, anyways. Ain't that the way of things: them that has is the ones as gets?" Nonetheless, he stepped back and dropped his hand. "Win, I was promised to Wilmington for

Christmas, and his sister's been casting out lures to me," he added plaintively. "Girl's got ten thousand at the least."

" 'Tis paltry, George," Drew said.

"Paltry to you, you mean. Me, I ain't got your money; got to come about ere the tradesmen get me. Got no address neither. Got to get a girl as don't note it, and the Wilmington chit ain't exactly full in the cockloft."

"Sir John's personal fortune exceeds seventy thousand pounds," Bagshot stated baldly. "It could even go considerably higher, depending on the final assessment of the manor."

"Seventy thou—*seventy* thousand?"

"Aye."

George returned, to drop into a chair next to where Drew stood. "Wilmington chit's got spots, anyway," he decided.

"How fortunate for her," his cousin murmured, suppressing the twitch at the corner of his mouth.

It was already quite dark when the hired cart drew up to the huge house, and Maria Jeffries stared through the spitting snow with misgiving. Jenny had often boasted of David's family's wealth, but until now she'd been inclined to think her sister had exaggerated.

"There must be some mistake," she said faintly.

"Yer asked fer Greystone Manor, mum, and that be it," the driver maintained stoutly.

"Aunt Mia, 'tis grand," Becca breathed in awe.

"Yes, it certainly is."

"Two shillings, mum. Though if they was expectin' ye, don't know why they didn't send the carriage."

Maria fumbled in her reticule for the coins, then counted them out into his worn glove.

Satisfied, the driver lifted their two portmanteaus to the ground. "A happy Christmas to ye and yer little girl, mum," he offered quickly as he scrambled back onto the seat. "Tell that butler Sims as how 'twas Willie Howell that brung ye." With that, he clicked the reins and the elderly nag slung into a slow gait, leaving them standing before the great porch.

"Well, Becca," Maria announced with far more enthusiasm than she felt, " 'tis time we are made known to your grandpapa." She picked up a portmanteau in each hand and started up the steps. "Sound the knocker, if you will."

The little girl skipped up the steps and lifted the brass ring, banging it loudly. They stood, shivering in the cold winter wind, waiting.

When the heavy door finally swung inward, Maria stepped forward with a boldness she did not feel. "Pray inform Sir John Grey that Miss Jeffries is arrived with his granddaughter, Rebecca Grey," she ordered the elderly retainer who answered. "I wrote, though I daresay he could not know the precise day."

Instead of stepping back to allow them entry, he shook his head. "I am afraid there's been a mistake, miss."

"This is not Greystone?"

"Aye, but—"

"Mr. Sims," she enunciated crisply, "I have not come all the way from Kent to be turned aside. I would speak with Sir John, if you please."

"I regret—"

"Aunt Mia, I am fr-freezing," Becca complained.

So was Maria. She brushed past the startled butler and set the heavy bags down. Taking off her gloves with the assurance of a grand lady, she once again faced the old fellow. "Perhaps you did not understand—this child is his flesh and blood. David Grey was her father," she added when he still did not move.

"He don't see anyone, miss—on his physician's orders. And I doubt 'twould be good for the little girl to see him now," he added, not unkindly.

At that moment, the door opened from one of the

salons, and a gentleman too young to be Sir John stepped out. Startled, she stared briefly, scarcely noting the impeccable tailoring of his clothing. He was, in truth, quite a handsome man, possessed of hair as black as Becca's, and he watched her with possibly the most arresting hazel eyes she'd ever seen. Even with her limited experience, she recognized him for a Corinthian of the first order. And by the rather impersonal expression on his face, it was obvious he was not nearly so impressed with her.

Sensing that she was at *point non plus* with the elderly butler, she appealed to him. "Sir, I pray you will see that Sir John is informed we are arrived. May I make known to you my niece, Miss Rebecca Grey? I am Maria Jeffries, her aunt on her mother's side. We are expected."

The hazel eyes betrayed a faint interest, then were veiled behind a studied boredom. "Er, there must be a mistake, Miss Jeffries. Sir John is scarce able to consider company."

"I wrote him the twenty-eighth of November that we were coming, sir." There was that in his manner that irritated her, for he did not appear ready to welcome Becca at all.

His first impression was that he faced an adventuress, but as he turned his attention to the little girl, Drew could see the resemblance to his late cousin. She stared back at him with David's wide gray eyes, and the blue-black mane of hair that streamed from beneath her bonnet reminded him of his own. He looked from her to the woman with her. Maria Jeffries was past the first blush, but certainly not much above twenty-five. Although trim enough of figure, there was little in either her clothing or her face to draw a man. In truth, she reminded him of nothing so much as a governess with her charge in tow.

"Rebecca, is it?"

"She was named for David's mother, I was told."

He inclined his head slightly. "I am Andrew Carstairs, Sir John's nephew."

"Viscount Swynford? David spoke of you often, calling you the best of his cousins."

"A dubious honor at best, Miss Jeffries."

"Surely you could assist us, if you will, my lord." When he lifted one black brow, she hastened to explain, "You knew, of course, that David died some six years ago. My sister, Jennifer Jeffries Grey, succumbed to a wasting illness in October, sir, and I wrote Sir John, asking if I might bring Becca here."

The eyebrow rose further, indicating his disbelief. "And he answered?"

"No, but neither did he refuse," she admitted candidly. "And as my brother will not assist us, I thought perhaps if Sir John saw Becca, he could not turn her away." When Viscount Swynford did not answer immediately, Maria sighed. "I know—'tis perhaps foolish of me to expect he would care for a child born of the union that estranged his son from him, but sometimes years change even the hardest of men." Her eyes met his steadily. "I have to try, my lord—for Becca's sake."

He looked at Rebecca Grey again, seeing the plain woolen pelisse over the simple blue cotton dress, and he actually felt sorry for both of them. It would do no harm, he supposed, to send them off with money. Aloud, he answered, "My uncle is quite ill, Miss Jeffries—so ill that we have been summoned to his bedside to await the end, I fear."

She paled as his meaning sank in, and for a moment the marble-tiled floor swayed beneath her. "Oh dear. That is . . . Surely you do not think he's dying, sir?"

He nodded. "Yes."

"I see," she said faintly. She sank into one of the reception chairs that lined the wall, too numb to think. "I was bringing Becca to live here," she managed hollowly. "I did not know . . ." Then, not knowing what else to say, she looked up at him. "But I must see him, sir. I must! There is nowhere else—that is, I must ask provision—"

"He is dying, Miss Jeffries," he repeated bluntly. "His physician does not expect him to live through Christmas, if you would have the truth of it."

The child's eyes widened until they seemed to dominate her small, heart-shaped face. "Aunt Mia, I want to go back with you. Please."

Maria was too late. She had spent money she did not have to see a man on his deathbed. For a moment, the only thought that came to mind was that she could not support Becca, that she'd gambled and lost. Mrs. Ransome would not allow her to keep her niece, she knew, and her brother, William, complained that he had enough mouths to feed. Salvaging what dignity she could, she looked up at Viscount Swynford again.

"As it grows dark already, I must ask for accommodations for the night, sir. Naturally, we shall leave in the morning, if you will order a carriage to take us back into Chester. I would ask, however, that if you cared for David at all, you will speak to Sir John's executor to see if enough money can be provided for Becca's education."

"What the deuce? Who the devil is this, Drew?" George demanded, coming out of the saloon.

"Cousin Rebecca . . . and her aunt, 'twould seem. David's daughter."

"Ain't got no . . ." The younger man peered at the little girl in dawning horror. "No! Win, come out here!" he bawled loudly. "Now!"

"Really, Mr. Allyn," Bagshot protested as he came out first. "Your uncle must not be disturbed by such outbursts."

But George rounded on him, lashing out with " 'Tis your doing, isn't it, you old meddler? Well, we ain't having it. You can tell this . . . this adventuress to take the brat back from whence she is come."

"George, whatever . . ." Edwin Allyn stopped to stare also.

"You behold Cousin George and Cousin Edwin," Drew murmured. "The pink is George," he added with a straight face.

"Come to turn Uncle Jack up sweet, Win. Plain as the nose on your face, it is. 'Tis the Jeffries woman's brat."

" 'Tis David Grey's lawful daughter," Maria retorted coldly. "I have my sister's marriage lines to prove it."

"Of course you do," Bagshot murmured soothingly. "Oh, dear, but—"

"I wrote. As I told Lord Swynford, I wrote, sir."

"Sir John has been unable to deal with his correspondence for some time. I regret . . . Well, I'd intended to give his letters to Swynford this evening," the solicitor admitted slowly. "In his illness, his affairs have become sadly muddled, I fear." He looked to Andrew. "You understand, do you not, my lord? As his closest heir, you—"

"Now wait a minute," George protested. "Drew's but a nephew, same as me and Win."

"I think he refers to the fact that Drew's mother was the older of Uncle Jack's sisters—gives him precedence of sorts," Edwin muttered, exasperated with his brother's open avarice.

Andrew turned his attention to Maria Jeffries and the child. From all he knew of the situation that had existed between his uncle and his son's wife, he suspected that there would be no mention of the late Jennifer Grey or her daughter in the will. And yet the heart he suspected he did not have went out to his small cousin. It was, after all, Christmas week, and by the looks of it, neither she nor her aunt prospered. And the young woman's still-stunned expression moved him also.

"I can promise you nothing, Miss Jeffries," he

found himself saying, "but I will attempt to speak with my uncle on the matter. I must suppose he knows of the child's existence, but whether he will acknowledge her or not—"

"No!" George screeched.

"I say, Drew, but—" Edwin protested.

"I think 'twould be a very good thing, my lord," Bagshot cut in quickly. "I have often thought 'twas ill justice in the first instant, you know."

"I will tell Mrs. Crawford to add two more places for dinner," Drew continued, unperturbed by George's outburst. "Then, in the morning, perhaps Mr. Bagshot will tell you how best to proceed in the matter."

"The devil he will! Just because you can afford to whistle a fortune down the wind don't give you the right to toss mine up with it."

Seeing that the thin young man's face now almost matched his claret coat, Maria shook her head. "Actually, my lord, I think Becca and I are rather tired, and—"

"But I'm hungry, Aunt Mia," the little girl complained. "At home, we would have eaten—"

"Hush, love. Perhaps a cold collation in our chamber, then. I shall ask your grandpapa's housekeeper."

"I am certain it can be arranged," Bagshot hastened to concur.

Mrs. Crawford, arriving from the back of the house, allowed as how both a chamber and a meal could be provided in a trice. A footman was summoned to carry the worn bags, leaving Maria and her neice nothing to do but follow them upstairs. Becca, awestruck by the ornately framed portraits of her ancestors that were hung to rise with the stairs, clutched Maria's hand tightly, asking, "Is one of them Papa, do you think?"

"I would doubt so, dearest. 'Twould appear they are all rather old."

Coming from the foyer below, George Allyn's voice carried loudly. "Who's to say 'tis David's brat?"

" 'Twould be difficult to deny it," his brother countered.

"And the woman . . . she looks like a governess, if you was to ask me."

"I suspect 'tis what she is," Lord Swynford answered.

"You going to let her stay?" Edwin asked.

"The devil! He ain't the only heir, Win. There's three of us, and don't you be forgetting it. He don't have the only say."

"Four," Swynford corrected him. " 'Twould appear there are four heirs, George."

"Is he awake?" Drew asked from the door.

Dr. Hatch rose from a chair beside the bed and stepped out into the hall. "Aye, but I gave him extra laudanum for the pain, so his mind wanders. Poor devil." He shook his head slowly. "By reason, he ought to have gone weeks ago, but he's fighting it."

"Understandable, I should think."

"Usually in cases of this sort, they are glad enough to depart this life. Your uncle is, I fear, in a great deal of pain."

"Do you think he will be able to understand if I tell him that David's—that his son's daughter—is here?"

"He has periods of great lucidity, my lord, but I would doubt tonight is one of them." Hatch looked back to where the old man lay propped amongst the pillows on his bed. "Still, when he is like this, one cannot know what he does or does not realize for certain. If you would sit with him, I'd only ask that you do not overtax him. 'Tis better if you speak rather than ask questions."

"All right."

Drew entered the room and waited for a moment, letting his eyes adjust to the dimness. Then he walked slowly to the bed, still shocked by the sight that greeted him. His uncle had been a large, robust man once, but now he'd shrunk measurably. His skin lay in sallow folds where it could be seen, and his once-piercing eyes were sunk deeply into the bony hollows of his face. As they were closed, Drew considered retreating, wondering if perhaps the morning would not be a better time to speak with the old man.

"Who is it?" the voice from the bed rasped.

"Andrew Carstairs. 'Tis Swynford, Uncle."

"Andrew." The old man peered through the shadows at him and struggled to sit. It was too much effort. He fell back among the pillows. "Bagshot sent for you—demned meddler."

"Yes. George and Edwin are come also."

"Don't know why." He paused as though to gain breath, then muttered, "A man as lives alone ought to be left to die that way, don't you think?"

Drew chose a chair and pulled it closer to the bed scarcely knowing what to say to this man he'd never particularly liked. "Perhaps we are come to share Christmas with you. There's naught to say you won't be here for holidays, is there?"

"Doing it too brown, Andrew." The faded eyes met Drew's soberly. "Demned charlatan has physicked and bled me to no avail. Now he don't do aught but dose me with laudanum." Even as he spoke, he winced. "A man don't want to sleep his last days, but there ain't no help for it, I guess. The pity's when the mind lasts longer than the body."

"I'm sorry."

For a moment, the eyes were sharp. "Sorry? What for? Not your fault, is it?" Then, as the pain seemed to intensify, he inhaled deeply and grimaced. "Besides, you'll get money when I'm gone, so don't pretend you'll miss me."

"I'm not exactly in dun territory, Uncle," Drew pointed out. "There is the Carstairs money."

"Aye. The Carstairs were always plump in the pocket." Sir John drew another breath and waited.

"Thought m'sister Olivia'd spend it, but she didn't live long enough."

"Perhaps you ought not to try to talk."

"No. What day is it?" the old man queried faintly.

"The eighteenth of December—one week before Christmas."

"Christmas." It was a weak, derisive snort. "You ought to be somewheres else—be young while you can. Don't see Edwin and George here, do you?"

"They are here," Drew reminded him.

"Oh. Vultures." Then, "Didn't want to come, did they? Surprised to see you, Andrew," the old man muttered. "Too fine a fellow, ain't you? Got better things to do than watch me die."

"Actually, you appeared the lesser of two ills, Uncle Jack," Drew admitted, trying to keep his voice light. "My other choice was a matrimonial trap, you see."

A pain took his uncle's breath away. "So you would do . . . your duty," John Grey gasped, holding his side. "Got . . . to have the . . . demned laudanum again." He half-raised up in the bed, straining toward the bottle that sat on the small table, then lay back weakly.

"I thought you just had some."

"Did, but it don't always work. Get it when I want it now. Don't want it, but . . . got to . . . worse at night."

Despite the fact that the room was rather chilly, the old man's forehead was wet with sweat, betraying his pain. "How much?" Drew asked, unstoppering the bottle.

"Twelve drops," his uncle gasped.

Drew picked up the empty glass and reached for the pitcher. Filling the glass less than half full of water, he carefully counted out six drops of the opiate. Hopefully, when it was combined with what he'd already had, 'twould be sufficient to ease him. He leaned to lift his uncle and held the glass to the old man's lips, waiting whilst he drank greedily. Then he laid him back onto the pillows.

For a time, his uncle was quiet, and Drew began to think he slept. He sat there, wondering if perhaps he ought not to attempt telling him of Rebecca Grey.

Then the old man spoke, and this time his voice was stronger. "They say a man's relations is waiting on the other side, Andrew." His eyes opened again. "What do you think?"

For a moment, Drew was taken aback. He'd not actually given the matter much thought yet, and theology was not terribly relevant to a buck of the *ton*'s life. And yet he felt the need to comfort the old man. "I don't know," he answered finally. "I'd like to believe that, I guess."

"No. I got nobody to wait for me there."

"Aunt Rebecca—"

"Humph! Ain't a chance of it!"

"Uncle, perhaps you should rest. It does no good to speculate with me, you know. I do not pretend to have any answers."

"Got eternity to sleep. No, she won't be waiting— I know it. Nor Johnny neither. Neither of 'em forgave me for David." He twisted his head until his eyes met Drew's. "But I wanted to punish the boy. How was I to know he'd die ere I did?"

Drew guessed it was the laudanum. "Uncle—"

"I thought I could put a stop to it, you know. All I wanted." His eyes welled with tears. "Didn't know . . . didn't want him to throw himself away on a nobody."

" 'Tis over, and you could not have known," Drew murmured soothingly.

"Wanted my blessing, Andrew. Even after they left here, he wrote me. I burned the letters. He was my son," he whispered.

As little as he'd liked his uncle, he felt sorry for him now. "We cannot look back at what we have or have not done. 'Tis today that matters—or so the vicars tell us. It is as much what you believe at the end.''

But the old man would not be comforted. "Told myself I . . . had another . . . when Johnny perished, the gel wrote me David had died . . ." He stopped, unable to go on for a moment. "Didn't even bring him home to bury . . . didn't want to see the gel . . . killed Meg. I know it." His voice was so low that Drew had to lean over him to hear. "No, they won't be on the other side." He reached a bony hand to wipe tears of self-pity from his cheek. "Just wish I could see David again." He turned his now-frail body to face the wall. "Just wish I could see my boy again."

Drew leaned back. It had been years ago—nearly a dozen of them, he guessed, for he'd been but just out of Oxford when his Cousin David had eloped with the governess of a family he'd met in Bath. There'd been a devil of a scandal, as he had been expected to offer for the eldest daughter of her employer with his father's blessing and encouragement. The unhappy result was a permanent estrangement when Sir John disinherited his younger son. And within six years, both David and Johnny had perished, one to illness, one to war.

For a time, Andrew considered how best to tell his uncle of the little girl, wondering if perhaps he ought to wait. Finally, he cleared his throat. "I think David forgave you, Uncle. Perhaps 'tis Providence, but David's daughter is come to see you now. She has the look of him even. Jennifer Grey is dead also now, and . . . " He stopped, wondering if the old man listened, for there was no sign, no word that he heard. "Uncle Jack . . ."

There was no answer. He reached to touch his uncle's shoulder, then realized that the two doses of laundanum had taken effect. Knowing that George and Win still waited downstairs, he sat there, staring into the lengthening shadows, thinking he ought to have broached the matter of little Rebecca sooner, but it did not matter, he supposed. If Sir John had wanted to reach out to his son's family, he could have done it anytime in the six years past, and he had not done it. There was nothing to say that he blamed Jennifer Grey any less now.

The thought crossed his mind that Rebecca Grey, aside from being his cousin's daughter, meant nothing to him. He'd not even been aware of her existence until an hour or so before. So why was he bothering with her? Why? He asked himself dispassionately. What difference did it make to him? Was it that he also felt the need to atone for a distant wrong? But he had not turned his back on David. It had been the other way around, hadn't it? Once he had wed his governess, David had never contacted any of them again.

But Rebecca Grey was in her father's image. That was it. There was that in those clear gray eyes that reminded him of a childhood long past. Besides, it was Christmas. Even if it were the grimmest holiday of his memory, it *was* Christmas.

It was the first time Becca had seen her aunt cry since her mother died. Yet there she sat on the edge of the elegant four-poster bed, her head bowed, tears streaming down her face, weeping almost silently. Becca laid a comforting hand on her shoulder.

"Aunt Mia . . ."

" 'Twas folly on my part. I ought to have waited for an answer," Maria acknowledged finally, wiping her face with the back of her hand. "But I thought if he saw you, that if only he could know you . . ."

"I don't mind it, Aunt Mia—truly I don't," the child consoled her. "I'd rather live with you than be a grand lady."

"Thank you, love," Maria sniffed, digging into her reticule for her handkerchief. Blowing loudly, she looked around her. "But 'tis here that you belong. Look at this place, Becca, just look at it! He could have given you so much more than I can. You are his flesh and blood, Becca, and by rights you belong here," she repeated. "David would have wanted this. I know it."

The little girl climbed into the bed beside her and slid her arms around Maria's neck. "Well, I'd very much rather be with you. I don't even care if Mrs. Ransome doesn't like me."

That was another thing. Maria would have to seek another position when they returned, for her elderly employer had made it quite clear that she could not come back with Becca. But it would never do to let on to the child. There'd been too much worry in her eight years already. Maria dried her eyes and forced a smile.

"Well, I daresay we will have to find another place, won't we?" She hugged her niece close for a moment, then said brightly, "You know, I cannot say I like Mrs. Ransome very much either. But possibly I can seek a position with a nice family, perhaps to teach, and they will not mind that there are two of us."

"Well, you could always marry Mr. Perkins . . . if he asks you," Becca ventured doubtfully.

"No. No, love, we are not quite so desperate as that," Maria answered definitely. "I should rather go into business than marry Mr. Perkins, I assure you. He is the sort of man who would make an offer merely to save the expense of a housekeeper."

"We could become modistes, and I still would have pretty gowns," Becca decided. "Mrs. Ransome says you are skilled with the needle."

"Not that skilled, I fear. No, 'twill have to be giving lessons to little girls."

"Is Lord Swynford truly my cousin?" Rebecca asked suddenly, changing the subject.

"If he is Sir John's nephew, I expect he is your first cousin once-removed. Why?"

"I just wondered what he is to me." Rebecca

slipped off the bed to look out the window. "Is he very rich, do you think?"

"I don't know. I have had neither the time nor the inclination to follow the *ton*, I fear." For a moment, Maria considered the viscount dispassionately, then sighed. "One cannot always tell by the clothes, Becca, for full half of the Corinthians and dandies are but one step from debtors' prison."

"Well, I thought him the nicest of my cousins." The little girl wrinkled her nose. "Cousin George," she pronounced with distaste, "is a quiz. And Cousin Edwin is dull, I think." She turned briefly to Maria. "Did you know they would not like me, Aunt Mia?"

"I had not expected to discover any of them here. I thought we should have the opportunity to acquaint ourselves with your grandpapa first. As for Lord Swynford's being any kinder than the others, we cannot know that," she added judiciously. "Perhaps he merely dissembles better."

"I didn't want to live here, anyway, you know."

"I know you did not," Maria said gently, "but—"

"Why did I never meet my grandpapa before?"

"He and your mama did not deal well together," Maria murmured in patent understatement.

"But why?"

" 'Tis too long a tale to tell now, dearest. Come, if we are to leave again tomorrow, which we might, we'd best get to sleep."

But Rebecca continued to stare through the darkness to the lamplit drive below. "Even if I didn't want to live here, Aunt Mia, I did want to meet him, you know," she admitted in a small, wistful voice. "He knew my papa."

"I know, but perhaps now it would be best if you did not," Maria answered quietly. "If he is so very ill, perhaps you ought not to remember him like that."

"I thought perhaps he would tell me of Papa."

"What would you like to know? I—"

"But you were not there when he was little like me." Rebecca took one last look outside. "Aunt Mia, it snows. Look, it snows."

The news did nothing to raise Maria's already low spirits. It was all of a piece, she supposed, for even fate seemed against her just then. "I don't care, love. It can come a storm for all that it matters now," she said tiredly. "Though I cannot say I relish spending another day with your papa's family."

"Do you think he looks like him?"

"Who? Oh, you mean Sir John? Well, he is much older, of course, and illness changes how one looks sometimes—"

"Like Mama?"

"Yes."

"She always said there was naught of her in me, that I resembled Papa. But I cannot recall just what Papa looked like, you know."

"She was right. Come on, you'll take a chill, Becca. Close the shutters and get into bed."

Reluctantly, the little girl did as bid. Slipping into the bed beside Maria, she snuggled beneath the thick covers. "I still wish I might see him," she sighed.

The room was dark, its walls alive with the grotesque shadows of night, and the slow hours ticked away monotonously, marked rhythmically by the clock on the table nearby. And the hot, gnawing pain vied with his nightmares, torturing him. They were all there at night, all the demons from his past, tearing at his soul, and he was powerless against them. He struggled restlessly beneath the weight of his blankets. Surely someone would come soon, surely someone would give him more laudanum to ease his body and free his mind.

There was a faint movement at the bottom of his bed. He felt rather than saw it. "Who goes there?" he demanded querulously. With an effort, he pulled himself up on his pillows and stared, straining to make out this new demon come to haunt him.

There was no answer, but something white moved. Telling himself it was but the bedcurtain blowing, he confronted it again. "Damme, speak up!" The pain caught him, robbing him of breath for a moment, as the white cloth seemed to float closer. Beads of cold perspiration formed on his brow.

As it neared, it took on form, stunning him. Through the deep shadows, he could see his younger son, not as he remembered him last, but rather as a small boy again. Despite the darkness, there was no mistaking him, for his hair was as black as ever against his white face.

The old man trembled uncontrollably, scarce able to believe what he saw. Despite all his fears to the contrary, his son had come to lead him across the valley between life and death. Tears of relief flowed freely, streaming down his deeply lined face.

"David . . . David . . . David! I did not mean . . . I never wanted . . . Come closer that I may see 'tis you," he babbled. For a moment, the boy hesitated as though he meant to flee. "No! Take me with you, I pray," John Grey called out. "Do not leave me again." Drawing upon every bit of strength he had left, he heaved his body up in the bed, reaching out to the apparition.

There were footsteps in the hall, and as the boy moved closer to him, the door opened, sending the flickering light from a lantern in a wedge-shaped slice across the floor. The boy stood rooted for a moment, his eyes huge and luminous in his pale face.

"Grandpapa?"

"Here now, what goes here?" Dr. Hatch demanded, stepping inside. Then, seeing the child, he was taken aback. "What the devil? Who are you?"

"David?" the old man gasped, falling back.

" 'Tis Becca, sir," she answered. "Rebecca."

"What are you doing here? I gave orders he was not to be disturbed," the physician snapped.

"I came to see my grandpapa," she answered simply.

"Well, be off with you," Dr. Hatch told her brusquely, opening the laudanum bottle. " 'Tis a fright you've given him. Of all the cork-brained things to do, girl . . ."

"What is it?" Still fastening the frogs on his brocaded dressing gown, Drew moved into the room. "Is he . . . ?"

"No. 'Twas the girl."

Rebecca's chin came up as she met his incredulous expression. "I wanted to see if he looked like Papa, sir."

"Get her out of here," Hatch ordered as he administered the opiate. " 'Tis no place for a child."

Drew's eyes traveled over her. She looked even smaller in her nightrail than she'd seemed earlier. The black hair, which had streamed over her shoulders before, was neatly tied back, probably to keep it from tangling in bed. She stood there, apparently unafraid, surprising him. When he met her eyes again, he was struck by the sadness and gravity he saw.

"You ought to be abed," he said gently.

" 'Tis what Aunt Mia will say," she sighed. Then, "You won't tell her of this will you?"

He looked past her to where Maria Jeffries stood in the doorway, her plain blue gown pulled on with such haste that she was still fastening the last of her buttons. "Er, I think she knows," he murmured, nodding significantly.

"Oh."

"Becca, whatever . . . ?" At a loss for words, Maria could only stare. "Oh, dear."

"Well, if we are to leave tomorrow, I was afraid I'd never see him, Aunt Mia," the child answered practically. "I did not mean to frighten him—truly I didn't."

"Of course you did not, but you should not have done this, Becca. You will return to bed immediately," Maria told her sternly.

"I'm sorry, Grandpapa." The old man lay still, his eyes closed, and did not answer her. "Good night, sir." Then, without another word to anyone else, she fled.

"What the deuce is the commotion?" George Allyn demanded, rushing in. "Is he . . . ?"

"What is it? Is Uncle Jack . . . ?" Edwin asked behind him.

"Is he all right?" Maria wanted to know.

"Will someone enlighten me? What the devil is going on here?" George moved closer to his uncle's bed, peering hopefully over Dr. Hatch's shoulder. "Did he go?"

"No. The little girl frightened him," the doctor answered as he straightened up. "No harm done, actually."

"No harm done?" George howled indignantly. "I knew we ought to have sent the brat packing—I knew it!" Turning around, he accused Maria. " 'Tis all your doing, isn't it? You wasn't about to leave without getting your hooks in him, was you? Well, I won't have it! Got no right to disturb an old man like that."

"I say, George, but—"

"Stay out of it, Win! I ain't—"

"Gentlemen, please! If you must dispute, I pray you will do so elsewhere," Hatch protested. "Sir John cannot rest amid turmoil."

Obviously stung by George's outburst, Maria faced Drew. "I am sorry, my lord. 'Twas a child's natural curiosity, I suppose, but—"

"What harm could she do? It isn't as though he can recover, Miss Jeffries."

"Yes, of course." She turned to leave also, then stopped. "Thank you for being kind to her, sir."

"Not at all. I never blame disobedient children for that which their elders have not taught them." He thought her shoulders slumped slightly, and he felt instantly sorry for his words. "And in Rebecca's case, the curiosity is understandable."

She spun around at that. "Yes, it is, Lord Swynford. As I am the only family she knows, she cannot be blamed for wishing to acquaint herself with any of you," she said evenly. "Good night, sir."

She left him standing there. He shrugged and walked over to the bed. His uncle's eyes fluttered open again as he leaned over and took the old man's hand, squeezing it.

"Would you have me sit with you awhile?" he asked.

"Aye."

"No! I won't have it, Drew. You ain't—"

"Would you rather stay?" his cousin asked. "You are most welcome to join me."

"Don't want to disturb him," George maintained stoutly. "Don't think you ought to either—that's all." Then, perceiving how he must sound to the old man, he asked cautiously, "You don't want me to sit with you, do you, Uncle Jack?"

"No."

"And you don't want the brat here neither, I'll be bound. I told Drew and Bagshot, but they—"

"Not now, George," his brother snapped irritably. "Two will get you three, she is gone tomorrow, anyway. I am for my bed, and I recommend you take to yours also."

It was then that the younger Mr. Allyn happened to look to the window, and his sense of ill-usage was complete. "Win," he said in a lower voice, " 'tis snowing. Damme if that ain't an ill omen."

"The laudanum will take effect ere long, sir," Hatch assured Drew. "Then he should sleep several hours."

"Don't want to sleep . . . not yet," the old man protested feebly. As the others went from the room and the door closed behind them, John Grey tried to focus on Drew's face. "Thought I saw David . . . thought I saw my boy," he whispered.

" 'Twas his daughter, sir. She and her aunt are but arrived. The girl's name is Rebecca."

"Rebecca." The effort was too great. The lids drooped over the dulling eyes. "Rebecca," he repeated softly.

"David's daughter."

There was no answer to that. Drew took a chair and leaned back, thinking that as soon as his uncle's breathing evened out, he'd leave. Until then, it was little enough to keep him company. He sat there a long time, listening to the steady ticking of the clock, unable to tell if Sir John slept or not.

Then he thought he heard something. "Huh?" he asked, rousing. "What?"

"Demned fool was right, Andrew," the old man said clearly. "Aye, 'tis an omen."

Instead of returning to his bed, Drew decided to look for the letter Maria Jeffries claimed to have sent. But as he came downstairs, he saw that light came from beneath his uncle's book room door, and upon investigation, he found the woman herself. She looked up guiltily.

"Oh, dear, I am discovered," she murmured apologetically. "Mr. Bagshot assured me that no one would mind in the least if I sought something to read."

Drew shrugged. "If you can discover anything worth reading. But I should think after what happened, you'd be with your niece."

Perceiving a hint of censure in his voice, she colored. "Becca fell asleep on the instant, sir. Alas, I, on the other hand, could not."

"No need to get on your high ropes with me, Miss Jeffries. I find myself unable to sleep either."

She looked toward the door hesitantly. "The others—"

"If you are afraid they will think I am trysting with you, you are very wide of the mark, my dear. Not even George would think you in my style, I assure you."

"How very comforting," she murmured dryly. "But I suppose I must count it a compliment not to be mistaken for that sort of woman."

"Unworthy of you, Miss Jeffries." He dropped his tall frame into one of the chairs still drawn up to the dying fire and reached for the brandy decanter. "Would you . . . No, of course you would not," he answered himself. "Got nothing else in here."

"I seldom partake of any spirits, sir."

"No, don't suppose you do. They don't offer much to governesses, do they?"

"I am not a governess," she retorted peevishly. "Though, if I were, I should not be ashamed to say so. 'Tis far better to admit to earning one's bread than to defraud tradesmen with empty promises as is common among the *ton*, I think."

Suppressing a smile, he warned her, "If you say that too loudly, you will offend Cousin George's sensibilities."

"You jest, of course. He has no sensibilities—or at least none that I have yet discovered."

He poured himself a healthy quantity of the brandy, then leaned back to sip it. "Tell me, Miss Jeffries, are you the adventuress George suspects?"

"If I were, would you expect me to admit it?" she countered.

"No."

She stared long into the glowing coals, then sighed. "Actually, I am companion to an elderly female, who is clutch-fisted, ill-tempered, and filled with imaginary ailments. For the princely sum of twenty pounds per year, I listen to her complain of her male relations and her health, sir.'' She looked up at him with an almost defiant set to her chin. ''She cannot abide children—not even her own grandsons.''

''Are you always so direct, Miss Jeffries?''

''In this instant, plain speaking serves me best, I think. As much as it pained me to write Sir John, as difficult as it is for me to forgive him for what he did to David and Jenny, I could not in good conscience wish to rear Becca as I live—not knowing that he could provide her with the things she deserves.''

''Which are?'' he asked curiously.

''I suspect you ask for amusement,'' she answered tiredly, ''but Sir John, were he to live, could give Becca an education and ultimately the opportunity to make a better life for herself. My sister was a governess and I a companion, but David Grey's daughter ought to be able to do better than either of us. I would even hope that someday she will be able to wed a gentleman of standing.''

''You do not mention money.''

''What Becca needs most, sir, is a home where she may experience the natural liveliness of a child. If wishing money for that makes me an adventuress, then I suppose I am. For much too long, my niece has been expected to be a small adult. Jenny was ill for nearly two years, you see, and there has been far too little levity in Becca's life.''

''No, if 'tis the truth, you are not an adventuress,'' he conceded. ''But is there no one else?''

That elicited a brittle, derisive laugh. ''My brother, William, one of God's so-called servants, has but a small living that he insists does not put enough bread on the table for his own five children. And his wife is the sort who would begrudge Becca every crumb she ate. But we will survive.'' She closed the book on her lap and rose abruptly. "Now, if you will pardon me, I find myself quite tired. Perhaps . . ." Glancing down at the title in her hand, she smiled wryly. "Perhaps *Husbanding the Land* will put me to sleep."

"Egad. Is that all there is?"

"No, but it seemed preferable to Sir Wilton Downey's *Treatise on the Proper Sowing of Corn*. The other bookcases—the ones containing the better selections—are locked."

"Sit down. Surely I can offer better diversion than that, my dear." When she remained standing, he rose also. "Obstinate female, aren't you?" he murmured.

"Yes. I suppose you are used to those who toadeat you."

"Alas, but there seems to be an excess of them," he admitted, grinning. "You, on the other hand, would appear impervious to my considerable charm."

"Well, as I have not the expectation of making a brilliant marriage, I am spared such lowering behavior," she pointed out practically. Yet as she spoke, her dark eyes twinkled. "Let us say that I am unfettered by matrimonial ambition."

"How wounding to male vanity."

"Don't be absurd, sir. I cannot afford to flatter. I would not for the world give any gentleman the wrong impression." She started toward the door. "Good night."

"Wait. As it appears that your plans have gone awry, what would you have Uncle John's heirs do for Rebecca?"

She halted. "I had hoped for a home for her, but—"

"But having discovered only three frivolous bachelors, there must be an alternate plan, I should hope."

"Yes. Failing that, I should ask for a fair share of Sir John's estate—to be held in trust for her, of course."

"And what for Maria Jeffries?"

"As I cannot take her back to Mrs. Ransome, I suppose I will have to ask for one hundred pounds per year that we may lease a cottage, preferably in a pleasant place. I should expect, naturally, to account for the money."

The meanness of the amount staggered his imagination, for he often spent that much on nothing. Still, he tried not to betray his surprise. "Naturally. What an uncommonly sensible female you are, my dear."

"I hope so. Good night, sir," she repeated firmly.

After she left, he finished his brandy. One hundred pounds per year. He spent more than that for his gloves, for almost everything, in fact. One hundred pounds per year. It made him wonder if perhaps in his own way he were not as useless a fellow as George. He could give one hundred pounds for anything and not miss it at all.

Leaning back, he soberly contemplated the few valiant coals left from the fire. Well, why not? 'Twas the season, he supposed, but somehow he felt good about the prospect of giving the money to Maria Jeffries. Perhaps it soothed his conscience for the life he led. There was no justice, he admitted it, for his world prized the beautiful empty-headed creatures whose sole pursuits were shopping and snaring wealthy, indulgent husbands, while it held no place for the shabby genteel females like the sensible Miss Jeffries. Indeed, but rather than accepting her sister, his uncle had driven his favorite son away.

He tried to remember David's wife, but he'd met her only twice. Idly, he wondered if she'd been dark-eyed like Maria. Those eyes, he decided, were Miss Jeffries' only claim to looks. And even then, she had to smile for the best effect. Abruptly, he heaved himself up from the chair. If he'd reached the point where he wasted thought on Maria Jeffries' eyes, he must be at least three sheets into the wind.

* * *

Maria was awakened with the news that Sir John wished to see her and Becca as soon as they could make themselves presentable. As it was still snowing outside, they hurried, hoping that if they had to leave, the roads would still be passable.

Once inside the old man's chamber, Maria paused to straighten the ribbon sash over her niece's best blue muslin gown. Then, with decidedly mixed feelings, she held the child's hand and approached the bed, not knowing what to expect of this man who had discarded his son because of her sister. Had desperation not tempered her bitterness, she could easily have hated him.

He was propped high against a bank of pillows, looking nothing at all like David had described him, for he was as pale as the tucked nightshirt that swallowed him, and his face was lined deeply. But his sunken eyes were strangely bright and alert as he watched them.

Just then, a maid came in, but he waved her off. "Don't mean to take the stuff yet—want to see the little gel first." Then, as if to explain, he added, "Opium dulls the mind as well as the body. Well, don't stand there—bring her up."

Becca's hand tightened in Maria's, then she stepped forward. Maria tried to smile, but could not. "May I present Miss Rebecca Grey, sir? 'Tis David's daughter."

Becca dropped a low curtsy, then rose to peer curiously at her grandfather. For a long, awkward moment, they stared at each other, then finally he spoke in a voice almost too soft to hear. "Aye. 'Twould be difficult to deny you, child. You have the look of him."

"My mama told me."

He looked up at Maria and reached a shaking hand to her. "Jennifer?"

"No, sir. I am Maria Jeffries, Jenny's sister." Then, unable to completely hide her bitterness, she added harshly, "Jennifer died two months ago—in a charity hospital."

His eyes clouded over and his mouth quivered. "I did not know . . ."

"Would it have made any difference, sir? Would you have done anything for her?" she asked, giving vent to remembered pain. Then, recalling herself, she brushed at her welling eyes almost angrily. "I should not have said that now, I suppose, for you are as ill as she was."

"She never asked for aid. She never wrote of the child. I did not know . . ." His gaze traveled again to Becca. "I did not know of her."

"David wrote you when she was born."

"Burned his letters." Again, his lip quivered as though he would cry. "Burned all of them." His frail hand stretched toward the child. "I have not the right, but I'd touch you . . . I'd feel your hand, Rebecca." To Maria, he directed, "Sit you down. Can't look up easily."

The little girl hesitated, then gingerly extended her fingers to be enveloped in his bony ones. He clasped them tightly, holding them, and his eyes filled with tears. Slowly, his other hand reached to explore her face as though to prove she were real. "David's little gel . . . Pretty as a portrait, ain't ye?"

"Her mother was pretty also," Maria reminded him pointedly.

"Aye, aye, so she was," Sir John admitted. "Well, so you are come to see your grandpapa, eh?"

Becca looked to Maria, then blurted out, "I was coming to live with you, but—"

"Hush, Becca," Maria warned her.

"Coming to live with me?" Astonished, he lifted his eyes to Maria. " 'Tis true?"

"Yes," she answered baldly.

"After . . . after . . . You would have let me . . . ?"

"Aunt Mia couldn't keep me," Becca explained.

Then, "I'm sorry you are sick, sir, but I'd rather stay with Aunt Mia," she added with childish honesty.

He winced visibly and his face paled. "Got to have the laudanum, after all," he muttered, exhaling. "Fetch someone, will you?" he asked the little girl. "Now."

"I'll go, sir," Maria offered.

"No. Got no time . . . got to talk . . ."

"All right. Becca, get whoever you can find and tell them Sir John is needful of his medicine."

It wasn't until he heard the child's steps on the stairs that he spoke again. Twisting his head restlessly against the pillows to hide his pain, he came to the point. "No time to beat about the bush, is there? What do you want?"

Taken back by his directness, Maria was uncertain how to answer without sounding like an adventuress. "It is not what I want, sir. I'd not ask you for a farthing, if there were a choice. I watched David die six years ago with no help from you, and I watched Jenny die this year, too proud to ask for anything for Becca or herself."

"Told you I did not know," he protested feebly.

"But you should have." She stopped, recalling why she had come. " 'Tis done, in any event. More to the point is what I am to do with Becca, sir." She drew in a deep breath, then plunged ahead. "I have no competence—none. Currently, I am employed as companion to an elderly widow, who greatly dislikes the noise and inconvenience of children. It was Jenny's wish that our brother, William, take Becca, but I have no hope that he will not begrudge her the food on her plate." Perceiving that he watched her closely now, she drew a deep breath. "It was my hope to bring Becca here, sir. You were, I had decided, the least of the evils, and I thought perhaps once you saw her, your heart would soften at least a little. I did not know of your illness, of course."

"Threw a spoke in the wheel, didn't it?" he acknowledged wryly. "Now, what's to do?"

"I cannot take her back to Mrs. Ransome's, sir. Perhaps a guardian—or, failing that, if I had even one hundred pounds per year, I could provide a home for Becca, but—"

"One hundred pounds?" His eyes narrowed as though he did not believe her. " 'Tis all?"

Her chin came up. " 'Tis all for now. Later, I would hope that one of your heirs would undertake to provide an education for her."

His hands gripped the coverlet, betraying the pain that gnawed at his insides. "Wish I had time," he gasped. "But the sand's about out of the glass."

"Yes."

"No. Won't do," he decided. "A spinster on her own ain't right to rear a little gel. Now if you was to wed . . . Don't suppose you—"

"I have no expectations, sir," she reminded him dryly. "And we were speaking of Becca."

"A pity. Best answer."

Before she could think of a suitable rejoinder, they were interrupted by Dr. Hatch and a footman, followed by Rebecca. She drew back to allow the physician to lean over him.

"Fagged out, eh? Simpson told me as how you would not take the laudanum, and now you are paying the piper, eh?"

"Aye."

"Twelve drops," Hatch ordered.

"Six."

"There'll be no relief."

"Eight, then. Don't want to sleep the last sand away."

"Make it eight. But if he complains give him more."

Realizing that her interview had come to an end with

no resolution, Maria rose reluctantly. "Becca, bid your grandpapa a good day."

"Not much good about it," Sir John muttered, pausing to swallow the opiate. Shuddering as he handed the glass back to the footman, he addressed Maria. "Going to speak to the nephews, but then I'd have her back. Don't care if she don't say anything. Let her bring charcoal and paper even. Aye, and you come also."

"Today? But—"

"What other time is there?" he countered. "And tell George to come up first."

After they left, the old man stared reflectively at the ornate ceiling, waiting. Whether it was from the laudanum or not, he didn't know, but he had a plan. If the Almighty would grant him but one wish, he'd try to make everything right.

"Christmas," he whispered aloud. "Give me until Christmas. 'Tis all I ask."

"I collect the interview did not go as you wished it?" Drew murmured when she sat down to breakfast. "I'm sorry."

"It is all of a piece, isn't it?" Maria answered tiredly. "I suppose I ought to have expected it. After all, even if he were well, there was naught to say he would have taken her."

"Where is she?"

"Becca?" She reached for a piece of bread and picked up her knife. "Mrs. Crawford took her to the kitchen with a promise of sweet buns and milk. Perhaps 'tis not very nourishing, but quite frankly I am a trifle blue-deviled just now, so I welcomed the offer."

"Hopes all cut up, eh? Poor Miss Jeffries."

Thinking he mocked her, she rounded on him. "There is no need to give false sympathy, my lord." She buttered her bread, then slathered on a layer of currant jam. "His greatest concern seemed to be my lack of a husband. And as I cannot see that remedied, we shall just have to hope.''

'' 'Hope springs eternal in the human breast,' '' he quoted.

"Pope's *Essay on Man*. And your attempt at levity falls on particularly deaf ears this morning,'' she retorted.

"You mistake the matter, Miss Jeffries. I admire your perseverance in the face of adversity. In fact, I have an offer to make you.''

"I beg your pardon?''

"Fifteen hundred pounds and a snug house in Hertfordshire. For the most part, the climate is salubrious, and you should want for nothing.''

For a moment, she thought she could not have heard him aright, but then there he was, smiling at her. She flushed to the roots of her hair. "Really, sir, but there is no need to insult me,'' she said coldly.

"What the devil?'' Then, seeing the indignation in her dark eyes, he realized she had misunderstood him. His grin broadened. "You think I would be such a rum touch as to offer you *carte blanche*, Miss Jeffries? And with my little cousin under the same roof? No, no, not at all. You are definitely not the sort of female I'd set up—not at all.''

The way he denied it was almost as lowering as the perceived offer. "Then what *were* you suggesting?'' she asked peevishly.

"What you said last night. I figured Rebecca must be about eight. Am I correct? And at one hundred pounds a year for fifteen years, you ought to be able to take care of her with some to spare. In fact, she'll probably marry before the money ends. If she wishes, I am not adverse to sending her off to a select seminary when the time comes.''

She looked down at her plate. "No,'' she answered finally, "I could not take your money, sir. It is one thing to ask her grandfather to provide for her, and something quite different for me to expect to hang on your sleeve.''

"My sleeve would scarce note it, Miss Jeffries. I can afford to see David's daughter cared for.''

"Nonetheless—''

"There you are, Miss Jeffries. Drew.'' George entered the room and dropped into a chair beside his cousin. "Looks like the snow's going to last forever, don't it?''

"The last I heard you were decrying it,'' Drew reminded him.

"Was I? Well, it don't signify now, I guess—gives me more time to make the acquaintance of little Rebecca and her charming aunt, don't it?'' He flashed an engaging smile at Maria. "Look prettier in the daytime, you know.''

"You seem to have had a remarkable change of heart,'' Drew observed with a trace of irony.

"Reality, old fellow—reality. Discovery set me back a bit, I admit it, but now . . . Well, it ain't right to abandon a little girl, is it?'' Noting his cousin's incredulous expression, he added defensively, "Dash it, but she's David's daughter, after all. Taking little thing, too. By the by, Miss Jeffries, where is she?''

"In the kitchen,'' Maria answered faintly.

"Don't suppose you'd like to go for a sleigh ride—with little Becky, of course?'' he asked hopefully. "I had it from one of the footmen that Uncle Jack's got a bang-up vehicle.''

"In this weather?'' Drew choked. "I thought you despised the cold. Besides, if it drifts at all, 'tis too deep for the cattle.''

"Where'd you get a notion like that? Dote on the weather, in fact—invigorating in the extreme.'' George reached to pour himself a cup of coffee from the silver pot. "And you, Miss Jeffries?'' he offered gallantly. "More?''

"Actually, mine is tea, but I thank you, anyway.''

"You always wear that cap?" he asked conversationally. "Shouldn't, you know—makes a man think you on the shelf."

"I am on the shelf, Mr. Allyn."

"Nonsense. Ain't a day above nineteen, I'll be bound—is she, Drew?"

"I'd say five-and-twenty," Drew guessed.

"Pay him no heed. He don't know a pretty female when he sees one, miss." Seeing his cousin's eyebrow lift, he added, "Well, daresay he does—just got different tastes that's all." He cut a lump of sugar from the loaf and dropped it into his coffee, while his cousin watched, bemused. "Likes the blowsy, buxom ones, you know. Me, I always favored the quiet, sensible females."

"Actually, I am five-and-twenty, Mr. Allyn."

"You don't say it! Don't look it at all, not at all." Glancing nervously at the door, he persisted, "Well, what d'you think? Want to take a hot brick and a carriage robe out in the sleigh? And if you think it too cold for the little one, we'll just go ourselves. Know you'd want to see the park—pretty place."

"Without an abigail?" Drew asked wickedly.

"Dash it, coz, but she ain't got one. Besides, I count her family, don't you know? We don't need anyone to play duenna amongst relations."

"I'll ask Becca if she wishes to go, but—" Maria rose.

"Is that all you mean to eat?" Drew inquired.

"Yes."

"Told you he liked the buxom ones. Me, I like slender females myself."

As Maria reached the hall, she heard George tell his cousin loudly, "Fine-looking woman, don't you think?" But then she could not quite hear the answer. Making her way to the kitchen, she mused over the strange turnabout in George Allyn's attitude. Well, she wasn't green enough to be taken in by it, not at all.

In the dining room, Drew was hard-pressed not to laugh outright.

"What the devil ails you?" George demanded.

"Miss Jeffries must think you've lost your mind, old fellow. If I didn't know better, I'd say you wished to give the impression that you were head over heels—a strange turn, given your earlier welcome."

"Got to . . . got to fix my interest before Win steals the march. Daresay the old gent's up there telling him the same as me. And she ain't a bad-looking woman," he added doubtfully. "Leastwise, she ain't an Antidote."

"Not at all. In fact, with the proper gowns and the services of a good dresser, she'd be more than passable. She's got fine eyes."

"You think so?" The younger man brightened visibly. "Well, daresay you ought to know—stands to reason, I mean. Regular out and outer, ain't you?"

"I am accounted a fair judge," Drew conceded, smiling.

"And you ain't funning me?"

"Not at all."

"Well, that settles it," George decided, relieved. "I ain't in the petticoat line, you know. Got a better notion of clothes than females. But if she ain't going to disgrace me, then I'm going to take her."

"The question, I should think, is whether she'll take you."

His cousin appeared to consider the matter, then shook his head. "If you are telling me she'd prefer Win to me, you've wounded me. Win's dull. Look at them coats he favors. No, only one as I'd fear is you, and you don't count in this, 'cause the old man ain't offering the deal to you. Told me you was too plump in the pocket to take it, and stands to reason he's got the right of that."

"How very observant of him," Drew murmured.

"I mean, everybody knows when Swynford's

caught, it'll be by an Incomparable, not by a nobody like Miss Jeffries. Uncle Jack said you know what you owe your title, after all. Me and Win, it don't matter. We cannot afford to be half so choosy in the matter.''

''A very lowering assessment of Miss Jeffries, don't you think?''

Ignoring the dry tone in his cousin's voice, George went on, ''Thing is, I got to worry about what Win'll tell her 'bout me, don't you know? Bound to say I'm a havey-cavey fellow just to warn her off.'' For a moment, he frowned, then his expression cleared. ''Just got to see that he don't get her alone, that's all. Well, best run. Have to get a notion of how to drive the thing ere we're off.''

''You've never driven one before? My dear George, I don't think—''

''Cattle's cattle, ain't they? Daresay won't make much difference, anyways.''

''Well, you'd best keep to the road, coz. Otherwise, you'll risk hitting the drifts,'' Drew advised.

''I ain't cow-handed,'' George retorted.

After he left, Drew poured himself another cup of now nearly tepid coffee and leaned back, feeling more than a little sorry for Maria Jeffries. Not only were her hopes for Rebecca quite cut up, but she was also about to be pursued by two singularly selfish fellows, each ready to court her not for herself, but rather for their Uncle Jack's money. A most unenviable circumstance, even for a paid companion.

Dispassionately, he considered Maria Jeffries, seeing again those dark, dark eyes. George was right: if she'd give over wearing that silly spinster cap, she'd probably look years younger. In a sort of mental exercise, he dressed her in a fashionable muslin, then a green silk, conceding that her plainness was more a matter of necessity than choice.

His thoughts turned to the past Season's beauties, particularly the reigning toast, Melissa Marchbanks.

Win had been right there: she was an empty-headed, but well-bred peagoose. And a man ought to have the right to expect more than that in a life's companion. He ought to get more than a bloodless marriage calculated on the basis of wealth for beauty. Somehow it was lowering to realize that despite his handsomeness, despite his address—despite all else, in fact—it was his money that made him a matrimonial prize.

"Oh, I thought Mr. Allyn was still with you."

He looked up, seeing Maria Jeffries with her niece hanging on her hand. The little girl's face was flushed with excitement at the anticipated sleigh ride, making her gray eyes sparkle. Despite her faded cloak, she was a taking little thing.

"Well, infant, where are your mittens?" he quizzed.

"Right here, sir," she responded promptly, lifting her free hand to display the black wool. "Are you going with us?"

"Not today."

She nodded, her expression suddenly quite sober. "Somebody must stay with Grandpapa, after all. He seems quite lonely, don't you think?"

"Becca—"

"Well, he does."

Outside in the hall, they could hear George stamping the snow from his feet. "Ready, Miss Jeffries?" he called out.

Drew rose from the table to watch idly out the window as his cousin bundled them into the brightly painted sleigh. An odd pang, for his own childhood perhaps, assailed him as he recalled an earlier Christmas when he and David and Johnny had been young, a Christmas when there was still magic in the season. His long-dead father had driven them to the mill, back when it was still in use.

Turning away, he thought of Rebecca Grey's plain black wool gloves. Well, if the snow stopped, he just might ride into Chester to see if a fur muff could be found. Children ought to have Christmas memories. That decided, he climbed the stairs to visit his uncle.

"Dash it, Drew, but they ought to be back by now," Edwin Allyn fumed. "Where the devil can he have taken them?"

"Your concern does you credit," his cousin observed, looking up from their uncle's voluminous correspondence. "Care to help me answer any of this?"

"Lud, no! As if I should know what to say. Best just wait until he's gone, you know. Then you can write 'em that."

But Drew had reached the piece he'd been searching for. Slitting open the envelope, he read,

Dear Sir John,

It is my sad duty to inform you that my sister, Jennifer Jeffries Grey, passed from this earth last month, leaving one daughter, Rebecca Grey, a child of eight years.

She is a taking child, whose appearance and temperament are very much reminiscent of your son. I think you will be pleased to discover she is quite lovely and intelligent, albeit more than a trifle solemn in disposition, which is surely understandable, given the loss of both her father and her mother.

As I am unable to care for her properly, and my brother, William, is already burdened with five children of his own, I am bringing Rebecca to you, in the hope that when you see her, you can bring yourself to accept her. I must ask you to make arrangements for her care and well-being.

I pray you will not reject Rebecca, for whatever ill you may think of the parents, she is still your granddaughter, sir, and she has suffered greatly. I ask you to welcome her into your home and your family, with the promise that, should you do so, I shall with sadness cut the connection between us.

We shall arrive in December, dependent upon when my employer, Mrs. Ransome, shall choose to allow me a holiday.

I remain, your servant in this matter,

Maria Jeffries

What it must have cost to write such a letter to the man who'd disowned David.

"How the deuce am I to pay court to the woman if George don't bring her back?" Edwin demanded peevishly. "Got no time, anyways. Ten to one, Uncle Jack's already got Bagshot redrawing the demned will."

"Tell me," Drew asked abruptly, his hand still on Maria Jeffries' letter, "what do you think of Cousin Rebecca?"

"Why the devil would you ask a thing like that? It don't make any difference what I think of the brat, does it? If I want the money, I got to take her—and the Jeffries woman, in the bargain."

"You could do worse."

"Easy for you to say. Don't see you offering for either of 'em, Swynford! But then, you don't have to—don't need the money, anyways. Me and George—we ain't got your pockets, you know."

"A man is leg-shackled a long time," Drew reminded him.

"Ain't it the truth! And I wasn't thinking of sticking my foot in parson's mousetrap for a long time—and not with a nobody neither," his cousin complained bitterly.

"In dun territory, Win?"

"Deep," was the succinct reply.

"Worse than George?"

"No, but that don't signify. Played where I can't pay, after all." He looked out the window again. "What's he doing, do you think? Keeping her out until she agrees to tie the knot?"

"How much?" Drew persisted.

"Twelve thousand."

That elicited a low whistle from Drew that made Edwin bristle. "At least I ain't like George. He owes fifteen if he owes a ha'penny." He was about to let the window hanging fall when he stopped. "Egad! 'Tis George—and he's alone and on foot. Drew, look at that!"

"Alone?" Drew rose quickly and moved to stand behind him, peering over his shoulder. "What the devil?"

"Must've turned him down," Edwin decided.

"No. He's limping."

Before Edwin could digest that bit of news, his cousin was already into the hall. "I say but, Drew . . ."

They had not long to wait. George stepped inside, redfaced from the cold, and stamped the snow from his feet. "Ruined a good pair of boots," he muttered, looking down.

"What have you done with Miss Jeffries? Where's Cousin Rebecca?" Edwin shouted at him.

"I'm damned near froze, and that's all you got to say?" George asked, aggrieved. Turning his attention to Drew, he explained, "Had to walk. Snow's getting deep."

"Where are they?" Edwin repeated awfully.

"Hit a stump under the snow, turned the silly thing over."

"Will you answer me?"

"Dash it, Win, I'm trying to! We was flung out of it; horses broke the traces and bolted."

"George . . ."

"Oh, devil take it! If you are so interested, you can go get 'em. Me, I tell you I am froze and you cannot even bring yourself to care about that. Walked miles, Win, miles."

"Is the Jeffries woman all right?" Edwin reached out to shake his brother. "Answer me!"

Drew understood his cousin's impatience, but he knew there was no hurrying George. "Where did you leave them?" he asked quietly.

"Old mill. Miss Jeffries has got a sprained ankle, I think, and Cousin Rebecca cut her face. Other than that, they are all right. Left 'em with the blanket out of the sleigh." His face betrayed his utter fatigue. "Tried to carry the Jeffries woman, but couldn't. I ain't a big fellow like you. And the brat was determined to stay with her."

"Inside?"

He nodded. "Broke the latch to get 'em in. By the time we was in, the horses was nowhere to be seen. Had to walk," he muttered again. "Got to sit—feet froze, I tell you."

"Get a footman and the housekeeper," Drew ordered. "He'll need a cold-water bath for his feet and hands."

"Where the devil are you going?"

"To see if there's a cart to be had. I don't think we can get a carriage through the drifts, but maybe a wagon—"

"You're going after them?"

"Of course I am!" Drew exploded angrily. "A woman and a little girl cannot survive out there. If you want to come, I'm happy for the company."

Edwin looked down at his tasseled boots, thinking it unlikely he'd ever get another pair like them. But there was a fortune to be had, after all. He hesitated, then gulped. "All right, but I am no hand—"

"If the road is impassable, we'll have to take a couple of nags. Can you ride a plow horse, Win? I don't want to chance ruining a thoroughbred."

"I can ride anything you can." Then, perceiving his brother's incredulous stare, he added defensively, "Almost anything, anyways."

"Good. Get some blankets and meet me at the stable." Already halfway up the stairs, he looked back down. "And we'd best take a flask of brandy if Miss Jeffries is hurt."

"You bungler," Edwin muttered to his brother under his breath.

Tears welled in the pale eyes as the slender young man nodded, "I know, Win, but I had to try. I got debts."

The interior of the abandoned mill was dim, musty, and made eerie by the wind that rattled the few remaining glass panes and banged the door beneath its broken latch. Maria huddled in a corner, trying to keep Becca and herself warm beneath the carriage rug, while watching the mice scavenging along the worn boards, looking for long-forgotten grains in the cracks.

"Aunt M-Mia," Becca chattered miserably, "are w-we going t-to stay at G-Greystone for C-Christmas?"

"I think we ought to, don't you?"

"Y-yes."

Maria's arms tightened around the little girl, holding her close. "It isn't much of a Christmas for you this year, is it?" she asked softly. "Poor darling."

"I don't m-mind it—t-truly I don't." But even as she said the words, her voice betrayed a childish wistfulness.

Maria's heart went out to her. "Well, we cannot do much, you know, particularly not since your grandfather is so very ill, and—"

"I k-know." She turned her head against Maria's breast and snuggled closer. "At least I have y-you, Aunt M-Mia."

Maria fell silent at that, for as far as she could see, they were likely to starve together. But there was no need worrying a child, not at Christmas. The thought crossed her mind that George Allyn, for whatever reason, was trying to fix his interest with her, and for a moment, she was almost tempted to encourage him.

Poor Mr. Allyn. How foolish he'd felt when they'd wrecked, and how ridiculous he'd looked trying to carry her. No, it would never do, she supposed, sighing. If she wed, she wanted something more than poor, frivolous, foolish Mr. Allyn. And it was unlikely that anyone else would ever ask her.

"Hallo! Miss Jeffries!"

She was startled out of her dispirited reverie by Viscount Swynford's shouted greeting, and relief flooded over her. "Over here!" she called back loudly. "We are over here!"

"Aunt Mia, 'tis Cousin Drew," Becca exclaimed, pulling away.

The door creaked inward, and he stepped inside, his face ruddy from the cold, his black hair dusted with snow. Incredibly, he was smiling.

"He has c-come for us, Aunt M-Mia—just like Lochinvar," Becca cried out as she ran toward him.

His smile broadened into a grin, and his eyebrow lifted. "Lochinvar, infant?" Looking past her to Maria, he could see the color that crept into her face. "As I recall the tale, Lochinvar was the fellow who threw the fair maiden over his saddle and eloped with her," he said wickedly. "My dear Miss Jeffries, I had no notion you tended to the romantical in your literary tastes."

Maria struggled to her feet, hobbling, her swollen ankle aching. "That was Sir Gawain, dearest," she muttered to her niece. Still blushing, she raised her eyes to the viscount's. "Becca," she explained quickly, "likes tales of knights and ladies." She tried to take a few steps, wincing. "I caught my foot beneath the runner, I think."

His grin faded. "You are fortunate you still have it then. Don't try to walk. Win, I've found them! Over here!" Reaching out to lift the little girl's hair, he inspected the cut that crossed her forehead. "Just a scratch," he reassured her, "but there's going to be a bruise. By the by, I brought brandy, should you need it.''

"Thank you, but no. And I think it was ice that cut her,'' Maria explained. "I tried to wash the blood away with the snow.''

"Mrs. Crawford will have a salve for it, I should think.''

Edwin Allyn came from the other end of the building. "There you are, Miss Jeffries. Cousin Rebecca. Dashed sorry I am that George deserted you, but we are come to the rescue.'' His voice boomed in contrast to his slight build. He stopped when he saw her leaning against the wall. "Devil of it is, the wind's drifted the snow, had to unhitch the wagon and ride the nags in.''

Drew's gaze took in the narrow skirt of Maria's dress significantly. "You'll have to ride in front of one of us. Can you hold on, do you think?''

"Aunt M-Mia's got good b-bottom,'' Becca volunteered proudly. "She was used to ride when she was l-little like me.''

"Well, I—''

"I want to ride with C-Cousin Edwin,'' the child managed through still-chattering teeth.

That gentleman shot her a look that bordered on dyspeptic. "Heh-heh. Best go with Drew, Cousin Rebecca. He's a better hand with the infantry.''

Rebecca shook her head. "He's b-bigger—he ought to take Aunt M-Mia so she does not fall.''

"We've got to get them out of here, Win. 'Twill be a miracle if they suffer no more than a chill from this.'' Before his cousin could protest further, Drew slipped an arm beneath Maria's. "Your pardon for the familiarity, Miss Jeffries, but I see no other way.''

"No,'' she murmured faintly. "I think I can walk.'' Biting her lower lip to stifle the pain, she took a few steps to demonstrate, but she could not help leaning on him.

"Nonsense. There is no need to sacrifice your ankle on the altar of modesty, my dear. Get the door, Win." As he spoke, he swung her up easily, ignoring her embarrassed protests.

"Come on, brat," Edwin grumbled.

"Becca, sir," the little girl reminded him.

"Worst snow in years. Don't know why George brought you, Miss Jeffries," the younger man said irritably as he hastened to make way for his cousin. "Stupid thing to do."

It was no easy task to lift Maria onto the bare, broad back of the horse without splitting the narrow skirt, but Drew managed. Handing her a blanket for her shoulders, he swung up behind her and slid his hands beneath her arms to take the knotted reins. She sat, perched precariously, her legs dangling off one side of the huge animal.

"I'm afraid I cannot do it all, Miss Jeffries," he murmured behind her ear. "You'll have to forget propriety and hang on."

Acknowledging the truth of that and telling herself that within a few days she'd never see him again, anyway, she half-turned against him and wrapped her arms around his waist. He pulled his driving cape closer about them, then leaned forward to shield her from the wind. The thought crossed her mind that he was nothing like his effete, affected cousins, for the arms that held her were decidedly strong and muscular.

"Are you all right?" he asked.

Conscious of the shamelessness of her situation, she turned her face into his shoulder to hide her embarrassment. "Yes."

Beside them, Edwin bundled both him and Becca in the other blanket. And looking down on the small, bonneted head, he was surprised to discover a certain sympathy for the child. "Ready, brat?" he asked. "Now, if you think you are about to fall, you let Cousin Win know of it, you hear?"

They rode silently, all of them intent on reaching Greystone in the blinding, swirling snow. And the farther they went, the less Maria worried about appearances. The cold gnawed through the blanket, his driving cape, her pelisse, and her plain muslin gown, until she was nearly numb. She clung to Andrew Carstairs for warmth, not caring that he did the same.

"Lochinvar, eh?" he said suddenly. "I've been likened to many things in my life, but never a gallant in armor."

"I think she must have meant Sir Gawain."

"Either way, she flattered me."

"We were grateful to see you."

He was conscious of how much smaller she seemed in his arms than he'd expected—nothing at all like what she'd appeared. It was her fine bones, he supposed. And as he held her, he could not help contrasting her with the more fortunate females of his acquaintance. He had not a doubt that had any of them found themselves thus in his arms, he would have been subjected to any number of enticements, all quite archly done and all designed to bring him up to scratch. Maria Jeffries, on the other hand, seemed more intent on warmth than flirtation.

"Where the devil is Miss Jeffries?" George demanded over his soup.

"After the turnover you gave her, I expect she has taken to her bed," his brother muttered sourly. "Cowhanded thing to do, George."

"You wouldn't have seen the stump neither, Win. Admit it!"

"I'd have stayed on the road. As it was, you nearly froze 'em, you know."

"Nearly froze me, you mean," George retorted. "They was inside."

"Actually, I believe Miss Jeffries is upstairs reading

to Uncle Jack,'' Drew said. "And Becca has been given a hot posset and tucked up for the night.''

"You know, she ain't half bad—Miss Jeffries, I mean. Didn't kick up a dust at all when we was overturned. Been thinking I could do worse, you know,'' George told Drew.

"Coming it too strong,'' Win protested hotly. "If she wasn't smelling of Uncle Jack's moneybags, you'd not give her a second look.''

"Couldn't afford to. Tell you what: five hundred says she takes me.''

"It seems to me,'' Drew cut in dryly, "that gaming is the last thing you ought to be doing—either of you.''

"Oh, collect you are right. Ain't got five hundred, anyways,'' his cousin remembered.

"She ain't taking you, you clunch. 'Twas you as nigh crippled her. Tell him, Drew, tell him how you had to carry the poor girl to the horse.''

"I'd very much rather eat in peace. As far as I can see, she'd be a fool to take either of you.''

"Now—''

"Got to,'' George countered smugly. "One of us is to take her and the brat—else we don't get the money.''

"Don't know why you are staying, Drew,'' Edwin said suddenly. "Nothing in it for you, after all. I mean, you ain't about to offer for her; you don't have to.''

"Uncle Jack is dying,'' Drew reminded him. "And 'tis Christmas.''

"Not this year,'' George decided glumly.

"There is a child in the house. We ought to consider that. Rebecca has lost her mother and she's about to lose the grandfather she just met. I was thinking that perhaps we ought to do something for her.''

Both cousins turned to stare at him. "Like what?''

"A few gifts, a few decorations for the front salon, maybe some carols—I don't know. Entertaining children is not precisely in my experience, after all.''

"Dash it, I'd make a cake of myself, Drew. I cannot sing an note," George complained.

"Me neither. Still, daresay Miss Jeffries would be pleased, don't you think?" Edwin pushed aside his soup bowl and leaned forward to rest his elbows on the table. "Give me a chance to get her a gift."

"You ain't leaving the place. Snow's too deep." But the notion was taking hold. "You don't think 'twill be remarked? I mean, with Uncle Jack—"

"It's his last Christmas," Drew answered simply.

As soon as the covers were removed, George and Edwin withdrew hastily to search for Maria Jeffries, while Drew made his way to his uncle's book room. From the closed door, it appeared deserted, but as he stepped inside, there was the faint light of a single candle. And as his eyes adjusted to the dimness, he could see Maria's head bent low over a book. He cleared his throat, prompting her to look up guiltily.

"Oh, dear, I am found."

"You ought to have more light."

"Actually, cowardly wretch that I am, I am hiding," she admitted.

Her brown hair was drawn back severely from her face, but the cap was gone, making her seem somehow younger and more vulnerable. He quietly closed the door and crossed the room to pull a chair up to the small fire.

"How did you get down here?"

"It was not a particularly graceful sight, but I hopped." She smiled ruefully. "Your uncle and Becca are both fast asleep."

"You missed dinner."

"Mrs. Crawford was kind enough to send up a tray for Becca and me, so we ate with your uncle ere Becca went to bed."

"I collect you are avoiding Win and George."

"Yes." She sighed heavily and looked into the fire. "Ridiculous, isn't it?"

"Understandable under the circumstances. I hope that my company is not quite so onerous?"

"No." Her dark eyes met his briefly. "You are beginning to be the only sane person in this house, I think, as you do not appear about to make me an offer."

"Poor Miss Jeffries."

"Well, 'tis the truth," she retorted with asperity. "And I have given neither of them the least encouragement, I assure you. But if I hear my eyes described as shining coals or dark gems again, I fear I shall become ill."

"Alas, but I fear I am partly to blame for that," he admitted candidly.

"You?"

"Well, I believe I said that you have lovely eyes."

"If you are going to join them, my lord, I will not be able to stand it. I am in no mood for Spanish coin from you either." Then, perceiving his eyebrow had lifted, she sighed again. "Your pardon, my lord, but I am out-of-reason cross, I guess. It has been a trying day."

"Ankle still hurt?"

"Only when I stand." She shifted her position in the chair and looked down at the volume in her lap. "Thankfully, Mr. Bagshot was able to discover the key to the cases. Poetry is infinitely preferable to treatises on farming."

"Scott?"

"Burns."

"You seem to have a taste for Scottish poets, Miss Jeffries."

"Sometimes. Actually, I read almost everything, although Mrs. Ransome despises Byron. But I suspect that has more to do with the scandals than with his work." She closed the book, marking it with her finger. "I read aloud to her whenever I can. 'Tis the best way to enjoy her library subscription. I order what I like, and she gets to hear it."

He looked down at her ankle, which was obviously quite swollen, and he knew it had to be painful. "I could see if there is any ratafia to be had," he offered.

"And open the door? I'd very much rather you did not."

"Then would you take some brandy?"

It was highly improper, and she knew it. In fact, it was highly improper just being alone with him. But just then she was beyond caring about convention. "I know I ought not," she conceded, "but it's been a difficult day. Besides, 'tis not likely I shall see you again after we leave, and I cannot think you would ever have cause to tell Mrs. Ransome."

He smiled. "A drop for your foot. 'Tis medicinal in moderation," he assured her.

"Yes." A faint, wry smile lurked at the corners of her mouth. "Though I must tell you that I know that for a whisker."

"But it is. I once had it prescribed for a cough." He uncorked the decanter and poured a small amount into a goblet. "A little won't hurt you." As she took it, he turned to pour himself considerably more.

She sipped just enough to taste, then made a face. He grinned boyishly. "It gets better when you are used to it."

Later, she was to wonder if it was the intimacy of the small room, the fire, or the brandy, but there was an appeal about him that went beyond his good looks. For a time, they merely sat there, each staring into the flickering flames, she sipping lightly, he drinking the distilled wine.

"Tell me, Miss Jeffries," he asked suddenly, "how did you come to this pass?"

"I beg your pardon?"

"How is it that you and your sister had to earn your

bread?'' He leaned back, watching her lazily. ''You
are of the gentry, are you not?''

It was an impertinent question, but nonetheless she
felt compelled to answer. ''When my papa died, my
mother was understandably lonely, I suppose. In any
event, she married a man more interested in her fortune than in her, and within two years, he had spent
it all. Then he left her for a younger, more handsome
woman.'' She took another delicate taste of her brandy
before meeting his gaze. ''We were fortunate in that
William was already ready to be received into orders,
and my sister was finished with Miss Marston's Select
Academy. She married David, and between them, they
somehow managed to keep me in school. David Grey
was, I think, the best of men, for he never begrudged
me the cost.''

''And so you became a paid companion?''

She nodded. ''Miss Marston knew of an elderly female who was desirous of having someone around to
read and to play cards. I took employment with a Mrs.
Winston in Bath, and we got on rather well. When she
died, her son gave me a character that gained me a
position with Mrs. Ransome. And that, sir, is all there
is to the tale.''

''Not quite. What are you going to do about
Becca?''

''Well, as my hopes of your uncle have come to
naught—through no fault of his now, I might add—I
mean to write Mr. Winston and Miss Marston, asking
for references that I may teach where Becca is welcomed.''

''You could choose between Win and George.''

''No.''

''Surely you must be aware that my uncle is offering
them money to take you, Miss Jeffries.'' For a moment, her expression went blank, and then the color
rose to her cheeks. ''So that explains it,'' she said

finally. "How very lowering for me, don't you think? I will, of course, speak to him of it."

"I suppose Uncle Jack had not the time to make any other provision," he added, certain now that she had not known. "And if you are capable of reforming a certain tendency to game, either of them would probably make an amiable husband."

"No. Foolish of me, I know, but I should very much rather be wed for myself."

"What about Becca?"

Briefly, she considered that he was probably enjoying himself hugely at her expense, for he could not possibly care what happened to either of them. But there was a certain sympathy in his hazel eyes. "You are of a very different world than I, my lord, so perhaps I cannot expect you to understand. Whilst 'tis common amongst the *ton* to wed for the shabbiest of reasons—and certainly Becca is not that—I cannot do so."

"Why not?"

"Terribly selfish of me, I expect, but she will grow up someday, and I should be left with a husband I had married for a very wrong reason."

"Is there a right one?"

Her color heightened again. "This is ridiculous, my lord. You cannot possibly wish to know what I think."

"On the contrary, Miss Jeffries, but I do. If Uncle Jack's plan fails, I might well be expected to take care of my little cousin."

"I should not expect much beyond assistance, sir."

"Still looking for Lochinvar, Miss Jeffries?"

Maria opened her mouth to deny it, then shut it. She turned to look again into the fire, and her expression grew distant. "Yes. Yes, I suppose in a sense I am," she answered slowly. "I should rather be alone than be like my mother. You must think me quite foolish, my lord."

This time, it was he who hesitated. "No. In fact, I

honor you for the sentiment, Miss Jeffries. As you say, in my set, there is very little room for the romantic.''

"How very sad for you, my lord. Whether we discover one or not, we all ought to cherish our dreams of having someone to love us, don't you think?'' She stared into her glass for a long moment, then looked up, her dark eyes sober. "I mean, there is such intimacy in marriage that there ought to be true depth of feeling. Otherwise, the arrangement must be little better than that between a Cyprian and her so-called protector.''

Her plainspeaking surprised him. "Often worse,'' he agreed, "for at least the Cyprian will pretend to love for the money. The gentlewoman will consider her birth and looks, coupled with the presentation of an heir, of course, fair exchange instead.''

"You sound as one burned,'' she chided.

"No. I have never discovered the female worthy of sharing my money or my life.''

"What a miserable, maudlin pair we are tonight, my lord.'' She lifted her glass and forced a smile. "Then may we both wish better for the other. May you discover a lady who would love you if you were poor, ugly, and untitled—and may I discover my very own Lochinvar.''

He touched his goblet to hers, grinning at the way she'd phrased the toast. "To Lochinvar.''

"And your lady,'' she reminded him.

"And my lady,'' he agreed.

"Foolish us, I suppose,'' she admitted after she drained the rest of her brandy. "We are more like to discover Alexander Pope was right, you know.''

"I hope not.''

He was watching her, his hazel eyes warm and disconcerting. The thought crossed her mind that a man ought not to look like that: it was unsettling to a female's peace of mind. And the last thing she needed was an absurd flirtation certain to lead nowhere. And yet she was reluctant to leave.

"Another brandy for your ankle?" he asked softly.

"Just a drop. I cannot go upstairs foxed, you know."

"Just a drop," he promised.

Warmed by the fire and brandy, they sat there, talking long into the night, covering such varied things as Scottish poets, the reformer Hannah More, the new industrialization, the future of gaslights in homes, female education, and just about everything either could bring up—except the empty state of their hearts.

Finally, when the clock struck two, she rose with an effort. "You must pardon me, my lord, but I find myself quite tired, and 'tis overlate. I think I shall seek my bed."

"Would you have help up the stairs?" he asked, rising politely.

"Thank you, but I have only to reach them, and then I shall pull myself up by the rail."

After she left, he sat again, this time to mull over the plight of Maria Jeffries and his small cousin. And there did not appear to be any good answer. Only the seemingly unthinkable. But he had to own that she was perhaps the first female of his acquaintance he could converse with beyond the commonplace. She had a good mind to go with her romantic heart, and the combination made her an Incomparable of a different sort.

And upstairs, once she'd struggled into her night rail, Maria Jeffries could not resist peering curiously into her mirror, studying her eyes. It was all a hum, she told herself, yet she had to admit she was really no different than any other female when it came to flattery. And somehow the thought that maybe he'd meant it lifted her spirits greatly. Foolish you, she chided herself as she slipped beneath the bedcovers. And when she finally drifted into that fanciful netherworld before sleep, the last thing she saw was a dark-haired, hazel-eyed Lochinvar riding his horse into the wedding banquet.

After a relatively sleepless night, Drew rose early, thinking to speak with his uncle. But when he reached the old man's chamber, he could hear Maria Jeffries' voice.

"You must not think me ungrateful, sir," she said gently, "but I did not ask for a fortune for myself, and I do not want one. All I wish for is a measure of security for Becca, nothing more. I don't want her to have to live as I do, and surely you can understand that."

"I told Edwin and George I'd expect—"

"I think I know what you told them, sir, and it simply cannot work. For one thing, neither of them really wishes to marry, and certainly not a nobody such as I am. And for another, I'd not wed where there was not the necessary affection." She leaned over the bed and took his hand. "But I know you meant well, and you must not think I do not appreciate what you have tried to do."

"Got to take care of Rebecca."

"And so you should. But do not be thinking me your responsibility also. If you would leave her money, I pray you will put it in trust for her. Perhaps Lord Swynford can be persuaded to administer it, for he seems to be about as decent as any of his set."

The old man sighed and his fingers closed over hers. "Thought to do some good in this world ere I left it. Never thought you was too proud to take it." His tired eyes watched her. "David . . . my boy . . ."

"You cannot make amends to me for what is past, sir, for I suffered no injury. And as Jenny is dead, there is only Becca."

"Got to have money to raise her, don't you?"

"Give us an income of one hundred pounds per year, and I promise you that I will rear a girl to make you proud. 'Tis all I ask. And when she is of an age, perhaps one of your nephews will be settled and able to bring her out modestly.''

Drew knocked to interrupt them. Maria looked up, but did not remove her hand from his uncle's. ''You are up early, my lord. I thought 'twas the fashion to lie abed until noon.''

''After only two brandies? What a weak, frivolous fellow you must think me.''

''No. I collect you are come to visit Mr. Grey?''

''For a little while. Then I'd like to breakfast with you ere George and Edwin put you on the run. There is the matter of Christmas, you know.''

''For Becca?''

''For all of us. I thought perhaps a few decorations, a wassail bowl, gifts for the little girl, and some carols, of course. You do play, do you not?''

''Yes, but—''

''You don't object, Uncle, do you?''

''Eh? No, no—give her Christmas.''

''Then 'tis settled. If the snow clears enough, we'll drive into Chester and buy some things. If not, we'll make do with whatever we can find. I am not above bribing Mrs. Crawford to discover something for Rebecca, you know.''

Perhaps it was because she was tired, or perhaps because she was no more proof to his unexpected kindness than anyone else, but she could not completely suppress the tears that brightened her dark eyes. ''Thank you, my lord.'' She withdrew her fingers from John Grey's and rose hastily, wiping her eyes with the back of her hand. ''Well, I daresay I ought to leave you two alone.'' With that, she fled.

''What the devil ails her?'' the old man wanted to know.

''Possibly a surfeit of George and Edwin,'' was the dry reply.

''She's a good girl . . . makes me wish I'd got to

know the sister.'' Sir John sighed heavily. ''Made a mull of everything, ain't I? Can't even do right when I want. Got no time for more mistakes, Andrew.''

Sir John's mind seemed clear. Drew glanced over to the laudanum bottle, and the old man followed his gaze. ''Ain't had any for hours . . . waiting to see my granddaughter.'' For a moment, his expression clouded. ''Don't want her to remember me as a fool . . . asked Maria to bring her up when I ain't befuddled. So little time . . .'' His voice trailed off almost wistfully.

''It is not the years, but rather the hours that we remember, Uncle John. When I look back, one year fades into another, yet I recall certain things Papa did and said more than others.''

''Aye. I remember David when . . . Well, it don't matter now does it? Got to think of Rebecca.''

''Yes.''

''Thought I could dangle my money for George and Edwin, you know: make 'em offer for the aunt and take care of the girl. Guess she don't like the idea none.''

''No.''

''Pity. She'd a been the making of either of 'em: got good sense, principles, too. Took me to task for it.''

''A remarkable young woman,'' Drew agreed.

''Got to think of something else. Just wish I had time.''

Drew picked at a nub of lint on his sleeve before answering. ''Make me Rebecca's guardian, Uncle.''

''You?''

'' 'Twould ease the matter for you, wouldn't it?''

''Damme if I know your lay, Andrew. Why?'' he asked suspiciously. ''It ain't for the money, I'll be bound.''

''I am not even sure I know the answer to that. Let us just say that I accept she is David's daughter and therefore a relation.''

"And Maria?"

"Cousin Rebecca will still need her."

"Let me think on it."

"I should not expect anything else."

"Andrew, I got to have six drops . . . cannot wait, after all. Take the rest after she leaves." He watched as Drew measured the painkiller. "You are a good man, Andrew—best of the lot."

"Not saying much for the lot, is it?"

Beads of perspiration formed on the old man's forehead as Drew lifted him. "Don't suppose you'd take Maria out of pity, would you?" he gasped.

"No." Then, seeing the disappointment in his uncle's eyes, he added, "You see, after thirty-three years, I find I am actually a hopeless romantic. And pity is a poor reason to wed."

Later, Sir John lay alone, listening to the clock counting away precious minutes whilst he waited for his granddaughter, wondering what his nephew had meant. It didn't matter, he decided, for he had one last plan.

To Maria's chagrin, the old man failed to correct George and Edwin Allyn's impression that she was going to be a wealthy woman. And she found herself turning more and more to the viscount, telling herself that he was literally her only ally in the place, for even Becca began to respond to the two brothers' attempts to win her.

Over the next several days, the household lost its pall as the staff, too long depressed by Sir John's impending death, responded to plans for the holiday. Mr. Sims, Mrs. Crawford, the cook, the maids, and the footmen all justified their efforts by pointing to the child. The best linen was aired and pressed, the silver polished, and new wax candles appeared everywhere. And gradually, with the preparations came the realization that they not only did it for Rebecca Grey, but they also were giving Sir John a send-off.

Anita Mills

Two days before Christmas, the snow had cleared and the main roads were dry enough to afford a trip into Chester. Leaving Becca to cut and paste and paint designs on a table by her grandfather's bed, Lord Swynford, accompanied by Miss Jeffries and her persistent suitors, went shopping. And when they returned, the carriage boot laden with packages, they discovered a footman hanging brightly colored streamers under Becca's direction in Sir John's bedchamber.

"Good little thing, ain't she?" George observed.

"Taking," his brother agreed. "If I was to have a brat, I'd as lief have one like Cousin Rebecca—after m'heir, of course."

"Miss Jeffries showing any partiality to you, do you think?" George asked cautiously.

"Deuced little," Win admitted.

"I've been thinking. We got her divided, don't you know? Poor woman don't know where to turn."

"I don't like it when you think, George."

"It ain't like that. Thing is, we got to quit quarreling betwixt us. It don't solve nothing, Win. Suppose we was to back off a bit. Let her decide, you know. And if 'tis me she takes, I ain't above sharing with you."

"What?"

"Well, it don't do me no credit for my only brother to go to Newgate, does it? No, I mean it: if she takes me, I won't let you go under," George promised.

For a moment, his brother stared suspiciously, but there was no guile in the younger man's pale eyes. "You mean it? You'd do that for me?"

"Would. Been thinking about Uncle Jack. We don't know how long we're here for, Win. And I'd as lief not go out with a dirty conscience. Besides, there ain't but two of us anymore."

"Egad." Edwin had to blot at a piece of dust that seemed to have caught in his eye. "Daresay you have the right of it, old fellow. Tell you what: if she takes you, there's no hard feelings—and if she takes me, I'll settle your debts.''

"Now, Win, I wasn't asking it of you."

"But you got to promise me to give up the gaming— nothing more than a little whist for low stakes."

"Nothing? But—"

"Nothing."

"Don't know if I can. Well, I suppose I can try." George brightened. "You know what we got, Win— we got insurance. She can take either one of us now."

"There you are, Cousin George," Becca called out. "Aunt Mia and Cousin Drew are ready to hang the bells and the kissing bough in the parlor. Come on."

"You go first, Win. I ain't no hand at that, not since Charlotte Hemphill caught me at Squire Trevor's."

"It don't signify," Edwin scoffed. " 'Tis just Christmas, that's all."

But as they entered the salon, Maria was holding the chair on which Drew stood, stretching to hang a rope of small silver bells from the chandelier. His task completed, he brushed them with his hand, setting them to tinkling. He climbed down to face her.

"Do you want to do the kissing bough next?"

"Uh . . ."

" 'Tis Christmas, Aunt Mia."

She turned to George. "Mr. Allyn?"

"Not me—that is, I don't like climbing."

"Cousin Edwin?"

"I ain't no hand—"

"I am." Drew walked over to pick up the piece of fir that Becca had twined with berries. "Come on, infant, I'll let you hang it over the doorway."

The little girl giggled. "Does that mean Sims will have to kiss Mrs. Crawford when he goes under it?"

"Only if he wants to."

He caught her at the waist and lifted her, holding her up as she twisted the wires around the evergreen garland. "Got it?"

"Yes."

Very gallantly, he set her directly beneath the doorway, then leaned over to brush her cheek with his lips. "There you are, poppet—the first of many."

"From one of the best," George chimed in. "Ain't every chit as gets kissed by Swynford, Becca."

"Do you think it's straight?" Drew asked Maria. When she walked over to inspect it more closely, he caught her hands and held them. "Got her, George."

"Me? Uh . . ."

"Oh, for heaven's sake," Edwin snapped. "Here . . ." He leaned to peck at Maria's cheek. "Nothing to it—hope you have as happy a Christmas as you can, Miss Jeffries."

"Thank you."

"Don't you have to kiss her, Cousin Drew?" Becca asked innocently.

"Little baggage."

His hands still holding Maria's, he leaned so close that she could feel the warmth that emanated from his body. And his beautiful hazel eyes were filled with mischief just before they became a blur. His lips touched hers lightly, and his breath caressed her cheek, then it was over.

"Happy Christmas, Maria."

She let out her breath and looked away. "And to you, my lord."

"Well, if that's done, let's warm ourselves with some punch. Then I got to fix my packages." George's eyes danced merrily. "I know a little chit as is going to be pleased, come Christmas morn."

When Maria went up to see Sir John just after dinner on Christmas Eve, she found him struggling to sit up. "Have 'em get my dressing gown. I ain't lying up here whilst everybody's down there."

"Are you quite certain you are able, sir?"

" 'Course I ain't able, but it don't matter. Fetch my

nevvies, will you?'' He eyed the laundanum bottle. ''And bring that, don't want it yet, but when George gets to caterwauling, I may be wishful of some.''

''Yes, sir.''

And when Edwin protested, the old man snapped, ''It's Christmas, ain't it? Got nothing to save my strength for, anyways.''

In the end, it was Drew who lifted him, and with George and Edwin edging down the steps on either side, he managed to get the old man down to the sofa, where Maria placed pillows behind him and covered him with a blanket.

Becca danced around him excitedly. ''Is it not grand, sir?''

Sir John looked up at the surfeit of painted stars, the bells, the streamers, and the evergreen garlands. ''Grand.''

''Aunt Mia, do we have to wait until morning?''

''It ain't really Christmas until then,'' George reminded her.

''But my grandpapa is down. In the morning, he won't see us until after 'tis done.''

Drew glanced at his uncle and could see the hunger in his eyes as he watched his son's daughter. ''Well, I don't see why not. After all, I seem to remember that the twenty-fifth is merely an arbitrary date.''

''I was wanting to hear Miss Jeffries sing,'' Edwin complained.

''You wretch,'' Maria hissed at him. ''If I play, you sing.''

''Music first, gifts later. Got to make it seem like Christmas,'' George maintained stoutly.

A bowl of steaming punch was produced to loosen the vocal cords, cups were passed, and the dessert tray brought in. As Becca settled onto the rug beside her grandfather, Maria took her place at the pianoforte. The fire blazed brightly in the hearth, and there was, despite everything, quite a festive air in the room. After a few tentative chords, Maria began an ancient carol. At first, only she and Drew and Becca sang, but as both the evening and the punch waned, George and Edwin joined in loudly.

When they stopped, the old man's eyes were closed. But as Becca began dividing the packages, he roused to watch. To his surprise, there was an envelope for him. With shaking hands, he opened it and read the childish scrawl, ''For as many hugs and kisses as you want, sir. Rebecca.''

''I'd have the first now,'' he whispered, choking back tears.

Most of the gifts were small: Maria received a pair of gloves from George, a box of writing stationery from Edwin, and a silver-handled mirror from Drew. In turn, they admired the lace-edged handkerchiefs she'd made them. But it was Becca whose eyes shone as she lifted the snowy fur muff from the tissue and held it up, exclaiming, '' 'Tis the prettiest thing I have ever had, Cousin Drew.'' Then, not to disappoint the others, she admired the little beaded reticule from George and the painted fan from Edwin.

''When you are done, I got something to say,'' Sir John said.

They all turned to the old man on the sofa, and he nodded. ''It ain't often a man is there to give his will, is it? But I wanted to tell you myself—thought about everything since the little one came—got nothing else to do but wait.''

The room went utterly quiet as everyone strained to hear Sir John's thin, weak voice. ''Made too many mistakes, and there's no saying this is right yet, but 'tis the best I know to do.'' His eyes rested on the younger Allyn, who'd gone white. ''I know you've been hanging on the expectation of my money for years, George. Well, the time has come, and whatever you get from me, 'tis all there is, you know. When it is gone, there ain't any more for you to stave off creditors with. Make myself clear on that head?''

''Yes.'' It was a whisper even lower than his uncle's.

''How much do you owe?''

''Uh . . .'' George flushed guiltily.

''I got to know as close as you can tell. So don't be cutting yourself low.''

''Tell it right, George,'' his brother advised.

''Easy for you to say, Win. You ain't as deep as me.'' He sucked his breath in and let it out slowly, looking away. ''Probably fifteen thousand.''

''Are you sure?'' Edwin demanded.

''No more'n sixteen, if I was to pay the tradesmen even.''

The old man nodded. ''I want you to submit it all—gambling debts, tradesmen's bills, everything—to Mr. Bagshot, George. He'll pay 'em all.''

''Even the butcher?'' the young man asked doubtfully. ''Somehow it don't seem right that—''

''All of 'em. I am giving you a new beginning, no debts and two thousand pounds to the good. Ain't many of us as gets to start again, but you got the chance, boy. Make it a good one.''

It was not precisely what his youngest nephew had expected, but it would lift a heavy burden from his thin shoulders. And he could have received far less. ''Yes, sir,'' he mumbled. ''Won't waste it.''

Sir John's gaze traveled to Edwin. ''As for you, my offer is the same: your debts and two thousand pounds. Go and game no more. Find yourself a good female and be a credit to your name.''

''Thank you, sir,'' Edwin murmured, relieved.

Twisting his head, the old man searched until he saw Drew. ''I suppose you guessed your share, ain't you?''

''I think so.''

''Now see here—''

''Close your trap, George,'' Edwin ordered curtly. ''You ain't heard him out.''

"Just so. I ain't leaving you a farthing, Andrew, not because I don't care about you. I do, in fact, probably more than the rest of 'em, but you don't need it."

"I never expected anything, Uncle Jack."

"Thought you didn't. Spend too much on clothes and cattle and maybe an opera singer or two, but you ain't exceeded your income. I like that. In fact, I'm hoping you can do as well for my granddaughter." His eyes held Drew's. "Naming you her guardian. I think you will see she is a rich woman when she is grown."

Drew looked to Maria, who sat on the pianoforte bench like stone. She had what she had asked for, and yet in that moment of triumph, there was no joy in her face. The parting was going to be painful. She blinked back tears.

"Putting my money in trust for Rebecca, Andrew—everything but what I just told. This house, the contents, everything. David grew up here and 'tis fitting that she does also."

"But what about Aunt Mia? Grandpapa, I don't want to leave Aunt Mia!" Becca cried.

"Hush, dearest," Maria choked. " 'Tis for the best."

"But I don't—"

"Ask Andrew about your Aunt Maria," Sir John advised, interrupting her. "I got a notion . . ."

"Well, 'tis settled then." Drew exhaled sharply. "One more carol, infant, and off to bed."

"But . . ."

Maria turned back to the pianoforte and started to play, scarcely able to see the keys. And one by one, the others in the room joined in the song, singing of a very different Maria in far-off Bethlehem, of another child born of the lineage of a different David. As the last notes sounded, Drew nodded to Edwin. "Can you and George get him back upstairs?" he asked.

"Think so. If not, get a footman to help." Edwin rose and stood behind Maria. "Almost sorry you didn't take me, you know. And I ain't in the petticoat line at all.''

"Thank you." Somehow, she managed to smile. "Good night, sir."

"Wish you the best, Miss Jeffries," George mumbled.

"You go on up, infant. I want to speak with your Aunt Mia." When the little girl hesitated, Drew bent down and put an arm about her. "The best is yet to come, little one."

"Go on, Becca," Maria ordered tiredly. "I shan't be long."

"But . . ."

" 'Twill be all right," Drew promised.

After they left, he closed the door behind them, then turned around.

Maria still sat on the bench. "Well, 'tis done, my lord. Becca is settled." She swallowed hard and tried to keep her voice from breaking. "I pray you will have her write to me."

"You can stay also," he said quietly. "In fact, I should be very disappointed if you go."

"I suppose Becca will need a governess, but—"

"I expect to hire one." He moved to stand directly behind her. "But what she needs more than that is a mother to love her, Maria. Oh, I know you cannot entirely replace Jennifer in her heart, but then neither would I replace David." When she said nothing, he reached to lay a hand on her shoulder. "I'm asking you to stay, Maria."

For a moment, her hopes soared, then reality dashed them. "You cannot pretend to any affection. It has only been a week, sir," she managed in a near whisper.

His fingertips traced along the bony ridge of her shoulder. "I won't say I have completely thrown my hat over the windmill yet, but I think it's headed in that direction. Everything I see in you I like more every day. Besides, there is a year of mourning, and during that time I expect to visit Becca often. There is no telling what we may discover in each other, my dear.''

"You are a lord, a Corinthian, a—''

"Lochinvar?'' he supplied helpfully. Stepping back, he sighed. "Rushing my fences, aren't I? Come on, you can sleep over it.''

"All right.'' She stood as though she were in a trance, then hobbled around the bench. "Good night, my lord.''

He waited until she'd reached the doorway, then as he leaned to open the door, he slipped in front of her. "Dreadfully unfair of me, I know,'' he murmured, taking her into his arms. "But it is Christmas, and it seems a shame to waste this.'' Carefully positioning her beneath the berries, he bent his head to hers. And this time, he did not brush her lips at all. When at last he released her, he grinned boyishly. "Devilishly impetuous fellow, Lochinvar.''

"Sir Gawain.''

"Was it?'' His hazel eyes were warm as they searched her face. "What do you say, Maria? If I hire a governess and a woman to play duenna, will you stay?''

"But you cannot possibly—'' she began helplessly.

"I promise that I will not wed for Becca, my dear. After all, when she is grown, I should still have the wife.'' Looking over her shoulder, he espied the mirror. "Don't forget my Christmas present, Mia. Every time you think I cannot possibly, you are to get it out and look at your eyes.'' When she still hesitated, he drew her into his arms again and kissed her thoroughly. "Well?''

"Perhaps it *was* Lochinvar,'' she decided.

"You'll stay?''

Smiling through misty eyes, she nodded. "Yes,'' she answered simply.

* * *

Surrounded by his family, Sir John Grey departed this world on Epiphany, confident at last of being met on the other side. And exactly one year later, Andrew Charles Philip Carstairs, fifth Viscount Swynford, took his ward's maiden aunt for wife, much to the astonishment of the *ton* and the delight of his relations. The only thing more curious than his choice of bride was the presence of a large white horse, saddled and ready to ride, at the wedding banquet. It was, they supposed, some sort of private jest.

Playing House

By

Mary Balogh

The logs in the fireplace were crackling and shooting sparks up into the chimney. The fire's warmth felt good to the young lady who had just come in from the cold and the wind and rain. She held her hands out to the blaze.

But she could not draw a great deal of comfort from the fire. She caught sight of the hem of her wool dress. It was heavy with wetness and streaked with mud. Her half-boots looked no better. And she wished she had not removed her bonnet and handed it to the footman with her cloak. Her hair was hopelessly damp and flattened to her head. And she knew that her nose as well as her cheeks must be glowing red.

It was cold outside, and the mile-and-a-half walk across the park to Bedford Hall had been taken into the teeth of the wind and into the driving force of the rain and had seemed more like five miles.

Lilias lowered her hands from the blaze and brushed nervously at her dress. The darned patch near the hem was more noticeable now that the fabric was wet. She looked down at her right wrist and twisted her sleeve so that the darn there would be out of sight.

She should not have come. She had known that as soon as the footman had opened the front doors and asked her, after she stepped inside, if he could take her to Mrs. Morgan. But, no, she had replied with a firmness that had been fast deserting her, she was not calling on the housekeeper today. She wished to speak with his lordship, if it was convenient.

She should not have come, a single lady, alone, to speak with a single gentleman. She knew she would never have dared to do so if she were in London or some other fashionable center. Even here in the country it was not at all the thing. She should have brought someone with her, though there was no one to bring except the children. And she did not want them to know she was paying this call.

And who was she, even if she had had a respectable companion, to be paying a call on the Marquess of Bedford? She was wearing her best day dress, yet it was patched in three places. She had had to walk from the village because she owned no conveyance or even a horse or pony. In two weeks' time she was to be a servant.

She should have come to the kitchen entrance, not to the main doors.

Lilias took one step back from the fireplace, suddenly feeling uncomfortably warm. If she hurried, she could grab her cloak and bonnet from the hallway and be outside and on her way home before any more harm was done. The rain and wind would be at her back on the return journey.

But she was too late. The door to the salon in which she had been asked to wait opened even before she could take one more step toward it, and he stepped inside. Someone closed the door quietly behind him.

The Marquess of Bedford.

Lilias swallowed and unconsciously raised her chin. She clasped her hands before her and dropped into a curtsy. She would scarcely have known him. He looked taller, and he was certainly broader. He bore himself very straight, like a soldier, though he had never been one. He was immaculately and fashionably dressed. His hair was as thick as it had ever been, but its darkness was highlighted now by the suggestion of silver at the temples. But he was not thirty yet.

His face was what had changed most. It looked as if carved out of marble, his jaw firm and hard, his lips thin and straight, his blue eyes above the aquiline nose heavy-lidded and cold. One eyebrow was arched somewhat higher than the other.

He made her a stiff half-bow. "Well, Miss Angove," he said in a voice that was softer, colder than the voice she remembered, "what an unexpected pleasure. You are the first of my neighbors to call upon me. All alone?"

"Yes, my lord," she said, clasping her hands more firmly before her and consciously resisting the impulse to allow them to fidget. "This is not a social call. I have a favor to ask."

His one eyebrow rose even higher and his lips curved into the suggestion of a sneer. "Indeed?" he said, advancing farther into the room. "Well, at least you are honest about it. Have a seat, ma'am, and tell me how I may be of service to you."

She sat on the very edge of the chair closest to her and clasped her hands in her lap. Someone had tamed his hair, she thought irrelevantly. It had always waved in a quite unruly manner and had forever fallen across his forehead. It had been a habit of his to toss it back with a jerk of the head.

"It is not precisely a favor," she said, "but more in the way of the calling in of a debt."

He seated himself opposite her and looked at her inquiringly. His eyes had never used to be like this. They had been wide and sparkling eyes, mesmerizing even. But then, they were compelling now too. They regarded her with cynical contempt. Lilias glanced down nervously at her sleeve to find that the darned patch was staring accusingly up at her. But she did not twist the sleeve again. Perhaps he would not notice if she kept her hands still. Except that she felt that those eyes saw everything, even the larger darned patch beneath her left arm.

"When you were at school," she said, "and found your Latin lessons difficult, Papa helped you during your holidays. You used to come to the rectory every morning for two successive summers. Do you remember?" She did not wait for a reply. "You would not tell your own papa for fear that he would be disappointed in you. And Papa would accept no payment for your tuition. You told him—I was there when you said it—that you would always consider yourself in his debt, that you would repay him one day."

"And so I did," he said in that quiet, cold voice. His expression did not change at all. "Your father has been dead for well over a year, has he not, Miss Angove? But I take it that the day of reckoning has come. What may I do for you?"

"I think less than the tuition for two summers would have cost you," she said hastily, wishing that she could keep her voice as cool as his. "I would not put myself in your debt."

His eyelids appeared to droop even lower over his eyes. "What may I do for you, ma'am?" he asked again.

"I want a Christmas for my brother and sister," she said raising her chin and looking very directly into his face. She could feel herself flushing.

Both his eyebrows rose. "An admirable wish," he said. "But it would seem that if you wait patiently for one more week, Christmas will come without my having to do anything about the matter."

"They are still children," she said. "My parents' second family, people have always called them. Philip and I were two years apart, and then there were eleven years before Andrew was born. And Megan came two years after that. They are only eleven and nine years old now. Just children. This is our last Christmas together. In two weeks' time we will all be separated.

Perhaps we will never be together again. I want it to be a memorable Christmas.'' She was leaning forward in her chair. Her fingers were twining about one another.

"And how am I to help create this memorable Christmas?'' he asked. His mouth was definitely formed into a sneer now. "Host a grand party? Grand parties are not in my style.''

"No,'' she said, speaking quickly and distinctly. "I want a goose for Christmas dinner.''

There was a short silence.

"Papa was not a careful manager,'' she continued. "There was very little money left when he died and now there is none left, or at least only enough to pay for our journeys in two weeks' time. The people of the village would help, of course, but they were so used to finding that Papa would not accept charity in any form that they now do not even offer. And perhaps they are right.'' Her chin rose again. "I have some of his pride.''

"So,'' he said, "instead of asking charity, you have found someone who is in your debt.''

"Yes,'' she said, and swallowed awkwardly again.

"And you want a goose for Christmas,'' he said. "Your needs are modest, ma'am. That is all?''

"And a doll for Megan,'' she said recklessly. "There is the most glorious one in Miss Pierce's window—all porcelain and satin and lace. I want that for Megan. She has never had a doll, except the rag one Mama made for her when she was a baby. I want her to have something really lovely and valuable to take with her.''

"And for your brother?'' he asked softly.

"Oh.'' She gazed at him wistfully. "A watch. A silver watch. But there are none in the village, and I would not know how to go about purchasing one for him. But it does not matter. Andrew is eleven and almost not a child any longer. He will understand, and he will be happy with the scarf and gloves I am knitting for him. The cost of a goose and the doll will not exceed the cost of tuition for two summers, I don't believe. Will it?''

"And for yourself?'' he asked even more softly.

Lilias gazed down at her hands and reached out to twist the offending sleeve. "I don't want anything that will cost money,'' she said. "I want only the memory of one Christmas to take with me.''

"Where are you going?'' he asked.

She looked up at him. "Into Yorkshire,'' she said. "I have a post as a governess with a family there.''

"Ah,'' he said. "And your brother and sister?''

"I have persuaded my grandfather to take Andrew,'' she said. "It took several letters, but finally he agreed to take him and send him to school. Sir Percy Angove, that is, Papa's father. The two of them never communicated after Papa's marriage.''

The marquess nodded curtly.

"And Megan is going to Great-aunt Hetty in Bath,'' Lilias said. "I am afraid I pestered her with letters too. But it will be only until I can earn enough money to bring us all together again.''

Bedford got to his feet and looked down at her from cold and cynical eyes. "Ah, yes,'' he said. "A suitably affecting story, Miss Angove. I must congratulate you on the manner in which you have presented it.''

Lilias looked up at him in some bewilderment.

His bearing was military again, his manner curt, his eyes like chips of ice. "You will have your goose, ma'am,'' he said, "and your sister her doll. Your brother will have his watch too—I shall see to it. You will have your Christmas and the memory of it to take into Yorkshire with you. I shall wish you good day now.''

Victory? Was it to be so easy? Was she to have more than a Christmas dinner to give the children? Was Megan to have her doll? And Andrew his watch? Andrew was going to have a watch! All without any struggle, any persuasion, any groveling?

Was this victory?

Lilias scrambled to her feet and looked up at the tall, austere figure of the Marquess of Bedford. She curtsied. "What can I say?" she said breathlessly. "Thank you sounds so tame."

"You need not say even that," he said. "I am merely repaying a debt, after all. You will wait here, ma'am, if you please. I shall have tea sent to you while you await the arrival of my carriage to take you home. I take it you walked here?"

He would not take no for an answer, although there was no apparent kindness at all in his manner. Lilias found herself gazing once more into the fire a few minutes later, having been left to take her refreshments alone. And after drinking her tea, she was to have a warm and comfortable—and dry—ride home.

She should be feeling elated. She *was* feeling elated. But uncomfortable and humiliated too. As if, after all, she were taking charity. She blinked back tears and stared defiantly into the flames. She was not taking charity. She was merely accepting what was hers by right.

He seemed to be made of stone to the very heart. Not once had he smiled. Not once had he given any indication that theirs was no new acquaintance. And he had called her explanation an affecting story. He had said so with a sneer as if he thought it contrived and untrue.

It did not matter. She had got what she had set out to get. More. She had not even been sure she was going to ask for the doll. But as well as that, Andrew was to have a watch. It did not matter that he had not smiled at her or wished her a happy Christmas.

It was at Christmastime he had first kissed her. It had been one of those magical and rare Christmases when it had snowed and there was ice on the lake.

They had been sledding down a hill, he and she the last of a long line of young people, all of whom had been trekking back up again by the time they had had their turn. And she had overturned into the snow, shrieking and laughing, and giggling even harder when he had come over to help her up and brush the snow from her face and hair.

He had kissed her swiftly and warmly and open-mouthed, stilling both her laughter and his own until he had made some light remark and broken the tension of the moment. It had been Christmastime. Christmas Eve, to be exact. She had been fifteen, he one-and-twenty.

It did not matter. That had been a long time ago, almost exactly seven years, in fact. He was not the same man, not by any means. But then, she was not the same, either. She had been a girl then, a foolish girl who had believed that Christmas and life were synonymous.

She turned and smiled at Mrs. Morgan, who was carrying a tray into the salon.

He had a daughter somewhere in the house, Lilias thought for the first time since her arrival.

The child tugged at her father's hand, trying to free her own.

"The water is running down my arm, Papa," she complained. A few minutes before she had told him that the rain was running down the back of her neck. "I want to go home now. Pick me up."

The Marquess of Bedford stooped down and took his daughter up in his arms. She circled his neck with her own arms and burrowed her head against the heavy capes of his coat.

"We'll be home in a twinkling, poppet," he said, admitting to himself finally that he was not enjoying tramping around his own grounds any more than she, being buffeted by winds and a heavy drizzle that seemed to drip into one's very bones. "The snow will come before Christmas, and we will build snowmen and skate on the lake and sled on the hill."

"Your coat is wet, Papa," she said petulantly, moving her head about as if in the hope of finding a spot that the rain had not attacked. "I'm cold."

He was clearly fooling only himself, Bedford thought, unbuttoning the top two buttons of his coat so that his daughter might burrow her damp head inside. Christmas would not come. Not this year or ever again. December the twenty-fifth would come and go, of course, this year and every year, but it would not be Christmas for all that.

Christmas had come for the last time six years before, when his father had still been alive, and Claude too. When he had been a younger son. When Philip Angove had still been alive. Before Spain had taken Claude and Waterloo, Philip. When life had been full of hope and promise.

Christmas in that year and in all the years preceding it had invariably been white. Always snow and skating and sledding and snowball fights. And Yule logs and holly and mistletoe. And family and laughter and the security of love. And food and company and song.

Christmas had always been white and innocent. How could there ever be Christmas again?

His brother—his great hero—had died at Badajoz. And his father less than a year later. And soon after that he had discovered that the world is not an innocent or a pleasant place in which to do one's living. Suddenly he had had friends by the score. And suddenly women found him irresistibly attractive and enormously witty. And suddenly relatives he had hardly known he had, developed a deep fondness for him.

In his innocence he had been flattered by it all. In his innocence he had fallen for the most beautiful and most-sought-after beauty of the London Season. He had married her before the Season was out.

Lorraine. Beautiful, charming, and witty. The only thing she had lacked—and she had lacked it utterly—was a heart. She had made no secret of her affairs right from the beginning of their marriage and had merely laughed at him and called him rustic when he had raged at her.

"Papa, open another button so that I can get my arms in," his child said, her voice muffled by the folds of his cravat.

He kissed one wet curl as he complied with her demand. He was not even sure that she was his, though Lorraine had always insisted that she was.

"Darling," she had said to him once, when she was very pregnant and fretful at being confined to home, "do you think I would go through all this boredom and discomfort for any other reason than to give you your precious heir?"

She had been very angry when Dora was born.

Lorraine had drowned two years later in Italy, where she had been traveling with a group of friends, among whom was her latest lover.

And the lures had been out for him again for almost all of the two years since. Women gazed at him with adoration in their eyes. Women cooed over a frequently petulant and rather plain-faced Dora.

The Marquess of Bedford ran thankfully up the marble steps in front of his house and through the double doors, which a footman had opened for him.

"Let's see if there is a fire in the nursery, poppet, shall we?" he asked, setting his daughter's feet on the tiled floor and removing her bonnet and cloak. "And buttered muffins and scones?"

"Yes, if you please, Papa," she said, raising a hand for his. But her tone was petulant again as they climbed the stairs side by side. "When will Christmas come? You said there would be lots of people here and lots to do. You said it would be fun."

"And so I did," he said, his heart aching for her as

he looked down at her wet and untidy head. "But Christmas is still five days away. It will be wonderful when it comes. It always is here. You will see."

But he was lying to her. The dolls and the frilled dresses and the bows would not make a happy Christmas for her. The only real gift he would be able to give her was his company. The choice had been between any of a number of house parties to which he had been invited alone, and Christmas spent, for the first time ever, with his child. He had chosen the latter. But he was not at all sure that that was not more a gift to himself than to her.

Where was the snow? And the young people? And the laughter and song?

"When will the rain end, Papa?" the child asked, echoing his own thoughts.

"Soon," he said. "Tomorrow, probably."

"But it has rained forever," she said.

Yes it had. For all of a week, at least.

He should not have come. He had not been home for almost six years. Not since leaving in a hurry with his father when the news about Claude had come. He should have kept that memory of home intact, at least. That memory of something perfect. Something pure and innocent. Something beyond the dreariness and the corruption of real life.

But he had been fool enough to come back, only to discover that there was no such place. And perhaps there never had been. Only a young and innocent fool who had not yet had his eyes opened

The rain was bad enough when he had been expecting the magic of his childhood Christmases. Worse by far had been that visit two days before.

Even Lilias.

She had been his first real love. Oh, he had lost his virginity at university and had competed quite lustily with his fellow students for the favors of all the prettiest barmaids of Oxford. But Lilias had been his first love.

A sweet and innocent love. Begun that Christmas when he had first become aware of her as a woman and not just as the fun-loving and rather pretty sister of his friend, Philip Angove. And continued through the following summer and the Christmas after that.

It had been an innocent love. They had never shared more than kisses. Sweet and brief and chaste kisses. He had been very aware of her youth—only sixteen even during that second Christmas. But they had talked and shared confidences and dreamed together.

A sweet and an uncomplicated love.

He wished he had kept that memory untainted. But the world had come to her too. He had wondered about her when he had decided to come home, wondered if he would see her, wondered what it would be like to see her again. He had been amazed to be told on his second day home that she was waiting downstairs in the salon for him. And he had hoped with every stair he took that it would not be as he suspected it would.

It had been worse.

The wet and muddy hem of her gown; the darned patches on the hem and sleeve—the second brought to his attention by the artful design to conceal it; the damp and untidy hair; the thin, pale face; the sad, brave story; the modest appeal for assistance; the ridiculous mention of a debt unpaid. He had seen worse actresses at Drury Lane.

He had been furious enough to do her physical harm. She had come to his home to arouse his pity and his chivalry, and in the process she had destroyed one of his few remaining dreams.

Could she find no more honest way of finding herself a husband? Did she really imagine he was so naïve? She had not even had the decency to wait awhile. She had been the first to come.

"Papa," Dora was saying. She had climbed unnoticed onto his lap beside the fire in the nursery and was playing with the chain of his watch, "it is so dull here. I want to go somewhere."

"Tomorrow, poppet," he said. "Mr. Crawford has two little boys, who will surely be pleased to see you. And the rector has a family of five. Maybe there are some little ones among them. We will call on them tomorrow, shall we?"

"Yes, please, Papa," she said.

"And I have another errand to run in the village," he said, staring down at his watch, which she had pulled from his pocket. "To see a little boy and girl, though they are not quite as little as you, Dora."

"Tomorrow?" she said. "Promise, Papa?"

"I promise," he said, kissing her cheek. "Now, nurse wants to dry and comb your hair again. And I need to change my clothes and dry my own hair."

Lilias set three pairs of mud-caked boots down outside the door of her cottage and looked down at them ruefully. Would it be better to tackle the job of cleaning them now, when the mud was still fresh and wet, or later, when it had dried? She glanced up at the sky. The clouds hung heavy and promised that the rain was not yet at an end, but for the moment it had stopped. The boots would not get wet inside just yet.

She was closing the door when her eye was caught by the approach of a carriage along the village street. The very one she had ridden in just three days before. She closed the door hastily. She did not want to be caught peeping out at him as he rode past. But she could not prevent herself from crossing to the window and standing back from it so that she could see without being seen.

"Ugh," Megan said from the small kitchen beyond the parlor. "It is all soaking wet, Lilias."

"Ouch," Andrew said. "Is there any way to pick up holly, Lilias, without pricking oneself to death?"

"Oh, mercy on us," Lilias said, one hand straying to her throat, "he is stopping here. And descending too. One of the positilions is putting down the steps."

The dripping bundles of holly, which they had all just been gathering at great cost to fingers and boots, were abandoned. Megan and Andrew flew across the room to watch the splendid drama unfolding outside their window.

"The marquess?" Megan asked, big-eyed. "And is that his daughter, Lilias? What a very splendid velvet bonnet and cloak she is wearing."

Andrew whistled, an accomplishment he had perfected in the past few months. "Look at those horses," he said. "What prime goers!"

Lilias licked her lips and passed her hands over hair that was hopelessly flattened and untidy from her recent excursion outdoors. The watch? Had he come to bring the watch in person? The doll had been delivered by a footman the day before, fortunately at a time when the children had gone over to the rectory to play with the children there. It had been carefully hidden away after she had smoothed wondering fingers over the lace and the soft golden hair. And the butcher had informed her that she might pick up a goose on Christmas Eve.

She wished she were wearing her best day dress again. She crossed to the door and opened it before anyone had time to knock. And she saw with some dismay the row of muddy boots standing to one side of the doorstep. She curtsied.

"How do you do, ma'am?" the Marquess of Bedford said. He looked even larger and more formidable than he had looked three mornings before, clad as he was in a many-caped greatcoat. He held a beaver hat in one hand. "I have been taking my daughter about to meet some of the children of the neighborhood."

"Oh," Lilias said, and looked down at the small girl standing beside him, one hand clutched in his. She was handsomely dressed in dark-red velvet, though she was not a pretty child. "I am pleased to make your acquaintance, my lady."

"This is Miss Angove, Dora," the marquess said.

The child was looking candidly up at Lilias. "We have brought you a basket of food from the house," she said, tossing her head back in the direction of the positilion, who was holding a large basket covered with a white cloth.

"Won't you come inside, my lord?" Lilias asked, standing hastily to one side when she realized that she had been keeping them standing on the doorstep. "And there really was no need." She glanced at the basket and took it reluctantly from the servant's hand.

"We have taken one to each of the houses we have called at," he said. "A Christmas offering, ma'am." He looked at her with the hooded blue eyes and the marble expression that she had found so disconcerting a few days before. "Not charity," he added softly for her ears only.

His daughter was eyeing Megan and Andrew with cautious curiosity.

"Do you think girls are silly?" she asked Andrew after the introductions had been made and Lilias was ushering the marquess to a seat close to the fire.

Andrew looked taken aback. "Not all of them," he said. "Only some. But then, there are some silly boys, too."

"Mrs. Crawford's sons think girls are silly," Dora said.

"They would," Andrew said with undisguised contempt.

"And do you squeal and quarrel all the time and run to your mama with tales?" Dora asked Megan.

Megan giggled.

"Dora," her father said sharply, "watch your manners."

"Because the children at the rectory do," Dora added.

"We have no mama to run to," Megan said. "And when Drew and I quarrel, we go outside and fight it out where Lilias cannot hear us and interfere." She giggled again. "We have been gathering holly. It is all wet and prickly. But there are so many berries! Do you want to see it? You may take your coat off and put on one of my pinafores if you wish."

"Megan," Lilias said, her voice agonized. One of Megan's faded pinafores on Lady Dora West?

"What is the holly for?" Dora asked. "And, yes, please." She looked at her father on an afterthought. "May I, Papa? Where did you find it? I wish I could have come with you."

"No, you don't," Andrew said. "My fingers look like one of Miss Pierce's pincushions. We found some mistletoe too. It is in the kitchen. Come and look."

Lilias found herself suddenly seated opposite the marquess in the small and empty parlor, the object of his silent scrutiny. She jumped to her feet again.

"May I offer you tea?" she asked.

"No," he said. "That is not necessary. We had tea at the rectory not half an hour since."

She flushed. "I am afraid I have nothing else to offer," she said.

"Sit down," he said. He looked over his shoulder into the kitchen, where the voices of the children mingled. "One of my men has been sent into town for your brother's watch, among other things. I shall have it delivered tomorrow."

Lilias felt herself flush even more deeply. "You are kind," she said. "And thank you for the other things."

More than ever she felt that she had begged from him and had been given charity. There was no unbending in his manner, not the merest hint of a smile on his lips or in his eyes. He was regarding her with what looked uncomfortably like scorn.

"Dora is lonely," he said. "She has never had children to play with. Until less than a year ago she lived with her grandparents.''

Lilias did not reply. She could think of nothing to say.

''Unfortunately,'' he said, ''when she does find playmates, she demands perfection. She wants them to be the sort of friends she would like to have. I am afraid our visits this afternoon have not been a great success.''

Lilias smiled fleetingly.

''Look, Papa.'' Dora was back in the room, holding up one small index finger for her father's inspection. A tiny globe of blood formed on its tip. ''I pricked myself.'' She put the finger in her mouth even as the marquess reached into a pocket for a handkerchief. ''Megan and Andrew are going to put the holly all about the house for Christmas. May I stay and watch?''

''It is time to go home,'' he said.

''But I don't want to go home,'' she said, her lower lip protruding beyond the upper one. ''I want to stay and watch.''

''We shall gather holly too, shall we?'' he asked. ''And decorate our house with it?''

''But it will be no fun,'' she said mulishly, ''just you and me. I want to watch Megan and Andrew. And I want to watch Andrew carve the Bativity scene he is making. We don't have a Bativity, scene, do we?''

''No,'' he said, getting to his feet, impatience showing itself in every line of his body, Lilias thought as she too rose from her chair, ''we don't have a Nativity scene, Dora. Take off the pinafore now. I shall help you on with your cloak and bonnet.''

''They have mistletoe, Papa,'' Dora said, making no attempt to undo the strings of her pinafore. ''They hang it up and kiss under it. Is that not silly?''

''Yes,'' he said, undoing the strings for her, ''very silly.''

''Can we have some, Papa?'' she asked.

"Yes," he said. "We will find some tomorrow."

"But it will be no fun," she said again.

"We will come with you," Megan offered, glancing at her brother. "Won't we, Drew? We know all the best places to look. Or rather, Lilias does, and she showed us today. Shall we come with you?"

The child looked almost pretty for a moment, Lilias thought, as her face lit up with eagerness. "Yes, you come too," she said. "We will need ever so much holly because our house is much bigger than yours. Isn't it, Papa? And mistletoe for every room. And Andrew can carve a Bativity scene just for me."

"No," Andrew said, "there will not be time. But I will bring the shepherd with me to show you. It will be finished by tomorrow."

Lilias found herself suddenly gazing into the marquess's eyes across the heads of the children and feeling decidedly uncomfortable. His eyes were cold and penetrating. And for the first time there was a half-smile on his lips. But she wanted to shiver. The smile had nothing to do with either amusement or friendship.

"Well, Miss Angove," he said, "it would be quite too bad if you were the only one to miss this merry outing. I shall send my carriage for the three of you after luncheon tomorrow and we will all go holly gathering together. You will do us the honor of taking tea with us afterward."

He did not ask questions, Lilias noticed. He did not even make statements. He gave commands. Commands that she would dearly have liked to refuse to comply with, for if one thing was becoming clear to her mind, it was that he disliked her. Quite intensely. Perhaps it was her temerity in reminding him of a long-forgotten debt that had done it. She could think of no other reason for his hostility. But it was there nonetheless.

And she was glad suddenly that he had come home,

glad that she had seen what he had become, glad that she could put to rest finally a dream and an attachment that had clung stubbornly long after he had left in such a hurry the very day after they had spent two hours together strolling the grounds of his home, hand in hand, looking at the flowers of spring and planning what they would do during the summer.

She was glad he had come back, for he no longer lived, that gentle and sunny-natured young man whom she had loved. He was dead as surely as his older brother was dead. As surely as Philip was dead. He had died six years before. She had just not known it.

He was holding her eyes with his own. He was obviously waiting for an answer, though he had asked no question. And how could she answer as she wished to do when there were three children standing between them, all eagerly anticipating the treat that the morrow would bring?

"Thank you, my lord," she said. "That would be very pleasant."

Very pleasant indeed, the Marquess of Bedford was thinking the following afternoon as the five of them descended the steps of his house and set off past the formal gardens and the lawns and orchards to the trees and the lake and the hill and eventually the holly bushes.

She was wearing a cloak that looked altogether too thin for the weather. And beneath it he could see the same wool dress she had worn for her first interview with him. Except that he had realized the day before that it could not, after all, be her oldest gown. The cotton dress she had worn when he and Dora had called upon her was so faded that it was difficult to tell exactly what its original color had been.

The children were striding along ahead, one Angove on each side of Dora, Megan holding her hand. Dora had had a hard time getting to sleep the night before.

He had sat with her, as he had each night since their coming into the country, until she fell asleep. He had sat there for almost an hour.

"We won't forget the mistletoe, Papa?" she had asked after he had tucked her comfortably into her bed.

"No," he had assured her, "we won't forget the mistletoe."

"Will you kiss me, Papa?" she had asked.

He had leaned over her again and kissed her.

"Under the mistletoe, silly," she had said, chuckling uncontrollably for all of two minutes.

"Yes, I will kiss you, poppet," he had said. "Go to sleep now."

But she had opened her eyes several minutes later. "Do you think Andrew will remember the shepherd, Papa?" she had asked.

"I expect so," he had said.

He had thought her asleep ten minutes after that. He had been considering getting up from his chair, tiptoeing out of the room, and leaving her to the care of her nurse.

"Papa," she had said suddenly, frowning up at him, "what is a Bativity scene?"

"A Nativity scene," he had said. "I'll tell you some other time. It is time to sleep now."

"It won't rain tomorrow, Papa, will it?" she had asked plaintively.

She had been excited about the promised outing with the Angoves. More excited than he had seen her since taking her from Lorraine's parents early the previous spring, a thin and listless and bad-tempered child.

Damnation! he thought now, and offered his arm to Lilias. Events could not have turned more to her advantage if she really had planned them. The afternoon before he had thought she had, but he had been forced to admit to himself later that she could not have done so. Too much had depended upon chance. She had not even known that he and Dora were going to call on her.

But she would take full advantage of the cozy family outing. He supposed he would be forced to listen to patient cheerfulness about the prospective post as governess and tender lamentations on the fact that the family was about to be broken up. Doubtless she would confide again her intention of reuniting them when she had made her fortune as a governess.

Lilias. He had not expected her to come to this. He looked down at her as she walked silently at his side. She had not grown since the age of sixteen. Her head still barely passed his shoulder. Her hair was still smooth and fair beneath her bonnet. But she was thinner. Her hand, even inside its glove, was too slender on his arm. Her face was thin and pale. Her dark-lashed gray eyes seemed larger in contrast. She really did look as if she were half-starved.

Damnation!

"I wanted Christmas for my daughter," he told her, realizing with a jolt as he heard his own words that that was exactly what she had said to him four days before about her brother and sister. "Christmas as I remembered it. I thought I would find it here. But I chose just the year when there is no snow. Only this infernal cold and damp."

"But it did not always snow," she said, looking up at him. "Just very rarely, I think. It was especially lovely when it did. But Christmas was always wonderful anyway."

"Was it?" He frowned.

She drew breath as if to speak, but she seemed to change her mind. "Yes," she said.

"I have your watch," he said. "It is at the house. I shall see that you have it before you leave after tea."

She looked up at him again, bright-eyed. "Thank you," she said.

Here we go, he thought. He had supplied her with

the perfect opportunity to heap upon his head reflections on how happy the boy would be during the coming years and how he would be able to remember his sisters and their life together every time he pulled the watch from his pocket. He clamped his teeth together and felt his jaw tighten.

He felt guilty suddenly. She so obviously *was* very poor, and it was so obviously true that the three of them were to be separated after Christmas. He just wished she had not decided to use the pathos of her situation to win herself a rich and gullible husband.

Except that he was not gullible. Not any longer.

She half-smiled at him and shifted her gaze to the three children, who were now quite a distance ahead of them. She said nothing.

Dora was skipping along, he was surprised to notice when he followed the direction of Lilias' eyes.

"This is where we got the holly yesterday," Megan announced a while later when they came up to the thicket. And then she looked at Lilias, a hand over her mouth, and giggled.

Andrew was laughing too. "We were not supposed to say," he said, darting a mischievous look at the marquess. "We were trespassing."

Lilias was blushing very rosily, Bedford saw when he glanced at her. She looked far more as she had looked as a girl.

"But these ones don't have as many berries as yours," Dora complained.

"All the good branches are high up," Andrew said. "We could not reach them yesterday. Even Lilias."

"It seems that I am elected," the marquess said. "Thank goodness for leather gloves. This looks like certain self-destruction."

Megan giggled as he stepped forward and his coat caught on the lower branches of holly. He had to disengage himself several times before he could reach up to cut the branches that were loaded with berries. His

upturned face was showered with water. Dora was giggling too.

Lilias had stepped in behind him to take the holly
as he handed it down. Her gloves and cloak were not
heavy enough to protect her from hurt, he thought,
and clamped his lips together as he was about to voice
the thought.

"Ouch," Dora cried excitedly, and giggled even
more loudly. "I have almost as big an armful as you,
Andrew. I have more than Megan. Oh, ouch!"

"You must not clutch them," Andrew said. "Just
hold them enough that they do not drop."

"Well," the Marquess of Bedford said when he
paused and looked behind him. "You look like four
walking holly bushes. Do you think you can stagger
back to the house with that load? Only now does it
strike me that we should have had a wagon sent after
us."

"Oh, no," Andrew said. "That would spoil the
fun."

"This is such fun, Papa," Dora said.

"Let me take some of this load," Bedford said,
reaching out to take some from Lilias' arms, "before
you disappear entirely behind it."

Her eyes were sparkling up at him.

"But, Papa," Dora wailed. "The mistletoe."

"Oh, Lord," he said, "the mistletoe. I shall go and
get some. You all start back to the house." But she
was loaded down. She would never get back without
being scratched to death. "Better still, drop your load,
Lilias, and show me where this mistletoe is. You children, on your way. We will catch up to you."

God, he thought, turning cold as she did what she
had been told—considering her load, she had had little
choice—he had called her Lilias. The witch! Her wiles
were working themselves beneath his guard despite
himself. His jaw hardened again.

She led him around past the thicket of holly bushes,

past the old oaks, to the mistletoe, which he had forgotten about. The old oaks! He had climbed them with
her, to sit in the lower branches, staring at the sky and
dreaming aloud with her. He could remember lifting
her down from the lowest branch of one—he could not
remember which—and kissing her, her body pressed
against the great old trunk, her hands spread on either
side of her head, palm to palm against his. He could
remember laughing at her confusion because he had
traced the line of her lips with his tongue.

"It was all a long time ago," he said abruptly, and
felt remarkably foolish as soon as the words were spoken. As if he had expected her to follow his trend of
thought.

"Yes," she said quietly.

He gave her the mistletoe to carry, being very careful not to lift it above the level of her head as he handed
it to her. And on the way back he took the large bundle
of holly into his own arms, against her protests, to
carry to the house.

"My coat and my gloves are heavier than yours,"
he said.

She brushed her face against the mistletoe as they
walked.

"I suppose," he said harshly after a few silent minutes, "you do not get enough to eat."

She looked up at him startled. "My lord?" she said.

"Your brother and sister do not look undernour-
ished," he said. "I suppose you give all your food to
them."

Her flush was noticeable even beneath the rosiness
that the wind and cold had whipped into her cheeks.
"What a ridiculous notion," she said. "I would have
starved to death."

"And have been doing almost that, by the look of
you," he said, appalled at his own lack of breeding
and good manners.

"What I do is my own business, I thank you, my

lord," she said. Her voice was as chill as his own, he realized. "I do not choose to discuss either my appetite or my means with you."

"You were quite willing to do so a few days ago," he said.

"Only enough to explain why I had to bring up the matter of that old debt," she said. "And I take it unkindly in you to refer again to a topic I confided only with embarrassment and reluctance."

He strode on, knowing that he was walking too fast for her, but doing nothing to slacken his pace.

"Stephen," she said. She sounded close to tears. "Why do you hate me?"

Stephen. No one had called him by his given name for years, it seemed. Lorraine had never called him anything but Bedford. He slackened his pace so that she was no longer forced almost to run at his side.

It was clever. Very clever. It almost unnerved him. It was too clever. She had overplayed her hand.

"I do not hate you, ma'am," he said, thankful to see the house close by. The children must be inside already. "What possible reason would I have to hate you?"

"I don't know," she said.

He gritted his teeth against the trembling of her voice. It was too overdone. Too contrived.

Lilias, he thought, and remembered the oak trees. And remembered Lorraine and dozens of admiring female eyes and more dozens of obsequious hangers-on. All with their various wiles and arts, and not a few of them with their sad stories and their outstretched hands.

Life might have been so different if only Claude had not died, he thought bitterly, standing aside so that Lilias might precede him up the steps and through the doors into the hallway of his home.

Lilias was putting the final stitches in a strip of faded blue cloth for Mary's robe while Megan was painstak-

ingly lining the manger with straw. Andrew was whittling away at a sheep that insisted on looking more
like a fox, he complained, a deep frown between his
eyes.

"But Joseph is quite splendid, Drew," Megan said
loyally. "He looks quite like a real man."

"And how lovely it will be," Lilias said, "to have
our own Nativity scene when everyone else has to go
to church to see one. What shall we sing?"

"Lully lulla, thou little tiny child," Megan began
to sing, and Lilias joined her, while Andrew held his
sheep at arm's length and regarded it with half-closed
eyes.

They all stopped what they were doing when there
was a knock at the door. Lilias rose to answer it.

Lady Dora West was dressed in dark-blue velvet this
time, in a small but dashing riding outfit. Her eyes
shone and her cheeks were flushed with color. She was
clutching her father's hand as she had two days before.

"We rode here on Pegasus," she announced as soon
as the door was opened, and Lilias could see beyond
her a magnificent black stallion tethered to the fence.
"Papa said we might call and see your decorations and
see Joseph if he is finished."

"I do beg your pardon if you are busy." The Marquess of Bedford was looking at her with hooded and
wary eyes, Lilias saw when she lifted her own reluctantly to his face.

Why had he come? The afternoon before had been
unspeakably embarrassing, especially after her outburst, when she had called him by his given name and
asked him such a foolish question. Instead of sitting
in the drawing room after tea while the children ran
excitedly about first that room and then the nursery,
placing the holly, and giggling over where to hang the
mistletoe, they had trailed almost silently after. Afraid
to be alone together.

She had not expected to see him again.

"Dora has quite taken to your brother and sister," he said. "She can derive no excitement from her nurse's company or from mine. She will be satisfied with ten minutes, I believe."

But by the time he entered the cottage, Dora had already thrown aside her hat and riding jacket and had run into the kitchen to lift from a hook behind the door the pinafore she had worn the last time.

"Oh, the holly," she cried. "It looks so lovely in here because the room is small. And the mistletoe is right in the center." She stood beneath it and chuckled. "Kiss me, Papa."

He did so, bending from his great height to take the upturned face between his hands and kiss the puckered mouth. Lilias turned away, a curious churning in her stomach.

"But that is supposed to be just for Christmas," he said. "Not for another two days, poppet."

Listening to his voice as he spoke to the child, not seeing him, she thought he sounded like Stephen. But, no, she would not think that. It was not true.

Dora was soon exclaiming over Joseph and laughing delightedly over the sheep when Andrew told her that is looked like a fox. She noticed Mary, who was already dressed in her blue robe.

"Oh, pretty," she said, fingering it.

Bedford seated himself, uninvited, his eyes on his daughter.

"We were singing when you came," Megan said, and began singing the same carol that had been interrupted by the arrival of their guests. Dora smiled and stroked Mary's robe. "You sing too, Lilias."

Lilias flushed. "Later, Megan," she said, and glanced in some embarrassment at the marquess, whose eyes had shifted to her. His expression was unfathomable.

"You used to sing," he said. "All the time."

She smiled fleetingly and wished she still had Mary's robe to stitch at. She had not yet started Joseph's.

"You used to go caroling," he said, frowning as if the memory had only just come back to him. "On Christmas Eve. We all used to go—Claude, Philip, Susan and Henrietta Price, the Hendays. But you used to lead the singing."

Lilias bit her lip. "We still go," she said. "Some of the villagers and I. The children too. We go around the village before church at eleven, and out to some of the cottages too if we know that someone is too unwell to come to church."

"Tomorrow night," Andrew said, looking up briefly from his work. "We had great fun last year. Mr. Campbell gave us all hot cider before he realized that some of us were children and ought not to be drinking it."

Megan giggled. Then she looked up, arrested by some bright thought. "You ought to come too this year," she said. "Dora can come. I will hold her hand. And you too, sir," she added magnanimously.

"May I, Papa?" Dora had leapt to her feet. She looked definitely pretty, Lilias thought, untidy hair and faded pinafore notwithstanding. "May we?" She danced up and down on the spot in an agony when he did not answer immediately. "Oh, please, please, Papa, may we?"

"You do not know any of the carols, poppet," he said. "And it will be too late for you. It will be past your bedtime."

"But Megan will teach me," she said. "Won't you, Megan? And Miss Angove. Won't you, Miss Angove? And I will go to sleep tomorrow afternoon, Papa, and sleep all afternoon and be very good. Oh, may we go too? Please."

"We will have to talk about it further," he said stiffly. He looked almost angry, Lilias saw at a glance.

"Right now we are interrupting work, Dora. And I have some errands to run in the village."

"But I don't want to go," she said. "You will stop to talk to people, Papa, and I will be dull. You go and do your errands and I will stay here. Miss Angove will teach me the carols."

The marquess stood up resolutely. "Put your pinafore away where you found it, now," he said, "and I shall help you on with your coat."

She stared at him her lower lip protruding beyond the upper.

"We will be very happy to have her stay, if you will agree," Lilias said softly. "It is good to have children here at Christmastime."

His eyes turned on her, hooded, inscrutable. He inclined his head. "Very well, then, ma'am," he said. He turned back to his daughter. "You may stay for an hour, Dora," he said. "But you must come without protest when I return."

Megan and Dora clapped their hands. Even Andrew looked pleased.

Lilias, standing at the door a minute later, watching the marquess swing himself into the saddle of his horse and proceed along the village street, was not sure if she had done the right thing or not, interfering between a father and his daughter. He had paused in the doorway and looked down at her.

"Another debt to call in?" he had said softly and icily.

She had not comprehended his meaning until he was riding down the pathway to the gate, and even then she was not sure he had meant what she thought he had meant. She hoped he had not. And she wondered again, though she wished with all her heart that she had not asked it, why he hated her.

They sang for almost the whole hour, sometimes the same carol over and over, while Andrew tackled the final feature of the Nativity scene, the baby Jesus, and

Megan arranged and rearranged the items already completed. Dora first helped and then stood at Lilias' elbow, staring fascinated at the tiny robe for Joseph that she was making.

Lilias smiled at her after a few minutes, when they were between carols. "Why don't you pull up that stool?" she said.

"Papa told me the story," Dora said when she was seated. "About the baby and the stable and the manger and the smothering clothes."

"The swaddling clothes," Lilias said with a smile. "That is what I will be making next."

"He is going to tell me again tonight," Dora said. "I like that story. I am going to learn to sew next year when I am five."

"Are you?" Lilias smiled again. "Will you like that?"

"Nurse is to teach me," Dora said. "But I am going to ask Papa if you can teach me instead. It would be fun with you."

Megan began singing another carol.

The caroling was not the only part of Christmas he had forgotten, Bedford discovered the following morning. And he really had forgotten that. He had always remembered Christmas as a white and outdoor affair. Everything else had become hazy in memory.

But there had always been the caroling and the lanterns and the rosy cheeks and laughter, and the glasses of cider and wassail until not one of them had been quite sober by the time they got to church. None of them had ever been precisely drunk—just smiling and warm and happy. How could he have forgotten? And how everyone had wanted to stand next to Lilias because she had such a sweet voice and such perfect pitch. He had won almost all of those battles.

Dora, restless in the morning because it seemed such a long wait until the evening—he had promised her the night before, much against his better judgment, that they would join the carolers—wandered down to the kitchen to watch the cook roll the pastry for the mince pies. And she fell into conversation with Mrs. Morgan, who was delighted to have a child in the house again.

And that encounter led, unknown to Bedford until later, to a visit to the attic to find the relics of Christmases past.

"Papa!" Dora burst into the library, where Bedford was trying to read, though it was hard to bring his thoughts to bear on the book opened before him. She was moving at a run past the footman who held the door open for her, and her face was flushed and pretty with an excitement that she could barely contain. "Papa, come to the attic with me. We have been looking at Christmas. The dearest bells. And the star! May we have an evergreen bough, Papa? Mrs. Morgan says there were always evergreens. May we? Do put down the silly book and come."

He put down the silly book and came. Or rather was dragged by an insistent little hand and a voice brimming with an excitement he had thought her incapable of.

And of course, he thought as soon as he looked into the opened boxes in the attic and dismissed a rather uncomfortable and apologetic Mrs. Morgan . . . Of course. How could he have forgotten? The evergreen boughs, decorated with crystal balls and bells that tinkled and twinkled every time a door was opened or a draft blew down a chimney. The evergreen boughs that had brought the smell of Christmas right inside the house.

And one year the candles on the boughs, until they had been forbidden forever after . . . after the great fire, when the branch had been singed black and a whole circle of carpet ruined, for he had collided with the bough during blindman's buff and tipped it over . . .

They must be only thankful that he had not burned too, his mother had said, hugging him while his father had scolded. And someone had been smothering hysterical giggles through it all. Lilias.

"May we have an evergreen bough, Papa? May we?" Dora's voice was almost a wail, there was so much anxiety in her tone.

"There are enough decorations here for a whole forest of boughs," he said with a laugh. "There used to be some in the nursery and dining room as well as a whole great tree in the drawing room."

"A tree, Papa. Just one whole tree in the nursery," she said, and reached up her arms to be picked up when he smiled down at her.

"Just one, then," he said. "We will go out and find one ourselves and cut it down, shall we? I think the rain stopped about an hour ago."

"Yes," she said, hugging his neck and kissing his cheek.

It was only when they were outside and she was tripping along at his side, her gloved hand firmly clasped in his, that she had her great idea. Though to her it seemed quite natural.

"We will take one for Megan and Andrew and Miss Angove as well," she announced. "Just a little one because they have such a small room. But there are so many bells and balls. We will take them before luncheon, Papa, so that I may still have my sleep ready for tonight. They will be happy, won't they?"

"I think they have enough, poppet," he said. "They are making their own Christmas. They will not want our offerings."

"Oh, yes, they will," she said happily. "You said Christmas is for giving, Papa. They will be happy if we give them a whole evergreen tree. Besides, I want to see the baby Jesus. He was not finished yesterday. Such a dear little manger, Papa. Miss Angove was going to make the smoth—the swathering clothes."

"Was she?" he said, his heart sinking. Christmas was for giving, he had told her, and she had just thrown back in his teeth. How could he refuse to give his daughter happiness?

"Just a little tree, then," he said. "Papa has only two hands, you know."

She chuckled. "But they are big hands, Papa," she said. "Miss Angove is going to teach me to sew when I am five."

"Is she?" he said, his lips tightening.

"Yes," she said. "It will be more fun with her than with nurse."

And so they found themselves little more than an hour later yet again knocking on the door of the cottage, Bedford found, Dora at his side, jumping up and down.

"I want to tell, Papa," she told him. The evergreen and the box of decorations, including the great star, were still inside the carriage.

And she did tell, rushing through the door, tearing at her cloak, and whisking herself behind the kitchen door for the pinafore just as if she had lived there all her life. And soon Megan was squealing and giggling and Andrew was exclaiming in delight and offering to accompany the marquess into the garden to fetch a pail of earth to set the tree in—a whole tree, and not just a bough!—and Lilias was clearing a small table and covering it with a worn lace cloth close to the window.

And there he was, Bedford discovered half an hour later, his coat discarded, his shirt sleeves rolled up, his neckcloth askew, balanced on a kitchen chair and pounding a nail into the ceiling. For the great star, it seemed, had not been brought for the Christmas tree at all—"How silly, Papa," Dora had said with a giggle. "It would be too big"—but to hang over the Nativity scene.

"Just look at the darling baby Jesus," Dora was saying in a voice of wonder while everyone else was gazing upward at the star Bedford was suspending from the nail.

And then they were all standing in the room, gazing about them at all the splendor and wonder of Christmas, just as if it had come already: the holly boughs and the tree hung with bells and crystal balls, all catching the light from the outdoors and from the fire, and the rudely carved Nativity scene with its bright and outsize star and its minute baby wrapped in swaddling clothes.

"Lilias is standing beneath the mistletoe," Megan said suddenly and in great delight.

Dora clapped her hands and laughed.

And he met her eyes from three feet away and saw the dismay in them and the flush of color that rose to her cheeks, and he was no longer sure that it was all artifice. It was a thin and large-eyed face. It was beautiful.

"Then I had better kiss her," Andrew said in a tone of some resignation. "Again." He pecked her noisily on the cheek and she moved swiftly to the window to still a bell that was swaying and tinkling.

"Time to go, poppet," the Marquess of Bedford said.

There was a chorus of protests.

"All right, then," he said. "Dora may stay for another half-hour. But no caroling and no church tonight."

Five minutes later he sank thankfully back against the velvet upholstery of his carriage. He had thought himself hardened to all feeling. He had thought that he could never be deceived again, never caught out in trusting where he should not trust. He would never be caught because he would never trust anyone ever again. It was safer that way.

His saner, more rational, more cautious, more hardened self told him that it was all a ruse, that she was an opportunist who was using all her feminine wiles to trap him and save herself and her brother and sister from a dreary and impoverished future.

His madder, more irrational, more incautious, more gullible self saw a mental image of her eyes lighting up when she saw the tree and the ornaments and their effect on the two children in her charge. And saw her below him as he stood on the chair, her arms half-raised as if she expected to be able to catch him if he fell. And saw the look of Christmas in her eyes as she stood in the middle of her living room looking about her. And the flustered look of pure beauty when she realized that she was standing beneath the mistletoe.

Had she known that she stood there? It was impossible to tell. And it made all the difference in the world. Had she known or had she not?

Even more important, did he care either way? Did he still regret that it had been her brother who had stepped forward to kiss her?

No, he must not, he thought, closing his eyes. He must not. He must not.

"Must I sleep all afternoon?" Dora asked him. "May we decorate our evergreen first, Papa?"

"We will do it immediately after luncheon," he said, opening his eyes and looking at her sternly. "And then you are going to sleep all afternoon."

"Yes, Papa," she said.

For the past few years Lilias had been the oldest of the carol singers. But none of the others had been willing for her to retire.

"But, Miss Angove," Christina Simmonds had protested when she had suggested it two years before, "what would we do without you? You are the only one who can really sing."

"Besides," Henry Hammett had added, with a wink for his friend, Leonard Small, "if one of the other girls were to start the carols, Miss Angove, the rest of us would have to either dig a trench to reach the low notes or carry a ladder around with us to hit the high ones.''

A deal of giggling from the girls and rib-digging from the young men had followed his words, and Lilias had agreed to stay.

She was not to be the oldest this year, though. Most of the young people were inclined to be intimidated when they first saw the Marquess of Bedford as one of their number. Most of them had only glimpsed him from a distance since his return home, and most of them were too young to remember that during his youth he had joined in all the village activities.

However, after singing at a few houses and consuming a few mince pies and a couple of mugs of wassail, they no longer found him such a forbidding and remote figure. And the usual jokes and laughter accompanied them around the village.

The younger children formed their own group, Dora firmly in the middle of them, clinging to Megan's hand. The marquess carried one of the lanterns and held it each time they sang, as he had always used to do, above Lilias' shoulder so that she could see her music.

She was very aware of him and wished she were not. Apart from the fact that the other faces around them had changed, there was a strange, disturbing feeling of having gone back in time. There was Stephen's gloved hand holding the lantern above her, and Stephen's voice singing the carols at her right ear, and Stephen's hand at the small of her back once as they crossed the threshold into one home.

She had to make a conscious effort to remember that he was not Stephen, that he was the Marquess of Bedford. She had to look at him deliberately to note the broadness of his shoulders and chest beneath the capes of his coat, showing her that he was no longer the slender young man of her memories. And she had to look into this face to see the harsh lines and the cynical eyes—though not as cynical as they had been a week before, surely.

She brought her reactions under control and bent over a very elderly gentleman in a parlor they had been invited into who had grasped her wrist with one gnarled hand.

"Miss Lilias," he said, beaming up at her with toothless gums, "and Lord Stephen." He shook her arm up and down and was obviously so pleased with what he had said that he said it again. "Miss Lilias and Lord Stephen."

Lilias smiled and kissed his cheek and wished him a happy Christmas. And the marquess, whom she had not realized was quite so close, took the old man's free hand between both of his and spoke to him by name.

In the voice of Stephen, Lilias thought, straightening up.

The children were all very tired by the time they had finished their calls and the church bells had begun to ring. But not a single one of them was prepared to admit the fact and be taken home to the comfort of a bed.

Dora was yawning loudly and clutching Lilias' cloak.

"I'll take you home, poppet," Bedford said, leaning down to pick her up. "Enough for one day."

But she whisked herself behind a fold of Lilias' cloak and evaded her father's arms. "But you promised, Papa," she said. "And I slept all afternoon. I was good."

"Yes, you were good," he said, reaching out a hand to take one of hers. "You may see the day out to its very end, then."

And somehow, Lilias found, the child's other hand made its way into hers and they climbed the steps to the church together, the three of them, just as if they were a family. People turned from their pews to look at the marquess, and nodded and smiled at them. Me-

gan and Andrew were already sitting in their usual
pew, two seats from the front.

Lilias smiled down at Dora when they reached the
padded pew that had always belonged to the marquess's family, and released her hand. She proceeded
on her way to join her brother and sister.

"But, Papa," she heard the child say aloud behind
her, "I want to sit by Megan."

A few moments after Lilias had knelt down on her
kneeler, she felt a small figure push past her from behind and heard the sounds of shuffling as Megan and
Andrew moved farther along the pew. And when she
rose to sit on the pew herself, it was to find Dora
sitting between her and Megan and the Marquess of
Bedford on her other side. She picked up her psalter
and thumbed through its pages.

There were candles and evergreen branches and the
Nativity scene before the altar. And the church bells
before the service, and the organ and the singing during it, and the Christmas readings. And the sermon.
And the church packed with neighbors and friends and
family. There were love and joy and peace.

It was Christmas.

Christmas as it had always been—and as it would
never be again. She had to concentrate all her attention
on her psalter and swallow several times. And a hand
moved toward her so that she almost lifted her own to
meet it halfway. But it came to rest on his leg and the
fingers drummed a few times before falling still.

She was saved by a loud and lengthy yawn and a
small head burrowing itself between her arm and the
back of the pew. She turned and smiled down at Dora
and slipped one arm behind her and the other under
her knees so that she could lift her onto her lap and
pillow the tired head against her breast. The child was
asleep almost instantly.

The marquess's eyes, when Lilias turned her head
to look into them, were very blue and wide open. And

quite, quite inscrutable. When the organ began to play the closing hymn, and before the bells began to peal out again the good news of a child's birth, he stood and took his child into his own arms so that Lilias could stand and sing.

His carriage was waiting outside the church, but Lilias refused a ride for herself and her brother and sister. "It is such a short distance to walk," she said.

He set the still-sleeping Dora down on the carriage seat and turned back to them. "I shall say good night, then," he said. He held out a hand for Megan's. "Thank you for inviting Dora. I don't think you know how happy you have made a small child." He took Andrew's hand. "You may come to the house the day after tomorrow if your sister approves, and we will take that ride I have promised you."

"Oh, ripping," Andrew said excitedly.

Bedford turned to Lilias and took her hand in his. He searched her face with his eyes and seemed about to say something. But he merely clasped her hand more tightly.

"Happy Christmas, Lilias," he said.

"Happy Christmas, Stephen."

She had said the words and heard them a hundred times that evening, Lilias thought as she turned away and made her way along the street with the two tired children. But the last two times burned themselves on her mind, and she felt herself smiling and happy . . . and swallowing back tears.

Christmas Day. Chill and dry but heavy with gray clouds out-of-doors. Warm with the glow and the smells and the goodwill of the season indoors. It did not matter that there was no soft white snow to trudge through, no snow to form into snowballs to hurl at shrieking relatives, no hills of snow to slide down and fall into, no ice to skate on. It did not matter. Christmas was indoors.

The goose was cooking, and the vegetables, saved from the summer's garden, were simmering. The plum pudding, part of the contents of the basket that had come from the hall, was warming. The light from the fire and the window was glinting off the crystal balls on the tree and off the star suspended from the ceiling. The bells occasionally tinkled when someone walked by and created a draft. And the baby Jesus, wrapped warmly in swaddling clothes in his manger, was being adored by Mary and Joseph, the Three Kings, an angel with one wing larger than the other, one shepherd, and one sheep, which might as easily have passed for a fox.

Megan was seated cross-legged on the floor close to the fire, rocking her new doll to sleep and gazing in wonder at the porcelain perfection of its face. Andrew was jerking his new watch from a pocket every five minutes to make sure that the goose was not being overcooked. And Lilias sat watching them, a smile on her face.

It was their last Christmas together, at least for a very long time. And their best for several years. She did not regret for a moment the humiliation she had had to suffer in going to the hall to beg for what she had needed to make it a memorable Christmas. And she did not regret that he had come to despise her and even hate her for that begging.

It did not matter. For now it was Christmas, and she had one week left in this cottage and with these children. And she had seen the wonder in their eyes when they had seen their presents that morning. They would have a day together that she would hug to herself in memory for many long months to come.

If there was a restlessness, an emptiness, a strange sense of something missing, then she would not think of it. For she could not bring back Papa or Philip, or Mama from even longer ago. She could not bring back the Christmases at the hall with their charades and blindman's buff and forfeits and sometimes their dancing. She could not bring back those rare and magical white Christmases when they had all spilled outdoors and been reluctant to go back inside even for the foods of Christmas.

And she could not bring Stephen back. For though he had stood beside her last evening when they had gone caroling and sat beside her at church, and though he had taken her hand in his at the end of the evening and wished her a happy Christmas and called her by her name, he was not Stephen. He was the Marquess of Bedford, serious and aloof. And he disliked her, even hated her, perhaps.

She must count her blessings—so many of them— and keep all her attention and all her love and hope within these four walls for today. She would not think of either the past or the future today.

She glanced across the room to the small table where the evergreen stood, and beneath it the box with the ill-fitting lid that Andrew had carved for her, and the carefully hemmed cotton handkerchief with the embroidered forget-me-not that Megan had made for her during stolen private moments over the past few weeks. She smiled again.

"I wish Dora could see my doll," Megan said. "Do you think she has had anything as grand, Lilias?"

"I can hardly wait for tomorrow," Andrew said, consulting his watch once more. "Do you think his lordship will let me ride one of his prime goers, Lilias?"

Dora was playing quietly with her own new doll. Indeed, she looked almost like a doll herself, her father thought, glancing across the nursery at her. She was dressed all in her Christmas finery with quantities of satin and lace, and large pink satin bows in her hair, which her nurse had dressed painstakingly in masses of shining dark ringlets.

The child was singing one of her newly learned carols to the doll.

They had opened their own gifts and distributed gifts
to the servants, but it was still barely midmorning.
Bedford turned to stare out the window. A gray world
met his eyes. Those were surely snow clouds over-
head, but they were stubbornly retaining their load. If
only it had snowed, he thought. He could have taken
Dora outside. He could have played in the snow with
her all day long and seen that flush of color in her
cheeks and that light of pleasure in her eyes that he
had not seen a great deal during her short life.

Perhaps he should, after all, have organized some
sort of party at the house. There had always used to
be a large gathering there for Christmas. But he had
come late and without a great deal of warning. Most
of the neighbors had made their plans for the day already.

Perhaps he should have accepted one of the numerous invitations he had received since his arrival. But
none of them had seemed to be for family gatherings.
It would have meant packing Dora off upstairs to
someone's nursery with other children while he was
entertained by the other adults. With cards, doubtless,
or dancing. He had been greedy for a Christmas spent
with his daughter. He loved her with an almost fierce
ache, he had discovered when he had finally taken her
from her grandparents' home the previous spring.

But perhaps he should have accepted one of those
invitations. Perhaps Dora would have enjoyed being
with other children instead of with him or her nurse
all day long. Perhaps he had been selfish.

Christmas Day suddenly seemed to stretch for many
long hours ahead of him. What were they to do for the
rest of the day? Their Christmas dinner was not to be
served until the evening.

"Papa," Dora said from beside him. She was still

cradling her doll in her arms. "Will you tell me a story?"

"Yes, I will," he said. "What will it be?" He leaned down and swung both child and doll up into his arms. "Shall we go for a walk or a drive afterward? Perhaps take your doll for some fresh air?"

"To Megan's?" she asked eagerly.

"It is Christmas Day," he said. "We must not disturb them today, poppet. Tomorrow Andrew is coming to ride with me. We shall have Megan come over to play with you, shall we?"

"But I want to see her today," she said. "I want to go now. I want to show Miss Angove my doll."

"Tomorrow," he said, hugging her. "You still have not told me which story you want."

"I want to go now," she said petulantly. "I want to see the holly and the tree and the baby Jesus and the star."

"But we have our own decorations and our own evergreen," he said, sitting down with her and settling her on his lap.

"But it's not the same," she said. "They are so much more cozy, Papa. Please may we go. Please!"

One thing he had discovered about himself in the past year, Bedford thought ruefully: he was incapable of exercising the proper control over his child. He knew that is was not good always to give in to her whims; he knew that he must stand up against her, for her own good as much as for his. But he could not bear to see pleading in her eyes and dash it to pieces.

He had so much to atone for: almost four years when he had scarcely seen her but had left her to the not-so-tender care of her grandparents. Lorraine had not wanted her; she had had no use for a daughter. Now he had to be both mother and father to her. There was no soft motherly presence to bring her the love and security so necessary to a small child. He had to provide that care himself. But he knew that he was allowing her to rule him, that eventually she would suffer from having no one to take a firm stand with her.

He sighed as he looked down into the pleading eyes of his child. Perhaps it would be easier to say no if he did not wish so desperately to go himself. This house was altogether too large and cheerless for two people, especially at Christmas. The cottage in the village was like a magnet to him.

Lilias was like a magnet. But he put the thought ruthlessly from his mind.

"We will take the carriage, then," he said, "and go immediately. Just for half an hour, to wish them a happy Christmas. No longer, poppet, because they will be busy preparing their dinner, and they will want to enjoy one another's company."

Dora's face lit up and she slid from his knee. "May I take my new muff?" she said. "May I, Papa? And may we take them gifts? I am going to give Megan my little pearls and Miss Angove my diamond brooch. What shall we take for Andrew?"

The marquess laughed. "Slow down," he said. "Gifts are a good idea, Dora, but nothing too valuable, or we will embarrass them."

She looked crestfallen, but her brow puckered in thought. "May I give Megan the new blue ribbon you bought for my bonnet?" she asked.

"I think that is a splendid idea," he said.

"And I could give Miss Angove the painting I did of you on your horse," she said. "Is it good enough, Papa?"

"I am sure she will be pleased," he said, hoping that his daughter would forget to identify the horseman when she presented the gift.

"But what can we give Andrew?" She was frowning.

"I'll wager he would like that seashell we found at Brighton," he said. "The one you can hold to your ear to hear the tide. Can you bear to part with it?"

Dora's face lit up again, and she darted off to find the three treasures. Bedford watched her go.

He really should not have given in on this occasion, should he? He must be the last person Lilias would want to see on this of all days. But just for half an hour. It would not quite ruin her day, surely. And it would make Dora's day.

It was Christmas morning, too early for the carriages of those going visiting for the afternoon. The street had been silent all morning. But it was no longer silent. It was Andrew who first remarked on the sound of horses and who crossed to the window to look out. Megan joined him there when it became clear that there was also a carriage approaching.

"It is Lord Bedford's carriage," Andrew cried. "And it is stopping here, Lilias. Oh, ripping! He will see that I have a watch, just like a man."

"Dora is with him," Megan cried. "How pretty she looks. And she has a doll with her. Do come and look, Lilias."

"I think one of us should think of opening the door," Lilias said, getting to her feet with a smile. And she passed nervous hands over her apron, realized she was wearing it, and removed it hastily. She was pleased that she was wearing her blue silk. It was true that it was no longer fashionable, but it had been worn so sparingly in the last few years that it was barely faded and not patched at all. She was wearing the lace collar that had been Mama's. And she had taken special care with her hair that morning because it was Christmas.

He was holding himself very straight. His expression was wooden. She would have said he was embarrassed if she had thought him capable of such feelings. But she had little time in which to stare.

"We have called for half an hour to wish you all a merry Christmas," he said stiffly.

But Dora was jumping up and down at his side and then pushing her way through the door. "We have brought you presents," she said in a voice that seemed designed to be heard by someone at the other end of the street. "And I have a new doll, Megan. Oh, and you do too. Ooh, she is pretty. What is her name? And see my new muff, Miss Angove? Papa bought it in London for me, though I did not know until this morning. I wanted to see the star again. Oh, it does look lovely. What smells so good? Does it not smell delicious, Papa? And here are your gifts. Open them. Oh, open them."

"Quieten down, poppet," the marquess said, bending down to remove her muff and undo her coat. He kissed her on the cheek, and Lilias felt that churning in her stomach she had felt before.

Megan and Andrew were soon exclaiming over their gifts while Dora shouted them both down, explaining that the ribbon had been meant for her but she had wanted to give it to Megan. And the shell she and Papa had found their very own selves on the beach at Brighton. And couldn't Andrew just hear the tide at Brighton when he held it to his ear?

Lilias sat down before removing the ribbon from the paper and unrolling her painting.

"Ah," she said. "How lovely. And you painted it yourself."

"Yes, I did," Dora said, climbing up onto Lilias' lap so that she could see the picture too. "That is Papa, but he does not look very much like him, does he? Papa is more handsome, isn't he? That is Papa's horse. His one leg is white, you see? Really he is not quite black, but I had to paint him black because my brown paint was not dark enough. I painted a sun, see?"

"It is beautiful," Lilias said, burying her face in the child's ringlets for a moment. "Quite the loveliest painting I have ever owned. I shall treasure it."

"Will you?" Dora looked up at her. "This is pretty." She laid one small forefinger against the lace collar. "Do you like my muff?"

But she did not wait for an answer. She wriggled down to the floor again in order to exchange exclamations of delight with Megan over their dolls.

The marquess was bent over Andrew, meticulously examining his watch, for all the world as if he had never seen it before, Lilias thought.

Dora accepted a mince pie, another of the offerings from the hall; the marquess did not. Dora sat very straight on a chair close to the Nativity scene, her usual pinafore protecting her dress from crumbs, her feet dangling above the floor.

"I like Christmas in your house," she told Lilias and Megan after telling them all about the distributing of gifts to the servants that morning. "I wish we could stay here all day."

The marquess, Lilias could hear with some delight, was telling Andrew about Tattersall's. He would make a friend for life. Andrew had a passion for horses.

"You *can* stay all day," Megan said. "Can't they, Lilias? Our goose is ever so big and there are enough vegetables to feed the five thousand. Lilias said so just a short while ago. We could play house all day. I could be mother and you could be elder sister. And the two dolls can be the babies. Andrew could be the father, but I don't suppose he will want to be. But that does not matter, does it?"

"I am sure his lordship must have other plans for the day," Lilias said quietly to Megan, but Dora had already slipped from her chair and crossed the room to stand beside her father's. She stood there, pulling at his sleeve.

"Papa," she said, "Miss Angove and Megan want us to stay for the rest of the day. There is lots of food, Miss Angove says, and Megan and I are going to play house all day. May we, Papa? Please may we?"

"Yes," Andrew said with some enthusiasm.

Wide-open blue eyes were turned on her, Lilias saw. Accusing? Assessing? Hostile? Incredulous? It was impossible to tell. She felt herself flushing.

"Impossible, Dora," the marquess said, getting to his feet. "We could not so impose. You agreed to half an hour, and that must be just about up."

There was a chorus of disappointed protests from the three children.

"You would be very welcome," Lilias found herself saying. "There really is plenty of food, and it would be such a treat for the children to have company."

His eyes burned into hers from across the room. And for me too, she told him silently. For suddenly there was no longer that elusive sense of something missing. There was excitement in the house and happiness. And Christmas was somehow complete.

And *he* was there. And there was a chance—she clasped her hands in front of her very tightly—that he would be there for the whole day. Her memorable Christmas would be memorable indeed, for she would remember him as Stephen. No matter how much he was this withdrawn and austere and even hostile marquess, in memory she knew she would erase all facts except the essential one: he was Stephen. And she had never stopped loving him. Maybe she never would.

If he stayed, she would be able to carry him with her in memory with all the other memories of this last Christmas with her family. It would all be complete.

"This is preposterous," he said, sitting back down again and looking distinctly uncomfortable. "Whatever will Miss Angove think of us, Dora?"

"Hurrah," Andrew shouted out. "He is going to say yes."

The girls squealed and jumped up and down on the spot. And when Dora climbed onto her father's lap to hug him and kiss him, Megan climbed onto his other knee and smiled adoringly into his face.

"Thank you," she said. "Oh, thank you, sir."

"Your sister is going to throttle me, little imp," he said, and to Lilias' amazement, he hugged the child close with one arm and kissed her cheek. "I had better go outside and dismiss my coachman. He might die of boredom and cold if we leave him out there for the rest of the day."

The children were enjoying themselves quite noisily. Even Andrew had been prevailed upon to join in the game of house and was currently sitting on a stool having his hair combed and parted down the wrong side by Dora.

They were having a good time, and that was what really mattered, Bedford thought. But what on earth must Lilias think of him for agreeing so weakly to stay for dinner and even for the rest of the day? He had instructed his coachman to return for him and Dora at eight o'clock.

Or perhaps he should not be feeling guilty, but angry. A few days before he would have been angry and suspicious. It would have been very easy for her to set the children on to trapping him into this domestic situation and leading him on to making her an offer.

But he found it hard to believe still that her every action since his homecoming had been conniving. And if it were, was it so despicable? She and the children really were in a desperate situation, and they really were facing a bleak future. Would it be so wrong of her to scheme to win for herself a husband who could lift the burden from her shoulders?

"I have never done this before, you know," he said now, looking rather dubiously at the goose she had asked him to carve. "The meat seems to want to come away in clumps rather than in neat slices."

Lilias laughed. "I have never done it, either," she said. "That is why I asked you." She was stirring the gravy. But she paused and looked at him in some concern. ''If any of that grease gets on your shirt, it will be ruined.''

He looked down at his white shirt. He had already removed his coat and waistcoat and rolled up his sleeves to the elbow.

''What you need is an apron,'' she said, and crossed to the hook on the kitchen door to fetch one.

''But my hands are greasy,'' he protested when she held it out to him.

''Lower your head, then,'' she said with a giggle he had not heard for years, and she slipped the neck strap over his head. She moved behind him, and there was a moment when her arms came around his waist to grasp the ties of the apron so that she could secure it behind him.

''There,'' she said, coming around to the front of him again to survey her handiwork. His hands were greasy, and he held them suspended in the air. ''The Marquess of Bedford in heavy disguise.'' She laughed. ''Oh, you do look funny, Stephen.''

But the smile froze on her face and faded, and color rose up her neck and into her cheeks, and he watched her swallow. The children's voices seemed very distant, even though they were just beyond the open door between the kitchen and the parlor. His eyes strayed to her lips.

''The goose awaits,'' he said lightly.

''The gravy will be lumpy,'' she said simultaneously.

They worked together in the small kitchen in an awkward silence.

The tension eased when they all sat down to dinner. But there was a heightened awareness that Bedford did not find altogether unpleasant. They sat at either end of the table, Andrew on one side of them and Megan and Dora on the other. Just like a family, all of them playing house in the warm and cozy little cottage. He met Lilias' eyes across the table and smiled. She looked down hastily and then back at him.

"Will you say grace, my lord?" she asked.

He had never in his life washed dishes. But when the plum pudding was finally eaten and they were all groaning with the good foods they had stuffed into themselves, he rolled up his sleeves and put on the apron again. The children giggled.

"Oh, you must not," Lilias said, flustered. "Please sit down in the parlor, my lord. The children and I will see to the dishes."

"No, this is famous," Andrew exclaimed. "You wash, sir, and Megan and I will dry."

"My thoughts entirely," the marquess said. "Your sister thinks I am incapable, you see, Andrew. We will show her, won't we? You may clear away the food, ma'am, and then we will all have something to do."

"I want to dry too." Dora had climbed onto a chair to make herself noticed.

"Oh, sweetheart," Lilias said, "you may help me put away. I really need assistance with that. Will you?"

Doing dishes had never been so much fun, Andrew declared half an hour later when the wet towels were being hung up to dry. Megan and Dora were still giggling over the cup that had slipped from the marquess's wet hand and smashed on the floor.

"Let's play house again," Megan said.

"Let's go for a walk," Andrew said.

"Yes." Dora jumped up and down on the spot. "Go for a walk."

"I am sure we all need a brisk walk of at least five miles," the marquess said, patting his stomach. He turned to Lilias. "You have been busy all morning, ma'am. Would you care to have a rest while I take the children walking?" He looked down at her hopefully. "Or would you care to join us?"

"I shall join you," she said. "Fresh air sounds wonderful."

Steady, Bedford told himself as he buttoned Dora's coat a few minutes later and pulled on his own great-coat. He must not become too mesmerized by the feeling of family he had had for the past few hours. Only Dora was his family. The other children belonged to Lilias, and she was not his family at all.

Perhaps she should have refused, Lilias thought as she drew her cloak about her and tied the strings of her bonnet. Perhaps she needed an hour alone in which to clear her head of this seductive feeling of warmth and belonging she had had in the past few hours. Perhaps she should not go walking with him, just as if they were one close and happy family.

But there was so little time left. Less than a week, and then a long and lonely life as someone's governess. And the long illusion that one day she would earn enough money to gather her family back around her again. Less than a week left with Megan and Andrew. Less than a week with Stephen and Dora.

No, she thought, pulling her gloves on resolutely, she was not doing the wrong thing. He had ordered the carriage for eight. That left them with six hours. Six hours. It was not long. She was going to enjoy every minute of it even if to do so was only to invite future pain. She did not care about the future. Only the present mattered.

Dora attached herself to one of her hands, Megan to the other. Dora skipped rather than walked, and entertained her companions with stories of all that her papa had shown her in London and Brighton. Andrew and the marquess were striding along ahead, deep in conversation—doubtless about horses, Lilias thought with a smile. She was glad for Andrew. He needed more male company than he had had in the past two years. But then, of course, soon he would have nothing but male company, their grandfather during holidays, other boys of his own age during term time. She shut the thought from her mind.

They walked to the lake on the grounds of Bedford Hall. It was looking very bleak and even had a thin layer of ice covering it.

"Yes," Andrew was saying excitedly as Lilias and the girls came up to him and the marquess. "If it stays cold like this, we will be able to slide on the ice in a few days' time."

The children were soon running around the bank, gazing eagerly at the film of ice.

Lilias had not realized how cold it was until she stopped walking. The wind cut at her like a knife. She glanced up at the heavy clouds.

"Snow clouds," the marquess said. "Are they just teasing, do you suppose? But I think not. I believe we are going to have our snow yet."

"Yes," Lilias said, "I think you are right." Her teeth were chattering. She shivered. She could feel him looking at her. She sought in her mind for something to say. There was an awkwardness when they were alone. They needed the presence of the children to create an atmosphere of ease between them.

"Lilias," he said. His voice was tight and withdrawn, the voice of the Marquess of Bedford again, despite his use of her given name, "your cloak is too thin. It must be quite threadbare. When did you last have a new one?"

She looked jerkily up at him. "It is quite adequate, I thank you," she said. "It is just this standing still that is making me cold."

"When did you last buy yourself anything?" he asked. His voice sounded angry. "Has everything been for the children in the last few years? Your lips are quite blue."

"Don't," she said. His face had that shuttered look it had had the first few times she had seen him. "It is none of your concern."

"Your dress," he said. "It was quite fashionable six years ago when it was new. You wore it for Christmas then. Had you forgotten?"

She stared at him, though she did not see him at all. She was blinded by hurt and humiliation. She *had* forgotten. She had felt pretty that morning. Pretty for him. She turned quickly away.

"It is none of your business," she said. "What I wear and what I spend on myself and the children is none of your concern at all. I am not answerable to you."

"No, you are not," he said, moving closer to her so that he stood between her and the wind. He lifted his head and his voice suddenly. "Andrew," he called, "your sister and I are going to begin the walk home. You may bring the girls along behind us. Don't let anyone set even a single toe on that ice."

"No, I won't, sir," Andrew called back.

He took her arm through his and hugged it close to his side. He walked at a brisk pace. And he plied her the whole way home with questions about her governess post: where it was and who the family were and how many charges she would have and how arduous the duties were likely to be. And he asked about Andrew, about what school he was to attend, how well he was likely to be treated by his grandfather, how much he looked forward to being away from home. He wanted to know about Great-aunt Hetty in Bath and how suitable a home she would be able to offer a nine-year-old child.

Lilias answered as briefly as she could.

"Why would your grandfather not take all of you?" he asked as they entered the village again.

"Papa defied him when he married Mama," she said. "He has never recognized us. I was fortunate to be able to persuade him to take Andrew."

"You are his grandchildren," he said. "He ought to have taken you. Did you ask him to?"

She shook her head. "I will not answer any more questions," she said. "I have arranged everything to my own satisfaction, my lord."

"In other words, it is none of my business, again," he said, his voice still angry. "You are right. But those children need you, Lilias. They are still very much children."

She stared stonily ahead to the cottage. The temptation to tip her head sideways to rest against his shoulder, to sag against the strength of his arm, to close her eyes and pour out all her pain to him was almost overwhelming. She was only thankful that for the return walk he had chosen to be the Marquess of Bedford rather than Stephen. She might not have been able to resist letting down her guard with Stephen.

He put fresh logs on the fire when they went indoors while she filled the kettle. By the time they were ready to settle into an uncomfortable silence, the children were home, and they brought with them again all the joy and laughter of Christmas—and, yes, the warmth too, despite rosy cheeks and reddened fingers and noses.

"Tell the Nativity story again, Papa," Dora begged when all outdoor garments had been removed and put away, climbing onto his knee.

"Again?" he said. "You have heard it three times already, poppet."

"Tell it again," she said, fingering the diamond pin in his neckcloth.

Megan was standing beside them. The marquess smiled at her—Lilias' heart did a complete somersault—and reached out his free arm to draw her onto his other knee. He told both girls the story, and Andrew too, who was sitting at his feet whittling away at the sheep again, trying to improve its appearance. Lilias busied herself getting tea.

The time went too fast. He willed it to hold still; he willed eight o'clock never to come. But of course it

did come. Stories and singing and charades and forfeits had passed the time merrily. Megan and Dora
were bright-cheeked and bright-eyed and very giggly
long before eight o'clock came, a sure sign that they
were very tired.

"But I don't want to go, Papa," Dora said, yawning
very loudly. "One more hour?"

"One more?" Megan pleaded.

Lilias was sitting in a chair opposite his own, her
feet resting on the hearth. She was smiling. She looked
very beautiful. Why had he not told her that out at the
lake? Why had he not told her that she looked even
lovelier this year in the unfashionable blue gown than
she had looked six years before? Why had he allowed
himself to get angry instead? Angry at a fate that could
treat her so? He wanted her to have everything in the
world, and instead, she had almost nothing. Why had
he not told her she looked beautiful?

"Not even one more minute," he told the girls.
"And, as it is, that coach of ours is late. Wherever
can it be?"

He got up from his chair and crossed the room to
the window. He pulled back the curtains, which they
had closed as soon as they had returned from their
walk, and leaned past the evergreen in order to peer
out into the darkness. Not that he had really needed
to lean forward, he realized immediately. It was not
dark outside.

"Good Lord," he said. "Snow."

It must have started in great earnest the moment
they had pulled the curtains. And it must have been
snowing in earnest ever since. There were several
inches of it out there.

"Snow!" There were three identical shrieks, and
three human missiles hurled themselves against him
and past him in order to see the spectacle. "Snow!"
There was a loud babble of excitement.

"Well," he said, "at least we know what has delayed the coach. It is still in the coach house and the horses in the stable, if Giles has any sense whatsoever."

Dora shrieked and bounced at his side. "We can stay, then, Papa?" she asked. "We can stay all night?"

He turned to see Lilias standing before the fireplace.

"She can share Megan's bed," she said hastily. "There will be room for the two of them. You must not think of taking her out if the snow really is too deep for your carriage."

"And you can share mine," Andrew said brightly.

The marquess laughed. "Thank you, Andrew," he said, "but I shall walk home. For days I have been longing to set my feet in snow. But I will be grateful to leave Dora here until morning. Thank you ma'am." He looked at Lilias.

She went upstairs almost immediately with Megan to get all ready. He took Dora onto his lap to explain to her that he would go home alone and return for her in the morning. But he need not have worried. She was so tired and so excited at the prospect of spending the night with Megan that she seemed not at all upset at being separated from him. He took her upstairs.

The door to one small bedroom was open. Megan was crying. The marquess stood still on the stairs and held his daughter's hand more tightly.

"Hush," Lilias was saying. "Oh, hush, sweetheart. You know we had a pact not to talk of it or even think of it until Christmas was well and truly over. Hush now. It has been a lovely Christmas, has it not?"

"Ye-e-es," Megan wailed, her voice muffled. "But I don't want to go, Lilias."

"Sh," Lilias said. "Dora will be here in a minute. You don't want her to see you cry, do you?"

"No-o-o."

The marquess looked down into the large eyes of his daughter and held a finger to his lips. He frowned.

Then he stepped firmly on the next stair. "Here we are," he said cheerfully. "Two little girls to squash into one little bed."

Megan giggled.

"Four little girls," Dora corrected him, indicating the doll clutched in her own arms and pointing to Megan's, which was lying at the foot of the bed.

Both girls giggled.

"Four, then," he said. "In you get."

Andrew was no less tired than the girls. He went to bed only ten minutes later. Ten minutes after that the giggling and whisperings stopped. It seemed that all were asleep.

The marquess was standing at the window, looking out into the curiously lightened world of freshly falling snow. Lilias was seated silently at the fire.

"Lilias," he said. He could no more think of the right words to say than he had been able to twenty minutes before. He continued to look out the window. "You must marry me. It is the only way. I cannot let you take on the life of a governess. And Andrew and Megan must not be separated from each other, or from you. You must marry me. Will you?" He turned finally to look across the room at her. And knew immediately that he had done it all wrong, after all.

She was quite pale. She stared up at him, all large eyes in her thin face. "No," she said, and her voice was trembling. "No, I will not accept charity. No."

But she must be made to accept. Did she not realize that? He felt his jaw harden. He retreated behind the mask that had become almost habitual with him in the past few years.

"I don't think you have any choice," he said. "Do you seriously think that, as a governess you will ever again have a chance to see your brother and sister? Do you imagine that you will be able to save even enough money to travel to where they are to visit? It will not happen. When you leave here, you will see them for perhaps the last time.''

She was sitting on the very edge of her chair, her back straight, her hands clasped tightly in her lap.

''Do you think I do not know that?'' she said.

''Andrew will not even be allowed to see you again,'' he said. ''He will be taken back into the fold, and he will be taught to despise you. Do you realize that?''

''Yes.''

He saw the word forming itself on her lips. He did not hear it. ''Megan will be an old woman's slave,'' he said. ''She will have a dreary girlhood. She will probably end up like you, a governess or a paid companion. Have you thought of that?''

''Yes,'' she said.

''Then you must marry me,'' he said. ''For their sakes, if not for your own. You will be able to stay together.'' His eyes strayed down her body. ''And you will be able to have some new clothes at last.''

He ached to buy her those new garments, to see the pleasure in her eyes as he clothed her in silks and lace and warm wool. He wanted to hang jewels about her neck and at her ears. He wanted to put rings on her fingers.

''You *must* marry me,'' he said.

She rose to her feet. He knew as soon as she did so that she was very angry. ''Must I?'' she said softly. ''Must I, my lord? Is this what your title and wealth have done for you? Do you talk to your servants so? Do you talk to everyone so? And does everyone kiss the ground at your feet and do what they must do? Is this how you persuaded your first wife to marry you? And did she instantly obey? Well, not me, my lord. I do not have to marry you, or anyone else. And if it is true that my brother and sister will live less-than-perfect lives according to the arrangements I have made for them, then at least we will all be able to retain our pride and hold our heads high. I will not sell myself even for their sakes.''

The Marquess of Bedford had trained himself not to flinch outwardly under such scathing attacks. He merely stared at her from half-closed eyelids, his teeth and lips firmly pressed together.

"Pride can be a lonely companion,'' he said.

"Perhaps so,'' she said. "But charity would be an unbearable companion, my lord.''

He nodded. "I will wish you good night, then,'' he said. "Thank you for giving Dora a bed. And thank you for giving her the loveliest day of her life. I know I do not exaggerate. I hope we have not spoiled your day.''

"No,'' she said. The fire of battle had died in her eyes. She looked smaller and thinner even than usual. "You have not spoiled our day. The children have been very happy.''

The children. Not she. The marquess half-smiled, though he feared that his expression must look more like a sneer. He picked up his greatcoat and pulled it on.

"Good night,'' he said again, pulling his collar up about his ears. "Don't stand at the door. You will get cold.''

He did not look at her again. He concentrated his mind on wading through the soft snow without either falling or losing his way.

She sat back down on the edge of her chair and stared into the fire. She would not think. She would not remember . . . or look ahead. She would not think. She would not. She would sit until some warmth seeped into her bones, and then she would go to bed and sleep. She felt bone-weary. But she would not think at all. Tomorrow she would work things out.

She would sit there until she was warm and until she could be sure that her legs would support her when she stood up. And until she could see to climb the stairs. She blinked her eyes determinedly and swallowed several times.

But she would not think.

She sat there for perhaps fifteen minutes before leaping to her feet suddenly and flying to the door to answer a loud hammering there. She pulled it open, letting in cold and snow. And she closed it again, setting her back to it, and watching in a kind of stupor as Bedford stamped the snow from his boots and tore off his coat and hat and threw them carelessly aside.

"Listen to me, Lilias," the marquess said fiercely, turning to her. But he stopped talking and looked at her in exasperation. He reached out and took one of her hands in a firm clasp. "No, don't listen to me. Come with me."

He did not take her far, only to the middle of the parlor. She looked up at him in mute inquiry.

"You will not even be able to slap my face," he said, drawing her against him with his free arm. He glanced upward at the mistletoe. "It is a Christmas tradition, you see." He bent his head and kissed her.

She stood still, rigid with shock. It was a hard and fierce kiss.

"Don't," he said against her lips. His very blue eyes were gazing into hers. "Don't, Lilias. Don't shut me out."

And then she could only cling to him and sag against him and eventually reach up to hold him more firmly by the shoulders and about the neck. He was no longer a slender boy, kissing her with the eager kisses of a very young man. He had a man's body, hard and firmly muscled. And his kisses were a man's kisses, deep and experienced and full of a knee-weakening promise.

But he was the same, nonetheless. He was Stephen as she remembered him as she had dreamed of him and cried for him, and as she had consigned to the most treasured memories of her young life. He was

Stephen as she had longed for him and yearned for him through six years when she might have married any of several other worthy men. Stephen, whom she had loved at the age of fifteen, and whom she would love at the age of ninety, if she lived that long.

She did as he asked. She did not shut him out. At long last, she lowered her guard and did not shut him out.

"Lilias." He held her head against his shoulder and looked down into her face. "I said it all wrong. I did it all wrong. Right from the start. Six years ago. How could I ever have left you? After Claude died, my father impressed upon me that I was now his heir, that I must put behind me all that was humble and beneath the dignity of a future marquess. And when he died soon after, I was dazzled by my own importance and popularity. I forgot you. I married Lorraine."

"I understood," she said, reaching up a hand and touching his cheek with her fingertips. "I did not expect any different. Even before you left, I never expected more from you. Only friendship and an innocent romance. I was very young. Too young to have any expectations of anything beyond the moment."

"I never allowed myself to think of you," he said. "You just became part of the dream of a perfect childhood and boyhood."

"I know," she said. "You became my dream, too."

"I did only one good and worthy thing in all those years," he said, "and had only one claim to happiness: I begot Dora."

"Yes," she said. "I know."

"I have had her only since last spring," he said. "And as Christmas approached, I knew I had to bring her here. I remembered that Christmases here were always perfect. I thought it was the snow and the sledding and skating. Memory can sometimes be so defective. I was wrong about that. But not wrong in the main. Christmas *was* always perfect here, and it has been perfect this year, even though the snow has only just come. It was because of you, Lilias. Because you were always there. And because you were here this year."

She turned her face in to his shoulder. "I wanted Christmas for the children," she said. "I did not know how I was to do it. But when I heard that you had come, I knew that you would be able to provide it. Not just with money, though that is what I ended up asking for and remembering that ridiculous incident of the Latin lessons. I just felt that I had to go to you and that you would make everything all right. But you had changed. I was frightened when I saw you."

"Lilias," he said, and held her head more firmly against his shoulder. "How can I say it this time without saying quite the wrong words again? If not for your own sake and your brother's and sister's, will you do it for mine? Marry me, I mean. Though I don't deserve it. I left you without a word. For Dora's, then? She needs a mother. You would not believe what a sullen and bad-tempered child she was when I first took her, and how petulant she can still be when she does not have her way. And I cannot say no to her, though I know I must learn how. She needs you, Lilias. And she loves you already. Have you seen that? I want you to be her mother. Will you? Will you marry me?"

She pulled her head free of his hand and looked up into a face that was anxious and vulnerable.

"No," she said, shaking her head. "Not for Dora's sake, Stephen. It would not be enough. And not for Andrew's and Megan's. That would not be enough either. And not for my need. Somehow I will survive as a governess."

He opened his mouth to protest. She set one finger lightly over his lips.

"For one reason only," she said. "For the only rea-

son that would make it work. Only if we love each
other. Both of us."

Wide blue eyes looked down into hers. "You have
been there for six long and unhappy years," he said.
"The dream of you. I brought my child to you this
Christmas, though I did not realize when we left London quite why I was bringing her here. The dream has
come alive again. Like a greedy child, I have Christmas and want to keep it forever here in my arms. I
don't want it to disappear tomorrow or the next day. I
don't want that dreary world back, Lilias. I don't want
to live without you. Yes, I love you. I always have, but
like a fool, I have repressed the knowledge for six
years. Will you have me?"

"So many times," she said, "I have told myself
how foolish I was not to let go the memory of you. I
had the well-being of two children to see to, and my
own, and I have had two offers since Papa died. We
could have been comfortable, the three of us. But I
could not let you go, even though I was so very young
when you left. Now I know I was not foolish, after
all. For whether you marry me or leave me forever
tomorrow, Stephen, you will always be a part of me.
I will never love any other man. There is only you."

He was quite the old Stephen suddenly, his eyes
dancing, his mouth curved into a grin. "Now, let me
get this straight," he said. "Was that yes or no?"

She laughed back into his eyes. "It was yes," she
said.

"Was it?" He stooped down suddenly and she found
herself swung up into his arms. He carried her over to
the fire and sat down on a chair with her. "God, Lilias, you weigh no more than a feather. The first thing
I am going to do with you, my girl, is fatten you up."

She clung to his neck and laughed.

"And the next thing I am going to do," he said,
"is take you to London and buy you so many clothes
it will take you a year to wear them all. And so many

jewels that it will take two footmen to lift you from the ground.''

Her laughter turned to giggles.

''But there,'' he said, shrugging his shoulder so that her face was turned to his again, ''I was always a fool, wasn't I, love? The costliest gown in London could not look lovelier on you than this blue silk. And anyway, those things are going to have to come second and third. A very distant second and third. There is something else I must do first.''

''What?'' she asked, reaching up to touch the silver hairs at his temples.

''I'll show you in just a moment,'' he said. ''But first you had better tell me what time you are planning to kick me out of here.''

''Mm,'' she said. ''Give me time to think about it. What were you going to show me, Stephen?''

He rubbed his nose against hers. ''How to play house properly,'' he said, grinning at her once more before seeking her mouth with his own again.

The Three Kings

by

Carla Kelly

Pay attention, Sarah, you silly, she told herself as she stood before General Clauzel—was it Bertrand? Did enemies have first names?—and tried to follow his French.

He was speaking slowly and distinctly for her benefit, eyeing her thoughtfully when he finished. He sighed and motioned for his orderly to come forward with quill and ink. He spread out the piece of paper before him, regarded her again and not unkindly, and began to write.

He scratched along on the paper as if he had all the time in the world, and then looked up. "Your name, *mademoiselle,* all of it, please."

Wake up, Sarah, she scolded herself. This will never do. Only a half-wit would doze off on her feet in the presence of so august an enemy. "You can sleep when you're dead," her brother James used to joke when she complained of exhaustion among the mounds of red tape in the library.

The library! At the thought of it, and of James, tears sprang to her eyes. They were large brown eyes, and quite her best feature besides her marvelous English skin and tidy figure. She had not slept in two nights because of that damned library and what happened there every time she closed her eyes and lived over the experience.

Sarah bit her lip and glanced at the general, who was watching her with a certain male trepidation that knew no language barriers. Had he been a German or a Russian, she would have stifled her tears at all expense to herself, but since he was French and this was Spain, she allowed her tears to well up in her eyes, magnifying them, and then spill onto her cheeks. She sniffed, stifled a sob, and was not at all surprised when General Clauzel leapt to his feet, took her in his arms, and patted her back in the foolish fashion men have attempted ever since Adam first consoled Eve over her sudden change of address.

Sarah let him console her and went so far as to rest her blond head against his chest. He smelled divinely of too much cologne, good French perfume that she had not smelled in years. Clauzel's careful embrace was a decided improvement over that of the old priest into whose care she had surrendered the still-warm James, and who had thought to comfort her, too.

Because General Clauzel was French, he knew what to do with his hands, despite his own discomfort. Sarah allowed him to pat her back because she was tired and in desperate need of someone to lean on, and because he was so comfortable and she needed that safe-conduct in the worst way.

At last Sarah made a movement and he released her. She scrubbed at her eyes with hands that shook, in spite of herself, and accepted the general's handkerchief.

"*Merci, mon général,*" she said in precise French. "Excuse my womanly weakness. These, sir, are trying times."

He nodded. "They are, *mademoiselle*. Please be seated."

She sat, and he returned to his side of the desk. He glanced behind him at his adjutant. "*Mon Dieu,* is it December twenty-second already? Where has 1812 gone?'' He looked at Sarah expectantly as he dipped the quill in the ink pot one more time.

"Sarah Brill Comstock,'' she said. "Lady Sarah,'' she amended.

She spelled Brill for him, overlooking the fact that he left the "h'' off Sarah.

The general finished writing, leaned back, and allowed his orderly to sprinkle the page with sand. When the sand was back in the bottle, he took the safe-conduct and waved it slowly.

"There it is, my dear, safe-conduct from Salamanca to the Spanish border, preferably Ciudad Rodrigo.''

Now that the deed was done, Clauzel allowed himself a touch of humor and began to tease her. "That means no side trips to Madrid to admire the paintings—the ones we have left there—or no jaunts to Seville to sketch those smelly gypsies. You are to take the most direct route southwest to Ciudad Rodrigo. The border and Portugal are not far, *ma chère.*''

Sarah nodded, her eyes on the safe-conduct. "As you wish, *mon général.*''

"You will, of course, leave immediately.''

Sarah nodded again, resisting the urge to grab the paper and sprint for the nearest exit, scattering soldiers before her. Instead, she took the pass and blew on it for a moment to make sure the ink had dried, hoping that she exhibited true British phlegm and that he could not see the beads of perspiration forming on her upper lip in that cold room.

"There is not a healthy horse to be had in all of Salamanca,'' the general said. "Your countrymen have seen to that in their—shall we say?—precipitate retreat. I can offer you a plug only, and there is no guarantee that someone else will not take it from you. But I do recommend that you hurry.''

She nodded, suddenly worn out with translating Clauzel's impeccable French. With a slight smile in his direction, she followed the orderly into the hall-way.

After James' shocking murder, the French had moved her to the university itself. Her protests at being separated from her clothes and other possessions had met only with a roll of the eyes, Gallic expressions better left untranslated, and laughter. She thought never to see her bandboxes again or the sturdy trunk that had traveled just that summer from Kent to Lisbon and then east over hot, shimmering roads to Salamanca in the wake of Wellington's army.

But there they were now, taking up the better part of the windowless little room. Sarah dropped on her knees in front of the trunk and pulled it open, pawing through her petticoats and chemises to the bottom. She pounded on the trunk in frustration. The money was gone. All she had remaining were the few coins in her reticule that the guards had somehow overlooked.

She sat back and waited for fear to wash over her. It did not. She felt nothing. She had felt nothing since James had staggered back from the archive doorway, his chest filled with blood, his eyes unbelieving, even as he shook his head in amazement, said, "Bless me, Sarah, what a plaguey turn of events," and then died in her arms.

The cold floor roused Sarah from her reverie. She touched the massive ring on her thumb, encircling it with her whole hand. While the breath was still sighing out of James' body and the soldiers still stood, transfixed, in the archive doorway, she had whisked the signet ring with the family crest off James' finger and crammed it on her thumb. There had to be something to take home to Papa.

"I will get it home, Papa," she said out loud. "I promise."

She looked over the clothes that had seemed so important to her only two days ago. She shook out her riding habit and, after a careful look around, closed the door behind her and hurried into the outfit. She pulled on two layers of stockings and glanced about her again.

The soldiers had piled James' possessions against the far wall. She hunted through his clothes, holding her breath against the familiar smell of the Caribbean lime cologne that he had favored, until she found his wool hunting shirt and pulled it on over her habit.

There was one thing more. She put her ear to the door and heard the soldiers coming up the stairs again. She darted to her pallet and raised the corner.

No one had disturbed the bloody papers that she had so carefully transcribed and that James had tossed in the air when the gun went off at such close range. The papers had fluttered about him as he lay dying. She had watched them settle on his body and had scrambled them together even as the soldiers were shouting at her and trying to drag her to her feet.

The papers lay hidden where she had left them, the blood brown now, old already, but not as old as the words from the fifteenth century she had been copying.

"Cristóbal Colón," Sarah whispered. "Christopher Columbus. Let us go on a journey." She stuffed the sheaf of papers into a leather pouch and pulled it over her head, easing it down the front of her riding habit, grateful for once that her generous bosom would distract any attention from the papers that nestled between her breasts.

For the first time since her interview with Clauzel, tears stung her eyes. Had it been only two days ago, before the soldiers had bashed on the archive door with their rifle butts, that James had remarked to her how much he was looking forward to turning those pages over to the Bodleian Library?

"Sarah, only think," he had said, his eyes sparkling, even though she knew how tired he was with the effort of translation. "Perhaps the last chapter

hasn't been writ on Columbus' first voyage, now that
we know the precise landfall. How I shall relish pre-
senting these papers!''

She sank back on her heels. "Ah, God, why did we
do it?'' she whispered.

When word had come to James through one of his
Continental sources about the possibilities in the Salamanca library, why had she allowed herself to be
swept along by his enthusiasm?

She had been as eager as James to hurry to Papa
with the news, and then to plead and argue and urge
Sir William Comstock to exert his considerable influ-
ence to permit them, in the name of scholarship, to
follow in the wake of the triumphant army. A word
here, some coins there, a promise given, and the deed
was done.

She thought of Papa and his great excitement. He
had kissed her on both cheeks, a thing of rare excess
in itself, and declared that the Comstock papers from
Salamanca would soon be as well-known as Lord El-
gin and his marbles.

The pleasure of presentation would be hers now, but
Sarah Comstock took no joy in it. She jammed her hat
upon her head, took one last look around the room,
and consigned herself to the French guards outside her
door.

The miserable horse that awaited her in the great
courtyard of the University of Salamanca looked as
resigned as she felt. Snow was beginning to fall. Sarah
turned her face up to the sky, absorbing in one last
breathtaking moment the venerable spires of ocher and
pink that she had clapped her hands over when they
rode in better style into Salamanca that summer. Never
mind that French soldiers in green uniforms ringed the
courtyard now. She did not notice them as she put her
fingers to her lips and blew a kiss to the university and
to James, resting in a vault of San Miguel in the Wall.

And there was Clauzel again, his kind face wrinkled

with worry. "You know the road to Lisbon?" he asked.

"*Oui, mon général*," she replied, her voice scarcely a whisper.

He gave the horse a prod. "It is never hard to find an army, Mlle Comstock. And they are not far."

She should have smiled at him at least. Throughout the misery of the last few days, he had been nothing but concerned—and aghast, at least in her presence— over the shocking death of her brother. "My dear," he had said over and over, "we do not fire upon scholars. I cannot understand how this happened."

No more could she. She nodded in his direction, dug her heels into the horse's side, and took her leave of the University of Salamanca.

Lady Sarah Comstock rode in silence for the better part of the day. Her early fears that someone would steal her horse or molest her soon disappeared. While nobody made a move to help her—and how could they, with the French back again?—the Spanish eyes that watched her from hovels and meticulously picked-over grain fields showed only respect, and some sorrow at her situation.

When she dismounted at noon for a nuncheon of water from a stream that tumbled ice-cold beside the road, she discovered a slice of bread and five dried-out olives in one of the innumerable shrines found on every Spanish byway. She sniffed the bread. It was not fresh, but it was bread.

"You see, sir," she said out loud to the saint, who looked at her out of mildly surprised eyes from his niche, "I am hungrier than thou art."

Sarah spoke in polite Spanish, such as she would use to address her betters or a recent older acquaintance. While not a superstitious person, she had no desire to offend the sensibilities of one who might consider, in this Christmas season, some heavenly intervention.

Snow was falling faster as she walked her horse into the afternoon, following the trail of Wellington's retreating army that had passed through Salamanca less than two weeks ago. There were broken bottles, bloody bandages, wooden biscuit crates that didn't even hold a whiff of victuals anymore.

She rode off and on as the shadows lengthened and the sun struggled out from its weight of clouds. Over one more rise, and the army was before her.

Her relief fled as quickly as it had come as she rose up in the stirrups and shaded her eyes with her hand. It was only the smallest group of soldiers and camp followers, the last straggling detachment from this part of Spain.

What did you expect, Sarah? she asked herself, and swallowed her disappointment. Wellington was probably sitting before a fire in Lisbon even now, writing up his report of the failed siege of Burgos and the retreat to Portugal. He probably didn't even know about this group.

She clucked to the horse and it moved faster, heading for the company of animals and the potential of food. As they bumped and jogged over the stony road, Sarah could make out the scarlet regimentals of British troops and the drabber brown of Spanish allies.

"Thank God," she said out loud.

Some of the horses were already milling around behind the picket line. Sarah sniffed the fragrance of campfires and the sharper smell of food cooking. Her mouth watered and she felt hungry again for the first time in several days.

She rode into the encampment and was met by a familiar face, hiding behind a layer of dirt and several days of whisker. Sarah held out her hand.

"Well, Dink, I didn't expect to see you here!"

Lord Wetherhampton—Dink to his Oxford cellmates—looked at her in some confusion. "Gracious,

Sarah, have a little pity and call me Lieutenant Markwell, at least!''

The officer on horseback next to him, dressed in Spanish brown, caught her attention out of the corner of her eye. He turned away quickly to hide a smile, even as his horse did a little dance in the snow.

''I'm sorry, Lieutenant,'' she amended as the Spaniard turned his back to her, his shoulders shaking.

And then it was Dink's turn to stare, as if he had only just then realized that he was looking at Sarah Comstock.

''Good God, Sarah, what are you doing here? And where is James? Don't tell me that brother of yours is still in Salamanca.'' He screwed up his eyes in that familiar gesture she remembered. ''Oh, I would like to thrash him.''

Sarah sighed. In another moment Dink would be dithering. She laid her hand on his arm, even as he muttered, ''Hookey will kill me for leaving you behind.''

''You couldn't have known we were there. James . . .'' Her voice changed and she looked down at her hand that grasped the reins. The Spaniard had steadied his horse and was facing her again, as if compelled to turn around by the despair in her voice. She looked at him instead of Dink. ''James is dead. Killed by French troops. Dink, I hope you can get me out of Spain.''

After the amazement on his face was followed by chagrin, she waited for him to utter the expected phrases of condolence and reassurance. Dink Markwell did none of those things. He sat on his horse, slapping his gloves from hand to hand, until Sarah wanted to grab him and shake him.

''Well, I'll do what I can,'' he said at last, but there was little resolution in his voice, and none whatsoever in his eyes.

He was on the verge of saying something else when a Spanish woman of indeterminate years stormed up to him and latched on to his reins. The animal snorted in surprise, but no more surprise than Dink Markwell showed as he lurched forward and clutched the saddle's pommel.

"We are hungry," the woman pleaded, her voice low and intense.

When her pleadings produced no look of interest on Markwell's rather spotty face, she tugged at the reins. "What are we to do, sir, we who stayed behind to nurse your wounded?" she asked pointedly, following his eyes with hers, forcing him to look at her.

She was joined by other women, and then by the children, who set up such a clamor that Sarah looked away in embarrassment. Trust Dink not to have a single clue what to do. She and Dink had grown up on neighboring estates in Kent, and she knew him too well.

After another moment of silence, followed by one last, desperate look around to see if there were someone else to take the burden, Markwell retrieved his reins and glanced over at the Spanish officer, who, like Sarah, had found something else to occupy his vision.

"Colonel, these are your people," he snapped in exasperation. "You tell them what to do!"

"Lieutenant, this is your command," the Spaniard replied. "I joined you only this noon, do you not recall? You have your orders. I have mine."

Dink wheeled his horse about in exasperation and faced his sergeant, who, with some difficulty, managed to compose his face.

"Sergeant, find these people something to eat," he ordered.

The sergeant saluted, grinned when the lieutenant turned away, and herded the little group toward the one remaining pack mule. The lieutenant watched him go and then dismounted and gestured to the Spaniard, who dismounted too.

"Colonel, since you remind me that my attention is

fully occupied by this ragtag, pestilential gathering of camp followers, stragglers, and God knows what else, I would ask you to be Sarah Comstock's escort. Lady Sarah Comstock, that is, until such time as we reach the battlements of Lisbon.''

The Spaniard bowed, but shook his head. "Lieutenant, I am going no farther than Ciudad Rodrigo." He looked back at Sarah. "And then I ride south along the border to Barcos to spend Christmas with my children. I am sorry, Lady Sarah, but there you have it."

Take it or leave it, she thought.

"Then you will be her escort until Ciudad Rodrigo," Dink said smoothly as he accepted a cup of tea from his servant. "Sarah, is it agreed?"

"I . . . I suppose," she replied, "if it is agreeable to the colonel."

She spoke in Spanish, and was rewarded with a flicker of a smile from the colonel.

She held out her arms to him, and he lifted her from the sidesaddle.

"Do you have many children, Colonel?" she asked as Dink handed her a cup of tea.

"Two," he said. "Two daughters. The young one is two, and will not remember me. The older is four, I think."

"But you do not know?" she asked, and then colored. The question sounded so impertinent, especially in Spanish, which is a peremptory language.

"It has been a long war, *doña*," was all he said. He took off his gloves and walked, stiff-legged, toward the nearest fire. Sarah noticed that he limped.

Lieutenant Markwell put his hands on his hips and watched him go. "He never said that much to me at one time," he said, his tone disagreeable, childish. He laughed then. "You must be an inspiration. God, these are dour people. One would think they were Scots, Lord help us."

Sarah could summon no reply. She felt less than

inspiring. Her backside flamed from an entire day in the saddle, and she was so hungry that tears sprung to her eyes when Dink's servant handed her a lump of nearly cooked horse meat. She scraped a little salt on it from the gray lump that the older Spanish woman offered her, and ate it with surprising relish.

The Spanish colonel—she did not even know his name—made no move to speak ,to her while she ate, and she wondered if she had offended him. And then she did not care. She gobbled up a handful of burned onions and washed it all down with beer.

"That was the worst meal I ever ate, Dink," she said as she passed the bottle to the private who sprawled next to her, half-asleep.

"Not exactly plum pudding and eggnog?" Dink rubbed his eyes and yawned. "Sarah, when we are next in London, I will take you to dinner at Claridge's."

"Very well, sir," she replied, and then spent the remainder of the brief meal in sleepy contemplation of the fire, her chin in her hand.

The Spaniard sat across from her through the fire, and she watched him, interested in him mainly because he was not interested in her, and there was no one else in her line of vision.

He was not a big man, and he was lean, but it was the leanness that comes from starvation. Probably if peace ever returned to Spain and he were given the opportunity, the colonel would put on pounds and flesh until he looked like the little priests who strutted about the University of Salamanca like so many pouter pigeons.

But now he was lean. Even his fingers were lean and elongated, like the hands of an El Greco saint she had seen in one smoky church or other. His hair was black and in need of trimming, and he wore a moustache shorter on one end than the other, as though he chewed on it.

His eyes were far and away the thing about the nameless colonel that drew her attention. They were a most startling blue, the blue of a subzero morning, the blue of ice rimming a deep pond.

She had seen enough blue-eyed Spaniards before, but none with eyes so pale, the pupils circled about with deeper blue. The effect was memorable. Sarah found herself looking at him through the flames, wondering about those eyes, until the sun went down and he turned into a silhouette.

He spoke to no one. When the sun was down, he had one of the Spanish soldiers tug off his boots. He sat cross-legged before the fire, gently massaging the instep of the foot that he favored. When he finished, he pulled on the boots again, wrapped his cloak about him, leaned his head forward against his chest, and was still.

Dink Markwell sat down beside Sarah. He followed the direction of her gaze. "That is an art I have not yet perfected, m'dear," he said, more to himself than to her. "I will be infinitely more rested when I can sleep sitting up." He laughed softly. "Think what an advantage it will be when I finally take my seat in the House of Lords." He winked at her. "Wouldn't James have a laugh at the thought of me in the House?"

He paused then, remembered, his eyes instantly sorry. "I am a beast, Sarah. Forgive me," he said. "It just doesn't seem possible that James . . ." His voice trailed off.

Sarah touched his arm and then rested her hand on the front of her riding habit. "I have saved his work, Dink. Oh, such wonderful things we learned about Columbus' first voyage." Her voice was animated, despite her exhaustion.

The figure across from her through the fire raised his head and watched her. She was not a person of much prescience, but Sarah Comstock was acutely aware of his gaze.

"You'll take it to Oxford?" the lieutenant asked.

"I will," she answered, surprised by the fervency in her voice. "No power can stop me. I will, Dink, I will."

And then she was filled with an enormous sadness that left her gasping for breath. With great effort she controlled it and sat once again in silence.

Dink was fidgeting beside her. "Well, old thing," he said at last, "you'll be in Lisbon soon enough. Colonel Sotomayor and I will see to it."

She swallowed her tears and leaned closer to the lieutenant. "Dink, what is his name? You never introduced us."

"I am sorry, m'dear."

Dink passed a hand in front of his eyes. "Can't believe how easy it is to forget the social graces in this scummy country. Luis Sotomayor, and there's more, of course," he whispered back. "How these garlic-eaters tack on name after name and then use the middle one baffles me."

"Alargosa de Menem," said the voice through the fire, not even raising his chin from his chest. "And it is not a scummy country, my lord. Devil take you Englishmen."

Dink leapt to his feet in confusion, looking about him for help and finding none. "Beg your pardon, Colonel. I am sure I did not mean any of that."

There was no reply. Sotomayor was silent. They might have dreamed his pithy comment.

Sarah sat alone for another hour, her eyes on the flames and then on the embers when the flames were gone and the others had begun to wrap themselves in cloaks against the snow that was falling again.

Sarah rose at last and shook the snow off her cloak. She tugged James' wool shirt up tighter under her chin and arranged her cloak around her again. There was no grass to cushion her sleep. She smoothed off a spot close to the fire, but away from the soldiers.

On the trip from Lisbon to Salamanca that summer, James had showed her how to burrow out a little hollow for her hips. Remembering him, she did as he had shown her so many months ago, and then sobbed out loud at the memory of James riding in the wake of the triumphant army; James in the archives, crowing over his discovery among the red tape; James lying still, his eyes wide open but not seeing her as the papers fluttered about.

Sarah took a deep breath and forced herself into silence. She lay down and drew her knees up toward her chest, her head pillowed on her arm. She closed her eyes.

It was hours later when she opened them. The Spaniard sat beside her now. He had covered her with his cloak, too. She sniffed and smiled to herself as she thought of Dink Markwell and his stupid prejudices. It smelled of horse and garlic.

Sarah made no sound, but the colonel seemed to know she was awake. He looked at her and he was deadly serious.

"Lady, do you know," he said in Spanish, "you would feel much better if you cried now."

She said nothing.

"No one will hear you." He looked about him elaborately, and his voice was dry and filled with something close to contempt. "Everyone sleeps. Even the guards your friend almost forgot to place until I reminded him. It would be a good time to cry."

Deep sobs shook her. Sotomayor sat close by in silence for only a moment before he wrapped both arms about her and pushed her head down onto his shoulder. In a pleasant baritone, he hummed a little tune that resonated in his chest and brought her surprising comfort.

Sarah let him console her. He hummed and rubbed her back until the tears were gone, replaced by a quiet calm that she wished would never end.

And then, suddenly, she was shy. She shifted her position and he released her immediately.

"You're awfully adept with weepy women," Sarah murmured, embarrassed.

He laughed. "I told you I have two little girls. Tempestuous creatures!" He sighed then and tugged on his moustache. "And Liria."

He said nothing more, and Sarah did not press him. After another moment he handed her a handkerchief. She wiped her eyes, blew her nose, and lay down to sleep, more reassured than at any time since she and James left Lisbon last summer.

The attack came at dawn, when she was most comfortable. All she was aware of at first was that someone—the colonel most likely—had whisked a cloak off her. She mumbled something and burrowed deeper in her own cloak.

"Get up."

The words were low and she might have been mistaken, but there was no mistaking the sharp slap to her backside.

Sarah sat up, angry now, even as she was still groggy, and ready to tell him what she thought, but the colonel was already running toward the horses, which had begun to mill around and whinny to one another.

No one else was up. The sky was dark still; it threatened snow. Sarah rose to her knees, mystified by the low rumble in the distance and the trembling of the earth under her. She looked in the direction of the horse herd, wondering that so few animals could cause such a sound.

And then she saw the French cavalry on the rim of the hill she had crossed only yesterday, and leapt to her feet, her heart in her mouth. She picked up her skirts and ran for the horses, the sound of the charge in her ears, and another sound of men wailing in high, banshee voices that raised the hair on her neck. In one wild moment, she remembered the stories the officers had told her of that terrible noise and how grateful she had felt never to have heard that eerie, warbling cry.

Her pitiful excuse of a horse that yesterday could scarcely put one hoof in front of the other was snorting and rearing now, its eyes rolling in terror. The colonel had managed to bridle the animal—how she couldn't imagine—but it would not stand still for her sidesaddle.

Other soldiers were up now, some running for the horses, others just huddling together in the fog of sleep. Sarah couldn't see Dink anywhere.

Her attention was yanked back forcibly to her horse. With a scathing oath, the colonel threw down the sidesaddle and leapt into his saddle. He held his hand out for her, but she backed away.

"I left my duffel bag by the fire," she said breathlessly. "Everything I value is in there. My clothes, some food. I can't leave it behind."

The French were firing now, some dismounted and taking deliberate aim at the British soldiers only beginning to wake to the chaos of early morning. Others had drawn their swords, and were slashing among the wounded.

"Lady, please," said the colonel. He leaned out of the saddle and tried to grab her, but she danced out of his reach, confused by the noise and the smell of gunpowder.

Driven by the demon of panic, she turned to run, heedless of the danger, crazy to gather up her few pitiful belongings and the odds and ends of James' scholarship in the Salamanca archives. She picked up her skirts and ran, mindful suddenly of the thunder of hooves behind her, and the horrible whooping and warbling that would not go away.

"*Dios mío,*" shouted the colonel as he leaned down

and grabbed the waistband of her dress, hauling her unceremoniously into the saddle in front of him.

Children were running about like rabbits now, women screaming, the wounded raising their arms for someone to help them into a saddle. Bending low over Sarah and without a backward glance at the others, the colonel sailed his horse over the picket line and down a small embankment, where he dismounted and pulled Sarah after him.

"We would only be followed," he said as he tugged her after him into the hollowed-out overhang of the dry riverbed. "Let us pray they have short memories, and other matters to occupy them." He whistled twice to his horse, which sank suddenly to the ground and lay still.

As Sarah watched, her eyes wide, all protest died in her throat. She offered no objection when the colonel clasped his hands over her ears as the main body of French cavalry struck the helpless troopers with an audible smack. She closed her eyes and made herself as small as she could against the dirt embankment, her fingers digging into the colonel's hands.

And then it was quiet. Colonel Sotomayor gradually removed his hands from Sarah's ears and then whispered to her, his voice a mere tickle. "Now it becomes dangerous. Don't even breathe."

She remained absolutely silent as the Spaniard grabbed the hem of her long riding habit and pulled it tight into their hiding place. The skirt was full and seemed to fill the space. As she watched, he dropped handfuls of dirt on her skirt until someone looking down from above would see no telltale fabric.

The eerie silence hummed in her ears. After several minutes of intent listening that seemed like hours, she tried to rise to her knees.

The colonel clamped his arms tighter around her waist. "Don't move," he whispered, and she had the wisdom to obey.

They lay close together, sheltered by the overhang of the embankment, and then in another moment, they were not alone. A group of soldiers stood above them on the bank. One of them even sat down, dangling his legs over the embankment and practically in Sarah's face. Her eyes wide with fear, she drew back as far as she could in the limited space and glanced at Sotomayor.

The Spaniard's face was devoid of all expression. He released his grip on Sarah's waist and fingered the cross about his neck, his lips tight together and thin. With his other hand he pulled the dagger from his belt and laid it across Sarah's lap.

After silence that stretched out like warm taffy, the soldiers finally stirred. Sarah flinched at the sound of a sword slamming home in its scabbard.

"Gone," exclaimed one of the Frenchmen. "And now what will we tell the general?"

"*Mon Dieu,*" said another. "We will follow, as we have been following. The border is far away in winter."

The others laughed.

"I wonder if Hook Nose can find the border by himself," said the first soldier.

After another long moment, the men left the embankment. Sarah let out the breath she had been holding. She was being followed, she assumed. That much was certain. What possible use could General Clauzel have with the Columbus' papers? Why had he allowed her to leave Salamanca with them in the first place? And he had seemed so kind. It made no sense to her.

Still not moving and scarcely breathing, Sarah and the colonel remained where they were, listening as the cavalry, augmented by the remaining animals of the British retreat, moved off to the west at a walk, and then a trot.

Colonel Sotomayor shook his head as Sarah stirred. "We will wait a little longer," he said. He grinned.

" 'Patience—and shuffle the cards.' You have heard this saying?"

She nodded. Not until another hour had passed did the colonel move. He climbed quickly up the embankment and whistled twice again to his horse, which rose immediately and scrambled up the embankment after him.

Sarah crept from the hiding space and then looked back in amazement. What a tiny space it was. She shook the dirt from her skirt and held up her hand to the colonel, who stood, hands on his hips, staring at the sight before him.

"Help me, sir," she asked at last.

He shook his head. "No, lady. Stay where you are."

Sarah sat down, suddenly cold at the thought of what lay above her. Dink! Where are you? Her eyes filled with tears, but she blinked them back.

Before her imagination forced her down blind alleys better left unexplored, the colonel returned. He dangled his legs over the embankment and then leapt down. He had a campaign hat in his hand, Dink's hat. Sarah took it from him and brushed at the dirt.

"They stole everything else." The colonel turned away and spat. "Even his smallclothes. *Dios mío*, I hate the French."

Sarah clutched the battered hat. The colonel nodded at the look in her eyes, and she did not have to ask anything. "The wounded, the soldiers . . . it is as you imagine. The women and children have fled."

He sighed and looked to the southwest. "The cavalry has moved down the road to Ciudad Rodrigo." He sighed. "I suppose we must go another way." He stood still, hands on hips again, as if working through his next strategy. He shook his head. "Happy Christmas," he muttered in English, and held out his hand to her.

Sarah hung back, suddenly shy and ill-at-ease with this competent man. "I am sorry . . ." She gulped and began again. "Sorry I gave you such trouble over the duffel bag."

"It is nothing," he replied, his hand still outstretched.

She held her own out. "You could have been long away from here, Colonel, if I had not slowed you down."

The colonel pulled her up the embankment. "I made a promise to get you to Ciudad Rodrigo, and I will keep it." He looked at her the way she used to stare at the menagerie in Philip Astley's Amphitheater. "Don't you English keep promises?"

"Of course we do," she said immediately, and then had the good grace to blush. "And I am impertinent to think you would not do likewise."

"You are," he agreed, his tone affable, friendly almost. "But we will overlook it."

The colonel mounted and pulled her up behind him. They rode quickly from the massacre, the colonel talking to his horse in the softest Spanish as the animal picked its way among the dead. Sarah buried her face in the colonel's back and tightened her arms around his waist.

There was nothing to say. The skies threatened snow again as Colonel Sotomayor followed the Ciudad Rodrigo road a mile and then turned south to another road, a shepherd's track through the scrub trees that shivered without their leaves and swayed in the biting wind.

Sarah relaxed as much as she dared, but she did not loosen her grip on the colonel. The silence stretched on, and she remembered Dink's joke that the colonel was not given to many words. She would have to supply the conversation.

"Sir," she began at last, "did you say that you had two daughters?"

He nodded, the subject covered.

She tried again in another mile, where the trees surrendered to a windswept valley.

"Sir, what are their names?"

He was silent for another mile or more, and then he sighed.

"Mariana and Elena."

"Beautiful names," she returned.

"Yes," he agreed. They were now on the other side of the wide valley. "My wife named them."

"Your wife?" Sarah asked, determined to pursue this line of inquisition to take her mind off the cold that bore down from higher mountains about them.

"Liria." He paused again. "She is dead."

"Oh, poor man," Sarah exclaimed involuntarily.

The colonel said nothing for many miles then, and Sarah did not force her conversation on him. The cold seeped up her legs and she wished she had taken the time to pull on a pair of James' socks before she left Salamanca. Her own hose were too thin for the Spanish wind.

"She died a week after Elena was born, trying to stop the French from burning our home."

Luis Sotomayor's words, coming as they did out of the air, startled her and she let go of him. The colonel reached around behind him and grasped her hand, and she regained her grip.

"I was away with Wellington's army. My sister in Barcos took my daughters into her household. I visit when I can. You see, we are all miles from home."

"How difficult for you," Sarah murmured.

The colonel nodded and directed his attention to the stony path before them.

"Was she pretty?"

Sarah could hardly fathom where such a rude question had come from.

Sotomayor shifted in the saddle, as if surprised, but he did not hesitate to answer this time.

"She was"—he hesitated—"about your size. She was . . . " Again he paused and then shrugged. "She was beautiful to me."

He said nothing more until long past noon, when Sarah's stomach set up an insistent growl that would not be silenced. She pressed her free hand against her middle and then laughed at the thought of her famished stomach suddenly reaching out through her skin to munch down her fingers, or turning about to gnaw on her backbone.

"Lady Sarah?"

She laughed and leaned her forehead against the colonel's back for a brief moment. "I laugh because I do not know how to deal with such a bit of social inelegance."

"Dios mío, you English," was all he said, but Sarah detected a smile in his voice, the first she had heard.

They rode until they were well into the trees again; then the colonel dismounted beside a trickle of a stream. He untied a tin cup from the front of his saddle, where he had lashed it tight so it would not rattle, dipped it in the stream, and handed it to her.

The cold water cramped her stomach and she made a face. The colonel drank the rest with evident relish and dipped it in the stream for more.

"You will forget for a while that you are hungry, if you drink some more," he said.

"I will not," she declared. "My stomach is not so easily fooled." Sarah pressed her hands to her middle. "Especially in December," she said, her eyes merry with remembrance, "when it knows there should be pasties, and fruited pies, and plum pudding, and a roast so thick, and goose with crackling skin . . . Oh, don't let me go on like this."

The colonel did not appear to be listening to her. His hands were on his hips again, the pose Sarah had already begun to associate with deep thought. A decision arrived at, he clapped his hands together and reached into the small canvas pouch next to the tin cup. He pulled out a small object wrapped in tissue paper and handed it to Sarah.

She pulled back the paper. It was a pear. No, it was not a pear. It was beautifully decorated marzipan, delicate green with just a blush of red.

"I have two of these, one for each daughter," he said as he took the candy from her, sliced it in half, and handed one portion back to her.

"Oh, I couldn't take their present," Sarah protested, even as her mouth watered and she longed to grab both pieces.

"I can," he said, and ate his share. "Even the one that is left, divided between them, will be such a treat."

Sarah ate the candy, holding the almond paste in her mouth until it melted, and remembering a time—was it only last year?—that she would have turned her nose up at Christmas marzipan and called it childish.

The colonel wiped his hands on his uniform. "Well, it is only fitting, I suppose that we should lose a gift. That is the way of the Three Kings."

"Three Kings?"

"Yes. They travel to Belén, bearing many gifts for the Child, and leaving things on the way for others who need them more."

To Sarah's surprise and utter delight, he struck a pose, threw back his head and sang:

> *Ya viene la vieja, con el aguinaldo,*
> *Le parece mucho, le viene quitando:*
> *Pampanitos verdes, ojas de limón,*
> *La Virgen María, madre del Señor.*

Sarah clapped her hands. "I heard that one night in Salamanca! Little children were singing it and teasing me for coins."

He bowed and grinned at her. "Ah, then you know about the little old lady and her presents of limes and lemons, and her basket too full."

Sarah nodded. "And isn't the second verse about the Three Kings that you spoke of?"

"Yes, yes. I will not tease you for coins." He winked at her. "Maybe other things, but not money."

Sarah blushed suddenly for no reason she could possibly think of. "It is a funny song."

"Yes, lady, and we have need of laughter." He touched her cheek with the back of his hand. "Let us go."

They walked the horse then, the colonel careful to keep well back in the trees. Silently, he scanned the horizon, his eyes alert, a frown on his face as he squinted into the distance.

Not pacified by marzipan, Sarah's stomach growled again.

"This is a hungry part of Spain, not like my part," the colonel said. "All armies prey here, and the *paisanos* are pardonably suspicious." He chuckled. "And I have no money to buy food, anyway, even if there were any." His tone became rueful. "I left Burgos in a hurry."

"Burgos? But isn't that in French hands now?" Sarah asked, and then wished she had remained silent, for the colonel said nothing more.

Sarah fingered her earrings, gold posts with diamond drops. Her reticule with its few pitiful coins seemed like a joke as she considered the journey ahead. Thank God I have my ear bobs, she thought. I can buy something to eat, if we ever come to a village. She looked about her at the enormous emptiness of the high Spanish plain. We might as well be on the moon, she thought, and tightened her grip on the colonel's belt even as she inched closer to him.

Sotomayor patted her hand. "Don't worry. It takes more than a day or two to die of hunger."

They reached the monastery of San Pedro entre los Montes after dark, long after Sarah had given up hope of ever seeing another building again. She had already memorized the weave in the back of the colonel's uniform cape and the way his hair curled over his ears.

Her entire horizon had been reduced to Colonel Sotomayor's back. She was weary with the cold, grumpy
with hunger, and too frightened to look around, for
fear of what she might see.

The colonel reined in his horse far short of the monastery's barred entrance. He handed Sarah down and
dismounted.

"Surely you could go closer," Sarah exclaimed,
dismayed at the pain in her legs.

The colonel shook his head. "Lady, I trust no one.
Not even priests."

She fell in beside him as he started toward the monastery, and the dogs began to bark. "You can trust
me," she said on impulse.

"I know that," was all he said.

He jangled the bell and Sarah jumped in spite of
herself. The tinny little sound seem to trumpet their
arrival. She pulled her cloak tighter about her shoulders and waited for the French to leap out of their
hiding places, screeching and yelling as before.

"Good evening, my son."

It was an old priest, his face a map of lines and
crevasses. He peered closer at Sarah. "And to you,
my daughter."

"Are there French about?" the colonel asked, moving closer to the half-open gate and pulling Sarah with
him.

The priest looked about him elaborately and winked.
"They have come . . . and gone." He put his finger
to his lips. "But not far. Come inside."

Silent, a black crow among the pale walls, the priest
led them into the refectory. Other priests—none looked
younger than Methuselah—huddled close to the fireplace. Other than a glance in their general direction,
no one marked their arrival.

"Is there something to eat?" Sotomayor asked, his
voice hushed.

"Be patient, my son. Sit down," said the priest,

who motioned to a bench far from the fitful warmth of the fireplace and left them.

Time passed. Sarah shivered and pulled her cloak closer. Sotomayor went to the door through which the old cleric had vanished. He stood there looking for a long moment and then stepped aside for the priest, who carried two bowls of gruel.

The fragrance of the cooked wheat tore at Sarah's insides. She smiled up at the priest and took the spoon he offered her. She was acutely conscious of eyes watching her. The other priests stared at the two bowls on the table.

Sarah glanced up at the colonel, who still stood in the doorway. "For heaven's sake, sit down and eat before the old man changes his mind," she declared, her voice louder and more strident than she wished.

Instead, the colonel came to the table and held out his hand for her. "I am sure you would be pleased to wash your hands."

Not really, she thought, her mind crowded with wheat that smelled more divine than a brace of roast pheasant. She sighed, took his hand, and let him pull her toward the kitchen.

Sarah stood still on the threshold. Four children stared up at her, children small and dwarfed by clothes rendered too large by hunger. No one moved. No one cried.

Sotomayor was careful not to look at her. "This is why the priests are not eating," he said. "Here is the washbasin, lady."

She made no move to wash her hands. Her stomach growled, and suddenly she was ashamed.

"Christ declared that the poor are with us always," said the priest behind her, "even in this time of His birth, my lady."

Sarah nodded, her eyes on a small girl, scarcely more than a baby, who stared at her out of grown-up eyes and leaned against an older girl.

"Have they anything to eat?" she asked when she could find her voice.

The priest shrugged. "The Lord provides."

Sarah put her hands on her hips in unconscious imitation of the colonel and then went back into the refectory. She gathered up the bowls and returned them to the kitchen, sitting on the floor and drawing the child onto her lap. She patted the floor beside her and the older girl sat.

Sarah handed the spoon to the older girl. "If you feed her a bite and take two yourself, that will be fair," she said.

Without a word, the child took the spoon in fingers that trembled, and fed her sister, who opened her mouth like a fledgling bird. Sarah cuddled the little one close and then looked up at Sotomayor.

"Well, Colonel, there are two other children. And didn't you say a while back that hunger was the best sauce?"

The ghost of a smile flickered across his lean face. "I did."

She nodded. "And I suppose you have that other piece of marzipan in your pocket."

"I do. It will divide nicely into four parts, and we will sniff the wrapper."

Sarah laughed and the little girl turned around, startled. Sarah's smile died on her lips as tears filled her eyes. "Oh, little one, have you never heard anyone laugh?" she whispered into the child's curls. "How long has this war been going on?"

And why was I never aware of it, back in England? she thought as she watched the colonel portion out the gruel among the other children and then divide the marzipan. She thought of the food she used to push around on her plate, the courses she ordered back to the kitchen because the garnish was not just so, or the meal slightly overdone.

Soon the gruel was just a memory. The child on her

lap licked the spoon clean and then leaned back against Sarah with a sigh.

It was a sound that went straight to Sarah's heart, and she sobbed out loud. Quickly Colonel Sotomayor took the little girl off her lap and tucked the child in the crook of his arm, singing to her, walking her close to the kitchen fire, which burned lower and lower.

Sarah wiped her eyes and got to her feet. She shook her reticule and was less than satisfied. She sighed and reached into it anyway, avoiding the colonel's eyes. She handed a coin to the priest, and it disappeared up his sleeve.

"You cannot always trust the Lord to provide, Father, especially in time of war, when so many others require His assistance," she explained, her voice low.

He nodded, bowed, and handed her a cup of hot water with a single potato peel in it. "Excellent for the digestion, my lady."

Sarah sipped the hot water without a murmur. With a smile, the colonel began to hum again and rock the child in his arms. Soon the girl slept, the spoon still tight in her hand.

Sarah came closer to the colonel. "She is asleep now, Colonel Sotomayor," she said. "You can put her down."

He nodded. He fingered the little one's curls, but his eyes were far away. He made no move to put down the child, but cradled her closer to his chest.

Is it Mariana or Elena that you are thinking of, Colonel? Sarah thought as she watched him with his small burden. She sat where she was on the floor and drank the rest of the hot water.

Suddenly she was in a pelting hurry to be off, to drag the colonel out the door and walk and walk until she could see the battlements of Lisbon. I will whine and cry and chivvy Wellington until he picks me up and tosses me on board the next frigate, man-of-war, or garbage scow bound for Portsmouth. And I will never, ever leave England again.

The older girl tugged on the colonel's sleeve finally, recalling him to the moment, and he stopped pacing the floor with the sleeping child. She held out her arms, and Sotomayor surrendered the baby. The priest shepherded the children out of the kitchen.

The colonel watched them go and then sank down against the wall on the floor beside Sarah. He closed his eyes and was asleep before she could complain. All her hasty words stopped in her throat as she looked at his face, as tense in sleep as it was when he was awake, the frown line between his eyes deeply etched. She went to the table to retrieve his cloak and bumped into a stool. At the slight noise, Sotomayor's eyes popped open and his hand went to his sword.

Sarah gathered up his cloak and put her finger to her lips. "Shh, Colonel," was all she said. She covered him with his cloak and he closed his eyes again. Without thinking, she touched his hair, smoothing it down, and then ran her finger lightly over the line between his eyes.

When she was satisfied that he would sleep, Sarah sat down next to him again. The little light from the fireplace gave off no heat, and as she watched, the embers winked out until the room was dark.

Sarah touched the leather pouch with the Columbus papers, the parchment crackling in her fingers. Sotomayor twitched in his sleep, but did not waken. The leather ties tugged at the skin on her neck, but she did not pull the pouch from its hiding place.

There was no comfortable place on the rough flagstones of the kitchen floor. After a moment of serious thought, Sarah scooted closer to the colonel and rested her head on his legs. He tensed, sat up from the wall, patted her hair, and then leaned back against the wall again. Soon he was breathing evenly.

The room was still dark when Sarah woke. A priest

knelt by the fireplace like a Muslim facing Mecca, trying to breathe some life into the coals. He blew and coughed and wiped his ash-filled eyes, then blew again patiently until the coal glowed again. In another moment Sarah heard the crackle of the fire and felt the colonel tense and then waken.

Sotomayor stared at her, as if willing his mind to register who she was and where they were. He looked no more rested than when he had closed his eyes the night before.

The priest rose from his obeisance to the fire. *"Dios los bendiga,* my son,'' he said. ''We have been watching the cut to the southwest where the French were camped. They have left. It would be good if you would do the same, you and your lady.''

''Have we outstayed our welcome already?'' Sarah burst out, stung by the priest's unctuous tone. ''Can't you see that the colonel is tired?''

The priest bowed and smiled. If anything, his tone was more intractable. ''My good lady, we have had enough of soldiers in this valley.''

Sarah opened her mouth to protest, but the colonel took her by the arm in a grip surprisingly strong, and pushed her in front of him to the doorway. ''But aren't we on his side?'' she whispered to Sotomayor as the colonel hurried her along.

''Lady, I don't press my luck,'' he hissed back.

''But . . .''

The colonel set his lips in a tight line and did not relinquish his grip, even though he slowed down. ''Oh, how can I explain it? They have all been at war too long. I am not sure we are on anyone's side, as you put it. We are only more trouble.''

''I refuse to accept that for an answer,'' Sarah stormed. She stamped her foot, furious with this stubborn man and all those countrymen of his who had raised intrigue to such a fine art. ''I'll have you know

I am an Englishwoman, and we expect answers that make more sense.''

He stopped in his tracks and threw up his arms. ''I don't care if you are that archpope of Canterbury. It's the only answer I have. Now quit nagging me.''

Sarah stared at him. To her horror, tears pooled in her brown eyes and trickled down her cheeks. She dabbed at her cheeks and sobbed, ''I don't understand you Spaniards. You're not at all like the English.''

Colonel Sotomayor shook his head, but there was a smile in his eyes. He held out his arms and she walked into them. He hugged her close, rocking her back and forth, until she felt like the little child in the kitchen last night. She sobbed into his shoulder in good earnest.

''Maybe if you spent less time in dusty archives, you would get to know us,'' he said at last. ''No, we're not like the English. Is that so bad?''

She dried her eyes and blew her nose on Sotomayor's handkerchief she had appropriated yesterday. ''I didn't mean it to sound so rude,'' she said.

He held her away from him by the shoulders. ''I know this is difficult.'' He put his arm around her shoulder and walked her across the courtyard to the stable. ''I wasn't going to tell you. Those children. They saw their parents cut down because they hid a British soldier. Some fool that wandered away from Wellington's brigade.''

''Oh, no!''

''Yes. You see, we are only more trouble.''

She nodded and sat down on the empty manger as the colonel saddled his horse. The animal nosed the manger and bumped her hip, searching for oats. There was nothing. Sarah sighed and went back into the monastery.

The children were sleeping in the refectory, jumbled together like spoons in a drawer. The air was so cold that Sarah could see her breath. She knelt by the older girl, who clutched her little sister to her, her grip tense even in sleep. Sarah watched them a moment, her resolution wavering.

"And now you must rely on the kindness of strangers, even as I? Ah, me," she said.

She looked around her. She heard the priests down the hall in the chapel, singing some out-of-tune morning hymn. Quickly she took the last coin from her reticule and placed it in the girl's free hand, curling her fingers around it.

Sarah patted the little one's head and smiled as the child nestled closer to her sister. Sarah touched the older girl, careful not to wake her. "You look resourceful, my dear," the Englishwoman whispered. "Make it last as long as you can." Sarah drew her cloak tight around her again and tiptoed from the dining hall.

The horse was saddled. Colonel Sotomayor gave the cinch another tug and turned to her. "We can get very close to the border this day," he said. "Excuse me a moment." He went back into the building.

Sarah shivered as the wind teased her skirts. Was it two days to Christmas? Was it one day? Had Christmas come and gone and left her still cold, still hungry, still in want? She rubbed her arms against a deeper chill. In all the days of trial since James' death, she had never felt quite so powerless.

It was an unwelcome emotion. She thought back to the only time in her life she had been hungry before, and it was the occasion of a horse ride through the Kentish countryside that went on much longer than she had anticipated. Even as her stomach had growled, she knew that at the end of the ride there would be food, and people to make a commotion over her. On the Spanish high plains, there was nothing like that. No one cared that she was hungry, or cold, or frightened.

She managed a crooked smile. Maybe that is why these people are such realists, she thought. They don't fool themselves. In another moment she was embarrassed at her harsh words to the colonel, at her childish behavior. Goodness, I haven't stamped my feet since I was in the nursery. Her cheeks flamed and she felt the most acute sort of misery, followed by a savage resolve to never be so foolish in front of Colonel Sotomayor.

She touched the front of her dress, feeling the outline of the leather bag. James, I will get this to Oxford. I will. The tears came back. It is my only Christmas gift of any value this year.

And there was the colonel in the arched doorway, pulling on his gloves. Sarah sighed, feeling immensely calmed to see him there. She smiled her biggest smile at him, the one that set the lights dancing in her eyes, the smile she usually saved for Almack's.

Surprised, the colonel smiled back. "You English are peculiar," was all he said as they hurried into the courtyard.

She stopped him with a hand on his arm. "Maybe if you would spend less time in dusty marches, you would get to know us." She lowered her head then, unable to look at him. "And I do apologize for my silliness."

He grinned at her and touched his forehead in salute. *"Muy bien.* I have already forgotten it."

He looked closer at her, his eyes troubled. "What is the problem, my heart?" he asked, the endearment out of his mouth unaware.

"I am afraid," she replied quietly, wondering if she had heard him right, then certain she had not. "Just . . . afraid."

The colonel took her by the hand and kissed her fingers. "I understand," he said, his voice as soft as hers. "I would infinitely prefer to be riding among my orange trees, with a little one in front of me in the saddle, helping me with the reins and ordering me about." He paused, and the memory filled his face.

He squeezed her hand tight. "But Spain has need of me now."

"Are you never afraid?" she asked.

"All the time. It is this way, Lady Sarah. When there is no choice, it's better to be brave."

He kissed her cheek quickly. "Let us leave this place. Now what are you staring at?"

"Colonel, you left your cloak in the refectory. I know you had it a moment ago."

He could not ignore her pointed scrutiny. A flush rose to his cheeks. "I thought I would help the Lord provide a little, too, as you put it, and the boys looked so cold. Now, are we going to leave this place or not?"

Sarah already knew better than to remark upon the colonel's philanthropy. Instead, she unfastened her cloak and handed it to him. "If you insist upon being Father Christmas—goodness, do Spanish children have Father Christmas?—then you had better take my cape and let me ride in front. That way, you can wrap it around both of us. I still have James' shirt, and it is quite warm."

He took the cloak, fastened it on, and lifted her into the saddle, swinging up behind her. He took the reins from the pommel and tucked his elbows in close to her sides. "Very well, Lady Sarah. I will not argue. And do you remember, Father Christmas does not come to Spain. There are the Three Kings on the sixth of January that children here look for." He leaned closer, his lips brushing her ear. "I tucked that coin under the edge of her skirt. She will still find it, and better yet, the priest will not. Was that the last of your money?"

Sarah shrugged. "It doesn't matter. You said we are close to the Portuguese border. The British army will feed me across Portugal to the sea. When I get to Lisbon, it's a simple matter to make an arrangement with a solicitor there on Papa's bank." She touched her earrings. "If worse comes to worst, I have these. We'll get by."

They rode into the early-morning fog, picking their way slowly along the stony path that led from the barren valley behind them to another barren valley before them. The colonel reined in his horse and rose up slightly in the saddle, looking over Sarah's head.

"See here," he said at last, pointing into the far distance. "I think it is the French. Well, they have not found us yet, and I have another path to try, once we leave this place."

He settled back down and put one arm around her waist as they began the steep descent. In another moment, his fingers rested against the leather bag that was outlined more distinctly under her habit. He moved his thumb across the pouch.

"Lady Sarah, what is that?" he asked finally. "I am rude to ask, but I am also curious."

"You needn't prod," she said briskly, and his hand left her waist.

Sarah tugged on the strings and pulled out the pouch. She spread out the closely written pages in front of the colonel's eyes and told him about their remarkable find in the Salamanca archives.

"You see, sir, everyone has assumed for years and years that any papers of Columbus would be in the Cádiz archives, or at Simancas." Her voice warmed to her subject. "James had an inkling about the Salamanca archives and he arranged for a friend to check his hunch. Here it is." Her voice grew doubtful then. "We stayed behind to copy it all."

"You stayed too long."

The colonel was silent then for a long time, and Sarah wondered if he had reverted once more to the monosyllables of yesterday. She folded the papers and replaced them in the pouch, dropping it down the front of her habit again.

"Was it worth it?" he asked simply, when they were in the safety of the trees again.

"I'm not sure," she replied. "I feel so angry at James for doing what he did and insisting that I stay with him, and Papa for urging us both on. And then I am angry at myself for not demanding that we leave with the army." She touched her chest. "And still, there are these papers. It is the only gift I have left to give, isn't it?"

She thought of the French then and turned around slightly to look at the colonel. "I need to tell you. It's only fair that I should tell you . . . Colonel, I think the French found out I have these papers and they are after them. I cannot imagine any other reason they seem to be looking for us, can you?"

He made no reply.

"I truly am sorry," she said. "I don't understand why they want these papers, but there it is."

"Perhaps they want to wish us Happy Christmas," Sotomayor said at last. "Lady, I did not know you were a dangerous lady when I agreed to escort you to Ciudad Rodrigo."

"I am sorry, sir. Please do not leave me now."

"Not a chance," and his voice was stiffly formal again. "I believe we already discussed Spanish honor on this issue."

"Oh, don't remind me," she murmured. "I always seem to be apologizing to you, Colonel." She turned around again. "I wish you would call me Sarah, Colonel, instead of lady." She smiled at him and then turned back to her previous view of the horse's ears. "I harbor a vast suspicion that you have many more titles than I, anyway."

"It's possible . . . Sarah. And you must call me Luis. I have titles and land, but the estates are all burned and the sheep and cattle run off."

"You can get more someday."

"I can get more someday," he agreed. "Right now, I would give it all up for a bowl of wheat mush."

Sarah laughed. "And a sausage."

"A piece of cheese."

"An orange."

He laughed then, too. "I have oranges, only they are on trees so far away." His voice was wistful as he tightened his grip on her. "You can't imagine the perfume when the blossoms come out in the spring. Liria used to . . . She would leave the windows open and the petals would fall all over the floor. It was beautiful."

His tone was so wistful that Sarah felt the familiar prickle of tears behind her eyelids.

"Do you miss her?" she asked suddenly.

Sotomayor showed no surprise at the bald question, even though Sarah blushed as soon as the words left her lips.

"*Virgen santa*, how I miss her," he said, unconsciously slowing his horse to a walk. "I was so far away, and so busy when she died. I would have given the earth to see her one last time . . ." He sighed and prodded his tired horse into motion again.

It was many words for the colonel, but he did not stop. It was as though Sarah's impudent question had opened a door closed too long.

"I miss her at night, Sarah, when I turn over and she is not there." He smoothed his hair. "I used to tease her about taking the middle of the bed and leaving me the sides, but I would gladly tolerate that again."

"Poor colonel," Sarah whispered. "Was it love at first sight?"

He laughed, and the free sound of his laughter relieved her. "No. Our papas arranged the whole thing. I didn't see Liria until the day we were married." His voice became reflective again, subdued. "We were just luckier than most."

He shifted in the saddle, and Sarah knew how badly he wanted to move about and walk off the agitation that her questions were causing.

"Do you know what I miss the most, all other things set aside?"

"No, Luis."

"When I used to do something she did not like, she would get such a look in those brown eyes and scold me and call me a thickheaded orange-grower."

Sarah laughed then, thinking of the times her father had peered over her shoulder and jabbed his finger at those places where her translations were weak. Or how James, his lips thin in that familiar gesture of agitation, would shake his head over her penmanship as she scribbled to keep up with his enthusiastic dictation.

"You can't seriously miss that, Colonel."

He slewed himself around to look her in the face.

"Sarah, when someone scolds you, that means they care. Don't you see? If people don't care about you, they don't say anything."

"I suppose I never thought of it like that," she replied.

"And then, when I was properly contrite, Liria would give me such a hug. Yes, I miss her."

"Now?" Sarah asked, her voice low.

"Well, not so much. The feelings are there, but they have changed. Time smoothes the emotions, like water on rock, and thank God for that. I am grateful for the time we had, and for our daughters, but life does go on . . ."

He was silent then, and she did not press him. The wind picked up and she shivered. The colonel drew her cape in closer. "But right now we are cold. Too bad there are no dead Frenchmen about."

She made a face. "What are you talking about?"

"On more than one occasion, I have dumped French bodies from caskets and burned the coffins to keep warm."

Sarah gasped and clutched the pommel. No, these people are not like we are. They are immensely practical, enormously resourceful.

"But didn't the smoke smell . . . well, funny?"

The colonel threw back his head and laughed. He hugged her tighter about the waist until she gasped again.

"You are a bit of a *pícara* yourself, no, Sarah?"

"No," she said firmly, and pulled his arms from her waist. "I would never dream of burning a coffin."

"Warm's warm, Sarah. Don't forget it. And also don't forget, trust no one."

They traveled in silence and hunger across high, wild-country, windswept land that seemed to stretch beyond her puny vision, out of the edge of her sight. What must it be like in the spring, when the oceans of grass were lime green again and lambs dotted the hillsides like so much cotton wadding?

But now it was stark and cold and frozen in the deepest winter such as she had never known. There was no snow. The ground was bare right down to the center of the earth. She shivered, grateful for the colonel's arms around her.

As the day wore on, they began to see houses, one here, one there, widely separate on the vast plain, and then closer together, as if seeking mutual comfort from the wind that never stopped. Luis circled the houses at a distance, coming no closer than was necessary.

Finally Sarah could hold back her complaint no longer. "Oh, Luis, could we stop for food? Surely someone—"

He cut her off. "Not as long as the French army is in front of us," he said. "They will be ordering every *campesino* to look for"—he paused, as if unsure what to say—"a woman in a blue cloak, and maybe a soldier, too." He shrugged and tightened his grip on her waist. "And if they are behind us, well, that would be worse. Then the French would know precisely where we are. We dare not trust anyone.''

The cold was making Sarah drowsy. She nodded to sleep, only to be elbowed awake by the colonel.

''No, Sarah,'' he said, his voice filled with an urgency that startled her, and yanked back the blanket of sleep. ''You must stay awake.''

He stopped his horse, plucked her off the front of the saddle, and set her on the ground. ''Walk alongside for a while. It will wake you up.''

She made no protest, where yesterday she would have sighed and scolded. Without a word, she took hold of the stirrup and plodded beside the animal, her eyes straight ahead. Soon she was colder than before, without the protection of her cape and the colonel's warmth, but she was wide awake. Hunger had gnawed a hole through her middle and lighted a flame in her forehead that kept her moving. Over and over she thought to herself, Will get these papers to Oxford, I will, I will.

Sarah didn't realize she was speaking out loud until the colonel leaned down and touched her head. ''Of course you will,'' he said. ''Come up now. I think you will stay awake.''

He took her by the elbow as she put her foot over his and climbed back into the saddle. She settled herself in front of the colonel with a sigh, pleased to the point of caricature to be warmer again. I can be content with so little now, she thought as the cloak came around her.

''Are you warm enough?'' he asked.

She nodded and rested her head against him, enjoying the comfort of his nearness.

They traveled a shepherd's path then, high into the mountains, rocky and difficult, and when they came out of the pass, the army was gone.

''Damn,'' the colonel exploded. ''I did a foolish thing.''

Sarah looked around. The plain was bare, with no sign of the French army before them raising a cloud of dust. The colonel swore again and turned around in the saddle. "Where are they now, Sarah?" he asked, more to himself than to her. "God take me for a fool."

"Perhaps they have gone back," she offered helpfully.

"Then I am the king of Spain, God bless that royal cuckold," was the colonel's reply. "Well, let us be more watchful."

The afternoon shadows lengthened across the land, which gradually yielded to a forested area, dotted with ice-flecked ponds and frozen grass. The colonel stopped frequently to allow his horse to graze, while Sarah dipped the tin cup over and over into the ponds and drank until her stomach gurgled. The colonel joined her, squatting on his heels, and accepted the cup from her.

"We're close to the border. I wonder that we have seen no Spanish troops yet, or British. They command a presence here." He drank and then tossed the rest over his shoulder. "Or, at least, they used to."

"Do you mean—"

"I don't know. I don't know anything right now," said the colonel, his voice filled with frustration. "I don't even know where the enemy is, and that is the worst blunder of all."

Sarah put her hand on his arm. "You have done magnificently, Luis. I would never have got this far with Dink."

He smiled at her. "You are more than kind, Sarah." He rose and pulled her up after him, looking at her. "I wonder that you have never married. Excuse the impertinence, but is there something wrong with the English?"

Sarah laughed and then pressed her hands to her middle. "Oh, that hurts! There is nothing wrong with Englishmen," she said, "only I suppose no one was ever interested in someone so bookish. I am what you would call a bluestocking. It was always more fun to tag along after James into archives than to bow and dance, and knot a fringe, or paint a dreary water-color." She looked about her. "But I would like to come back here in the spring and try something else in oils. Spain is not watercolor country."

The colonel shook his head and then bowed play-fully. "You have my permission when—*ojalá*—there is peace again, to paint my orange groves in the south. In fact, it may be that I will insist upon it."

"Insist?" she teased playfully, delighted at the way his blue eyes widened when he smiled.

"Yes. I have been known to order people about. For their own good, of course, dear lady." he said.

She clapped her hands and curtsied back. "We shall see about your orange groves. Are there archives nearby?"

"Silly woman," he scolded, but there was a twinkle in his eyes. "Did no one ever tell you that brains are a frivolous ornament on a woman?"

"Many times," Sarah replied quietly, "but I chose not to believe them."

"Brava, bravissima," the colonel said as he helped her to her feet. "My Liria was a woman of great in-telligence. Thank God she was smarter than I."

He limped back to the horse and just stood there watching the animal. He shifted his weight from one foot to the other.

"Do you know, Luis, you should have your foot looked at by the British doctors when we get to Ciudad Rodrigo."

He turned around in surprise. "What? What are you talking about?"

"Well, your limp," she said in confusion.

He shook his head. "It will be better soon enough. Nothing to worry about."

They rode into the afternoon. Dark was coming fast

as the valley narrowed. Sarah could see lights in the near distance. She pointed to them.

"Ciudad Rodrigo?"

The colonel shook his head. "No. Probably La Calera, or maybe Cailloma."

He started to say something else, but jerked forward, a grunt of surprise forced from him. Nearly thrown from the saddle, Sarah grabbed the pommel and then the reins as they fell from his hands. In another second, the colonel's head drooped onto her shoulder, and she felt a wet warmth spreading over her back.

"Colonel Sotomayor!" she screamed as she pulled back on the reins and the horse stopped. The animal tossed its head, nervous at the smell of blood, sidestepping even as she tugged on the reins. The colonel was a deadweight against her. She reached behind and felt him.

"Don't stop, Sarah," he said, his voice heavy, sleepy, and faint in her ear. "I think we found the . . . the . . ."

"French army," she concluded, her thoughts jumbled together. Not this, not now. They fired at someone in a blue cloak. It was meant for me.

Without another word, Sarah grabbed for the colonel's hands and pulled them around her waist. She held them there until he managed to dig his thumbs into the waistband of her riding habit.

With a savage tug of the reins, she wrestled the colonel's horse under control and then dug her heels into the animal. They shot across the plain, the exhausted animal grunting in its exertions.

The colonel managed a look over his shoulder. "Nothing," he muttered. "Where are they?"

Sarah looked back once as twilight settled in, and the sight drove all hunger and cold from her mind. It was a column of troopers, not riding fast in pursuit, but loping along like wolves to the rear of a wounded deer, animals of prey with all the time in the world.

She headed toward the village, and the colonel tried to take the reins from her.

"Not there," he gasped. *"Dios mío,* Sarah, not these border villages. They have even less loyalty than the *campesinos.* Find a small farmhouse, anything else."

She ignored him and forced the horse into a gallop, her heart and mind trained on the village. "At some point, Colonel, you have to trust someone," she murmured, and then rubbed her cheek against his in a gesture of comfort.

His breathing grew more labored as he leaned so heavy against her back. "Sarah, I wanted to tell you something," he gasped.

"Can it wait?" she said. "Oh, please don't exert yourself. Luis, just hang on!"

They galloped into the village as dark took hold, still in front of the soldiers. She rose in the stirrups and then covered her mouth with her hand to stifle a cry. French soldiers were camped across the bridge just beyond the village. As she watched, another detachment rode in from the north.

What have I done! she thought wildly.

And there was the village. The comforting smell of wood smoke greeted her and made her mouth water, even as her stomach grew into a tighter ball from fear. As she sat on the lathered horse, wondering what to do next, a procession of villagers wound their way through the street, singing. At their head was a woman wrapped in blue, seated sidesaddle on a donkey. A bearded man led the animal, and children skipped alongside.

The colonel opened his eyes at the singing. "God bless us, a *posada,"* he said. "Oh, Sarah, help me off this horse."

She sat where she was, remembering. Was it only

nine days ago that she and James had watched a similar procession wind its way through the narrow streets of Salamanca, as Joseph sought a bed for Mary? This was the ninth night. Soon he would knock and knock and then the innkeeper would finally let them in.

Sarah threw herself from the horse and steadied Luis as he dismounted and then dropped to his knees. She ran to the head of the procession, which had stopped in confusion.

Her hands clasped in front of her, she ran to the Joseph. "Oh, please, please help us," she cried. "The French."

Startled, the man stepped back and stared at her. He shook his head.

Tears sprang into Sarah's eyes and then she realized that in her agitation she had spoken in English. She took a deep breath and tried again in Spanish, her words tumbling out. "The French! They are after me. Oh, please, the colonel said not to trust anyone, but I must."

There was silence, and then sudden activity as the villagers swarmed around her. Almost quicker than sight, some grabbed the colonel, ripping off a waistband and cinching it tight around his middle, stopping the bleeding, while another took his horse by the reins and ran with it into the darkness.

As she watched in openmouthed surprise, the children stomped in the dirt and covered the blood on the ground, while a woman gently removed the bloody cloak and motioned to Mary, who leapt from the donkey, pulling off her cloak as she ran to Sotomayor. She whirled the cape around his sagging body as Joseph lifted the colonel in his arms and placed him on the donkey. He pulled the veil far over the colonel's face and took his place at the head of the procession again, even as another man, singing loud again, jerked Sarah to his side and covered her with his cloak.

The procession moved on again as the French troopers rode into town and shouted at them to stop. The villagers continued to move until the officer spoke to them in terrible Spanish.

"Have you seen any strangers in this village, one of them bleeding?"

Joseph shrugged. He looked up at Colonel Soto-mayor. "María, you would have noticed, wouldn't you?"

The colonel shook his head. Sarah clenched her fists and turned her face toward the villager who held her tight.

Joseph looked back at the soldier, who scowled and struck him.

"Damn you villagers," the man shouted. "I know he is here, and that woman!"

Joseph only wiped the blood from the corner of his mouth and rested an arm on the colonel's leg. "We are only poor pilgrims on our way to Belén, if it please your worship. Honorable sir, it is the ninth evening of our *posada*. Soon the Child will be born." He gestured toward the colonel. "I must find a place for María this night. Let us pass, noble one. It is a small thing we do, something we have done for centuries."

As the Frenchmen stood beside the colonel and Joseph, the other soldiers ran down the procession, peering at the villagers. Scarcely breathing, Sarah burrowed in closer to the man who held her. The soldier scrutinized her and passed on down the line.

The French stood together in conference at the head of the procession. The colonel swayed slightly in the saddle, and Sarah bit down on her knuckles and closed her eyes. She clutched at the leather pouch under her habit, cursing herself for being such fearful trouble to the colonel and wondering why she had not thrown the papers away hours ago, to let them flutter about the landscape. What terrible secret did they hold? Were they worth a man's life?

She let her breath out slowly as the soldiers moved

off. The leader returned and shook his fist at Joseph.
"Continue your procession, you superstitious savages," he shouted, and struck the man again for good measure.

Joseph reeled under the blow and then bowed again. "Happy Christmas to you, my lord," he said.

As the soldiers watched, the procession moved down the street to another door. Joseph let go of the colonel and knocked on the door.

A man with an apron drooped about his paunch opened the door. "What is wanted?" he bellowed, and then sang in old, pure Spanish as quaint as the writing on the Columbus papers. "We have a party within, and our house is full of travelers."

Joseph bowed his face to the ground. "We seek a room for the night," he sang, gesturing to the colonel. "Here is María, great with child, and it is her time. Oh, sir, is there room in this inn?"

"Please sir, I am weary," sang the woman who stood beside the colonel and steadied him. "Please, sir, it is the Christ Child."

The French soldiers drew closer again, intrigued by the ragged pageantry before them. Sarah gritted her teeth. Would they never go away?

Joseph looked about him as if he had no greater concern than María, who clutched at the donkey's mane with bloodstained hands. Gently he covered the colonel's fingers with the edge of the robe and sang to the innkeeper again, adding something at the end of the song that made the man's eyes widen.

The innkeeper nodded then and gestured to Joseph. "All may enter and find rest," he sang, his voice loud and with a certain defiance that gave Sarah hope and put heart back in her again.

Joseph bowed low once more and lifted María from the donkey. The colonel groaned and his head flopped against the man's shoulder.

The French troopers applauded. "Such acting,"

shouted one, and tossed a coin to the colonel. "Three cheers for María!"

The soldiers shouted their approval, laughed, and then moved off down the street toward the campfires across the bridge. The villagers poured into the house, throwing off their cloaks and gathering around Soto-mayor, who lay in front of the *nacimiento*. He opened his eyes as Sarah knelt beside him and gripped his hand. Slowly, slowly, he drew her hand closer, kissed her fingers, and fainted.

One of the women led Sarah to a stool close to the fire as Joseph cut away the colonel's uniform and the men gathered around to offer advice. They chatted companionably among themselves as Joseph and another man poked and prodded the colonel, and then uttered "Ahh," and plinked a ball into a basin.

A call from one of the men brought a wife close with a sewing basket and more advice, followed by grunting and shallow breathing from the colonel, and then a long silence that was even harder on Sarah's nerves. She leapt to her feet, but the woman pulled her back and handed her a bowl of wheat mush.

Famished, Sarah ate the mush as a call went out for cloth. The usurped María offered her petticoat, which was accepted and ripped into strips and wrapped tight around the colonel, who had long ago drifted into unconsciousness.

Her eyes on the men, Sarah ate another bowl, wondering how she could sit there in that room and stuff herself as the drama of life and pain unfolded in front of her. I shall have such a story to tell the neighbors back in Kent, she thought, and then dismissed the idea. They would never believe her.

In another minute the colonel, swaddled in María's petticoat and clad only in his smallclothes, was carried into the next room and put between rock-warmed sheets. Sarah followed and watched from the doorway as the priest blessed him and the innkeeper's wife drew the blankets up to his chin. She glanced at Sarah and put her finger to her lips.

"He will feel much better in the morning, my lady, and so will you."

Feeling strangely empty, Sarah went into the other room again. A pallet was prepared for her close to the fire, and she sat down upon it. Joseph came and stood before her.

"Accept the hospitality of our village, my lady," he said simply, and held out his hand to her.

Sarah got to her feet again and took his hand. "I cannot express my gratitude, *señor*," she said.

He patted her cheek. "There is only one payment, my lady. You must do likewise for another."

She nodded. "Thank you," she said again, and sat down, more tired than she had ever been before in her life.

As she sat staring into the fire, one of the women brought the colonel's bloody clothes to her and held out the boots. In her hand was a wad of paper, tightly folded.

"My lady, you should see this. It fell out of the colonel's boot."

Mystified, Sarah accepted the paper and unfolded it. She frowned over the tiny writing, pages of numbers and letters. They made no sense to her at first, but as she studied them, a growing chill covered her body. She moved closer to the fire. They were regimental numbers, French regiments, and a census of artillery. She put them aside and picked up the other papers, also in French. She saw the name Soult, and Ney, and the signature of . . . She looked closer: Bonaparte.

The letters dropped from nerveless fingers. Sarah took a deep breath. "And you thought the French were after you, you silly widgeon," she whispered. "Colonel Sotomayor, you dear, wonderful aggravating man! What game have you been playing?"

And then suddenly Sarah was furious with him. She

tried to resist the anger that shot through her like a
ball from a French carbine, irrational anger that left
her weak and shaking as it passed quickly.

She folded the papers again, her mind going a thousand miles an hour, even as her body cried out for
sleep. The colonel had mentioned Burgos once and
then brushed past the word as though he had not said
it. "Were you spying on the French, Colonel Sotomayor?" she asked out loud.

The papers formed a sizable wad in her hand. "No
wonder you had such a limp, Colonel," she said in
English, and then laughed.

The woman beside her looked at Sarah in concern.
Sarah touched her arm. "I am not hysterical, *señora*,"
she assured her. "But I am so tired."

The woman nodded and spread back the blanket.

Sarah shook her head. "If you do not mind, could
we carry this into the colonel's room? I would feel
better if I were there when he woke up."

"Very well, my lady."

They carried the pallet into the room where Joseph
kept watch over his unconscious María. He beamed at
Sarah and helped make a space for the pallet at the
foot of the bed.

Sarah lay down then, clutching the papers tight in
her hand, and was asleep before Joseph pinched out
the candle.

When she woke, startled out of sleep by a dream of
soldiers in pursuit of Joseph and Mary, the colonel was
sitting up in bed, letting himself be fed by the lady of
the house. Two bright spots of fever burned in his
cheeks, but he was single-minded in his devotion to
wheat mush. Someone had wrapped a shawl around
his bare shoulders, and his curly hair was tousled.

He winked at Sarah, and she smiled back, noting
the very small seep of blood through the bandage.

He followed her glance. "Our host is a barber,

Sarah, or so his good wife tells me. We fell into excellent hands.''

Sarah nodded. She straightened herself around and then sat on the end of the bed until the woman spooned in the last of the mush and wiped the colonel's mouth. She withdrew from the room, a smile on her face.

Without a word, Sarah held out the wad of paper. He took it from her, wincing as he leaned forward. He spread the papers out as she had done the night before, looking at them as if for the first time.

''Bless my soul,'' he said at last. ''Where could these have come from?''

Sarah glared at him. ''You know perfectly well,'' she said indignantly. ''Why didn't you tell me I was riding with the most dangerous man in Spain?''

He tried to shrug, winced, and then gave it up as a poor attempt. ''I thought you would be afraid.''

She could only sigh and look away.

''Happy Christmas, Sarah,'' he said, and her cup ran over again.

''How could you do that?'' she scolded, and shook her finger at him. ''When I found those papers last night, and realized what a game you have been playing—''

''No game,'' he interrupted, a twinkle in his eyes that mystified her as much as it enraged her.

''You made me so angry! I wanted to march in here and clobber you with your own boot.'' She paused for breath and narrowed her eyes. ''But I never throttle people who are down, no matter how much they deserve it. Consider yourself lucky, you . . . you. . . . ''

''Thickheaded orange-grower?'' he offered helpfully.

She stared at him and nodded slowly, realizing exactly what he meant and why he was looking at her with such love.

''Yes, you marvelous person. I don't wonder that Liria used to scold you.''

"As you just did, *querida.*"

"Well, someone has to," she finished lamely, too shy to look at the man in the bed.

The colonel moved carefully, made a face, and lay back against the pillow. "I wish I were equal to this occasion, Sarah. Maybe in a few weeks." His eyes widened with that hopeful look in them she was coming to consider as indispensable to her own happiness. "I am a rapid healer, my heart."

She laughed and watched his face a moment, admiring the beautiful blue of his eyes, grateful, at least for the moment, to see the frown gone from between them. She thought of what Joseph had told her the night before, and made up her mind.

Sarah held out her hand for the papers, wiggling her fingers when he seemed reluctant to part with them. He sighed and put the wad into her hand.

Sarah pulled the leather bag from the front of her habit and opened it. She removed the safe-conduct from General Clauzel and waved it in front of his eyes.

"These papers will fit in my boot as well as yours, dear sir, and I have this safe-conduct. I will ask these good folk to point me in the direction of Ciudad Rodrigo and be on my way."

"Oh."

"That's all you can say?"

He held out his hand to her and she got off the end of the bed and came closer.

"Lean down, Sarah."

She did as he said, and he kissed her lips. "That's for luck," he said, and then kissed her again, a kiss that belied his infirmity. "And that is for Colonel Sotomayor. In fact . . ." He stopped, winced, and sat up again. "I wish I could stand up. Sit down, will you? Right here."

He moved his legs and she sat beside him. "I tried to tell you earlier, you know, back there on the trail."

He paused and chewed on the end of his mustache.

"It is hard to put into words, Sarah."

"Think of some," she said, and twinkled her eyes back at him.

"I love you," he said simply. "Marry me."

Sarah smiled and kissed him. "Concise as always, but so effective, Colonel Sotomayor. Yes."

"Even more concise. You will be a fine Spaniard, my love."

He kissed her again and several more times, to make up for his taciturnity.

"I'll be back, Luis," Sarah said a moment later, when she could speak again.

"I wouldn't chance it now, Sarah. Not until it is safer."

She rose quickly even as he grabbed at her, and stared at him, her hands on her hips. "I don't care what you think. I am coming back as soon as these papers are in British hands."

He smiled. "The answer I was hoping for. Very well, Sarah. Are you in charge now?"

"For a while. Until you are better. Someone must see that you arrive in Barcos at least in time for the Day of Three Kings, and we cannot always expect our Lord to provide."

Luis crossed himself. "He tries, my dear, He tries, but Spain has always been a difficult child." He took her hand. "Be careful, my heart."

She blew a kiss to him and went outside. Joseph stood by the front door, watching the French across the bridge as they doused their fires and mounted.

"I can offer you the loan of a donkey, my lady. It wouldn't be safe to take the colonel's horse," he said when the troops moved off down the road to Ciudad Rodrigo.

"I would welcome it, Joseph. Oh, what is your name? I do not know it."

He smiled. "It is better that way."

"I do not even know the name of this village, Joseph, where the pilgrims of Christ live,'' she said in her most elegant Spanish.

He bowed. ''And I will not tell you that, either. Better sometimes that you know nothing, especially if the French ask you. And they will, my lady. You must go through them to reach Ciudad Rodrigo.''

''Pray for me, Joseph,'' she said simply as she took off an earring and tried to hand it to the man.

Joseph stepped back and held up his hands to ward off her gift. ''No, no, my lady. We did not do this for money.''

She pressed the earring into his hand. ''I know that. But can you use it to buy food for the village?''

He held up the earring, turning it this way and that in the morning light. ''This is valuable.'' He handed it back with a wink. ''Save it for when you fall among the English again, lady.''

She laughed and put it back in her ear. ''Happy Christmas, Joseph.''

She did not encounter the French until far into the afternoon. The donkey acquitted itself admirably, picking a surefooted way on the rocky ground that gradually, almost imperceptibly, began to slope away toward a flatter, more gentle land. They were leaving behind the highest places of Spain.

By shading her eyes and squinting into the afternoon sun, Sarah was able to make out Ciudad Rodrigo.

''Thank God,'' she said out loud, ''and Merry Christmas to me.''

And then the French were upon her. They rode leisurely toward her on the trail. Her heart in her mouth, Sarah dug her heels into the donkey and forced it to continue at a sedate pace toward the soldiers. Finally she dismounted and stood beside the donkey, saving them the trouble of ordering her to the ground. She held her head up and twined her fingers together so they would not shake.

They came close, wary at first, and then riding with

confidence when they saw it was only a woman—and a small one at that.

As they looked her over, Sarah stared back and allowed a sigh of relief to escape her. They were not the same troops that had tracked them into the village last night. She looked until she found the man with the most gold braid, and sighed again.

He had a rough face, a peasant face, and the hardened look of one who had spent all his adult years in the service of Bonaparte. His skin was coarse and lined from years in the outdoors, facing into the turbulent winds that blew all across Europe. He was a peasant, she was sure of it, one of the many who had risen from the ranks through a lifetime of soldiering. He probably could not read.

"You are the Englishwoman."

It was not a question but a statement, delivered in a flat, uncultured voice that further betrayed humble origins.

"I am," Sarah answered in French. "Lady Sarah Brill Comstock, of Mansfield, Kent. I am on my way to the British lines in Lisbon, and I have a safe-conduct."

"Then produce it, *mademoiselle.*"

Sarah pulled the safe-conduct from her pocket and handed it to the lieutenant, who looked at it a long time. Sarah came closer and pointed.

"See you there, sir, it says, 'General Bertrand Clauzel.' "

She had pointed to her own name. The lieutenant nodded and Sarah could barely contain herself. So you cannot read, sir. I thought as much.

He nodded finally and handed it back to her. "Where is the colonel?"

She did not attempt to hedge about the issue. She raised her head as her eyes filled with tears. "He is dead, sir, killed last night from ambush."

The lieutenant held out his hand. "Give the papers

to us then, my lady. That wily wolf we have tracked from Burgos would never permit them to be lost.''

Sarah said nothing. The lieutenant came closer. She gritted her teeth as he drew his sword and calmly put the point at her neck and flicked at the leather string.

"Mademoiselle, I suggest that you present it to us before we are forced to strip you right here on the road.''

And find the notes in my boot, she thought. Never. With steady fingers, Sarah pulled out the pouch. The tears spilled onto her cheeks as she opened the bag for the last time and pulled out the Columbus papers.

She smoothed them out for one last look, remembering the long hours in the archives, James' great joy at finding Columbus' diary, and the feverish race to copy it all down as the French closed in. She handed them to the lieutenant with a great show of reluctance.

He snatched them from her as she sobbed.

"He told me never to let those fall into your hands," she cried, noting that the other soldiers backed away, uneasy with her tears.

"Ah, but here they are," said the lieutenant, looking at the words in old Spanish that told of Columbus' first voyage, with the exact readings of that first landfall. "The entire troop strength of every army we have in Spain." He bowed over Sarah's hand and kissed it. "How good to have this back again, *mademoiselle.* Such a Christmas present you have given me."

He turned and waved the Columbus papers to the others before folding them and tucking them into his tunic. "A promotion for the lieutenant, no?" he shouted, and his troops cheered.

Sarah dried her eyes. "May I go now, sir?" she asked. "I would remind you that I am an English-woman, and not entirely friendless in the world.''

"You may go." The lieutenant eyed her donkey for a moment and then waved her on. "Because it is

Christmas, and I am in a fine mood, we will not take your donkey.''

"So good of you,'' she murmured. And may I be far from here when your superiors in Burgos shout you out of the room for the Columbus papers and strip you down to private.

The lieutenant helped her mount and handed her the reins. Sarah nodded in his direction and continued down the road to Ciudad Rodrigo.

When the troops were out of sight, she patted the donkey. "I should be sad, of course,'' she said. "All that James and I worked for is gone, but truly, Señor Burro, I have carried out Joseph's condition, have I not? I have returned a favor to a . . . friend.'' She smiled—"And it would please the Three Kings.''

Her voice lingered over the words, and Lady Sarah Comstock made another resolve.

She arrived in Ciudad Rodrigo at dark, and was met at the city wall by a detachment of the 45th Foot. They looked scarcely better than the French troops, dirty and wearing uniforms long past repair or the efficacy of a scrubbing board. They smelled no better, either. Sarah wrinkled her nose and thanked the good Lord that it was winter.

She soon found herself in the middle of a group of officers, who hurried her into the stable that made up headquarters. She told them who she was, sat down, and calmly extended her right foot.

"If you would be so kind, sir, I have something that will interest you in that boot.''

With a puzzled smile, the officer pulled off her boot. Sarah thanked him prettily and reached inside, extracting the wad of paper.

"Colonel Luis Sotomayor sends Christmas greetings to the Marquess of Wellesley and apologizes that he could not carry these to Lisbon in person.''

At the mention of Sotomayor's name, the major grabbed the papers and took them to the table, spreading them out and then uttering a low whistle. The others crowded around in silence that was broken by loud huzzahs and soldierly embraces.

Sarah smiled at their exuberance. "Little boys," she whispered. "Why must you go to war?"

The major remembered himself then and returned to Sarah. "The colonel?" he asked.

"He was wounded in ambush, but he is well enough. I told him that I would see the papers safely to Ciudad Rodrigo. Can I trust you to carry them to Lisbon?"

"Oh, most assuredly, Lady Comstock," the major replied. "And you, too, of course. In no time, we'll have you safely home in England."

Sarah shook her head. "No, I think not."

The major stared at her, but he was too well-bred to say what he thought.

"No, sir, I will return to that little village. The colonel will need my help in getting to Barcos, where his children await him." She put up her hand when the major attempted argument. "I am over twenty-one, sir, and I know my own mind. I would ask the loan of another donkey, if you can spare one."

One of the subalterns spoke up, his voice eager, impulsive. "Lady Comstock, you may take my horse. Nothing is too good for such a heroine."

She smiled at his eagerness but shook her head. "I would not get very far on my way with such a steed, sir, before someone from some army or another relieved me of it. No, I prefer a donkey—and a modest one, at that."

She looked at the major. "Sir, if you could spare a little food, it would not be wasted."

"Of course, Lady Comstock," he said, "but, really, I must protest."

Sarah touched his arm. "I know that you mean well, sir, and I thank you, but I will return to the village and go to Barcos and you cannot stop me. If you confiscate Joseph's donkey, I will walk."

The officers were silent then, the air tense. Then the major smiled and shook his head. "Very well, if you are sure."

"I have never been more sure."

Sarah looked about her at the other men. "There are two little girls in Barcos waiting for their father. There will be no visit from the Three Kings without a little help from you."

The major bowed. "I think we can find some candy about. You there, Monroe."

"Sir," said the eager man who would have given his horse away.

"That scarf about your neck is so colorful. Good enough for a Spanish lady of . . . of . . ."

"Four years, sir, I believe."

"Excellent. And I believe I have a doll I was saving for my own daughter. I can easily procure another."

"Capital," Sarah said.

"Two dolls, sir," said another officer. "For the other one who is . . ."

"Two."

"You will stay the night, won't you, Lady Comstock?"

"Oh, yes, and with pleasure," Sarah said, taking off her gloves. "I have several letters to write."

The letter to James' Oxford don would be difficult. She would not even mention the Columbus papers. That scholarship would have to rest now until someone else in distant years came across the papers again, if anyone ever did. She sighed, clasped her hands together, and then put Columbus from her mind.

The letter to her father would be no easier. He would grieve for James and not understand what she was doing.

He might even disinherit me over this marriage, she thought as she watched the officers' cook bustle about over the simple meal. A pity Papa's so high in the instep about deference due to English titles. He would only get all tight about the mouth if I told him that the Sotomayors were prominent in Spain at the time of Trajan, back when his Comstock ancestors were still painting themselves blue. Ah well. Father cannot tamper with that little legacy from my mother, and it will be enough to rebuild the estates and buy cattle. And perhaps if Papa has Sotomayor grandchildren with those beautiful blue eyes and blond hair . . .

The major stood before her again, suspiciously blurry.

Sarah dabbed at her eyes and accepted the battered cup he held out to her. She raised it high.

"A toast to Christmas, Lady Comstock, and a prosperous new year for all of us."

"Hear, hear," she said, and drank deep.

The Christmas Star

by

Sheila Walsh

Winter had set the lake diamond-hard, like a jewel in the glittering necklace of fountains strung out beyond the gracious west front of the Duke of Wyvern's Palladian-style country seat. Frost, as luxuriantly thick as snow, blanketed the famous avenue of cedars of Lebanon and clung with precarious sparkling beauty to the oaks and elms whose bare black branches etched their complex tracery against the blue of the sky.

Distant laughter rang out on the clear cold air. Four eager figures, diminishing in size from first to last, ran along the path to the lake, swept and sanded earlier by a small army of gardeners boys.

They halted at the lake's edge, momentarily diverted by the spectacle of their elders disporting themselves in a manner that any self-respecting mama would have condemned as unseemly. However, their own mamas were still safely and warmly ensconced within doors, and the three youngest members of the party, overcome by the lure of the ice, could wait no longer to join in the fun.

There was a frantic scramble to secure skates, the bigger children helping the smallest, with the exception of the elder of the two girls, who stood motionless, gazing out across the lake with a wrapt faraway expression.

"Come on, Lou," urged fifteen-year-old Philip, son

281

of the duke's eldest daughter, tugging at her sleeve. "You're supposed to be in charge."

"It's no use, Pip." Joanna, his cousin, though a year his junior, was already showing evidence of a strong practical streak. "Lou's gone off into one of her air dreams. Anyway, we can manage perfectly well without her. Give me your hand, Jason—you're sure to fall if you don't."

"No, I shan't!" The outraged cry of her seven-year-old brother changed to squeals of pretended terror as he was hauled unceremoniously onto the ice, but the sound soon faded to merge with the laughter of their elders.

Louise Beresford, left alone, scarcely noticed their departure. Every Christmas it was the same, she thought, and every year the sheer beauty of it took her breath away: the way nature fashioned the most intricate patterns from every bush and blade of grass, transforming the duke's parkland overnight into a white fairy-tale world touched now with golden sunlight, a world where anything was possible, where at any moment a prince might appear and vow his undying love.

For the last few years her godmother had invited her to Wyvern for one whole week at Christmas—a magical week that had more than compensated for the dispiriting frugality of the other fifty-one. No, that was not fair, for it had not always been so. It was not Papa's fault that the war against Napoleon had taken such a toll of his business that they were now obliged to skimp and scrape.

But this year was different. This year she was to stay on as companion to the duchess, which meant that for a while at least she would cease to be a drain upon her father's meagre resources. For, without a dowry, and with nothing exceptional in the way of looks to commend her, she could scarcely hope to make an advantageous marriage. And as her younger sister, Ellie, was now of an age to help Mama with the younger ones, the need to find a paid position had become imperative. The offer from the duchess had come out of the blue, and seemed to her mama like a sign from heaven. "Only consider, my dear—it will not be in the least taking a menial position among strangers. To be sure, Cousin Arabella has not actually mentioned the question of payment, but she was ever a generous soul, so I have no doubt you will receive at least as much as poor old Miss Fiddlestone. Also, she is bound to take you about with her, and who knows where that may not lead."

That was typical of Mama: always looking for a silver lining in every cloud. But Louise, for all her tendency to dream, was more of a realist. Companion might sound comfortable enough, but she found something infinitely dispiriting in Mama's unintentionally comparing her with the amiable but dowdy Miss Fiddlestone. However benevolent the duchess might be, Louise feared many would make the same analogy. She sighed, put on her skates, and prepared to follow the children.

And then her heart leapt into her throat, for with a cold hiss of blades on the ice he was there, just as she had always imagined him: tall and straight, a cloak trimmed with fur swirling about his legs to reveal a glimpse of pale breeches and shining boots beneath. There was a golden aura about his head, highlighting a face that set her imagination racing, its high chiseled cheekbones and sensuous mouth reminding her of pictures she had seen of a corsair. Even as the thought crossed her mind, his dark eyes crinkled into a quizzical smile that seemed to be meant for her alone . . .

He had seen her arrive with the others, had seen them rush away, leaving her standing, and his curiosity was aroused. Perhaps it was that she could not skate and was afraid to venture farther. He moved closer, gliding over the ice with lazy effortless grace.

She was taller and rather older than he had at first supposed, though her slight, rather shabby figure, together with a curious air of other worldliness, lent her a certain youthful vulnerability.

"You are perhaps in some difficulty, *mademoiselle?*"

The face that lifted to him was delicately pointed, a little pinched with cold, and quite unremarkable except for the eyes—enormous eyes the color of violets as they emerged shyly from the woodland undergrowth each spring, thickly fringed, and wide open now with the force of some elusive emotion that made one forget her plainness.

"If you are nervous of the ice," he prompted gently, "I would be most happy to assist you."

"Oh, no!" How rude that sounded. Louise pulled herself together and tucked an errant strand of dark hair back under her bonnet. "You are very kind, *monsieur,* but truly, I am well able to manage. I was simply admiring the scene. Don't you love to see everything so white and sparkling?"

He laughed softly and the light faded from her eyes. "Forgive me. I do not laugh at you. It is only that in Russia we have so much snow that it holds very little novelty for me."

So he was Russian. Louise's passionate interest in far-off places made her long to know more, so that for a moment she forgot to be shy. "I thought you must be French, for all that you speak English so well."

There was a wry note in his voice. "It has long been society's custom in my country that French is spoken in preference to our mother tongue, which is thus confined mainly to the peasants. As for my English . . ."

But Louise could see Lady Amelia Revel moving purposefully toward them across the ice, and knew that her brief exhilarating interlude must end; the duchess's youngest daughter was only two months her senior, though she cultivated an air of consequence that made her seem much older. The prospect of being patronized by Amelia in the presence of this most compelling stranger was more than she could contemplate. Uttering an abrupt apology, she sped away to join the children.

"Prince Andrei, I hope you were not being pestered."

"Not in the least, Lady Amelia," he said gallantly, looking down at her heart-shaped face delightfully framed by the swansdown-trimmed bonnet. "Tell me, who is she, the rather fey young woman?"

Amelia tossed her head. "Oh, Lou isn't anyone of account—just a kind of poor relation. Mama is her godmother, I believe. She has always taken pity on Lou at this time of year, and now that she is coming up to eighteen, I believe she is to stay on as a companion to Mama. Poor Miss Fiddlestone is far too old to be of any practical use and has gone to live with a sister." Her laugh trilled on the cold air. "With my brothers and sisters forever bringing their offspring for visits, I daresay Lou will prove invaluable, coming as she does from a large family herself." Amelia saw the prince's thoughtful glance stray to where Louise had by now linked hands with the children and was encouraging the little one to attempt more adventurous moves. To distract him, she laid a gloved hand lightly on his arm. "Should we not return to the others?" she said a little archly. "Otherwise, I fear they may gain quite the wrong impression."

Louise did not see him again that day, but she managed to discover from James, the head footman, that his name was Prince Andrei Zarcov, distantly related to the czar, and a captain in the czar's own regiment. It came as no surprise that he was a prince, for she had known from that first instant that he was special. He was also, James told her, related to Count Lieven, the Russian ambassador, and was in England on private business. Eager to know more, she gently quizzed the duchess as they went over the arrangements for Amelia's birthday ball, which was to be held three days after Christmas and would be attended by everyone of note from miles around.

"Such a charming young man, is he not, my dear?" the older woman enthused, needing little encouragement to indulge in a comfortable gossip. "And so fortuitous that Madame de Lieven should have tempted him to spend Christmas not five miles away at Charlcombe with my dear friend Emily Burridge." The duchess lowered her voice. "I believe that Count Lieven chooses to remain in London. So diverting, but then I daresay he has long since become reconciled to the intrigues of his charming countess, who is well-known to have an eye for a handsome face."

Louise said nothing. It was not her place to question the morals or lack of them among the *haut ton*. The duchess did not appear to notice her silence.

"I am not at all sure that the prince returns Madame de Lieven's regard, however. In fact, I could not help but notice that he looked with more than a little partiality upon my Amelia. So, as our own guests are not expected until Wednesday, I have decided to invite Lady Burridge and her party to dine with us tomorrow evening. Not that I would dream of casting out lures, but there can be no harm in throwing the two young people together. I do try not to be partial, yet I have to confess that I think Amelia quite the most beautiful of my daughters."

Although she had been taught that "Beauty is as beauty does," and that in this respect the duchess's youngest daughter's nature left something to be desired, Louise stifled the unworthy thought and agreed that Lady Amelia's looks were very fine, and yes, her fair loveliness did frequently acquire an almost breathtaking translucence under the soft glow of candlelight.

Prince Andrei would be a great fool if he were not already well and truly smitten.

The dinner party, said the duchess, must be something quite out of the ordinary, which caused the chef to throw a tantrum. Much of the ensuing diatribe was in Monsieur Jacques' native tongue, which was happily beyond the comprehension of his minions. The gist of it seemed to center upon the insensitivity of those who expected him to perform miracles with the feast of Noel but a week away, and eight guests expected in three days' time, not to mention the birthday ball. His creative genius was stretched to the limit. He could no more! It fell to Louise to soothe his bruised spirits, to subtly convince him of the wider implications of producing a *chef d'oeuvre.*

"Only consider, Monsieur Jacques," she coaxed, "a Russian prince and the Countess Lieven, a lady of the first importance. I daresay they will be accustomed to dining with kings and emperors, but I believe that you are capable of surpassing anything that the kitchens of the finest palace could contrive."

"Sans doute, mademoiselle," he declared pompously. "With one hand tied behind my back."

"Well, then? Only consider: glowing accounts of your culinary skills will surely spread far and wide." Louise hoped that this rather dubious means of persuasion would not come to the ears of the duchess. "Were he ambitious, a man might climb as high as he chose on the recommendation of such important people." It was enough. Already his eyes were glazing over as he gave his mind wholly to his art, and she wisely rested her case.

Louise had scarcely any time to herself from that moment on. When she was not helping tne duchess with her arrangements, she was entertaining the children and keeping them out of the way of their elders— a task that their governesses were only too happy to leave to the willing girl, while they put the babies down to rest and sat toasting their toes around the nursery fire exchanging confidences.

This arrangement suited the active younger members of the family very well. "We have much more fun with you," Philip explained, speaking for all of them as they helped the garden boys collect great boughs of greenery to decorate the house.

"I daresay you do." Louise ruefully surveyed their disheveled clothing, the streaks of dirt already being smudged across cheeks by less-than-clean gloves. "I only hope I shall not earn myself a scold for allowing you to run wild."

This brought shrieks of mirth from the children, which quite drowned out the ring of hooves, so that she was not aware of the high-perch phaeton being driven at a spanking pace around the wide curve of the drive until it was almost abreast of them.

Prince Andrei hauled back on the reins and sat watching their efforts with amused interest. It seemed to Louise, clutching her bundle of holly, that she was the target of his whimsical gaze. As the warmth crept into her cheeks, she prayed that it would seem no more than the natural result of her exertions.

"You fill me with nostalgia, Mademoiselle Louise," he said. "When I was a child, I too used to go with my brothers to collect the Christmas greenery from the forests surrounding our country estate."

It irked her to be counted in with the children, and she was thus ill-prepared for his next comment, which seemed to be invested with an altogether more provocative implication.

"We made also a mistletoe bough, and beneath it we stole kisses from all the pretty girls. Do you have such a custom?"

Louise gave him back a prim look, determined not to be embarrassed by his outspokenness. "I imagine most countries enjoy similar customs, sir."

"I imagine they do," he agreed, the laughter now

brimming wickedly in his eyes. "Were I not promised to the Lady Amelia, I might be tempted to pursue our discussion and discover what further delights we have in common."

He was plainly teasing her, but she could not bring herself to respond as Amelia might have done, with arch smiles and coy glances. Even if her situation had been otherwise, it was not in her nature to play the flirt. Instead, she dipped a brief curtsy. "Forgive me, your highness, but I must return to the children."

"Of course," he agreed gravely. "I would not for the world keep you from your duties." He tipped his hat to her in a final audacious gesture and gathered up the reins.

"He is really quite jolly for a prince," Louise heard Philip telling his sister. "Not in the least toplofty. We had a splendid conversation yesterday when we were out on the ice."

"Aunt Amelia is well and truly smitten," Joanna said in a disgusted voice. "Sighing over him like a regular wet peagoose. I heard Miss Trumper say she was going all out to marry him."

"You shouldn't listen to other people's conversations," Louise admonished rather more sharply than was her wont.

"Oh, governesses don't count," Philip averred off-handedly, and did not notice how quiet Louise had become.

A companion is not so demeaning as a governess, she thought, swallowing a rather horried lump in her throat. But there were times when she seemed to be in a kind of limbo—caught between upstairs and downstairs, not quite knowing her place. And for all that she had always been a favorite with the duke and that the duchess was kindness itself, treating her almost as a daughter, not everyone was as charitable, so that she was quickly learning to accept snubs as part of her lot. But no good ever came from repining. "Do all with a cheerful heart," her mama was used to tell her, "and sooner or later you will be rewarded."

So, "Come along," she said with determined cheerfulness. "Jason is working much harder than the rest of us."

That afternoon Louise helped to decorate the dining table under the watchful eyes of the housekeeper, Mrs. Bright, and Melton, who had been his grace's butler for more years than he cared to tell. The silver epergne that formed the centerpiece had been burnished until it gleamed, and Louise begged Mrs. Bright to allow her to arrange the flowers in the little vases that graced each of its ornately swathing branches: simple Christmas roses with their delicate waxy petals and dark-green leaves mingling with exotic hothouse blooms of deepest red. Nestling among the greenery were ripe peaches, also from the hothouse, and apples, their skins brightly polished.

"You've made a right good job of that, Miss Louise," Mrs. Bright said, nodding approval. "Wouldn't you say so, Mr. Melton?"

"A very tasteful arrangement," the butler allowed in his unbending way.

"I've never seen it look finer," the housekeeper enthused. "It's not easy. Took me many a year to master it. You've obviously got the knack."

He won't know that I've done it for him, Louise thought dreamily, but *I* shall know.

She was kept busy that evening almost until the guests arrived, running between the duchess and Amelia, and Amelia's sister, Lady Treadwell, who was mother to Philip and Jason—a comfortable pleasant lady who resembled the duchess in both looks and temperament. The Marchioness of Bute, wife of the duke's son, Gerald, was less easy to like. She was thin and sharp, draped herself in a number of shawls, and complained constantly to the long-suffering marquess of the drafts and inconveniences of her father-in-law's vast mansion. Louise sometimes wondered how she had managed to produce such a bright practical child as Joanna.

It was the marchioness who had first dared to question Louise's inclusion by the duchess at family meals. "When you are alone, it may be unexceptionable, but in company she is plainly ill-at-ease and has absolutely no conversation. I am sure she would be much happier among her own kind."

"But we *are* her kind, Maud." The duchess, though pleasant, was coolly firm. "Her mama is not only my cousin and a very dear friend, she is also, like me, a Deveaux; our pedigree, I may tell you, goes back a great deal further than the Revels of Wyvern. Mr. Beresford, too, is a gentleman of good sound country stock, much respected by the duke. To be sure, it is very unfortunate that he suffered such an appalling reversal of fortune as a result of the war, but he is far from alone in that. I don't understand the workings of the stock exchange, but I do know that many people were similarly ruined. It is even more unfortunate that, as a result, Louise's chance of making a good marriage has also been set back for the present, but who knows? She is still very young and her papa may yet come about. In the meanwhile, since we have always been particularly fond of the child, I am only too happy to take her under my wing."

Her daughter-in-law had known better than to pursue the argument, but Amelia was less tactful when later she had raised particular objection to Louise's being present at the dinner in honor of Prince Andrei.

"She is such a mouse. I vow our guests will think her odd."

"Nonsense," declared her mama, finally losing all patience. "True she is not forever putting herself forward, but Louise has very pretty manners when the occasion requires it of her." She anticipated her daughter's determination to pursue the matter. "No, Amelia, I do not wish to hear another word."

No one troubled to ask Louise what she wished to do. Given the choice, she would by far rather have been excused. The mere thought of being plunged into such exalted company was daunting enough and made her feel faintly sick. But hopefully, if she answered politely when spoken to and did not draw attention to herself, she might manage to remain inconspicuous.

Lady Burridge's party arrived in high good humour amid a flurry of snow, the cloaked figure of the prince solicitously escorting a dark vivacious lady who must be the Countess Lieven. In the course of shedding their outer garments and the greetings that followed, few people noticed the slim figure in a simple unadorned dress of cream muslin who moved among them, quietly ensuring that everything was going forward as the duchess would wish.

Prince Andrei noticed, however. Even as he laughed and talked with the rest of the party, his eyes frequently sought her out. Now she was with Lady Burridge's youngest son, a shy gawky youth with a nervous stammer. Under her gentle ministry, the prince saw William gradually relax and even laugh at something she said.

Louise was placed next to William Burridge at dinner. Amelia, seated at her father's end of the table, with the prince at her side, would not doubt be pitying her, but in fact it was the best thing that could have happened, for in striving to set the young man at ease, Louise quite forgot her own shortcomings. When the ladies retired to the drawing room, leaving the gentlemen to their port, Lady Burridge made a particular point of thanking her.

"Poor William," she said with a sigh. "He was ever a delicate child, so he never went away to school as did my other sons, or mixed with children of his own age. This Christmas he is having his first taste of company, and is finding the whole business of making polite conversation something of a nightmare.'' Her ladyship smiled warmly at Louise. ''I have never seen him so much at ease as he is with you, my dear.''

Louise felt a small glow of satisfaction. ''I have a brother very like him, ma'am, so perhaps it makes us better able to converse. Indeed, your son has a very lively mind . . .'' Louise hesitated, wondering if that might sound patronizing.

But Lady Burridge beamed. ''Do you really think so? That has always been my opinion, but Lord Burridge has always thought me overpartial. I must tell him what you say. William does not care for sport of any kind, you see, and so they do not always . . .'' She stopped, aware that she was in danger of criticizing her husband. ''Ah, well, I daresay time will tell,'' she concluded vaguely, and turned away.

Louise waited until the gentlemen rejoined the party; then, as soon as she could do so, unnoticed, she slipped from the room and made her way along the wide upper hall to a small salon at the far end. No candles lit this room, though a fire gleamed dully in the grate, but with the curtains thrown back and a full moon flooding the white world outside with silver light, she found her way easily to the window. She sat on the wide-cushioned seat, half-hidden by the curtain, with her feet drawn up to support her arms, one hand cupping her chin.

It was so peaceful after all the laughter and talk of the drawing room. Here at last she was free to think of Prince Andrei. She did so, extolling his graces without inhibition, for he was so far removed from her in every way that she could weave her dreams as she chose, untrammeled by hope or expectation or the least regard for reality.

Small wonder that Amelia had looked at him with stars in her eyes, for only a block of wood could remain unmoved by so magnificent a figure, even if one were obliged to share him with the possessive Countess Lieven, who was on his other side in pride of place next to the duke. Prince Andrei's white dress uniform was stiff with gold braid, setting him apart from every other man in the room, but his charm of manner easily outweighed a natural hauteur that signified his pride of race. The prince might so easily have allowed Madame de Lieven to monopolize him with her brilliant conversation, but instead, he had listened and murmured something that made her laugh and turn to the duke for support. At that point Prince Andrei turned and gave the radiant Amelia his whole attention, appearing to hang on her every word. Louise liked him for that, even if it did appear to confirm that the duchess was right in supposing that he was more than a little interested in her daughter.

Louise was so lost in contemplation that she did not hear the door open and close, and was therefore not aware of a pale figure approaching until a soft accented voice murmured seductively, "See! how she leans her cheek upon her hand: O! that I were a glove upon that hand, that I might touch that cheek . . ."

She sat unmoving, her breath caught in her throat, preventing speech, half-afraid to look around lest the exquisite lines of poetry be but a figment of her imagination. Then a faint shudder ran through her and common sense asserted itself. She sat up, swung her feet circumspectly to the floor, and smoothed her skirts, clasping her hands neatly within their folds in an effort to appear composed. "Your highness is familiar with the works of William Shakespeare?"

He came to sit opposite her on the window seat and she could see his silvered features quite plainly, noted the appreciative curve of his mouth as she sat so demurely. "Very much so, Mademoiselle Louise. You see, we had a good Scottish nurse who ensured that we were properly educated before ever our tutor took us in hand, which accounts for my fluency in your language." His smile deepened. "Not that Miss MacCall had much time for *Romeo and Juliet.* 'Romantic pap,' she called it, as I remember. *Macbeth* was more to her taste."

Louise laughed, suddenly less in awe of him; somehow, in the dark, he seemed less grand, less beyond her reach. Also a small illogical part of her rejoiced that he must have followed her deliberately, or he could not have known she was here. Why, she knew not, and for the moment she did not care.

"You will be missing your family at this time, I daresay?" he said.

"Very much, though I have not spent a Christmas at home for some years." A small sigh escaped her. "However, we do not entirely forgo our family celebrations, for we keep the feast of St. Nicholas earlier in the month as our special day."

"Oh, but this is quite extraordinary. In our country, we also celebrate the feast of St. Nicholas. He is the patron of Russia. Did you know that? On the night before the feast day all the little children hang up their stockings, and at midnight there is a great Mass in the cathedral." The prince leaned forward eagerly. "So? This gives us a kind of bond, yes?"

His enthusiasm infected Louise. "I suppose it does, though I fear my family's simple festivities have little in common with such magnificence."

"Oh, but that is unimportant." His careless dismissal of so much grandeur amused her, but in a moment his mood changed and he sat staring at a place somewhere beyond the window, all teasing forgotten. "Mademoiselle Louise," he said abruptly, "I wish to ask a favor of you, and in view of what you have told me, I have every hope that you will consider it kindly."

She could not imagine what he could possibly want of her that he could not more appropriately ask of Amelia. She studied his profile. Moonlight etched the aristocratic line of cheek and jaw, giving it the pure opalescent beauty of alabaster, and she had an irresistible longing to run smoothing fingers over those classic contours. Her face burned in the darkness and she clasped her hands more tightly together lest they acquire a will of their own.

"I wonder," he continued, not appearing to notice her silence, "if the duchess can spare you for maybe two hours tomorrow, would you consent to take a drive with me?"

If he had wished to deprive her of speech, he could not have devised a more perfect way of doing so. Louise began to wonder if he were mad, or simply a little drunk. Her mouth dry, she stammered, "Surely, your highness, Amelia would be—"

"No, no," he cut in imperiously. "The Lady Amelia is a delightful creature, but she would not be in the least suitable. It is you I wish for most particularly."

Louise found her imagination boggling at the most obvious implication of his words. She scarcely knew whether to be outraged or to dissolve into giggles at the sheer absurdity of supposing that he might wish to ravish her. She steadied her voice. "If your highness could perhaps explain more clearly?"

"I cannot. Not here, not now. You will have to trust me." He stood up and turned to stare down at her, saying with a harsh urgency. "If you agree, what follows must be a matter of the greatest secrecy between us. It seemed to me that you had the kind of integrity that . . . But perhaps I was mistaken."

"Oh, no!" Louise sprang to her feet, still not fully comprehending, but resolved to follow her instinct, which told her that whatever his problem, it was of the utmost importance to him, and he had done her the signal honor of placing his trust in her. "Of course I agree, and you may count upon my discretion."

"Good." He nodded. "I thought I could not have

so badly misjudged you. When is a good time for you to be free?''

It seemed to Louise that she would never get away on the following morning. The duchess, having slept late, was only too eager to discuss the success of the previous evening over a cup of hot chocolate. "All went remarkably well, I think," she mused complacently. "Prince Andrei could scarcely take his eyes off my dear Amelia, but who could wonder at it? The new blue spangled gown made her look positively ethereal. Why, even her papa remarked that she was looking very fine, and he seldom notices such things." Louise murmured agreement. "As for Jacques, he truly excelled himself. I hope Melton will have told him so. Madame de Lieven was most impressed.''

"I'm glad. He did put himself to considerable trouble to make everything as perfect as possible for you.''

"Then I shall make a point of visiting the kitchen myself in order to commend him.''

Louise smiled. "He will appreciate that, I'm sure.'' She replenished her grace's cup and said diffidently, "I wonder, ma'am if I might be spared for a little while later on this morning? There is something I particularly wish to do.''

"My dear child, of course!'' The duchess opened her sleepy eyes wide. "As if you need to ask! You must not be thinking yourself forever at my beck and call. Besides, we have been invited over to Charlcombe for nuncheon. Did I not tell you?'' She sighed, settled herself back more comfortably against the pillows, and sipped her chocolate. "Of course, with our guests due tomorrow, there is much still to be done. But you will not be away long, I daresay.''

As Louise had no real idea, she avoided committing herself, and just for a moment was irritated by the constraint, however benevolently manipulated, of be-

ing obliged to account for her time. She seized the first
opportunity that offered to escape.

"Oh, and I have just remembered," the duchess's
voice floated after her. "I believe Maud wishes to con-
sult you about the hem of her gown. She caught a heel
in it late last evening and dares not entrust it to her
maid, for the silk lace is very fine. But she has so often
heard me boast of your deftness with a needle."

"I will make a point of seeing her ladyship." But
not now, Louise thought, avoiding the marchioness's
room. And without further ado she ran to collect her
cloak, after which she crept past the nursery wing and
down the backstairs until she reached the door leading
to a quiet back corridor that housed the gun room and
the muniments room. From here she could leave the
house unobserved. Or so she thought.

"And where do you think you're going, young
woman?"

She turned guiltily as the question was barked at
her. The duke stood framed in the doorway of the gun
room, a handsome fowling piece cradled across his
arm. He was a big man, possessed of a pair of spectacularly bushy eyebrows that gave him a look of
fierceness. But Louise had long since seen through the
disguise, and of all the family, he was the person who
most engaged her affections.

"I am escaping for an hour or so," she whispered
conspiratorially. "Don't tell anyone you've seen me."

"Good for you," he said. "Got a secret beau, have
you, eh?" He chuckled as the color flooded her
cheeks. "Well, get along and enjoy yourself, wherever
y're off to. You can trust me to throw 'em off the scent
if they come looking for you."

The snow was not lying too thickly, and her pattens
kept the worst of it from her feet as she hurried down
the drive. Even so, her toes were soon numb with the
cold, which, in spite of the brilliant sunshine, nipped
cruelly at hands and feet. Was it the same frosty air

that caught in her throat, making her gasp for breath, or was it the thought of being alone with Prince Andrei? If only she did not have to meet him in such a hole-and-corner way. A tiny rebellious corner of her mind longed to have him drive up to the front of the house, as he had for Amelia. But that was wishful thinking.

It was more than a mile to the nearest gate, and by the time she arrived, her relief at seeing the phaeton already waiting overcame all other considerations. The prince was pacing the ground.

"Ah, good, you are prompt. Quickly now, you must be frozen, but I have a fine fur rug to put around you." Without further ado, his hands spanned her waist and she was lifted high and deposited as lightly as thistle-down in the awesomely high seat. A moment later the carriage dipped and swayed as he stepped lightly in at the other side and settled beside her. He reached for the rug and tucked it around her until she was co-cooned in the softest fur. It was such unaccustomed luxury that she sighed with the sheer pleasure of it.

"Ah, poor little *dushka,*" he exclaimed. "I should not have asked so much of you, but we do not have far to go."

"I don't mind, truly." Louise had no idea what *dushka* meant, but it had the ring of an endearment and did more to warm her than any number of fur rugs. He shouted something in Russian and for the first time she noticed a small wizened man who had been holding the horses and who now let go and scrambled nimbly up to a perch seat set perilously high behind the carriage.

It was some moments before the horses were into their stride and Prince Andrei was able to give his attention to her once more. "Well, now—are you feeling less cold, Mademoiselle Louise?"

"Thank you, yes." In fact, her hands and feet were

coming painfully back to life, but not for one moment would she admit to any discomfort.

He chuckled softly. "You are a remarkable young woman, do you know that? I, a complete stranger, ask you to do this crazy thing without giving you a word of explanation—and you agree almost at once."

"It seemed to be very important to you," she said simply.

"And for you that was enough?" His glance was quizzical. "Were you not just a little apprehensive of my motives?"

Had she seemed too willing? Given him the wrong idea? "Not really," she said with deliberate lightness. "Since I am nothing out of the ordinary, I could not suppose you would go to such lengths to carry me off."

The prince laughed aloud. "Oh, I like you, *mademoiselle*. But you should not underestimate your charms. They are not so obvious as some, yet there is a refreshing openness about you that warms the heart. And now I have embarrassed you," he added in his droll way as the sudden dip of her bonnet brim hid her face from him. He addressed himself to her bowed head. "Well, to make amends, I shall tell you a story. It is a sad little tale, and will, I trust, explain my reason for wishing to enlist your aid."

Louise looked up, her interest at once engaged.

"Certain families in Russia," he began more seriously, "have a long history of serving the czar. The Zarcovs are thus privileged, as are the Melinkoffs, whose country estates adjoin ours. The ties between our two families have always been very close, so it was quite natural that I and my brothers and sisters grew up alongside the Melinkoff children. We were almost as one family. There were three boys, but Irena was the Melinkoff's only daughter. I was enslaved from the first. She was some years younger than the rest of us, but to my eyes she was as gentle and beautiful as an angel.''

There was so much feeling in his voice that it brought a lump to Louise's throat, and even a little jealousy to her heart, except that she had no right to be jealous.

''By the time she was sixteen,'' he continued, ''she was enchantingly lovely, and it had long been agreed that we would become betrothed on her seventeenth birthday. But Count Melinkoff betrayed us. He had always been a compulsive gambler, and in that fateful year he took one chance too many, losing virtually everything he owned to one of Moscow's most astute rogues, Count Kirinsky. With ruin staring him in the face, Melinkoff did the unforgivable . . .''

Louise was by now hanging on his words, gripped by the story, the presentiment of what was to come chilling her far more than the coldness around them.

''He made a deal with the debauched Kirinsky, who had made no secret of his desire for Irena. He would bestow upon him the hand of his innocent young daughter in marriage if the count would return to him the bulk of his fortune.'' The prince was so absorbed in reliving the events that Louise's exclamation went unnoticed. ''I was away in St. Petersburg with my regiment, and by the time the news reached me, it was too late. They were married.''

For a moment Louise could not speak. Then, ''How dreadful for you—and for her, too,'' she whispered.

The prince gave her a bleak smile. ''A melancholy tale, is it not? But I do not tell you simply to engage your sympathy, much as it is appreciated. The story does not end there. Being a creature of impulse, I left St. Petersburg without permission from my commanding officer and rode to Moscow, arriving uninvited at a ball given by the czar and attended by Kirinsky and his new bride—the only thought in my mind to challenge the count, there and then. The flimsiest of pretexts would have sufficed, just so that I might rid the world of him. But Irena begged me not to create a scandal, not simply because it would bring the anger of the czar down on my head, but because it would enrage her husband, and she would be the one to suffer. And she would suffer cruelly, for unless I killed Kirinsky there and then, he would revenge himself upon her the moment they arrived home. The fear in her eyes made me certain that she spoke the truth. You may imagine my feelings. I left the ball that night plotting murder in my heart, but before I could act, my colonel—a strict disciplinarian—ordered me back to Petersburg under guard. Shortly after the Kirinskys left for a belated honeymoon, traveling through Europe.

"And that was the last I heard until about two months ago when I received a somewhat incoherent letter from Irena, from Paris, telling me that she was on the point of running away to England and begging me to come to her aid. Her governess had been an Englishwoman, a Miss Enderby, who had retired to live in Wyvern village several years ago."

"I see," Louise exclaimed. "At least, I think I do."

They were approaching the outskirts of the village that formed part of the Wyvern estate. The state of the road was such that the prince was obliged to negotiate a passage for the phaeton with some care.

She waited until he had cleared his way before continuing. "Would I be right in thinking that it was not entirely chance that led Lady Burridge to invite you to Charlcombe?"

"Not entirely," he agreed dryly. "How astute of you. In fact, I took Madame de Lieven into my confidence. Many people proclaim her an intriguer, and perhaps she is, but I know of no one better able to keep a secret when required to do so. Also, she has little love for Count Kirinsky. So, it was she who arranged this Christmas visit."

"And you have found her—your Irena?" Louise

thought it the most romantic story she had ever heard. Her own feelings for the prince, far from being dealt a blow, were becoming every minute more achingly real, but because he was already way beyond her reach, she found herself able to contemplate his love for his childhood sweetheart without rancor.

"I have found her," he said quietly. "But all is not as simple as one would wish. Two weeks ago she gave birth to a child—a son—and she is terrified that Kirinsky, in his fury at being deprived of both wife and heir, as well as being made to appear foolish in the eyes of his Parisian friends, will find her before she and the child are fit to travel. Miss Enderby is a good dependable woman, and George, her general handyman, will keep watch and notify me at the first hint of anyone asking questions in the village. There is also Irena's own servant, a brute of a fellow. But Irena is ill-at-ease, and it occurred to me that the company and support of someone young and trustworthy, a young woman like herself, might help Irena to feel less lost and frightened."

Louise was much moved. Impulsively she withdrew her hand in its neatly darned glove from beneath the rug and laid it on his sleeve. "I am honored that you chose to confide in me. I will gladly help in any way I can."

"Thank you." He covered her hand briefly with his own. "Irena speaks excellent English, so there should be no problem." Thereafter he was obliged to give all his attention to the horses as they swung around the village green and approached a small cottage set a little way apart from the rest.

Miss Enderby must have been watching for them, for she was at the door almost before they had stopped, a woman no longer young, but with a trim upright figure. The prince set Louise down in the tiny porch, where he made the two ladies known to each other. Then, while he had a few words with his groom, she swiftly removed her pattens and left them on the porch, and surrendered her cloak to the older woman, who presently ushered her into a small cozy living room where a fire burned brightly.

Louise turned to find herself being scrutinized by a pair of intelligent blue eyes, and smiled shyly. "Will I do?" she said.

Miss Enderby nodded briskly. "Forgive me. I wasn't sure what to expect. A young man's judgment, even that of a prince, is not always to be trusted."

Louise blushed. "No, and to be honest, ma'am, although I could not refuse his plea, I am a little apprehensive of my ability to be of use. My free time is very restricted, but if you think I can help, I am very willing to be guided by you." It was obviously the right thing to say, for Miss Enderby bade her come to the fire and make herself comfortable.

"What that poor child needs now, more than anything, is someone of her own age to talk to. She is still inclined to dissolve into tears at the least thing, though of course one may attribute that to weakness. It is barely two weeks since the birth of her son, and she did not have an easy time. But I think I may claim to know her as well as anyone, and I am convinced that she is holding something from me. If you could gain her confidence, perhaps she may feel able to tell you."

Louise did not think it very likely that Irena would confide in a stranger. "The prince has told me a little of her background. But might her behavior not be explained quite simply by the growing fear that her husband will find her?"

"No, no. She has made no secret of that." Miss Enderby was adamant. "No, this is something more, and I will not deny that it troubles me."

The door opened on a draft of cold air to admit Prince Andrei, who strode in, bringing with him an aura of vitality. "Well, now," he said, shrugging off his cloak and looking from one to the other. "You have become acquainted, yes?" and without waiting for answer, "Tell me, Miss Enderby, how is the little one today?"

"Much as ever, sir. But you will see for yourself."

Louise followed him up the tiny staircase into a little room whose white walls offset the brightly colored curtains. The prince was obliged to lower his head to avoid the beams of a steeply sloping ceiling as he approached the bed in the corner. Here, her figure making no more than a slight impression beneath the cheerful patchwork counterpane, lay one of the loveliest creatures Louise had ever seen. The silvery hair, drawn back from her brow and coiled into a thick plait that lay across one shoulder, exposed a face that was an exquisite oval in which every feature was perfection. Her skin, though scarcely less white than the pillows that supported her head, had a delicate translucent quality, accentuating eyes of a startlingly clear jade green, their fretfulness turned to joy as she saw the prince.

"Andrei!" She held out her hands and he enfolded them in his own.

"And how are you today, *ma mie?*" he inquired, lowering himself gently onto the bed beside her. She made a little moue. "Ah, well, you will soon feel much better, for I have brought Miss Louise Beresford to you as I promised." And as Louise lifted her gaze from contemplation of the tiny sleeping baby in the cradle beside the bed, he drew her forward. "Mademoiselle Louise, this is my dearest little Irena."

"*Mademoiselle.*" The green eyes considered her with guarded interest. "Andrei has told me much about you. It is good of you to come."

"I am very happy to be here, Countess."

The eyes clouded. "No! You must not call me by that dreadful name," she cried, fretful once more. "I will not have it. I am Irena—only Irena."

Louise bit her lip and glanced swiftly at the prince. "Of course you are," he said soothingly. "But it is perhaps a little impolite to shout at your visitor?"

At once Irena was repentant. "Please. Come and sit beside me and we will talk."

"Excellent," agreed the prince. "And I will go downstairs to sit with Miss Enderby. If I am fortunate, she will offer me a glass of her excellent homemade wine." He stood up, head hunched to avoid the beam above him, and gave her a lopsided smile. "This room is not big enough for all of us."

When he had gone, Louise drew forward the low nursing chair and sat beside the bed. She did not know quite how to begin a conversation with this young woman whose life had been so very different from her own.

In the end, it was Irena who said abruptly, "Andrei told me that you also have been obliged to leave a loving family. Will you not miss them?"

Louise heard the wistfulness in the question. "I already do. But I mean to write them long letters and they will write back to me. And that way it will not seem so bad. Also I hope to go home from time to time."

"Home . . ." There was such a wealth of feeling in the single utterance that Louise cursed her clumsiness. Ready tears sprang into the lovely eyes. "I no longer know where is my home."

"Oh, my dear Irena, forgive me. I spoke without thinking."

"No, no, you must not be sorry." She stretched out an impulsive hand and Louise, grasping it, felt the febrile pulse. "If we are to be friends, there must also be complete openness, and if that sometimes makes us sad, then we shall comfort each other. Yes?"

"Very well, if that is what you wish."

"Andrei has also told you about me—about the hopes we once had?"

"Yes. You have had a terrible time." Through the hand she still held, Louise felt a long shudder. "Worse perhaps than anyone knows?"

"Much worse," Irena whispered, and then, as if the words were forced from her, she cried passionately, "I have said little to Andrei, for assuredly he would seek out Victor and kill him if he knew one half of his cruelty. I told myself it was my duty to stay with my husband, but one can only take so much, and once one has known a great love, then it eventually becomes impossible to continue . . ."

"So you ran away? That must have taken a lot of courage, and with your baby on the way—"

"But that is why I had to leave, don't you see?" Irena was becoming more excitable, and Louise wondered if it was wise to encourage her. But, once started, she could not be stopped. "Count Kirinsky is not a fit person to have power over a child, especially if . . ."

She stopped, biting her lip, and Louise was convinced that she had been on the verge of saying something of importance. But after a moment she shook her head and continued in a subdued voice, "Even so, for a long time I was a coward, but then I realized that if I was to escape, it must be before the baby was born. It was not easy. My maid, all the servants, had been chosen for me by the count, so I could trust no one. No one, that is, except an old manservant to whom I had once shown kindness when Victor ill-treated him. And Mishka it was who arranged everything and brought me to England, to Miss Enderby, and he remains to watch over me still."

Louise could see that she was tiring, so she smiled and glanced at the cradle. "Well, you are safe now, and you have a lovely baby boy. You might almost say a Christmas baby, so he should be truly blessed."

"Oh, I do hope so," Irena whispered, tears of weakness rolling down her cheeks. "Because nothing must happen to him. I shall know no peace until . . . until he is quite, quite safe. And, you see, Victor will be so very angry. He will be searching for me even now. And sooner or later he will learn of my connection with Miss Enderby. I know it.''

Louise stood up and leaned close to her. ''Please, do not distress yourself. You must know that Prince Andrei will never permit any harm to come to you or the child. Trust him.''

''Oh, I do. But . . .'' Again it seemed that she would say more. And again she bit back the words. ''You will come again, very soon?''

''The very first chance I get,'' Louise promised.

In the downstairs room, two pairs of eyes turned to her.

''I doubt she told me anything you do not already know,'' she confessed. ''But I believe you are right: there is something she cannot bring herself to say, and although we got on very well together, one visit is not enough to establish such a fine degree of confidence. I have yet to win her complete trust. Perhaps, if I can come again very soon . . .''

''My dear girl, you may come as often as you can be spared,'' Miss Enderby said briskly. ''Which, with Christmas almost upon us, is probably not often enough.''

''I daresay I can contrive some excuse,'' Louise said. She added with a chuckle, ''The duke may prove an ally. He thinks I have a secret beau. Also there is a small gig in the stable that I have been permitted to use on occasion when something is required from the village in a hurry.''

Prince Andrei was unusually quiet on the way home. He had gone up to see Irena before they left. Louise wondered if she had perhaps said something to him. Snow was in the air once more, and when they came to the gates of Wyvern, he turned in and continued on up the drive.

"Sir, is this wise?"

"Entirely," he said. "I would not think of permitting you to walk all that long way back to the house when you have done me so great a favor."

"I achieved very little, I fear." Louise turned impulsively to him. "Is Irena really in as much danger as she thinks?"

"More, if anything," he said without hesitation, his voice hardening. "I know Kirinsky. He is a vindictive man; he will not rest until he finds her and, more importantly, his heir. I pray God that I can intercept him before he can wreak his vengeance upon her."

Louise shivered and he instantly reassured her.

"Come, we must not despair. Irena is well-protected, though I have warned Mishka not to show himself in the village. Fortunately Miss Enderby speaks Russian sufficiently well to keep him in check. Between us all we shall keep her safe."

They rounded a curve in the drive and Wyvern House came into view. Again, Louise begged him to set her down. "If we are seen, it will appear so odd."

"Nothing of the kind," he declared. "It is all very simple. I saw you trudging wearily along and with great gallantry took you up."

"Yes, but it wasn't quite like that and I am hopeless at telling lies."

The prince winced comically. "Such an unpleasant word, and scarcely applicable in this case, for it is no less than the truth that I did see you and did take you up; that it all happened rather earlier in the day is but a trifling juxtaposition of the facts."

"For shame!" Louise laughed aloud. But because she had no wish to leave her warm place at his side one moment sooner than she had to, and because she very much wished to be driven to the front entrance in style just once, she gave up the argument and savored the moment. She was less happy, however, when he insisted, in the interests of her immortal soul, on escorting her up to the drawing room, where the ladies of the family were assembled, so that he might explain how he had come upon her.

"Ah, there you are at last, my dear," the duchess said.

"Really, Lou! We have been looking everywhere for you." Amelia sprang up crossly and then saw the figure behind her. Color flooded her cheeks and her manner changed instantly. "Prince Andrei! We were not expecting . . ."

"Indeed not. Such a pleasant surprise," her mother interposed smoothly. "Do, pray, come to the fire."

"Your grace is most kind." He moved forward and greeted each of the ladies in turn. "I came but to deliver Mademoiselle Louise safely." His account of their meeting was delivered with such aplomb and with such a sublime disregard for the finer points of truth that Louise was lost in admiration, though she was aware of Amelia's frowns and knew there would be questions later.

"How very kind of you to take pity on the child," the duchess was saying. "You must permit me to offer you some refreshment."

"Thank you, madam, but I have been away some considerable time, and if I do not return to Charlcombe, Lady Burridge will be sending out search parties, in the fear that I have lost myself." His smile and the bow that accompanied it encompassed them all, though his glance lingered—or so it seemed to Louise—on Amelia. "But I shall give myself the pleasure of calling upon you again very soon."

Amelia lowered her eyes very prettily.

"You will be most welcome," said the duchess.

"And you will be coming to my birthday ball," Amelia said quickly. "It is to be masked, you know."

"Yes, indeed. I look forward to it with the greatest

pleasure." He carried her hand to his lips in a brief
salute before turning to leave. Louise had remained
near the door, and as he passed her, he paused and
said so that no one else could hear, "You see how
simple it all was? Such a harmless deception—the
fruits of a misspent youth, perhaps?"

In spite of herself, a smile lifted the corners of her
mouth. It did not go unnoticed by Amelia, who had
endured the boredom and disappointment of the visit
to Charlcombe, which had been nothing without the
prince's presence.

"And what was that all about, pray?" she demanded when the door closed behind him. "Putting
yourself forward in that ingratiating way. As if Prince
Andrei would look twice at you."

Louise flushed, but said nothing.

"Have a care, Amelia," the marchioness murmured
with gentle malice. "Cattishness is not at all becoming."

Lady Treadwell said in her amiable way, "I am sure
Amelia doesn't mean to be horrid, Maud. It is simply
that she is used to having things very much her own
way. I suppose it comes of being indulged from birth,
being the youngest and much the prettiest of us."

"That does not excuse rag manners." There was an
unusually acerbic note in the duchess's voice. "Prince
Andrei has been about the world a great deal, I daresay, and will have learned to judge what lies behind a
pretty face."

"But, Mama—"

"No, Amelia. I do not wish to hear any argument.
Louise, do go and take off that cloak; it is soaking wet
around the hem and you are trailing it on the floor.
Besides, we cannot risk you taking a chill with such a
busy time ahead."

For the rest of that day and the whole of the next,
Louise had not a moment to call her own. "Oh, my
dear, will you just . . ." and "Louise, if you can spare

a moment, would you kindly . . ." rang in her ears until she scarcely knew which way to turn. And of course there was still the decoration of the house to be completed. Over the last year or two it had somehow become accepted that her natural artistic flair should be employed in the disposal of the greenery, which meant that she and a small army of servants, with the children in gleeful support, spent hours wreathing the public rooms with great swags of holly and ribbon, and painstakingly threading the banister rail of the grand staircase with trailing ivy. And all to be completed before the first guest arrived.

Always at the back of Louise's mind, however, was the thought of Irena, and whether she was safe. She made time briefly to take the children skating in the hope that Prince Andrei might again be there, but the lake was deserted; everyone, it seemed, had other things to do. So it was that, with one thing and another, it was Christmas Eve, with all the guests assembled and settled in, before she could find an excuse to leave the house. The marchioness's gown was still awaiting her ministrations, and she conceived the notion of needing to visit the village dressmaker in order to find just the right shade of silk thread with which to repair the damage.

"I suppose if you have nothing suitable, you will have to go," said the duchess. "Although I'm sure I cannot see why Maud must needs wear that gown at all when she has others just as becoming."

"If I were to take the gig, I shouldn't be too long away," Louise suggested casually. "The roads are now reasonably free of snow."

"Well, if you think you can cope, my dear. We really cannot spare anyone to drive you just now."

Miss Potts, the dressmaker, lived in the center of the village and always knew what was going on. As she hunted for the thread she required, Louise was able to gently quizz her about the small community—

how they would spend Christmas. "I expect there will be one or two strange faces about the place as people have friends and relations to visit with them?"

"Well, of course, I never like to inquire too closely, not being one to gossip," confided the birdlike woman. "Miss Enderby, of course, has that poor sad young relative staying with her. So very young to be having a baby, and no sign of a father, though a young gentleman has been visiting in the last few days—a gentleman of some importance, so it would seem . . ." She hesitated as though inviting comment. Louise wondered for a moment whether her own presence had been noted, but concluded that it had not as the dressmaker continued, "Miss Enderby keeps herself very much to herself. An odd woman. Mind you, she spent many years in foreign parts, and I always think it rubs off . . . Ah, I believe this is the color you require." She held up the silk, and rather frustratingly the conversation moved on to sewing matters.

However, Louise was reassured; if anyone had been asking questions, she felt sure that Miss Potts would have known of it.

Miss Enderby further reassured her. "Though I shall be happier in my mind when Prince Andrei is able to move Irena to a safer place of shelter. She has been a trifle feverish in the last day or so. She is having to feed the child herself, of course. Dr. Waters has been unable to find a wet nurse, but he assures me that this little setback is no more than a touch of milk fever, and I have the greatest faith in his judgment. Even so, her present situation is far from ideal."

Louise dared not stay long, though she managed a few minutes with Irena. She did look unnaturally flushed, and having professed herself delighted to see her new friend, she turned her head restlessly on the pillow and seemed disinclined to talk, except to complain that Andrei had not been to see her since the previous morning.

"I imagine his hostess will have arranged many diversions for her guests. I daresay the prince cannot be forever excusing himself."

But Irena would not be soothed, and Louise returned home with a heavy heart and a vague feeling of disquiet that lay at the back of her mind despite all attempts to reason it away; even the insistence of the children that she should come up to the nursery to help them wrap their gifts could not quite banish it.

"Are you feeling unwell, Lou?" asked Joanna upon finding her for the third time staring into the fire, a piece of ribbon wound between inert fingers. "You've been looking glumpish all afternoon."

Louise came to with a start and explained that she was simply a trifle tired.

"You're probably sickening for some hideous disease," Philip said, delving with ghoulish glee into the realms of his imagination. "Can I have your helping of Christmas pudding if you die, Lou?"

But this was going too far for Jason, who began to cry, and the uproar that followed brought the governesses hurrying in like avenging crows. "I am surprised at you, Miss Louise," said Miss Trumper with pursed lips. "Allowing them to get so overexcited."

"If you wish your charges to be little models of perfection, perhaps you should keep a better eye on them," Louise said with an unaccustomed tartness that made everyone stare. "The upset was all something and nothing, anyway, and if children can't let go a little at this time of the year, when, pray, can they?"

It was very rag-mannered of her, and she had no doubt that word of her behavior would reach the ears of the duchess, but for once Louise didn't care. She was tired—so much so that she excused herself from dinner that evening. It was unlikely that she would be missed. Quite the reverse, in fact. And there was still the marchioness's gown to be repaired. She sat quite late into the night, mending the lace by the light of

her candle, and when she finally slept, it was but fit-
fully, her sleep plagued by dreams of Prince Andrei
and the shadowy figure whom she supposed was Count
Kirinsky fighting a duel in Miss Enderby's tiny cottage, Irena and the baby writhing on the floor between
them.

Nevertheless, Christmas Day itself was enjoyable. It
began with a short service in the small private chapel.
The children with their governesses and as many of
the family and guests as could rouse themselves in time
listened to the unctuous voice of the chaplain intoning
the familiar words of St. Luke "And it came to pass
in those days . . ." after which they sang carols with
varying degrees of enthusiasm around a manger made
by the gardener's boys with real straw from the stables.
Thereafter the children hurried through breakfast so
that they might open their presents, which kept them
happily occupied for some time.

Louise fell to thinking about her own family. They
would have gone to the midnight service and would
now be enjoying the simple pleasures so carefully contrived by her parents. She suddenly felt very much
alone. Although a few of the duchess's guests were
known to her, she had very little in common with
them. She wondered what Prince Andrei was doing?
Probably much the same as the gentlemen at Wyvern
who had gone riding, while the ladies were either still
closeted in their rooms or making desultory conversation in the drawing room.

She hoped the prince would find time to visit Irena.
How frightened that poor girl must be, trapped here
in a strange country—a girl of her own age, but unused
to fending for herself and for the present unable to
even attempt to do so. Again, Louise was aware of
that feeling of disquiet as she tried to imagine what it
must be like to be responsible for a tiny life, knowing
that danger constantly threatened. Miss Enderby was
an excellent woman, but she was no longer young, and

if anything should happen . . . Tomorrow, she vowed.
I will go again tomorrow, come what may.

With so much to be done, the day passed quickly.
An extra pair of hands was more than welcome, and
in spite of all the bustle, and Jacques being at his most
temperamental, she found the true spirit of Christmas
much more in evidence belowstairs than above.

At dinner she was seated inconspicuously next to Sir
Roger Beamish, a rather jovial older man whom she
knew well enough to be at ease with him, for although
he liked to flirt, he was quite harmless. He told her
she was looking "very jolly."

"New gown, what? Most becoming—fine as fivepence!"

"Thank you, Sir Roger," she said with a smile. "It
is kind of you to say so."

"Not kind at all, m'dear. Simple truth."

Louise was not displeased with the gown. The duchess had presented her soon after her arrival with the
length of crepe in a soft moss green. "I bought it for
Amelia, but she does not care for the color," she had
confided. "And I've no doubt that with your needle-
work skills, you will be able to contrive something
very passable. I think it quite a pretty color, myself."

In an unaccustomed fit of rebellion Louise had
longed to reject it as Amelia had done, but in the end,
practicality won. She possessed few-enough dresses
for her needs. Besides, the duchess meant well; and
she had been right: it was a pretty color.

Benevolence had been further heaped upon her
when, earlier that morning, the duchess presented
Louise with a dressmaker's box. With trembling fingers Louise had pulled aside the tissue wrappings to
lift out the most beautiful ball gown she had ever
seen—of lavender blue crepe trimmed with tiny shimmering beads, and in separate wrapping, a delicately
fashioned mask, embellished with the same beads.

"The duke was most insistent that you should have a new gown for the birthday ball," said her grace complacently, "and I agreed with him. So I hope that you will accept this as a little extra Christmas gift from us both. My maid, Partridge, contrived to measure one of your dresses when you were otherwise occupied so that it would come as a complete surprise."

Louise stammered her thanks and could hardly wait to take it to her room in order to try it on—only in case it should need alteration, she told herself. But the gown, with its brief bodice and tiny puffed sleeves, fitted perfectly. The color echoed the violet blue of her eyes, and somewhere among her incoherent thoughts lay the knowledge that Prince Andrei would be at the ball two nights from now. Of course, Amelia would outshine her by far, but might he not, if only for an instant, notice how fine she looked?

On the following morning, the ladies lay abed while the majority of the gentlemen braved the rigors of the weather, which threatened snow, to shoot over his grace's covers. Prince Andrei was one of several sportsmen among Lady Burridge's guests who drove over to join them. Louise saw him briefly as she helped to hand cups of hot punch before they set out. There was no opportunity to say anything of a private nature, but as he prepared to leave, he looked intently into her eyes and murmured, "Please, I wish to speak with you when we return."

Throughout the morning, she found many an excuse to hover near the side door, and was therefore on hand to see the shabby carriage that came hurtling around from the main drive making for the kitchen quarters, driven by a man she immediately recognized as Miss Enderby's handyman, George. He pulled up on seeing her, and she hurried out, heedless of the spasmodic swirls of snow, and ran a soothing hand over the horse's steaming flanks.

"Eh, miss, I'm that glad to see you. It's tekken me long enough as it is," George gasped, leaning down. "Been all the way to Charlcombe, I have, only to discover that Prince Andrei was here all the time."

All Louise's lingering disquiet surfaced once more. "Something is wrong! The young countess . . . ?"

He shook his head. "She's only middling fair, but it en't that." A gust of wind snatched at his muffler. "There's bin a man asking questions 'round the village," he said, catching the errant muffler and tucking it back inside the collar of his greatcoat.

It was what they had all feared. "What kind of man?"

"Sharp-looking cove—could be a groom or some such, wanting to know the whereabouts of a perticler young woman as might have arrived recent-like. There's no knowing how much he was told, so Miss Enderby sent me straight off to fetch 'is highness. Only, like I said, it's taken me longer'n I thought, so if you'd be so good as to let 'im know quick as I'm here—"

"But I can't." Even as she explained, Louise's mind was racing. "The best thing I can do is to write a note for him and get someone—one of the stable lads, possibly—to ride out after the shooting party. They've been gone some time, but with the weather as it is, they may not have gone very far."

"You do that, miss. And if you'll pardon me, I'll be gettin' back to Miss Enderby. I'm none so happy at leaving her alone. Time's going on, and I don't reckon as we've that much to spare."

"No—wait! I'm coming with you. The note will only take me a moment." Without waiting for an answer, she picked up her skirts and ran down the passage to the muniments room. It was locked, but she knew where the key was kept. She found pen and ink and, after a brief search, paper. "Dear sir," she scrawled,

"Matters at the cottage grow urgent. Have gone with George. Please come with all speed." She signed it, folded it several times, and wrote his name on the front. As she turned to leave, she saw a cloak belonging to the duke's agent hanging on the back of the door and seized on it with relief. There was no time to fetch her own, and although it would be much too big, it would keep out the weather.

"Drive 'round to the stables," she told George, gasping out the directions as she scrambled up beside him and wrapped the cloak around her as best she could.

A few more minutes and they were on their way to the village, leaving behind them a very junior stable boy who was even then mounting a hastily saddled horse and riding out in pursuit of the shooting party.

All seemed quiet enough when they reached the cottage. Louise saw the muslin curtains move and guessed that Miss Enderby was keeping watch. She hurried to open the door, and though there was no doubting the warmth of her welcome, Louise saw the older woman's glance lift worriedly to probe the drifting snow in search of a familiar tall masculine figure.

"The prince will be along very soon, ma'am," Louise promised reassuringly as she removed her cloak, shaking the snow from it in the porch before allowing Miss Enderby to take it from her. "Meanwhile, George is going to stand guard. He'll let us know the moment he sees or hears anything. Now, do tell me quickly whether there have been any further developments."

"Not as yet." There was less crispness than usual in the older woman's voice, and Louise guessed that the strain of waiting was beginning to tell on Miss Enderby. "But I fear that time may be running out. George will have told you about the stranger?"

"Yes. That is why I am here."

"It is very good of you, my dear, but I cannot hide from you the fact that I was so hoping to see the prince. I am relying on him so much to know how best to deal with Count Kirinsky."

"He will come . . . very soon," Louise reiterated, explaining the reason for the delay. "But if he does not come in time, we shall contrive something."

Miss Enderby sighed and smiled a little helplessly at Louise. "How confident you sound. I am very glad to have you with me, my dear, though I feel guilty lest being here places you in danger. There was a time . . ." She shook her head. "But now I am grown too old for such alarms and excursions."

Louise did not feel at all confident, but clearly Miss Enderby needed someone to lend her support. "Well, let us see what can be done. First, how is Irena?"

"The fever has subsided, but she is still rather weak. Naturally, I have said nothing to her about—"

"No. Well, there is no point in upsetting her until we are sure. If the count should come, we must find some way of diverting him. Do you have anyone here that we can call upon besides George and Mishka?" Louise frowned as she shook her head.

"Oh, well, it is of little consequence. We shall contrive something." Louise peered out the window, shivering with a mixture of excitement and fear as an idea began to take shape in her mind. It could be dangerous, but desperate situations demanded desperate measures. "I will go up to see Irena while you watch the window." At the door, she paused. "Tell me, is there anywhere in the cottage where she might hide if the need arose? Somewhere not immediately obvious to the eye?"

Miss Enderby obviously thought she had taken leave of her senses. There was a hint of the governess in her reproving tone. "In a place this size? My dear girl, you have only to look about you. One couldn't hide a mouse in here, and certainly not from a man as ruthless as Count Kirinsky is, if half I have heard is true.''

"Well, please give it some thought,'' Louise begged, unabashed. "I have an idea, and if it can be made to work, I do not anticipate that the count will wish to make a thorough search of the house, so as long as Irena is safely concealed.''

She whisked out of the room before the old lady could ask any awkward questions. Upstairs, she found Irena raised high on her pillows, leaning wearily toward the cradle as she rocked it gently.

"Poor little Paul, he is sleeping at last, I hope,'' she said softly, extending her free hand to greet Louise. "He has not had a happy time these past few days.''

"But you are feeling better now?'' Louise asked, sitting on the edge of the bed.

"Oh, yes. Soon I shall be well.'' Irena allowed her to take over the rocking and lay back. "Andrei is not with you?''

"No, but we are expecting him shortly.'' Preoccupied as she was, Louise did not guard the tone of her voice quite carefully enough.

"Something is wrong? No, you need not lie to me. I know it. I have felt it all morning. Victor has discovered me—yes?''

"No. That is . . .'' Oh, well, the damage was done now, and perhaps it was for the best that Irena should be prepared. "My dear, do not distress yourself. We are not yet sure about the count. But if he is here—''

"He must not find me. He must not find Paul. *Dieu!* What am I to do?''

"For a start, you must keep calm,'' Louise said sharply. A display of hysterics was the last thing they needed at this moment. But Irena seemed not to hear her.

"Andrei will come, he must come! He will kill Victor for me!'' She began to sob uncontrollably.

Louise stood up, leaving hold of the cradle, and grasped Irena firmly by the shoulders. "Stop it," she ordered, giving her a sharp little shake. "Do you hear me? You will not help yourself or baby Paul by working yourself up into a state. There is much to be done, and perhaps not much time to do it."

The sobs subsided. "You do not understand. He must on no account be permitted to even see Paul," Irena murmured piteously.

"My dear, don't—"

"Paul is not Victor's child," the small voice continued as though Louise had not spoken.

The admission was totally unexpected, and was followed by a great echoing silence broken finally by Paul's grizzling cry. Almost without thinking, Louise's hand stretched out to set the cradle in motion once more. So, this then was what Irena had been keeping to herself?

"Does anyone else know?" she asked, and was surprised by the normality of her voice.

"No."

Not even to herself would Louise admit that the relief she felt had anything to do with her fear that Andrei might have sired the child. "Well, then," she said. "Surely there is no reason for your husband to suspect?"

"The red hair of the Kirinskys is unmistakable among the men of Victor's family," Irena whispered. "And, as you can see, Paul is very dark, as is his father."

"And who is his father?" Louise asked, holding her breath.

But before she could receive any answer, there was a sound on the stair. "Louise?" She heard the urgency in Miss Enderby's voice and went at once to the door. "A traveling coach has just driven into the village square. It will be here at any moment. I had hoped it might be Prince Andrei, but . . ."

Louise's heart gave an apprehensive lurch, but calmness was now of the essence. "The hiding place?" she asked, low-voiced. "Have you thought of anywhere?"

"There is a cupboard beneath the stairs, but Irena is so weak, and it is very cramped."

"No matter. Mishka can carry her down, and hopefully she will not have to be there for long. You have spare blankets?" In the room behind them the baby began to bawl lustily. With one last despairing look, Miss Enderby went to the chest in her own room and returned with two big fleecy blankets.

"Good." Louise took them from her, and seeing the older woman's rather dazed expression, she gave her a sudden reassuring smile. "I have not gone mad, I promise you. Now, if you could fetch Mishka . . ." Louise hurried back to the bedroom.

Irena was attempting to get out of bed, one hand clutching the cradle, her eyes dilated with fear. "He is here," she whispered. "I know it."

"Hush," Louise said quietly. "My dear, I want you to do exactly as I tell you. There is no time to explain." As she talked, she wrapped the blankets around the shivering girl, and above the cries of the baby a heavy footfall sounded on the stair. "See, here is Mishka, come to take you downstairs, to a place where Count Kirinsky will not find you."

"And Paul, too . . . my baby. I must take my baby with me."

"Paul will be quite safe, I promise you." Louise grasped Irena's hands and willed her to believe. "You may trust me not to let any harm come to your baby, but he must remain here and you must not make a sound until the count has left. Your whole future may depend upon it."

Miss Enderby hurried in and, behind her, the great bearlike figure of Mishka filled the doorway. Irena gave a hiccuping sob and, with one last agonizing look at her baby, allowed herself to be lifted and carried from the room.

"He knows what to do? And that he must on no account allow the count to see him?"

"He knows," said Miss Enderby dryly. "I only hope that you do." She jumped as the door knocker rattled imperatively. "Oh, dear God! It must be—"

"Nightgowns," Louise said urgently, unpinning her hair and shaking it free. "Where are Irena's clean nightgowns?"

A faint gleam of hope came into Miss Enderby's eyes as she began to realize what Louise meant to do. She hurried to a drawer and pulled out a clean gown. "Are you sure you want to do this?" And when Louise nodded impatiently, "Will it work, do you think?"

The door knocker rapped a second time.

"It has to work! We will say that I am your godchild, disgraced by a nobleman." Louise's voice was muffled by the gown. "Go now and let him in." She leaned over the crib and lifted the red-faced baby, who stopped crying momentarily and opened wide his bright button-black eyes to stare at her. "Well, young man," she told him, "it's up to you and me now."

As his mouth began to pucker again, she heard the voices below: Miss Enderby's measured tones against the heavier, more authorative ones. She scrambled into the bed and pulled the bedclothes up tight around herself and the baby. It was not a moment too soon. She heard swift decisive footsteps on the stair and Miss Enderby exclaiming angrily, "Sir, I must protest. My goddaughter is far from well—"

"Goddaughter! *Mon Dieu!* Do you take me for a fool?" A man strode into the room, loomed over her. "Irena," his harsh voice rose above the baby's cries.

Louise slowly emerged from the bedclothes, her face flushed, wide-eyed and frightened, her dark hair fall-

ing in a disheveled mass across the child. His mouth
dropped open in an expression so ludicrous that she
felt a sudden desire to laugh. The urge lent a very real
edge to her impassioned "Aunt Jane! Oh, help me,
someone," which brought Miss Enderby running in
on cue.

"Now, see what you've done! How dare you force
your way into my house, frightening this poor girl half
to death, as if she hadn't enough to bear. To say nothing of her child, poor mite. As for the neighbors . . .
The disgrace! I shall never be able to hold my head up
again in the village."

Louise, peering through the wild curtain of her hair,
could hardly believe what she saw. Miss Enderby, having entered into the spirit of the charade, was in her
element. The count, meanwhile, was looking more and
more angry. He was handsome in a florid fashion, and
his hair was certainly as red as fire beneath the high-
crowned hat that he had not even bothered to remove.
He had also a temper to match.

"This is some kind of trick," he snapped. "I was
informed that my wife—"

"Wife, indeed! Would that it were so." Miss Enderby paused dramatically. "But since there are two
of you claiming knowledge of my godchild, it seems
that matters are more shameful than I had supposed.
Louise," she demanded with awful sternness, "I want
the truth. Is this the fine nobleman who ruined you
and not that other one?"

Louise choked, turned the choke into a splutter, and
took refuge in fresh tears as she denied it vehemently.

"I repeat, I was informed that my wife," the count
continued, addressing himself to Miss Enderby with
barely contained fury, "who was Irena Melinkoff before her marriage to me and who ran away from our
Paris apartment in a fit of pique some weeks since,
heavy with child"—his eyes strayed consideringly to-

ward Louise—"had taken refuge in this vicinity. Do you deny, madam, that you were once Irena's governess?"

"Certainly not. I was—still am, very fond of the child. We occasionally correspond. But as for her being here—"

He swept on arrogantly, "Or that it is something more than coincidence that your godchild"—there was something approaching a sneer in the word—"should just happen to have given birth to a bastard child. And that Prince Andrei Zarcov, her onetime lover, should have been seen visiting this cottage?"

"You go too far, sir," Miss Enderby snapped in her best governess manner. "We do not have to endure your insults or your accusations. I must ask you to leave."

He turned on her in a fury. "I will not move from here without first seeing the child."

At this point there was a disturbance below, followed by the urgent sound of feet on the stairs. Prince Andrei burst in, and was obliged to stop, for the tiny room was fast becoming filled to overflowing. Louise had never been so glad to see anyone.

"Kirinsky! What the . . . ?"

Before he could ruin everything with a word, she flung out an imploring hand and exclaimed dramatically, "Andrei! Oh, how glad I am to see you. This person is trying to make Aunt Jane believe that he is the father of our child."

"Yours?" the count thundered, turning on him.

There was a moment of silence. Then, ignoring both the count and the question, the prince moved to kneel beside Louise, being careful not to disturb the baby who had grown tired of all the fuss and fallen asleep. He gathered her fingers into his hands and laid them gently against his cheek. "You are quite safe now, *ma petite*, you and little Paul. This creature has not harmed you?"

"No." She smiled tremulously. There was no need to act, for his closeness, the feel of his skin against her own, disarmed her totally. Unaware of the extent to which her eyes betrayed her, she confessed, "But I had begun to fear that you would not come."

"Well, I am here now." For one magical moment his lips brushed hers. Then he stood up and faced the count. "Now, Kirinsky." His voice was silky soft. "We will go downstairs now, if you please, where you will answer to me for your deplorable behavior."

The count's fury was tightly leashed. "Gladly." He ground the word out. "When I have seen the child."

Again time seemed to hang suspended until Louise said calmly, "You are very welcome to see him, Count."

She drew back the fine lacy shawl and watched his expression as he gazed down in silence at the tiny face, the thick cap of black hair. As if she had prearranged it, the bright eyes opened, blinked up at him, and closed again. She could almost hear the count grinding his teeth.

"Dear Paul, he is so very like his father," she said, rubbing salt in the wound.

The count's eyes met hers and it took all her considerable resolve not to shudder. He offered no apology, bowed stiffly to Miss Enderby, and strode from the room, followed closely by the prince, who paused only to say softly, "I shall want words with you later."

Not until he was safely downstairs did either woman speak. Louise lay where she was, not daring to move until she was certain that the count had left. After all the high tension, she felt suddenly deflated, and not a little fearful for the prince's safety. "Will they fight, do you suppose?" she asked in a small voice.

Miss Enderby glanced sharply at her, but only said, "Who knows what men will do. They are nothing but overgrown boys, after all."

"I suppose they are, but I do not want a death on my conscience." Especially not his, she thought, and all because of her silly playacting, the memory of which, now magnified out of all proportion, returned to haunt her. There had been a look in his eyes as he left the room—not anger, exactly, but something very close. In her attempts to convince the count, had she perhaps been carried away, acted her part too well?

"For goodness' sake don't brood. What is done is done." Miss Enderby was all governess once more. "Whatever the outcome, Irena at least should be safe for a while."

"Yes, of course," Louise said. The thrill of pitting their wits against the count and winning returned momentarily, and her eyes warmed as she regarded the older woman. "My dear ma'am, you were quite splendid."

"Oh, as to that, I simply followed your lead." But she looked pleased just the same. "To be completely honest, I have to confess that despite the circumstances, I found the whole experience curiously exhilarating. Still, for all that, you took a great risk. I shudder to think what would have happened had things gone wrong."

"True. I dared not even contemplate it at the time. Poor Irena. One can only pity her, being married to that dreadful man. It doesn't at all surprise me that she ran away."

"Well, do you know, it does surprise me. She was always a sweet, rather biddable child. I had not thought her capable of showing so much initiative."

Louise remembered the girl's earlier confession. Perhaps the governess didn't know her onetime charge as well as she thought. However, it was not her place to betray confidences.

"I think . . . Yes, I am almost sure that was the front door closing," said Miss Enderby, breaking in on Louise's musings. A moment later, Prince Andrei was up the stairs and in the room, his expression so severe that Louise felt her heart sink.

"You have not . . ."

"Killed him?" he finished for her in clipped tones. "No. Once again, regrettably, the circumstances favored him. But I left him in no doubt that I should not be so generous a third time. You will doubtless be pleased to know that for the moment your little charade seems to have had the desired effect. The count means to pursue his inquiries elsewhere." His eyes took in the sight of them, with Louise still in her self-appointed role, and a gleam of wry incredulity stole into his eyes. "As for you, are you both grown so tired of living that you attempt such a blatant flirtation with danger?"

Miss Enderby grew a trifle pink.

Louise swiftly exonerated her from all blame and, to give the embarrassed woman's thoughts a fresh direction, drew her attention to the sleeping child. "I really do think you might safely put him back in the crib now. My arm is grown quite stiff, and if I don't move soon, I vow I shall swoon away with the cramps." As soon as Miss Enderby had relieved her of her burden, she pushed back the blankets and swung her legs out of the bed . . . and found herself in the prince's firm clasp, being lifted bodily to her feet, her dark hair spilling over her shoulders.

"You would not swoon easily, I think," he said. And then, very softly, "You must have been mad."

"Not mad, just desperate. There simply wasn't time to weigh the risks." To cover her blushes she began to struggle with the ribbons at the neck of the nightgown, which she had tied tightly in order to conceal her dress. A moment later his fingers moved hers aside and accomplished the task so nimbly as to suggest that he was not unfamiliar with the task. Filled with confusion, she rushed into speech again, aware that she was gabbling. "I hope you did not mind my . . . my behaving as I did toward you? I had not meant to be so familiar, but when you came bursting in like that, I was so afraid that you might inadvertently betray us." He made no attempt to help her out as she concluded lamely, "I suppose it was a crazy thing to do, but it was the only scheme I could devise at a moment's notice, in order to protect Irena until you arrived."

Miss Enderby, who had been observing this exchange with some interest, clapped a hand to her mouth. "Oh, my good Lord, Irena! That poor child."

The prince quirked an eyebrow. "I had been wondering about Irena's part in all this. What exactly have you done with her?"

But Miss Enderby was already hurrying downstairs, leaving Louise to explain. She did so, all too aware of his intent, half-amused gaze upon her.

"I hope Irena will not have taken any harm," she said. "You had better go to her. I will follow as soon as I have made myself respectable once more."

"Must you?" he murmured wickedly. "Such a pity. To my eyes you appear quite charming as you are." But he went.

When Louise arrived downstairs with her hair neatly coiled once more and the creases smoothed from her gown, Irena had been extricated from her hiding place and was huddled on the sofa in front of the fire. She looked much too pale, and the fear had not quite left her eyes, but the prince's arm was around her and her head was against his shoulder. Feeling decidedly *de trop*, Louise wandered through to the kitchen beyond where Miss Enderby was wreathed in a delicious aroma of mulled wine.

"Can I help?" she asked as the older woman filled a jug and set it on a tray with some glasses.

"You can bring that plate of shortcake through, if you will," Miss Enderby said, preceding her with the tray. She poured the wine and passed it around. "You'll drink every drop of that, young lady," she declared as Irena attempted to push it away.

Louise settled in a nearby chair. "I'm sorry you have had such a wretched time," she said, resolved not to let the obvious intimacy between the young girl and the prince affect her.

"Oh, no! It is nothing. I owe you so much!" Irena's face was streaked with tears, but she was quite calm. "If I had not behaved so foolishly in the first place . . ." She took a sip of the wine as if to draw courage from it, and her eyes held Louise's for a moment. "It is time, I think, for me to explain." And haltingly she began to tell them about the baby's father: how she had met the young American diplomat, Paul Weston, at the Paris home of Monsieur Gallatin, the American Ambassador, and how they had fallen in love at first sight.

Miss Enderby listened with pursed lips after a brief flicker of shocked surprise, but Louise was more interested to know how Prince Andrei was taking the news. She could read nothing from his expression.

"It was not how you think," Irena exclaimed. "Paul is everything that Victor is not, charming, considerate and honorable. He would never have proclaimed his love for me, had I not encouraged him." Irena blushed, but continued resolutely, "I was by then quite desperately unhappy, you see, and here was fate offering me a glimpse of paradise. You would be surprised how devious one can become when such a temptation presents itself. Victor thought me so biddable that he never suspected for one moment."

"But surely, if this man truly loved you—" Louise began.

"He did, he does," she cried passionately. "But in

the end everything happened too quickly. Monsieur Gallatin had urgent letters for Washington, and Paul was obliged to leave almost at a moment's notice. He begged me to go with him, but it was impossible. By then I was *enceinte* and Victor, elated at the prospect of an heir, was watching me very possessively.'' She shuddered. ''Paul promised to return with all speed, but as time passed, I grew terrified in case the child was not Victor's, and I knew that I must get away. Mishka delivered a letter to Monsieur Gallatin's house, to await Paul's return, telling him where I would be. The rest you know. It was wicked of me not to confess the whole when first I came here, but I did not know how to begin . . .''

Her voice died away. In the tiny room, the only sounds were the ticking of the clock and Irena's uneven breathing. Then Prince Andrei murmured, ''Come now, *chérie*. Do not distress yourself. All may yet right itself.'' His arm tightened around her, and with a convulsive little movement she buried her face in his shoulder and began to cry.

Miss Enderby gestured to Louise to follow her. In the kitchen she said softly, ''Well! I would never have believed it, had she not told us herself.'' Louise made no immediate reply, and she looked at her more closely. There would be more than one heart in danger of breaking this day, it seemed. ''How blind men can be,'' she observed tartly to no one in particular. And Louise, whose sympathies were wholly with the prince, sighed. ''Yes, indeed.''

''You already knew about the child, I think.''

Louise came out of her reverie to say apologetically, ''Only that the count was not the father. Irena told me just as Mishka came to carry her downstairs. There was scarcely time to take it in, let alone confide in you, though perhaps it made my part a little easier to play.''

"Hmp," muttered Miss Enderby. "When I think of the trouble I took to teach that child right from wrong. Heaven knows where it will all end. She will remain with me, of course, but even if this young man does eventually come for her, the matter has no easy solution—unless, that is, Irena elects to live in sin for the rest of her days. To tell you the truth, nothing would surprise me now."

But the day was not yet over.

Her fragile energy all spent, Irena presently allowed the prince to carry her, exhausted, to her bed, where he left her with Miss Enderby, who proceeded to sponge her tearstained face, put her into clean linen, and tuck her up warmly while the baby, worn out by all the to-do, slept on.

Louise was thus left alone with Prince Andrei. Her heart ached for him, and not a little for herself. She was already experiencing a sense of anticlimax; odd that she should feel so unaccountably flat when things had turned out better than anyone could have hoped but a few hours ago. It must be reaction, she told herself. A small sigh escaped her.

Prince Andrei roused from his contemplation of the flames at the sound and turned to see her sitting dejectedly in her chair beside the hearth. "Poor Mademoiselle Louise," he said gently. "It is fatiguing to be cast in the role of a heroine, is it not?"

For some reason she could not explain, his sympathy made her angry. "I wish you would not say such foolish things. I am very ordinary and only did what anyone would have done in the circumstances."

If he was taken aback, he did not show it. Instead, he knelt on one knee beside her and put a hand gently under her chin, drawing her around to face him. "No," he said softly, his eyes gleaming like dark velvet in the firelight. "You are not ordinary at all. In fact, I do not think there is anyone quite like you in the whole world.'' She caught her breath, and to her intense mortification, she found tears suddenly rolling down her cheeks. He drew back at once and the tears flowed faster.

''Oh, how stupid of me,'' she cried, vexed beyond all measure.

Prince Andrei stood up, a wry smile warming his eyes. ''No, it is I who am stupid. You are suffering just a little from reaction, I think.'' He refilled her glass and his own with mulled wine. ''Come, we will drink to the success of your valiant escapade . . . and be happy, yes?''

''Yes, of course.'' It would be foolish, after all, to read more into his behavior than mere kindness.

He frowned, hearing the listless note in her voice. ''And then I shall take you home. We can do no more here, I think.''

At that moment the back door opened to admit George in an obvious state of agitation. ''Beg pardon,'' he said on seeing them, ''but you wouldn't 'appen to 'ave seen the big Russian anywheres about?''

The prince's eyebrow lifted. ''Mishka? No.'' He glanced at Louise.

She shook her head. ''But he was warned to keep out of sight.''

''Aye, that he was, miss. Only he's not where he should be, if you take my meaning,'' George said darkly. ''Or anywheres else as I can see,'' He turned back to Prince Andrei. ''Which being the case, there's somethin' out here as I think your highness should come and tek a look at . . .''

They were gone some time. Miss Enderby came downstairs, and was surprised to see Louise alone. She explained briefly about George and then asked after Irena.

''Already asleep,'' said the older woman dryly. ''Clearly she does not suffer from a troubled conscience.''

"She is very young, ma'am," Louise said in mitigation.

"No younger than you, I'll warrant."

"Perhaps not. But I would not for the world have been in her shoes this past year."

Miss Enderby looked at her in silence for a moment. "You're good girl," she said abruptly. And then, "I'm going to make a restoring pot of tea."

They were well into their second cup when Prince Andrei returned with George. Both were looking unnaturally grave.

Miss Enderby sighed. "What is it now? I doubt I can stand any more shocks today."

"I am sorry, ma'am," said the prince. "Would that my tidings were more pleasant."

"Very well. Out with it. As long as you do not mean to tell me that that dreadful man has come back . . ."

He seemed to be measuring his words. "I think it very unlikely that he will do so ever again."

"Oh, no," whispered Louise, seeing at once where he was leading.

"I have to tell you, ma'am, that Mishka is nowhere to be found, and that George has found the body of a man on the ground beside your cottage. I have seen him, and although his topcoat and hat are missing, he has the general appearance of a groom or coachman."

Miss Enderby's hand fluttered to her breast, but her voice was firm. "Not to be mealymouthed about it, you think he was the count's coachman and that Mishka killed him in order to take his place."

"Almost certainly. My own man saw nothing untoward, but it could well have happened before we arrived."

"In which case, one is forced to the conclusion that Mishka means to put period to the count's life also."

Prince Andrei nodded. "I am very much afraid he does."

"Is there no way you can stop him?" Louise asked impulsively. They both looked at her, Miss Enderby in some surprise, Prince Andrei enigmatic. "Oh, I know the count is a horrible man, and his death would come as a great relief to Irena, but . . . Well, I was thinking of poor Mishka. What will he do afterward? Where will he go? He speaks no English."

"Oh, I believe Mishka knew exactly what he was doing," the prince said, not unkindly. "His hatred for Kirinsky was just as great as his devotion to Irena. To keep her from further harm and secure her future, I have no doubt he would hold his own life cheap. That being the case, he would surely see this as the perfect opportunity." He shrugged. "And who are we to deny him that opportunity? Even were there any way to stop him, I am not sure I would try."

Louise could appreciate that there was a certain justification in his line of reasoning, but particularly at this season of goodwill, it seemed to her such a cold-blooded philosophy. She could only suppose that gentlemen saw such matters rather differently, but he was not just any gentleman and she felt curiously let down.

Her return to Wyvern had a strange air of unreality about it. So much had happened that it was as though she had been away for a very long time and was coming back as a stranger. She had feigned sleep during the journey, and although she could feel the prince glancing at her once or twice, he made no attempt to disturb her until they drew to a halt at the front steps when his hand brushed her face lightly.

"Wake up, *dushka*," he murmured. "We have arrived. And do not fear, I will see his grace and explain everything." So saying, he stepped down and came around to her side of the carriage. Without a word he lifted her and carried her over the snow, not setting her down until they were admitted by Melton, who

stiffly expressed his relief at seeing her and sent a footman scurrying to inform the duke.

Deprived of the all-too-brief closeness of the prince's
arms, Louise felt as though she were parting with a
bit of herself and would never be quite whole again.
Silly, she thought, and wrapped the too-large cloak
more tightly around her.

"Are you all right?" Prince Andrei asked with a
concern that might have touched a chord in her, had
she not known that it stemmed merely from kindness.

The arrival of the duke spared her the necessity of
answering. He looked more austere than she had ever
seen him, although his eyes betrayed his relief upon
seeing her, apparently safe and unharmed.

"We had no idea what to think, d'ye see, when you
couldn't be found. Bella thought that you might have
gone home, but I said you wouldn't leave without saying so." His glance moved to Prince Andrei and his
brows drew into a fierce frown.

Louise opened her mouth to speak, but the prince
was before her. "Sir, things are not as they might
seem, and if you will accord me a few minutes in
private, I believe I shall be able to explain all to your
satisfaction."

"Explanations are certainly in order. I confess I'm
mystified by the whole thing. You'd better come into
the library."

Louise said, "I do hope the duchess has not been
distressed by my absence, dear sir. There was no time
to leave a message."

"Hmp! Well, of course she's been worried, not a
doubt of that. I mean, it ain't like you to go off without
saying, and to make matters worse, what with first one
and then another asking where you were, it ain't been
the easiest of days for Bella. In the end, she told 'em
all you'd taken to your bed with a chill."

"Oh, dear!"

"She don't know yet that you're back; so, if I were you, I'd slip up the back way to your room and leave me to tell her."

"But . . ." Louise looked from one to the other.

"Go along," said the prince, not ungently. "I will explain better alone."

Louise resumed her duties the following day, and if she seemed unusually subdued, this merely lent credence to the fiction of her brief indisposition. There had been recriminations, of course, although the duchess had in the end accepted Prince Andrei's explanation together with Louise's profuse apologies for having caused her so much worry.

"But I still do not understand how you came to be involved," she said, gently complaining. "It seems quite extraordinary that the prince should turn to you, of all people, for help."

Louise tried not to resent the note of condescension as she agreed. "I can no more explain it than you, ma'am."

"Oh, well, you are safe, and that is all that matters. And the whole story is known only to the duke and myself. But I do exhort you, my dear child, to be less impulsive in the future. Prince Andrei might be thought unexceptionable, but to be going off with any gentleman in that way can only lead people, should they hear of it, to imagine the worst."

Amelia had not been told the details, but she knew that, for the second time in a matter of days, Prince Andrei had brought Louise home, and she had not been slow to accuse her of deliberately putting herself in the prince's way. "I vow I could laugh if it weren't so pathetic."

But Louise would not be drawn, and with her birthday on the morrow, Amelia soon found more important things to occupy her mind.

* * *

The day of the birthday ball dawned fine and dry. A crisp frost had made the less-used roads somewhat treacherous, but there was every hope that it would not seriously impede the progress of the hundred or so guests who would be setting out later in the day, and the duchess was profoundly relieved when the orchestra arrived from Bath in good time.

For the past two days the house had worn an air of bustle as every servant who could be spared had been engaged in the preparation and decoration of the huge ballroom, which was seldom used. The children, who were in danger of getting under everyone's feet, were confined to the nursery quarters when they were not out-of-doors. By the day itself every polishable surface gleamed, the two great chandeliers had been unswathed from their holland covers, their lusters washed and buffed so that they might shine like diamonds when lit by hundreds of candles. Now, the flowers and ferns were brought in from the hothouses and banked about the room. In the kitchen, Jacques was absorbed in creating a feast to be remembered. It was impossible for Louise to remain in poor spirits with so much going on.

Amelia, too, having been showered with gifts and good wishes, was in charity with everyone, Louise included, her moodiness quite forgotten. Her happiness had been crowned that morning when her papa had presented her with an exquisite *parure* of sapphires, its necklace fashioned like a tiny waterfall, as were the earrings. "Oh, Mama," she cried, trying the complete set on for the umpteenth time and turning this way and that to catch the sunlight. "Are they not the prettiest you ever saw? I cannot wait for this evening. I vow Maria Datchett will die of envy, for they cast her pearls quite in the shade."

"I hope she does not," exclaimed the duchess, but

indulgently. "Lady Datchett is a dear friend, and I could not wish her only daughter ill!" The laughter that followed was spontaneous, and just for a moment Louise felt shut out and very much alone.

It was with mixed feelings that she faced the evening, for she had not seen Prince Andrei since he had disappeared into the library with the duke two nights ago. Her spirits lifted considerably, however, when she received a letter from Irena full of her incoherently expressed gratitude. With the letter came a tiny padded box, beautifully wrapped, inside which she discovered an oval amethyst pin edged with pearls. "I could bring to England very few of my treasures," Irena had scrawled, "but this was given to me many years ago by my mother, and I wish you to have it as a remembrance of me—and please to come and see me whenever you can spare the time . . ."

Louise thought the pin a hundred times prettier than Amelia's sapphires and resolved to wear it that evening on her gown. As usual, she was left with little time to prepare, but she brushed her dark hair until it shone and bound it up with lavender ribbon, coaxing one or two curls to fall across her brow. She lifted the gown and felt a shiver of excitement run through her as its silky slip slithered and settled against her skin. She smoothed down the soft crepe overdress and fastened the amethyst pin to the brief bodice and turned to the inadequate mirror. Even the yellowing glass and lone candle could not dim the reflection that stared back at her, bright-eyed. Suddenly everything was perfect. This would be Amelia's night, but it was Louise's first ball, and she was determined to enjoy it to the full.

"You look like a princess," Jason exclaimed when Louise looked in on the children before going down, as she had promised. "And your eyes are all shiny purple like those beads on your dress."

"Thank you," she said, laughing at his awed face, all pink and cherubic from sitting near the fire. "But I doubt I can compete with Amelia."

"Well, I agree with Jason," Joanna declared. "Amelia may well be very pretty-pretty, but you look elegant. Don't you think so, Phil?"

"Oh, fine as fivepence," he muttered with an embarrassed grin.

"Boys," Joanna exclaimed in disgust.

But their artless remarks put an extra sparkle in her eyes and she was still smiling when she arrived downstairs, which earned her further compliments, summed up by the duke's: "Never seen you look finer, m'dear. You should wear that color more often."

Louise was content. She had no desire to rival Amelia, who looked like a fairy-tale princess in white spider gauze, scattered with tiny silver stars that caught the light with every movement of the flimsy material. Pale-golden curls framed her face, and against the delicacy of her skin, the sapphires gleamed like blue fire, echoing her eyes. This was Amelia's night, after all, and any gentleman in his right mind must surely find her irresistible.

Nevertheless, Louise was glad of her pretty mask when from nine o'clock onward the guests began to arrive for the ball, for it enabled her to watch Prince Andrei's face as he caught his first glimpse of Amelia. She had thought her own feelings well-schooled, but watching him raise the dainty hand to his lips and hold it there for a timeless moment, she experienced a stab of pain so violent, it took her breath away.

"Miss Louise?"

Dimly she heard the tentative voice, became aware of the youthful, rather gangling figure hovering at her side.

"F-forgive me, but I recognized you at once," said William Burridge. "I wonder, would you stand up with me for the opening country dance? I f-fear I am not a very experienced dancer.''

Louise shook free of painful thoughts and smiled at him; thanks to the mask, he would not notice that the smile did not reach her eyes. ''How kind. I would be very happy to dance with you. I, too, lack expertise.'' She was rewarded by a faintly audible sigh of relief.

The duke formally opened the dancing by leading his daughter out, his pride in her evident throughout. But to judge from the eager crowd that had surrounded her from the first, it was clear that she would be danced off her feet the whole night, and it came as no surprise to Louise to see Prince Andrei claiming the cotillion that followed the country dance. They made a perfect pairing: he in his dress uniform and she in her floating silvery gauze. But by then Louise had her feelings well under control.

It had come as something of a surprise—though a pleasant one—to discover that she did not want for partners herself. Perhaps there was something about the anonymity of being masked that freed people from their inhibitions. Once or twice she even found herself indulging in light and harmless flirtations with gentlemen she hardly knew. Occasionally she was aware of the prince's glance sweeping the room, but with a little ingenuity she was able to arrange that their paths did not cross. Sooner or later they would have to meet, but it would be better for her peace of mind if it were later.

Supper had been arranged for midnight, and there was only one waltz to go before the supper dance. Louise and her sister, Ellie, had managed, amid much laughter, to learn the steps of the waltz when it first became the rage, but she had never been afforded the opportunity to display her doubtful skills on the ballroom floor. Both William and Sir Roger had confessed themselves unable to master its intricacies. ''Can't teach an old dog new tricks, m'dear," Sir Roger had said wryly.

Louise resigned herself to the inevitable, and rather than face the frustration of watching others when her feet longed to take wings, she decided to go and see if the supper preparations were complete. She had almost gained the door when an urgent hand on her arm stayed her.

"Beautiful stranger," said the well-loved voice, "you cannot think of leaving now, when I so wish you to waltz with me?"

She turned slowly, panic and something else she could not name almost depriving her of speech. "Sir, I am not . . . you cannot wish . . ."

"But I do wish, very much. I have been wishing all evening. Come."

He was very much the corsair as she had first seen him, proud and a little reckless, his eyes glinting through the slits in his mask. His voice, seductively persuasive, robbed her of all resistance.

Without further protest, Louise allowed him to lead her onto the floor. And then she was in his arms and the music began. If I never know such joy again, I will remember this, she told herself dazedly as they dipped and swayed and a myriad lights swirled above her. Vaguely she was aware that he was holding her much closer than the duchess would think seemly, his hand warm and possessive through the thin stuff of her dress, but she didn't care. Just for this moment they were beyond the reach of mere mortals. Only when it was too late did she realize that he had waltzed her right out of the ballroom and into one of the small anterooms leading off it.

"Your highness," she remonstrated as he shut the door.

"Ah, so you do recognize me," he murmured.

"Well, of course I—"

"Then why, pray, have you so studiously avoided me for the whole evening?"

"I haven't!"

He laughed softly. "Not many days ago you told me what an unconvincing liar you are, and now I find that it is true." He waited for her to speak, and when she did not, he reached out to remove her mask, tossing it with his own onto a nearby sofa. "It is very becoming, but I would so much rather see your dear face." He watched the tide of confusion suffuse her. "My poor little Louise, do I go too fast for you?"

"Yes . . . That is, no!" She scarcely knew what she was saying. "I don't understand what it is you want of me."

Prince Andrei took her hands and held them against his heart. "It is really very simple. I love you. I love your simplicity and honesty, and the shining courage that makes me want to cherish you. What I *want* is to have you with me for the rest of my life. I want your face to be the first thing I behold in the morning and the last I see at night."

It was a beautiful impassioned speech, heartbreakingly beautiful, but for all that, it did not mention marriage. Yet, even as Louise struggled to believe in miracles, a small doubting voice at the back of her mind reminded her that just so had he loved Irena but a short time ago—until she put herself beyond his reach. Instinctively, her fingers closed on the little pin.

He had recognized it immediately and now his hand came to cover hers. Beneath it he felt the wild uneven beating of her heart. "Irena treasured that gift from her mama," he told her. "She must think a great deal of you to have parted with it. Please God she will soon find her happiness." Something in Louise's stillness made him look down into her face, and what he saw there made him exclaim softly, "Oh, my dearest girl, you have nothing to fear. Irena was but my adolescent dream. *You* are my reality."

He bent his head, and his mouth found hers. It was a gentle lingering caress, but it set her on fire with its hint of leashed passion, and she was lost. As if he sensed it, his arms came around her, his kiss deepening in intensity, and she gave herself up to it, knowing with absolute certainty that, with or without benefit of matrimony, she would follow him to the world's end. The thought hardly shocked her at all.

"So?" he said, his dark eyes brilliant as he looked down at her. "You feel it, also, this belonging together?"

Louise offered a trembling smile and laid her head against his coat. "I feel it, your highness, but I still can't believe it."

"You will, very soon," he assured her. "And my name is Andrei. You made free of it once, remember? Now I long to hear you say it again." Looking up shyly, she obliged him. He kissed her again, and several minutes passed in foolish delights before he put her away a little. "My dearest, I am not a patient man. To use Irena's words, you have given me my glimpse of paradise, and now there is no going back." From the inside pocket of his coat he drew out an oblong velvet case. "There has been no time to arrange for your betrothal ring, but for now perhaps this trifle will suffice."

Had he really said those words? If so, he must surely mean . . . Her mind swam with the full realization and her fingers were trembling as she opened the slim case. "Oh! But it is beautiful," she whispered, staring in awe at the complete circlet of amethysts set in gold, each cluster of stones with a tiny diamond at their center. She touched one reverently. "They are like little stars. And how well they match Irena's pin."

"Pure coincidence. I chose amethysts because they spoke to me of your eyes." The prince took the circlet from her and fastened it about her neck. "It is just a Christmas *bibelot.*"

"But I have nothing for you," she cried.

"The gift of your love is all and more than I could wish for." He lifted her fingers to his lips before drawing her hand into the crook of his arm. "And I tell you now, I do not intend to wait a moment longer than need be to claim my bride. The duke already knows of my intention, but perhaps now is a good time to tell the duchess also so that everyone may know. And tomorrow we shall go to ask formal permission of your parents."

Her cup was now filled to overflowing, but Louise found her sympathy going out to the duchess. She had entertained such high hopes of a match between Amelia and Andrei—how odd it was to think of him thus—and had voiced them freely among her friends. It would come as a bitter blow to discover that he had chosen her godchild instead. Louise was less concerned for Amelia's feelings. Inevitably her pride would be hurt, but her heart was never truly engaged and she would soon find consolation elsewhere.

Even so . . . "Andrei," she asked tentatively, "would you mind very much if we did not mention anything tonight? This is Amelia's birthday ball, after all, and I have no wish to steal attention away from her." His face wore its silent, rather arrogant look and she rushed into speech again before he could refuse, her tone beseeching. "We could put the necklet back in its box and keep our secret for a little while longer. In fact, I would prefer it. I need time to pinch myself occasionally, to grow used to the whole miraculous reality of your love for me."

The prince drew her close again. "You think I am blind? I know very well why you are doing this, but how can I refuse you when it is one of the qualities in you that makes me love you so much?"

At last she and Andrei could dally no longer, and in turning to leave, Louise saw that the curtains of the anteroom were still tied back. In the star-strewn velvet sky beyond, the moon rode on its back. One star shone brighter than all the rest, and she drew Andrei's attention to it.

"It is the Christmas star," she said softly. "I shall wish on it, and my wish shall be my gift to you."